ARUSHA

J. E. KNOWLES

Spinsters Ink
2009

Attitude Books
P.O. Box 242
Midway, Florida 32343

Printed in the United States of America on acid-free paper
First Edition

Editor: Katherine V. Forrest
Cover designer: Linda Callaghan

ISBN: 10 1-935226-09-6
ISBN: 13 978-1-935226-09-3

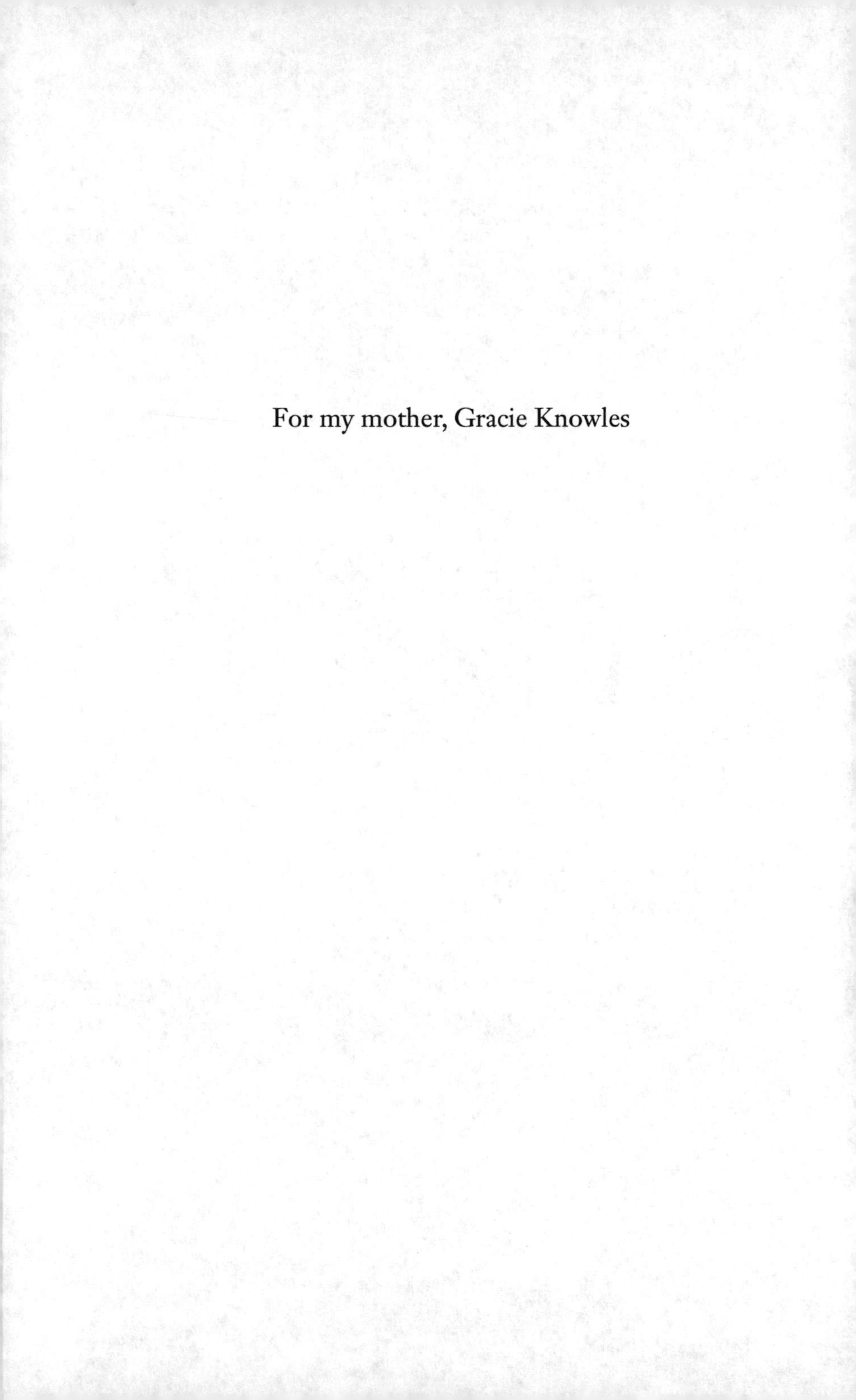

For my mother, Gracie Knowles

Acknowledgments

To Trish Hindley, thank you. I owe a great debt to a wonderful group of writers: Dan Chalykoff, Carol Lawlor, Sandi Plewis and Andrejs Rosts. They were the first to read substantial portions of this novel, and supported my writing at a time when very little else was going right. Many other writers have helped me, in particular Diana Armstrong, Vincent Lam, Lee Lynch, Kim Moritsugu, David Adams Richards and Marnie Woodrow. To work with Katherine V. Forrest as editor is my honor and pleasure. I am grateful to publisher Linda Hill and her colleagues at Spinsters Ink, and of course you, the readers. Thanks to Paul Gallant, who was my editor at *Xtra!*, and to Matthew Firth for publishing my fiction. Special thanks to my brother Ben, with whom I can always talk about the artistic process. I thank Charma, Jen, Heather, Millie, my grandparents, the other Linda, Pat, Ann, Kathi, Kate, Jodie Manross and the countless musicians who inspire me. I've never been a teacher, but I have the deepest admiration for those who have shared that profession with my fictional characters, including my parents, who have been together for more than forty years; my friend Fritz Bernshausen; and many of the women and men who taught me in the public schools. Finally, eternal gratitude to my companions in Tanzania: Frank, Janet, Bob, Rachel and Penelope. *Solo Deo Gloria*.

Chapter 1

Advent 1988

Not one of Edith's students was looking forward to Christmas vacation more than she was.

"Billy," she said, "what is Newton's first law?"

"Huh?"

"You do not say 'huh' to me, you may say 'what' or 'ma'am.'" Was she teaching eighth grade or first? "A body in motion tends to remain in motion until something happens to change that motion. Billy?"

"Ma'am?"

"What is Newton's first law?"

"I don't know."

She again recited, "A body in motion tends to remain in motion until something happens to change that motion. Yes, Julie?"

"Or at rest."

"Thank you." Not for the first time this school year, Edith gave up on Billy. And today, the whole class was raring to go home and beat up their little brothers and sisters. That was why

Edith had saved the sodium demonstration until now, as she did every year.

"Now listen, people. We've talked about the periodic table and what happens to this column." She thwacked her finger against the giant, full-color poster on the wall. "Sodium and potassium. Today, I'm going to demonstrate with some pure sodium how the element reacts with water. Watch."

A tray of water was set up on her desk. When she dropped in the silver-white piece of sodium, there was a bright flash, an explosive sound, and the class was momentarily awed. They were always awed, and even for Edith there was that second of nervousness that her hair, which this year was in a rather large perm to match the perms of other forty-year-old women, would go up with the sodium. But just bits of the element stuck to the ceiling over her desk, already studded with sodium bits from fifteen years of the day-before-Christmas-break.

"Miz Rignaldi, do it again!"

She used to tell students, "I am not Miz Rignaldi," but now she accepted that they would never pronounce Mrs. as two syllables. Billy Lowry could barely cope with one, and his daddy was just as ignorant, never mind if he too was a so-called teacher. It wasn't being stupid that was so bad; it was plain ignorance. Edith knew Bill Lowry, Sr. didn't teach a thing. All his students knew it too, happy though they might be about it. Just because he coached boys' baseball he thought he didn't have to know anything, let alone share it with a class.

Edith always thought of it that way, boys' baseball, though it went without saying as only boys could play. Girls played softball and powder-puff football. None of it made sense. Anyway, with a daddy like Bill no wonder Billy sat in the back of the class saying "I don't know" like those were the only words he did know, didn't matter how many times she stood there and handed him the answer. She would have paddled her own kids if they'd been such smart-alecks when they were this age, only a few years ago.

"Sorry, you all, I can't do it again," she said. As if the school would, or could, pay for extra chunks of sodium just to keep her classes entertained. No, leave them wanting more. That's what the great entertainers always did and sometimes that's all she thought she was, an entertainer, trying to keep the class on the edge of its collective seat. She wished she did have something else to blow up.

It seemed like an entire day passed before lunch break, and then she would have to entertain three more times. At lunch, except on the days she had lunchroom duty, Edith could snatch half an hour for herself. Well, less than half an hour because her bladder was full and she'd probably been holding it since first period, like today. And not really for herself because the lounge would be full of other teachers, all itching for a cigarette or gossip, or both. When you got right down to it, it was lucky she had time to eat at all.

The toaster oven, the one that worked, was in use, so Edith joined the lineup figuring she'd smoke on the way. Pam Bailiff was right in front of her, all hairspray. Maybe it was just the memory of sodium but Edith was almost afraid to light her own cigarette, for fear of sending Pam's perm up in flames.

"How's it going, Edie?" Pam said.

"All right. Haven't seen you in a while."

Pam dragged on her cigarette and shook that perm. "Lunchroom. I should've only had Monday to Wednesday last week, but I had to cover."

Edith nodded. None of the other teachers called her Edie, but Pam was married to her cousin Charlie and couldn't break the habit. Edith supposed that made them cousins-in-law.

When the bell rang at two thirty no one was more thankful to be out of that building. She'd been up since six o'clock, as she had been most mornings of her working life. Even when Jeremy and Dana were babies, there'd been a feeding at that time, not to mention two a.m. which she didn't even want to remember. And they hadn't grown to sleep in on the weekends, either. As kids they were up by seven, wanting their breakfast, the whole day ahead of them. Not a habit to discourage.

Neither she nor Joe could ever sleep in late. The flip side was getting out of school in the afternoon but only an outsider thought teachers finished working at that time. Lesson planning had just begun. Public school teaching was a full-time-plus, year-round job, vacations notwithstanding. About the only day of the school year Edith didn't plan when she got home was today, and that was only because she had cooking, baking and wrapping presents ahead of her. Even the decorating she hadn't gotten done the previous weekend.

Joe could've fucked mud. That's what his brother Steve would say. Steve was in the navy and Joe hardly ever saw him, but sometimes these less-than-welcome memories came flooding in. Usually when he was alone, in the bathroom of the house he shared with Edith and their children. All his life, from sharing with his brother to his college roommate to his wife, Joe Rignaldi had never had so much as a room to himself.

He felt bad about spending so much time in the bathroom, but it was the only way he could get through the unbroken days of family togetherness. This was his second time today. Sometimes he would make it through the day with just one quick trip to sexual release; other days, he needed three or even four. Rarely, he would skip a whole day. But it was Christmas and being penned up in the house all day only increased his priapic frustration.

Even the gym would be closed for the holidays. Joe didn't really work out, just used the pool. He found swimming the next best thing to solitude, and enjoyed seeing others without having to talk to them or even make eye contact. It was so different from school where he always had to be talking: to his classes, other teachers, students in the hall.

Sometimes Joe worried about his kids, especially his daughter. Dana was sixteen and seemed never to have a boyfriend, which was fine with him, but he feared she was naïve. He wanted to impart to her how strong the male sex drive could be, to warn her. But Joe knew from television that a father could not talk to his daughter that way, or there'd be some 800 number she could call.

It was a desperate feeling, like being trapped in a smaller and smaller space, the size of this bathroom or a single cubicle in the staff washroom. Joe knew it was a trap of his own construction, and part of the franticness of his desire, as his hand moved up and down, was that he'd asked for this but could not quit it. He couldn't go back and he didn't see his way forward. Maybe, if he got desperate enough to articulate it, he could get past his wife. But never his mother.

He cleared his throat, zipped up his pants, flushed. He had about a minute to think with the water on, then to dry his hands deliberately on that little purple towel, look in the mirror, ensure his face was not too red, or his nails too dirty. He ought to unscrew this medicine cabinet, put it up a little higher on the wall, now that Edith was the shortest person in the house at five foot six. That would be the handy thing to do, a proper man's job. Give him a little more time in the bathroom, as well.

Some of those guys in the gym were so built. His brother Steve had always lifted weights, kept dumbbells under the bed and such, but they weren't a bulky family, they didn't have that build. One guy in particular was not tall like himself but man, was he built. You couldn't help but notice him, and he knew it, too, spent all his time strutting around in front of the mirrors. Maybe after Christmas Joe would do something about this mirror. He could hear pots and pans out in the kitchen.

To Edith, the house had a totally different aroma at Christmas. It wasn't that hard to explain: there were real pine needles among the decorations, there was always something cooking, a little more fat than usual in the food, an awareness of gravy hanging over the kitchen and every room into which the air of the kitchen wafted. The house was a little warmer than usual. Not that it was ever cold. Joe sealed all the windows and doors, there was never any worry about that.

Joe took care of possible emergencies. He wasn't one of those husbands you couldn't count on in any kind of a situation. There were always flashlights in case the power went out, which it often did even though they were only a couple miles out in the country. Flashlights, and D batteries to go in them. There was a kerosene heater, and extra fuel in the winter. There was even a four-wheel drive in the driveway, though it was a minivan, not the kind of shiny toy men sometimes bought when they had made it while still young, or when having a crisis in middle age.

Not like Joe to have an ordinary midlife crisis.

On this twenty-third of December, he seemed to be spending most of his time in the bathroom. She tried not to wonder what unpalatable compulsion kept him in there, just as she tried not to wonder what Jeremy or Dana were doing when they came and went continually, in and out of the bathroom. There were plenty of mirrors in the house, a huge one over Dana's dresser, but if she ever so much as glanced in it Edith couldn't tell. Most girls pushed their mothers to let them wear makeup at what Edith thought was a ridiculously young age. But, not pushing, she'd bought Dana a small selection, pale blush, no foundation or anything. It sat there, in front of the unused mirror, and though she hadn't checked Edith doubted any of it had been opened.

If only—and this was a feature of modern plumbing whose time she wished had never come—the bathroom had not opened right off the kitchen. So the effluvia and the spray meant to cover it, which only drew one's attention to the fact that a stink was there, kept mingling with the browning onions, the not-yet-scorched flour and milk, whatever else she was preparing on the stove. She wished that, instead of spraying, her family would just strike a match. Flame, at least, was a smell that might reasonably occur in connection with cooking (rather more often than desirable, in Edith's case).

No, Joe was dealing with Christmas stress, or whatever you wanted to call it, in his own way; no one else's way would do, even if he was just backing the minivan out of the driveway. Her way, the way she got through almost every day whether stressful or not, was chopping onions. The smell, for one thing, tended to make her family's eyes water and keep the kitchen clear. Edith was immune, or nearly immune, to the onions. When the tears did indeed need to come for some other reason, they were a good excuse.

Joe emerged from the bathroom, a purple towel in his hands. "Can I throw this in the hamper, or do you want me to take it to the basement?"

That depended what was on it. "Just take it downstairs, please. I'm about to do a load anyway."

Edith went rooting in the most cluttered of her kitchen drawers for the old can opener. It was manual, like everything they had, a thin, rusty implement not easy even to grip. But she wouldn't think of replacing it. It was the only one she'd ever owned, and dated from a time in her life when "What's for dinner?" meant "Where's the can opener?" She'd learned to cook, of course; all the girls of her generation had. Learned to sift flour before baking and break eggs into a separate bowl to make sure they weren't rotten. She'd even taught her children—both of them. Somewhere she had a picture of Dana with a blue kerchief tied around her head, and an apron, earnestly mixing something in a bowl.

Edith opened a can of beans. There was always that smell following the snapping open of the can, like someone had just made gas in the room. A wonder she could tell sometimes, with the bathroom right there. She took a match from the top cupboard, where she still kept matches even though the children were grown, and struck it. That would cut through all smells.

Dana came in, looking like she'd slept in clothes she'd pulled from a pile of other people's discards. "Something burning in here?"

"I struck a match." Edith decided to let her think she'd been in the bathroom; it didn't matter. "I'm heating up these beans for you."

Her daughter crossed the room, examined the empty can. Edith said, "It's tomato sauce, not pork and beans. I read the label."

"I always read the label."

Before Dana could go anywhere, Edith said, "You can get out some dishes to set the table with. We'll be eating in a little while."

"I'll be right back," Dana said, and disappeared into the bathroom.

The sky had gone dark, but there was no snow. There was unlikely to be any snow, even up on the Blue Ridge, before the new year. Edith switched on the multicolored lights that hung over the kitchen window. She preferred white lights. Down the road, there were houses decked out in red, green, blue, not to mention the neighbors who went crazy putting reindeer and Santas all over the yard. Some were tasteful, just a glimpse of a tree through the picture window or, if the right kind of tree grew there, in the front yard. But the roads here lacked sidewalks and there wasn't any opportunity to see these things except from a car.

After supper, Joe reminded Dana to help her mother with the dishes. For someone who could remember all the presidents' names when she was ten, it was remarkable how Dana could forget this daily chore without her father's reminder. As far as Edith knew, Joe himself had never washed or dried a dish in his life.

He was useful in other ways. Their age and generation notwithstanding, both of them brought who they really were into this marriage. If it happened to closely match what was typical for a man's or woman's "role," that was pure coincidence.

"Is there football on this weekend?" Edith asked Joe when he returned to the living room, paper in hand.

"I think there might be a basketball game on Christmas Day. Why?"

It drove her crazy, his habit of asking why about everything. She took it as a challenge, or reproach. She'd never been very good at answering the question when a young child persisted in asking it, and could scarcely tolerate it from her husband. Fortunately, he never seemed to expect an answer.

Neither of them had seen Jeremy much since the vacation began. He would be in his attic room listening to one of his rock bands. She'd rather he turn the music up in his own part of the house than blow his ears out with the headphones. She was grateful that he preferred the bands that purported to talk about something other than hell. Edith was not much of a believer in the Satanic rock argument, but she thought hell was already talked about entirely too much in church.

Now, reassured by the thump from upstairs, Edith joined Joe on the couch in front of the television, which was not on.

Joe finally spoke. "You think he's on drugs?"

"What?"

"Do you think Jeremy is taking drugs?"

"No," she said, and she didn't. "What a thing to say."

"I don't really either," Joe said, "but he's just so pale."

"We're white people, Joe. It's winter and he spends all his time in the attic, or at that bricked-in school." She reached for the paper, needing to busy her hands. "I wish the high school at least had some windows, like your school. It's not like kids would be jumping out of them; it's all on one floor."

Joe continued to look directly in front of him, at the blank screen. "I don't recall doing that when I was in high school."

"What, jumping out the window?"

"No, I mean just listening to the stereo all the time, no friends."

"It was different. You put on a record and people listened to it, or you played your own music. We liked different music." She crossed to their old stereo, searching in the stack of Christmas records, stuff she'd grown up with. "What would you like to listen to? Choral or instrumental?"

"Can we just talk for now?" His voice sounded choked, and he held his palms together in front of him, elbows on knees. She saw strain in his face. Joe did not usually want to "just talk."

"All right." She sat down, then started up again. "Do you want something to drink?"

He turned to her, visibly agitated. "I need to ask you to consider something with me." He took a deep breath. "I need to ask you to revisit our arrangement."

This was not right, not the way Joe talked. He didn't use clinical phrases; he certainly didn't sit there, talking, holding his hands still. She got up. "I need you to stop this."

"Stop what?"

"Talking like this. It's Christmas, Joe. What can we possibly resolve at Christmas?"

The thunderous music from upstairs continued, but through the ceiling there was a new, very strange percussive noise. What now? Edith ran up the stairs, opened the attic door and was hit by something heavy. A pair of shoes.

"Jeremy? Oh dear Lord." She advanced on her son, who was pitching around on the floor. "Joe!"

He came quickly. It appeared that Jeremy's shoes, which

were perpetually untied after the fashion of boys his age, had been kicked free in the course of a fit. “Call the rescue squad,” Edith said in her command tone. “I’ll take care of him, just call the rescue squad.”

The rescue squad was at the house before she thought to tell Dana, who looked disappointed to have missed all the action. In contrast to Jeremy’s room, Edith found Dana’s silent and the light dim. I need to get her a hundred-watt bulb to replace that sixty-watt.

Edith would have gone to the hospital, but Joe said he’d go instead. She felt as if her home were being invaded by paramedics. They came in, all bundled up in their black uniforms, and surrounded her son. They ascertained that he was having a seizure (yes, she could have told them that). It proved difficult to hold Jeremy down. For a skinny high school boy, he showed remarkable strength.

“Is it drugs?” she asked, for Joe more than for herself.

“No, ma’am.” The older paramedic had curly hair and a red face. “He’s having a seizure.” They’d just told her this, and he repeated it patiently, as if explaining the same thing over again to a slow child.

“I know that.” Her voice must have been rising in pitch more than she thought, because Joe looked over at her, his eyes heavy with meaning. She hoped he could read hers: Not now, Giuseppe. Now is not the time to talk about our arrangement.

The paramedics managed to sedate Jeremy, and off they went in the ambulance, Joe riding along. He did have first-aid training from the school. Edith hated to think of him as the strong man, taking over while the mother of his children fell apart in the driveway.

She stood for several minutes after they’d left, before realizing she was wearing nothing over her clothes. But she didn’t feel cold. She didn’t feel hot either, as with anger. Numb.

She’d make a fresh pot of coffee. There was very little in life that could not be endured more tolerably with a good cup of coffee. She used to say “and a cigarette,” but she’d stopped smoking in the house when the kids were born (ahead of her time in one way). Now she didn’t have any cigarettes when she wanted them.

The door of the little house next door opened and out came her mother-in-law, wrapped in a housedress. Isabella was the only person Edith knew of, outside of movies or TV, who either wore housedresses or would call them that. This one was a pale pink-and-green checked thing, not warm enough to be worn outside in December, even in Tennessee. But Isabella produced a cigarette, and offered it to her, and Edith didn't send her back inside.

"Jeremy had to go to the hospital," Edith said. "Some kind of fit he's having."

"I saw the whole thing from my window, honey." Isabella, though a Northerner, had perfect pitch, and after twenty years "honey" flowed through her speech like milk in the Promised Land.

"I'm sorry I didn't come over and tell you."

"It's all right, honey. Joe went with him."

"Yes."

"How is Joe?"

This struck Edith as an odd question, since Isabella saw her son every day, and ate most meals with them. "He's okay," she said. "I mean, he's probably concerned about Jeremy right now. It's not drugs."

"Of course not."

The two women stood for a moment, smoking companionably. Edith looked at Isabella's hair, which in texture resembled tinsel before it was taken out of the box of decorations, and was thankful her own hair was just beginning to gray. She finished her cigarette. "Come on inside, Mom. It's too cold to stand out here without a coat or anything."

The lights in the window of the big house were a foggy glow in the dark evening. Once inside, Isabella began rummaging around the kitchen. She was several inches shorter than Edith, and for this reason claimed the drawers closest to the floor as her own. Edith could not imagine why anyone would ever need so many sizes and types of wooden spoons.

"You want me to cook tomorrow?" Isabella didn't wait for an answer. "Christmas dinner, you're going to be too busy with that, honey. I'll cook for tomorrow."

Isabella was a wonderful cook, but many of her recipes depended on mysterious stocks and pot liquor that she sealed away in margarine containers in the back of the refrigerator. Sometimes it was impossible to find margarine. "If you're cooking with meat stock," Edith said, "remember Dana won't eat it. We'll have to give her cottage cheese and seeds or something."

Isabella tapped the side of her own head, as if trying to rid it of any notion so silly. "It's that girl you ought to worry about, honey," she said. "The boy is fine. That girl, she's too skinny. You know they have a disease for that now, honey. Nervous disease."

"Dana runs, Mom. She runs, that's why she's skinny. She's not anorexic."

"I'll make chili," Isabella said. She continued to putter and hum, leaving Edith feeling superfluous in her own kitchen. Who started Christmas Eve dinner on the twenty-third? The dishes from supper were still draining in the rack, but Isabella paid no attention to them.

Edith wondered, for no longer than a second, whether she should confide in her mother-in-law that something was going on with Joe. There was nothing much to tell her, and though Edith regarded Isabella as a friend and mother, the details of her marriage were not something she often discussed with anyone. How strange that it should be by her daughter-in-law, not her son, that Isabella was kept abreast of next-door's intrigues.

Now the big house was filling with the smell of browning onions and hot chili peppers. Isabella believed in cooking extra and saving the leftovers, and clearly she'd decided to prepare tomorrow's chili tonight, in quantities that Edith couldn't believe were necessary, even if Jeremy came home and was able to eat. She forced calm breaths, remembering that this was an emergency and she could not afford to lose control. Jeremy was a senior, he would be applying to colleges soon. Well, he should be. That was another thing she had to deal with in the new year. There was a lot.

She sighed as Isabella piled ground chuck into a skillet

and began browning that too. No point in trying to explain vegetarian to her, Isabella was convinced her granddaughter was too skinny and needed meat on her bones.

Edith knocked on Dana's door and it opened at once. Dana was chewing gum, but not the bubble type, thank the Lord. "What's wrong with Jeremy?"

"I don't know yet," Edith said. "Dad went in the ambulance."

They stood there a moment, regarding each other, very close in height now that Dana had stopped growing. The wood of the door shone softly in the light of the desk lamp. That reminded Edith. "Let me get you a brighter bulb for that lamp."

"I tried a hundred-watt, it got too hot."

The desk was veneered with a darker wood. It was a sturdy, if old piece of furniture, and had a leg that had to be held straight if you ever attempted to move it. Like the Royal standard typewriter sitting on one end of it, the desk had belonged to Isabella in her school days. In fact Isabella, not Edith, had taught the girl to type. "J, H, J, space," Isabella had drilled her granddaughter, and the manual keys clattered across the page.

Joe came home later, but they didn't talk much. He assured her that Jeremy was fine, that the staff was monitoring him overnight and would have a much better idea what was going on tomorrow. Then he shut himself in the bathroom for what must have been the billionth time that day.

In bed, Joe went to sleep right away, and Edith was left lying there. This was a reversal of their usual pattern. She tended to fall asleep quickly, from sheer exhaustion. They often slept in an embrace, or at least touching, which she suspected was not common for couples in their nineteenth year of marriage, but she never read those articles in the women's magazines so couldn't be sure. Some nights, though, like this one, she would lie in his arms and still feel like the loneliest person in the world.

Edith wasn't stupid. She was a teacher herself; she'd been to college too. She had not been one hundred percent surprised at Joe's little announcement, only at its timing. It was a measure of his integrity, or of her trust in it which wasn't exactly the same thing, that he had spoken to her first, rather than going off and rearranging on his own. Most husbands would not bother to mention it first.

She knew she would not be going to sleep for a while, so got up, felt for her slippers and padded out into the living room. She was always more comfortable in rooms lit by lamps; overhead lights didn't flatter anybody, and she hated them, especially the fluorescent kind that lit her classroom all day.

The *Poudre Valley Crier* lay scattered around the floor. She found herself wanting a cigarette again. Isabella's fault, though she didn't care much for her mother-in-law's brand. Those sweet-smelling, old-lady cigarettes. Edith thought of them and the craving subsided.

She picked up the section of the paper that wasn't news, since she wasn't in an intifada mood. The cartoons—all black and white—were in the back, but she found her eyes drawn to Dear Abby. The letter today was from a woman whose marriage could not, in Abby's opinion, be saved. Abby said that in all such cases "the woman loses" and advised her correspondent to seek counseling.

And for this she got paid. Well, Edith wasn't going to lose. She was not, by nature, a confrontational person, but she had not gotten through the last two decades, with the family she had, by listening to Dear Abby. She had a quiet confidence in her family that other wives and mothers could not afford (she did read those articles in the women's magazines and discussed them with her friends, at church or elsewhere). She knew, for example, as well as Isabella did that her son was not on drugs, knew it even if Joe, confused as he was, did not. She knew that Joe, confused as he was, was honest with her, and had always been honest with her as far as he could be. Sitting down together each evening for supper was an achievement these days. She knew there were families with no such thing as a dinner table or a regular gathering round it. If people didn't grow up together, she wondered, not for the first time, what did they have to miss once they left home?

She barely slept that night. She just lay there, listening to Joe breathe. She was awake again some time before six. On weekdays she always got up at six, shuffled out before any of them, washed her face, and turned on the heaters and the stove. With one bathroom everybody could not get up at exactly the same time.

But today was a vacation day, and though she couldn't stay in bed, there was no reason to wake the household either. She went into the kitchen, wrapped in a terrycloth robe, her slippers soft on the linoleum and her hair defiantly ugly. The floor was scarred from a thousand dropped knives, worn from scrubbing out spatterings from cans. It was difficult for her to draw a line of propriety in that kitchen. Domestic or war room, in Edith's mind the kitchen was a theatre of almost all human existence. This was where Jeremy had fallen off the counter, having gotten up there she didn't know how, and busted open his mouth and needed stitches, and she'd had to call the rescue squad then too because Joe wasn't home. That was where Joe had stood when he last told her, several years ago, of his ongoing struggle with feelings that weren't going away, but that he still wanted to control them and needed her help. She had stood there, with the rangehood light on, stirring something continuously (the secret to not burning anything, she'd learned too late from Isabella). Then she'd spoken, and that too, in its way, had left blood on the floor.

Now she started the coffeepot—opening the fresh can of grounds, she just loved that fresh coffee smell—and took her own few minutes in the bathroom, studying the lines around her eyes and her untamable perm. There were more lines than there had once been, and she supposed she could attribute them all to her husband, but where was the originality in that? She peered more closely, plucked a few stray hairs from between her eyebrows.

She hadn't bothered to close the bathroom door. Intimacy meant not caring what someone saw you doing, though she'd had more of a sense of privacy than the rest of her family in the early years. For most of the children's lives, they and their father would use the bathroom or bathe or dress with the door wide open, it didn't matter who was there.

Joe was in the shower when the ancient percolator finished

its business and Edith poured her first cup. If she had had cigarettes in the house, she'd have gone out on the porch and had one right then, with her coffee. This was why she'd started keeping them in the car.

The phone call came and Jeremy was all right, but he had epilepsy. She wanted to go to the hospital right then, before eating, but she also wanted to avoid the appearance of panic. Then Joe came into the kitchen, wrapped in his robe, his full head of hair still wet. "Let's eat first," he said. "They won't be ready anyway, we'll just be sitting there. Bacon, you want some bacon?"

She didn't think she did, but if she smelled it frying she knew she'd want some, as with coffee or tobacco. Joe never cooked, but Isabella was there before Edith even dressed, the scent of those cigarettes still clinging to her housedress and curlers. Isabella peeled off a slab of bacon strips and threw them in the skillet. They sizzled and sweetened the air.

Dana appeared, looking pale, but maybe that was Edith's imagination. She made no acknowledgment of the bacon smell. Edith set cereal boxes and a glass of juice down in front of her. "Jeremy's all right, we're going to pick him up after breakfast."

"How are you, Mom?"

"All right." She paused before returning to the subject of Jeremy. "He has epilepsy."

Dana looked up. "So he's going to keep having fits?"

"I don't know." Edith gulped at her coffee. Did epileptics necessarily keep having seizures? Her instinct was to look this up at once, but the library was closed. She was a science teacher. That was the first step of the scientific method, to find out everything that was already known about a disease, before you set about experimenting. On real people and real lives.

"Jeremy will be fine, honey," Isabella said. She placed the crisply fried bacon on a pewter tray kept for that purpose. She never lined it with paper towels, as Edith did, and the resulting mess drove Edith crazy, although Isabella was conscientious enough to drain bacon fat away into a container, to save for what? Mardi Gras?

Isabella set the tray down in front of Dana, who continued

to munch on flakes of some kind. Edith poured coffee for Dana and Joe. "You want some coffee, Mom?" she said to Isabella.

"Honey, I've had two cups already."

What did Isabella do so early? Did she lie awake all night too, worrying about her son, her grandson, her skinny pale granddaughter? She didn't seem like a worrier. More of a putterer. If she ever relaxed it must have been at her own house, because she always seemed to be busy over here. Edith didn't object. She didn't want to fry bacon.

Eventually they all sat down, after Isabella had fried some eggs, which Dana wouldn't eat because they had touched bacon grease.

Breakfast was a peaceful grazing. Normally, on Christmas Eve, Edith would have put on some music. She rarely was up and awake without at least a radio on; she enjoyed the clamor. But under the circumstances, quiet was welcome.

She and Joe barely exchanged a word on the drive to the hospital. Early in their marriage she had not found silence comfortable; she was not used to it. When someone else was present, she felt the need to fill silence with words. She used to talk and talk, growing more and more agitated, while Joe stared at the road or at his plate or into space, and she would wonder whether he was listening to her or even knew she was talking. It didn't matter what it was about, she just needed to have a conversation. They were more used to each other now, but she was secretly convinced she'd done most of the accommodating and letting go. And she was sure he felt the same way.

Chapter 2

Dana twisted her fingers through her hair, the bedroom door bolted against intrusions, her mind racing around in unproductive circles as it always did. She couldn't wait to get home from school for the vacation and now she couldn't wait to go back. What was the point of being here? Nothing happened unless you counted Jeremy's so-called seizure and she didn't count it. So he had a fit. She loved her brother but he got all the attention; he had that attic room all to himself. Jeremy could ask to live in a barn and Mom would say it was okay. And Joe, well, Joe wouldn't object to anything, didn't matter who did it. Dana was sure of this although neither she nor Jeremy had ever put it to the test.

She always thought of her father as Joe, even while calling him Dad. Dad was what Mom called him, to Dana and Jeremy, and calling either parent by a first name was out of the question. To Mom. Joe couldn't care less. He didn't smoke anymore but otherwise seemed so old-fashioned, classic coat and hat, a glass of wine every night even though Mom didn't drink.

Dana adored her father in that way that was more wanting

to be somebody than loving him for himself. Hero worship, wanting to dress that way, if she had a trench coat and fedora which Mom would certainly never let her wear to school. On the wall behind her was a poster of *Casablanca*, and she wanted to be just like Bogart. Just like Bergman, if Mom was asking.

At Christmas Mom wouldn't allow the TV on any more than it usually was. "Only if there's a special program. You may turn it on for a specific program, a movie, ball game, but we are not going to be one of those families that turns on the TV before they turn on the lights." Not that there was anything much Mom would let them watch.

Nothing to do indoors but read, and the only magazine her parents subscribed to was *U.S. News & World Report*, because they got an educators' discount. It was the most conservative of the three weekly news magazines, but Mom said that was not why; it was just the cheapest. Mom was a big believer in the cheapest.

Dana'd already read this week's U.S. News from cover to cover. She could tell Reagan how to balance the budget right now, if he gave a shit, lame-duck Republican. She had a copy of *Campus Life* from her church youth group but it was so irrelevant, all this stuff about witnessing to non-Christians, of whom she knew none, and how to say "no" to drinking at parties which Dana didn't go to, had never seen anybody drink except for Joe and Isabella's nightly glasses of wine.

Campus Life was flipped open to the only part she always enjoyed reading, and had already read. It was a column entitled "Love, Sex, and the Whole Person." She would read and reread this no matter how little it had to do with her own life. The less, the better, in fact. If it weren't for the admonitions of "Love, Sex, and the Whole Person," if she didn't have its painstaking enumerations of degrees of petting and what teenagers should and should not do, she would know nothing about sex at all. Nothing good, nothing about why it was something to look forward to, so hard to resist. Didn't seem hard to resist to Dana. Her parents had met when they were twenty-one and probably been virgins when they married. If it weren't for her and Jeremy's existence, she'd think they were virgins now.

Poudre Valley Memorial Hospital was built on the site of a fort where gunpowder had been produced during the American Revolution. The patriots, as Edith had been taught to call them in school, had named their settlement after the French word for powder, since the French were allies and the British enemies. Next door to the hospital was a reproduction of the fort, and an adjoining museum with displays on how the Tennessee Valley Authority had changed the landscape of the state during the 1930s. Unaka Lake, like all lakes in this part of the world, was artificial, created by a dam. The fort and museum were places everybody who grew up in Poudre Valley had been to at some point, but no one actually wanted to go.

The glass doors of the hospital opened automatically. They had been modernized since Edith gave birth here, but the hospital smelled the same. It was liquid Lysol, not that horrible spray. She hadn't been here since Jeremy had to get stitches in his chin, ten years ago.

They didn't keep people in the hospital overnight much now. She had a semi-private room when Jeremy was born, but a year later, with Dana, she took a room on the ward to save money. She still remembered the difference in how she'd been treated among people who couldn't pay. She could taste the difference like blood in her mouth.

Joe strode up to the reception desk and announced, "I'm Giuseppe Rignaldi and this is my wife, Edith. We're here to see our son, Jeremy Rignaldi." Edith half expected a stage door to open. But maybe Joe remembered that this was a different receptionist than the one he'd seen before, and wouldn't know them.

They walked through the antiseptic halls—at least she hoped they were antiseptic. When she hugged Jeremy, he seemed very relaxed about it, for a teenage boy. He must still have been a little shaky. As so often in the history of her family, Edith felt that she alone stood between them and the hungry world that would devour every semblance of normality. Jeremy had enough problems; she would not allow him to be threatened by her magnifying his illness.

"We'll get you a bracelet," she said. "Medic Alert. We'll get you that and then if you're ever—"

"He knows," Joe said. "They gave him a pamphlet already."

"Okay." Edith knew she really should listen. "What did it say?"

Jeremy sighed. "Just because I have epilepsy doesn't mean I can't live a normal life."

He wanted to handle it by himself. Couldn't she just let him do that? He was seventeen and when she was seventeen... "All right, Jeremy. When we get home, you can eat. Are you hungry?"

Jeremy nodded. As always. Sometimes Edith wondered if her son was ever comfortable speaking words. As a teacher, she was convinced (and Joe shared her professional opinion on this) that Jeremy's quietness, his few words in class, had more than a little to do with his mediocre grades through the years. Teachers thought he was shy and that, for many of the Rignaldis' colleagues, was at least as bad as never knowing the answer; either way, he didn't raise his hand in class, ever. There was educational theory to the effect that boys dominated classrooms, but Edith had never seen it. It was Dana who dominated every room she was in, whether they wanted her to or not.

Just because Jeremy had epilepsy didn't mean he couldn't live a normal life. This reminded her of an old joke, which she risked telling in the van on the way home.

"So a man goes to his doctor and the doctor tells him, 'You'll need surgery on your hands.' And the man says, 'Will I be able to play the violin?' And the doctor says sure and the man says, 'Oh, great. I never played it before.'"

She laughed, and heard corresponding rumblings from her husband and son. She could usually get them to laugh by laughing herself, and that was a saving grace. Now was definitely not the time to start being upset; now was lunchtime.

Dana was pissed, so fucking pissed all the time. She didn't know at what; there was no direction to it. She just knew whatever she was doing, wherever she was, she wanted to be somewhere else. At sixteen she already wondered what the point of achievement was. She'd achieved everything that was expected of her so far and was bound to go on doing so.

There was a stack of college leaflets next to her stereo. These had arrived after Dana checked a box on the SAT indicating that she would like to receive them. She'd imagined glossy brochures from Harvard or Columbia, but no, those places didn't need to recruit and certainly not down South. Her recruitment leaflets were coming from the women's colleges, which Dana hadn't realized were still in operation.

She dropped the needle on a new album. She still said that, "drop the needle," although you could hardly buy conventional records anymore, and when you did they were cheap bendy vinyl, scratched the first time you played them. Lousy cheap fakes. Dana only sang along when, as now, she was alone in the house. She didn't need Grandma Isabella coming in here and whistling. How could you whistle to stuff like this? It had to drive Jeremy out of his fucking mind.

She stood at the mirror, rows and rows of bottles lined up in front of it. Many of them had been found in the ditch behind the house, sorted and cleaned, every size, shape and color of glass. It was Isabella who had gotten her started on this collection when Dana was in the sixth grade. The country roads were not really made for walking along, they didn't have lines down the middle let alone sidewalks. But Isabella would take a stick (in case of strange dogs) and stride off on her morning constitutional just as if she were still living in suburban Chicago. Dana used to walk with her, in the summer, and they picked up trash from the roadside, rusty cans and paper too, but especially bottles, which people threw from their car windows or just set down in the ditches behind their own houses, letting the occasional hard rain overflow and carry the trash downhill to somebody else's property. No one outside the so-called city limits of Poudre Valley seemed to think there was anything wrong with this. But Isabella was from a real city, and she picked up trash. Or maybe it was for the opposite reason, and Isabella really cared about the country more than anyone who was from here. Joe was the same way.

Dana's bottle collection ranged from what looked like an old apothecary bottle, small and blue, which when she recovered it from the ditch was packed entirely full of mud, to a huge Jim Beam bottle that had pride of place at the center, although (or because) Mom was not very happy about it. Dana had a Dr. Pepper bottle from before they changed the logo, which she'd deliberately bought from the last vending machine in Poudre Valley still stocked with glass bottles—one of the few in the collection she hadn't found in a ditch.

The green Grolsch bottle was her favorite, with its unique flip top and ceramic cap. She held it now, lovingly, like a microphone. Her hair was swept back from her face in a way she imagined a singer's should be. She reserved a ponytail for when she went running. It was pretty boring, running around and around the perimeter of their two acres and timing it with her watch, but you'd have to be suicidal to run along the road. Isabella would ride a bike, believe it or not. But it had been a long time since she'd found a bottle Dana didn't already have.

Now the ponytail was down, and Dana shook back and forth and screamed along, "I wanna be a door!" She watched her own expressions in the mirror, not knowing what she was singing about or to whom, any more than she knew what she intended to defend her family against when, at night, she would pick up the Grolsch bottle by its neck, wielding it like a weapon, ready to break over an intruder's head.

Dana did not particularly enjoy running, but she couldn't stand being cooped up in this house all the damn time. No one smoked in the house, but you could smell it on their clothes, and did Mom really think Dana didn't know she smoked as much as Isabella did? Dana hated smoke, and would cough loudly any time anyone smoked near her. This embarrassed Mom. Dana thought it was pretty rich of teachers to tell students never to smoke, show pictures of blackened lungs and all, when you knew they ran for a cigarette every chance they got.

The song ended and, in a paroxysm of emotion, she smashed the microphone into the floor. Only she used too much force, and the glass shattered. Oh well, there would be more Grolsch bottles where this one came from.

"Dana?" It was Mom.

Shit, they were back.

"Dana, can I come in?"

"Yeah." She unlocked the door.

The look of shock was out of all proportion to what was, after all, only a piece of trash. "What were you doing?"

"Nothing."

"Get the dustpan."

While Dana finished cleaning up the broken glass, Edith set about the business of bread, sliced ham, cheese, opening a jar of mayonnaise. Joe rooted in the cupboards for pickles and potato chips.

She knew his being there meant he was still trying to tell her something. She opened the fridge, pulled out a half-empty two-liter bottle of Coke, hoping it hadn't gone flat.

Right behind her, he said, "When was the last time we made love?"

She nearly dropped the bottle. This was a breach of protocol; there was no telling when Isabella or the kids might come wandering in. "I don't remember," she said. "Do you?"

"No."

"Do you want to?" She was aware of using the same tone with which, in a moment, she would ask if anyone wanted a pickle.

He stood there, the unopened bag of Lance's chips in his hands. He had lines around his eyes, as she did, that hadn't been there eighteen years ago. He looked back at her with a kind of extract of tenderness, from which all the residue of passion or romance had long since faded, if it had ever been there at all. "No," he said.

"Then what do you want? Want to start doing the dishes?" She had not meant to sound so irritated, but what was he talking about sex for? She didn't remember how long it had been and, frankly, that wasn't her fault. Well, if he wanted this conversation now, she would let him have it. "What exactly do you want to reconsider? I reconsider every day."

"Do you?"

"I think about it—why I'm here, whether I want to be. The end result is the same, I just don't take it for granted like so many people do."

"The end result is the same?" He was reverting to one of his most annoying habits: turning everything she said into a question. As if she were a child in his class.

"Yes. Why wouldn't it be?" She grabbed a block of pre-sliced American cheese. "We own a house. We have children. Your mom lives next door. Oh, not to mention we teach in the same school system. Then there's church. And it goes without saying, we have one bank account and one MasterCharge. Can I stop now?"

"Inertia."

As if to prove him wrong, she set the cheese on the table. "A body in motion."

"Or at rest," he said.

"Or at rest."

"Which is it?"

Isabella came in at this point. Discussus interruptus. A regular feature of their so-called love life.

She wasn't the kind who claimed they never contemplated divorce, only murder. It wasn't the end of her marriage she contemplated, so much as the possibility of not having one in the first place. She thought, not infrequently, of an imaginary universe, a parallel one, in which she and Joe had never married. They joked, not very often, that theirs was an arranged marriage, arranged by themselves.

In the parallel universe life was quite similar to the way it was now. She and Joe were friendly, they didn't spend a whole lot of time talking to one another but neither did they fight; there existed between them the distant memory and the possibility of being sexual, but they did not indulge.

And sometimes, Edith thought, looking out at the brown, winter-stripped landscape, sometimes she wished not to be married, more than anything in the world. Not to divorce Joe, not to end a marriage already nearly two decades old, but never to have taken a step that no one, even they, had the words to explain. She had heard that to be married to one's friend was a stroke of good fortune that would make her the envy of most women. If only they knew.

There were radio programs and columns in the magazines, and Edith observed them curiously, like yet another parallel universe. Always, the advice was to be realistic, to be forgiving, not to expect one person to fulfill all your needs: partner, friend, lover, father to your children. Always the advice was to the only people who were paying attention, the wives. Settle down, ladies, the advisers seemed to be saying. Don't ask for so much.

The fields outside were desiccated and, on Christmas Eve, it would have been appropriate for snow to be lying there, but instead there were the shreds of last year's tobacco crop, row on row. The hills rolled up toward the horizon, turning to shades of pink and blue without the green, since all the trees were deciduous. Edith remembered, as a child, getting her first pair of glasses—it turned out she was very nearsighted—and the optometrist told her, "Now you'll look up into those hills and see things you've never seen before." She squinted and scrunched up her eyes, as she was used to doing before she got glasses, but didn't see anything new. She was aware, though, that what the doctor said sounded like something out of the Psalms.

Thinking of the Psalms made her want to confess, so after lunch she said to Joe, "I had a cigarette with Mom last night."

There was a pause, but there usually was before Joe spoke. "Those things smell terrible." He must have meant his mother's brand.

"I know," she said. "I guess I was worried about Jeremy."

"Don't worry." Joe had never learned that saying this guaranteed she would worry the rest of the day about whatever it was.

He did wash the dishes, and then he and Dana, separately, went outside. Edith hoped they were not walking along the road, since no one expected pedestrians there or ever slowed down.

At holidays, their lives were measured in meals. She relaxed a little since she knew Isabella's chili was coming tonight. Then church, always a little uncomfortable on Christmas Eve because many families either weren't there or had extra relatives visiting them. The church was Methodist, without high-church, Mass-like trappings; the congregation didn't know whether or when to stand up or sit down.

Dana sat in the pew, palms flat to her thighs. She could feel them sweat. The best thing about this church was that she could wear pants and nobody cared. Only she and one other girl ever did, but Dana didn't give a shit if she was the only one.

The new youth minister, who organized activities for the young people up to and including high school, was named Eric Dufresne. He seemed too pretty to be a man, and he had long hair. Looked like Jesus, Mom said, but Dana didn't see it that way.

Like everyone else she knew, from the age of thirteen, Dana had been obsessed with sex, and perceived it everywhere. She was grateful to be a girl, if only because the boys were so obviously in distress, she could almost hear the thunk under their desks when some cheerleader type (student or teacher) walked into a classroom in a V-neck blouse. A girl didn't have to worry about that. Guys probably didn't even think girls got a hard-on, since it was something they couldn't see. It was like the existence of God.

Dana spent the service staring at the back of Eric's head, four pews in front of her. His hair was even brushed out like a girl's. Clayton, who sometimes played the organ as well as cut hair, was more of a man than that, in fact Dana thought Mom was too fond of Clayton. Too fond of someone.

After the service, when the candles had been extinguished and left in a box by the door, Dana saw Eric greeting people on the front step. He was with somebody and she walked right by him, though he did see her, and smiled at her just for a second. Not long enough to tell she wasn't smiling back. Then she had to wait for Mom, who found time to speak to everybody. Dana saw, from where the car was parked, that Mom was shaking hands with Eric and she imagined their eyes, intent on one another, and that thin girlish palm in her mother's hand.

Fucking hypocrites.

Edith took the moment of candle lighting before "Silent Night"—an episode that used to terrify her, she was so sure the kids would light each other or themselves on fire—to look about the church building. She had been coming here for most of her life and so it was familiar enough that she was always careful to refer to it as the church building. She had been taught that "the church" did not refer to a building, but to the people, and not just to this congregation but to the worldwide church, "triumphant" as Julie Andrews sang on one of their Christmas records. Had she listened to Julie Andrews yet this season?

She glanced at the familiar glass-pane Jesus and sheep, barely visible now except by reflecting the lit tapers held high for the second and third verses of "Silent Night." The church—Joe and their son and daughter to the left of her, other people she'd known since her childhood, and their children and even grandchildren, dangerously holding flames—was in shadow, between the dark outside the windows and the miniature lights that soaked up all their reflection. In recent years Edith had watched, surprised, as "the family" became the political building block for the church, as Reagan's America seemed to require the nuclear family as much or more than nuclear weapons. Edith considered herself a conservative, but it was mostly celibacy, not the family, that she read about in her New Testament.

No one talked about celibacy anymore, certainly not in the grocery-store magazine world that was nothing but sex. No one talked about following the exhortations of the apostle Paul (you used words like exhortation if you'd been reading Paul most of your life). But it was a commitment as much as any marriage could be.

Edith extinguished her candle, the lights coming up, and she saw Eric Dufresne, the youth minister, coming down the aisle and he did have pretty hair. Pretty as a girl's. She wished she had hair like that. She did once, in her student days. Long and brown, not a streak of any kind, and she had covered it with a blond wig because that was the fashion of the time.

Cousins, aunts and uncles were swarming around the pew. Jeremy was subdued. Edith did not get to him in time to stop Aunt Lanie from asking, "Jeremy, how are you feeling? We heard about your fit."

"Aunt Lanie, Merry Christmas," Edith said, interposing herself between Lanie and Jeremy's scowl. All he needed was to feel even more the focus of attention. "Did you get your hair done up that way for Christmas? It looks real nice."

"Oh, thank you, honey." Aunt Lanie cupped one fine-boned hand around the spherical surface of her hair, which was tightly curled and appeared, in the light, to have a purplish sheen. "Clayton done it for me."

"Is he here?"

"Oh, honey, Clayton's playing the organ for one of his other churches. Presbyterian, I think. He'll play for anybody, even the Catholics." Then Aunt Lanie seemed to catch herself. "Is that where Isabella's at?"

"She always goes to midnight Mass on Christmas Eve," Edith said. It had come as a revelation to her aunts, each of the last eighteen years, that her mother-in-law was still Catholic, and chose to go to her own church. Joe used to accompany her but then he was asked to be a deacon for the church Edith's family attended.

Aunt Lanie saw Jeremy shuffling off toward the back of the church, and turned back to Edith. "How's he doing? With that epilepsy."

"He's fine. Aunt Lanie, it'd be better if you don't just ask him about it flat out, right now. He's a little bit sensitive."

"Oh, he's a teenager. I remember how they are, honey. Always frowning, never a word to say. Your cousin Charlie was the same exact way, I mean the same face. Look at the family pictures."

Edith smiled. It was no use talking to her aunts about children; they already knew everything from raising her cousins, all thirty of them. Not all of them in this church tonight, praise be. Certainly not Charlie, whose teenage frown she remembered well. It was not the same as her son's face at all. Charlie had been a stupid boy, deliberately stupid, the kind of child Edith had struggled with her entire teaching career. He had continued being deliberately stupid throughout high school, only graduating because Aunt Lanie and Uncle Claude required it of all their children, and now he was a fat policeman, eating doughnuts at the jail nights and pulling over black men who drove through town. Though what they were doing in

Poudre Valley, Edith wasn't sure. Getting out as fast as they could, probably.

At the door to the church she forced herself to smile extra sincerely at Eric, and shake his hand, and say some warm words, since she had had envious thoughts about him during church. Envious wasn't even the word; jealous was. She saw Joe shake his hand and talk to him also, and Joe didn't talk much. She was sure he was as conscious of Eric's hair, his pretty young face, as she was.

She pushed her mind back to cousin Charlie on the way home, not wanting to say anything to Joe in case it came out sounding choked. Joe drove slowly to avoid the patches on the road that had frozen when the temperature dropped. Edith had noticed that people like Charlie, the ones who held up the class with concentrated (not innate) stupidity, somehow graduated into adult life, and were doing all right. They faced no consequences for their youthful antics, paid no price. In fact, Charlie was not badly paid, at least compared to a public school teacher. He got respect and carried a gun. She wondered at what point it had ceased to matter whether one knew what one was doing, or anything much at all.

"Mom," Dana said from the backseat, "are we going back to church in the morning?"

"What?" Oh, it was Sunday. And she was so tired. "Yes, I guess we will."

"Is Grandma going to midnight Mass with Dad?"

Edith didn't answer, forcing Joe to speak. "Yes, uh-huh. I'm just going to drop you all off and she should be ready to go."

When they pulled into the driveway, Isabella was ready. She crunched out over the gravel to the car, wrapped in a ball-length black coat that appeared to be but was not actually made of fur, and waved a pink handkerchief drenched in perfume. "Edith, honey," she said through the passenger side window, "I was just over at the big house, putting my presents under the tree." No matter how long they lived near each other, Isabella never talked about their house and her house; it was always "the big house" and "the little house." "Somebody called, about Clayton."

Edith stepped out of the minivan and reached to open the

side door, but the kids were already out. "Who was it?"

"I don't know, honey." Isabella buckled herself in. "I'll see you in the morning. Merry Christmas."

"Merry Christmas, Mom."

The minivan pulled out and Edith was left alone, standing under a very dark, very clear sky. Something she would miss if she ever moved from the country.

Who would call on Christmas Eve? She hoped nothing had happened to Clayton. She needed him to apologize for the state of Aunt Lanie's hair.

The old rotary phone sat on the kitchen counter. When it rang, it startled her. The voice was low. "Miz Rignaldi?"

"Yes."

"Joe there?"

She answered before thinking to ask who it was or why he needed to know. "No, Joe's gone with his mother to church." She felt reflexively guilty asking, "Who is this?"

"You the science teacher?"

"Yes."

His voice was unhurried. He spoke as if he had all kinds of time to visit, this early on Christmas morning. "I was in your class in the eighth grade."

"Yes, well, most people were." Edith's manners took over, a smooth gear clicking into place. "If you grew up in Poudre Valley."

"I never forgot your class." He paused. "You failed me."

"I'm sorry, I don't know who you are."

"I couldn't even read. Do you understand what I'm saying? I just could not read."

"I'm sorry," she said again.

"Your husband really not home?"

She was silent, and knew that made her sound more alone.

"You need to stay away from that girly hairdresser."

There was a click on the line but it wasn't a hang-up, it sounded like someone on the party line. One thing Edith didn't love about living in the country. She heard a snickering sound.

"I seen that fairy Clayton down at the bus station," he said. "Guy could get hisself killed."

"Who is this?"

"Watch out for Clayton Fucking Faggot."

The line went dead. Edith stood with the receiver still in her hand. She was gripped by the fear that it could be a near neighbor.

She walked to the door that led to the attic stairs. There was no sound coming from Jeremy's room, hadn't been since he came home from the hospital. Perhaps loud music didn't agree with his medicine.

She unclenched her fists and opened the door to the basement, just wide enough to feel a tool rack hanging on the wall next to the stairs. It held a mop, a broom and a couple of softball bats, one of which—the aluminum one—Edith put her hand around now, and removed it quietly, shutting the door so that no one would hear. The bat felt light but solid in her hands.

She'd grown up playing with wooden bats and they made a more satisfying cracking sound, but as a weapon this one made her feel more secure. She remembered the grip from her youth, and figured she could get one really good bash in the head in before a criminal could turn it against her. This thought made her queasy, but then there'd been a fair amount of adrenalin kicking around in her body for days.

She was aware of the throbbing of blood in her head, the muscles of her fingers around the grip of the bat, swings taken long ago on school playgrounds around East Tennessee. The hours of her life spent scuffing a toe against a dusty base, waiting for anyone to recall she was there, came back as a single muscle memory, concentrated into the bones clenched tightly around her weapon of choice, the twist of trunk and shoulders, coiled in readiness at the sound of someone fumbling with the knob of the back door—

There was a juddering crash! as Edith, responding with all her childhood might, swung the aluminum bat directly into the door. Glass from the window showered the kitchen floor, though the door itself remained intact. She felt a pain in her shoulder and heard Joe, only mildly agitated, say, "Edith, what's the matter with you? You broke the damn window."

She looked down at the bat in her hands, did not know what to say. Joe reached through the frame of the window and turned on the switch for the overhead light. Edith turned and saw that Dana had emerged and was clutching the Jim Beam bottle she'd found in the front yard, thrown from some passing pickup truck.

"Mom, are you nuts? I was getting ready to brain some burglar."

The attic doorknob turned and Jeremy shuffled in, looking worse than usual. He saw the broken glass on the floor and looked at her with a mix of bewilderment and accusation.

"Edith," Joe said, "give me the bat." He took it from her kindly, as if only his calm stood between them and a crazed rampage. Though she doubted she had another swing like that left in her unpracticed arms. She sank into a chair.

Joe stood looking at the back door, so-called not because it was really in back but because no one ever unlocked, never mind used, the front door. "We're not going to be able to fix that until after Christmas. Even if I could do it, I can't get any material."

"I'm sorry," Edith said, in the same tone she'd used on the phone. "I heard fumbling, and I thought somebody was trying to break in."

Joe sat down and motioned for the kids to do the same, but they remained where they were. "I was just getting out my key. It always takes me a minute."

This was true. How many years had they lived here, and yet he never was ready to walk in the door, would invariably fiddle with his keys for a full minute while the rest of them wasted sixty precious seconds of their lives hopping from one foot to the other. Four people, one bathroom.

"Well." Joe headed for the basement. "I've got some plastic I can tape over that till we can get it replaced. Jeremy, help me out please."

The men set about their task, a veneer of common life as thin as plastic on a window. Joe didn't even seem curious as to why she'd had the bat in her hands. She looked over at where Dana had been standing with the bottle, but she'd returned to her room.

It was just before two o'clock Christmas morning when they finally got to bed. There were still no questions forthcoming, so Edith said, "How was Mass?"

"Fine. Mom got to talking to the priest afterward." Joe lay silent, as he did for long stretches of their nights—months, years. "She was home when you broke the window, if that's worrying you. She won't have heard it."

Edith couldn't stand the lack of curiosity, so she told him she was sorry to have broken the window, but someone, a former student, had called asking if Joe was home and saying ugly things that scared her. She left out the part about Clayton.

Joe was remarkably calm. "You know how young men drink."

Always the Italian, the Yankee pagan who drank real wine and prayed to Mary when he thought no one was looking.

"Leave the ball bat in the basement."

Chapter 3

After Jeremy had hung up the extension in his attic room, he'd thought, That should do it. Didn't know it would send Mom for the ball bat. God.

Jeremy had put Bear, his Skoal-dipping friend, up to the phone call. Bear was a pretty slow kid. Didn't matter to Jeremy, he liked hanging out with slow kids, was used to being called one himself.

He wasn't a reader but he could pick up anything on guitar. Right now he was learning Pink Floyd's "Wish You Were Here." He started thumbing the opening notes. He hoped Bear's call would make his mom stop letting Clayton paw all over her, that's all.

Dana said that whenever Mom went to get a haircut, or saw Clayton at church or anyplace, he would always hug her and kiss her, on the cheek but still, just touch her all the time. Made her sick, Dana said. She thought Mom and Clayton were too close, and that was why Dad was so unhappy. But it made Jeremy sick for a different reason.

Jeremy hated girly guys, not so much on account of them being fags or not, but because girls always seemed to like the girly guys best. Why was that? Fairies that would suck you off at the bus station for free, which girls wouldn't do. Well, maybe girls that hung out at the bus station would.

For chrisssakes, look at Dad. Elementary school teacher. Jeremy couldn't count the times kids had made fun of his dad for that, even though those same kids had loved Mr. Rignaldi back when they were in his class. Fucking hypocrites, as Dana would say.

The smell of incense wafted (Mom's word) around the attic. Mom hated incense, and she would always nag him if she smelled it, worried that he was going to burn the whole house down. Now that he'd had a fit she'd probably bug him even more. Look how tense she was, busting the door. Didn't she see he was just trying to keep the house together himself? He was the same person, wouldn't let anything stop him.

Christmas was a Sunday. When the alarm woke Joe after only a few hours' sleep, he heard Edith beside him say, "I hate it when religion gets in the way of my holiday."

They both laughed, then dragged themselves out of bed and the family off to church, though they'd barely been home.

Joe began to regret even trying to have a talk about things. Look at that Eric Dufresne, divinity student, twenty-five years old and not even a girlfriend, let alone a wife. What a struggle he must have. Joe watched him in a bow tie, looking as dapper as someone could with long hair. Dana didn't like him but Joe didn't see anything wrong with him, just another earnest white kid with a Bible, far as he could tell.

The church was hung with holly and pine, but it looked different in the daylight. It was a sunny morning for December, and the stained glass cast its patterns on the old worn floor and across the aging pews and their aging occupants. There were plenty of kids in the church, who would normally be having junior worship at this hour under Eric's leadership, but he and his old guitar were in the main sanctuary this morning. It was a holiday for him too, and the children filled up the church and sang carols along with the rest of them.

For Christmas dinner, the custom was for the entire Wheeler family, all Edith's cousins, to get together at one of the houses, either theirs (with Joe's mother cooking) or Aunt Anna's. This year it was Anna's turn. Joe was glad of this, not because Aunt Anna was his favorite—Edith said Lanie was her favorite aunt—but because no one would have to explain the broken window. He could tell something was preoccupying Edith because she barely sang along to the service, but it must have just been a nicotine fit because no sooner had they pulled into Aunt Anna's driveway than she hopped out, not waiting for him to turn off the engine. "Charlie!" she called, almost running to see her cousin the policeman at the end of the driveway. He was having a cigarette and Joe saw him offer her one too.

Jeremy and Dana followed him toward the house. Uncle Jimmy, Anna's husband, hefted himself down the porch steps and shook his hand. "Joe, Merry Christmas," he said. "Warmest Christmas we've had in a while."

"Yes, sir," Joe said. "How are you, Uncle Jimmy?"

"Pretty good, doing pretty good. How them kids treating you down at the school?"

"Well, they're pretty young kids, don't get in too much trouble. One of them had to go to the principal's office last week though. Hated to do it, you know, Mr. Tanner likes to paddle them."

"It's the only thing you can do, sometimes, ain't it?" Jimmy's eyes lit on someone who had just pulled in. "Excuse me, son."

Joe walked into the party, and wished, not for the first time, that there was wine at Wheeler family gatherings.

Edith smoked a cigarette with Charlie, gut hanging over the waist of his blue jeans, a ridiculous number of zippers on his jacket. These boys—Edith would never think of them as men, though they were the same generation she was. They finished and went inside for the meal.

The house was a riot of people, dressed mostly in sweaters patterned red and green. It was too warm inside for sweaters but they had to be worn once a year. There were too many cousins to sit all at a table, even if you didn't count the kids, so Uncle Jimmy called everyone to attention and said grace before the buffet opened and people started dishing up their own food. A bird had been carved but there was ham besides, and potatoes and gravy, mounds of biscuits, and vegetables that had been salted and boiled till every last vitamin had been wrung out of them, in the Southern tradition. Edith had brought a fruit salad in the hope that it would offset a little of the salt and fat, which couldn't be doing anyone much good in this age of stress, particularly the uncles with their ever-expanding girth. She didn't worry so much at home. Joe was leaner than any of the boys.

"Our Father in heaven, we thank thee for all thy many blessings," Uncle Jimmy prayed, and there were scattered "Amens" when he finished. Isabella's was always the most emphatic, a fact Edith found curious. She had not thought this was a thing Catholics did and maybe it was just an attempt to blend in. She wondered if Isabella's own lack of a large family, despite being Italian, drew her closer to her in-law Southern brood.

"I guess Jones couldn't make it down this year," Aunt Anna said when the table was crowded round with people, the others having gone off to perch on the arms of couches or wherever they could fit. Anna was fairly relaxed about the use of her house, which was just as well. It had been more than a few years since Anna's brother Jones had been home for Christmas, and they had stopped expecting him.

"You talk to Jones much, Edie?" Aunt Anna tried again. Her hands were full of serving spoons but her eyes were on her niece.

"Not much." Not for years.

"He's probably on vacation, Florida maybe," Uncle Jimmy said. He put up his hand to indicate that Aunt Anna had heaped enough potatoes on his plate. "Thank you."

"He likes to go someplace warm in the winter," Edith said.

"It's warm here, today," said Uncle Claude, Aunt Lanie's husband.

Aunt Anna shook her head. "Why would anybody be

by themself at Christmas when they have family." It wasn't a question.

Edith was sure, even if Jones had gone away alone, he wasn't alone now, but she wasn't about to tell Anna that. Discussing her uncle was bound to bring comments about the city, the North, and all the odious people Anna had heard (but did not know from her own experience) lived there.

Throughout the 1970s, Edith's Uncle Jones had had limited contact with his family in Tennessee. The Christmas outing to Poudre Valley was as much time as he would concede to his place of origin, and even this must have become too much, since his last visit had been in 1982. Edith had kept up with him through very occasional phone calls; Jones never wrote letters, and that was unusual in their family. A few years ago the phone calls had trickled away to nothing. This hurt Edith to a degree she could hardly express, but in a vague way, she understood.

"Church was nice this morning," Anna said. "I hate it that you have to wait until church on Sunday to learn the true meaning of Christmas anymore. Children are so ignorant now. Isn't it true you can be arrested for telling the true story of Christmas in the public schools?"

"No," Edith said. Joe put a hand on her arm.

"Well, not around here, maybe. I daresay people wouldn't allow it. But technically, didn't they pass a law that it's illegal to say the name of Jesus in the public schools?"

"Aunt Anna, every child in Poudre Valley knows who Jesus is."

"But that could change. First the Lord's Prayer, then the manger scene and what's next? Pretty soon the only place it will be safe to be a Christian is in church."

Edith wished, for a moment, that Anna had decided to talk about Jones instead. It wasn't really her brother Anna had a problem with; it was this strange urban legend of a world she didn't know, except by reputation, much as Edith knew the world of other marriages through Women's Council and the magazines at the Piggly Wiggly. When it came to the public schools, though, there was no reason for Anna to be so ignorant. Everyone's children had gone to them, and two teachers were sitting right across from her at the dinner table. Joe thought Anna did it deliberately to provoke them, but Edith couldn't impute such a motive to her aunt. After all, she had a good heart, which, being a Southerner, Edith would "bless" at every opportunity.

"Maybe that wouldn't be such a bad thing," Joe was saying now.

"I beg your pardon?" Aunt Anna seemed surprised by an interruption from Joe, who spoke so rarely.

"For the only place to be a Christian to be church." Joe did not look up from scooping his mashed potatoes, and his hands were steady but Edith's, in her lap, were not.

"What on earth do you mean, Joseph?" She would call him that, though she knew it wasn't his name.

"People get complacent. When the early church was persecuted, Christians were passionate about their faith. Now it's just taken for granted."

"Well, I don't know as much as a schoolteacher, I'm sure," Aunt Anna said. "But I certainly don't take my faith for granted."

"Who wants another roll?" said Aunt Lanie. She thrust the basket eagerly in front of Joe and Anna, who ignored her. Edith took it, unfolded the red-checked cotton cloth, retrieved a roll, and bit into it. She tasted nothing; her mouth was completely dry.

"I didn't mean you, Aunt Anna." Joe smiled the broad, full-toothed grin that had won over so many Southern women, beginning with his wife. "I just meant, when Christianity is taken for granted as the background of a culture, it loses some of its power. Like everybody celebrating December the twenty-fifth, whether or not they have, you know, a personal relationship with Jesus Christ."

"Yes. That's right," Aunt Anna said. If it were true, it must have been what she was saying. "You know, you don't sound like a Catholic at all."

"Aunt Anna," Edith said in despair.

"Mrs. Rignaldi," Aunt Lanie tried again, "would you like some more of this sweet potato casserole?" And Isabella must not have heard Aunt Anna's remark about Catholics, because when Lanie got Isabella's attention—it took a couple of tries, she was a little hard of hearing—she agreed with a smile.

Aunt Anna did not comprehend that what she'd said was anything less than a compliment. She gave that shake of the head that always meant the people around her were idiots, but she would pray the Lord to take their brains away and create in them new brains, clean of all these unworthy thoughts that the Tempter had been allowed to slip in.

Joe did not respond to the present insult, and the conversation moved on. Edith chewed her roll, over and over, trying to moisten it. It was not clear to her if Aunt Anna or the cloud of last night had ruined dinner. The uncles around her had no trouble salivating, downing their food as if they'd had no breakfast and didn't expect supper either. None of them looked as if they'd ever been young, like her cousins had once been, flat-stomached and throwing a football around the backyard. Joe was older than the boys playing out there now but he still belonged with them, separated from his own generation by the absence of sloppy joes around his middle.

As long as people were eating around the table, the television would not go on. This was one of God's laws, Aunt Anna's finger once again in the dike of secular culture. Edith happened to agree with her on this point, painful though it was.

The meal did end, finally, people so stuffed they could not even face the pies, which would be there a few hours of football later (played or watched, albeit in the living room). Edith needed another cigarette so took her own exercise, joining other guilty cousins on the back porch. Aunt Anna did not allow smoking in the house, either, said it gave her a headache. It was also profoundly unladylike, something she was sure Edith could only have picked up in the urban North, despite heaps of redneck evidence.

Since cousin Charlie was a policeman, Edith had to tell him about the phone call. Goodness knew Joe wouldn't take it seriously.

"City bus station," Charlie said. "Not a place I would go if I was—a lady."

Edith wondered how long this cigarette would take. "You

still pick up free doughnuts behind the Krispy Kreme after midnight?" This was one perk of his job Charlie was particularly proud of; he boasted about it as if it were health insurance.

"Most nights."

He was useless. "See you at the piano."

It was Aunt Anna's custom, when evening came and everyone was full of pie, to plunk down at the old piano and hammer out Christmas carols. It wasn't as bad as it sounded. She really could play and besides, for whom were they singing? Only each other and the Lord.

In the kitchen, Isabella was saying, "Dana, don't you want a piece of pie?"

Dana's eyes turned toward her as if she were surprised to be addressed. "What kind of crust is it?"

"Oh," Edith said, "Dana's a vegetarian, remember, Mom? She won't have anything that's made with meat, not even the turkey."

"Lard," Dana said. "There's lard in pie crust, Mom."

"There probably is the way Aunt Anna makes it." Back to running interference. "Come on, have a cup of coffee with cream." There would be no peace until she got some calories in the girl, some fat, to be exact.

A young cousin was at the piano, flexing her fingers to "Heart And Soul," the universal exercise of out-of-tune pianos in church basements and rural homes. Very Christmasy. Edith poured a coffee for herself and one for Dana, adding generous shots of cream. She also poured a glass of peach Hi-C for a little cousin who had followed them to the kitchen, and they went back in the living room. Automatically, Edith scanned the room and noticed her son was missing.

"Joe," she said, "where's Jeremy?"

"Playing football?"

She doubted that. "Have you seen him? I didn't see him outside."

"Well, unless the van's gone, he can't have gone far."

One of the things Joe was always complaining about, that he thought was so wrong with where they lived, was that you had to have a car to get anywhere, even to buy milk and bread.

You could not ride a bike safely; often there wasn't even room for one car to pass another. This was a normal state of affairs to Edith, since she'd grown up with it, but she could see how someone from Chicago would find it difficult to adjust.

She checked, but the minivan was still in the driveway, blocked in by other relatives' cars and blocking others in its turn. It was an industrial, boxy-looking thing. Edith had a classroom and filing cabinets at school, but Joe was always hauling crates of materials back and forth, and she frequently did too. She hated to work in the classroom after school, much preferred to prepare at home now that Jeremy and Dana were older and no longer depending on her constant attention. Except for occasions like this, when they were supposed to be participating in family events, both of them could normally be found in their respective rooms, listening to their own music. Edith had been skeptical about the quality of homework produced under such circumstances, but Dana assured her that the music helped her concentrate, and her grades didn't seem to suffer so Edith let it go.

She was worried about Jeremy, though. It didn't seem wise for him to be somewhere unknown and unaccounted for, so soon after his diagnosis. But she didn't want to draw attention to him by talking about it in a roomful of aunts. Anyway, they were singing.

The room was cheerful and loud—even Joe was swaying his lean body, sharing a song sheet with one of the boys, and lending his bass to the general cacophony. Joe was a true bass, not one of those baritones who sort of crept down there; the low notes were his natural range. The windows and everything between them were bright with decorations. Fake greenery adorned the piano and the other furniture. Nonetheless, Edith felt a melancholy in her bones, as if her arm had just now remembered to ache from swinging that bat. It was something that came to her every Christmas night, the knowledge, even in a mild Southern clime, that the one redemptive feature of winter was now over, the anticipation finished, and now nothing remained but to wait out the bizarre season when it might be six degrees one morning in January and the lilacs trying to come out the next. At least up north winter looked like something; you knew what to expect. It was ugly, dirt and snow ugly, and it was cold and it would be that way into March, if not April. Whereas March here was lions and lambs, a whole peaceable kingdom of weather to look forward to. The thought of it made her rub her temples.

"Hi, Dorothy." She took a song sheet from the cheery cousin who would never be mistaken for a dieter. Scarcely the same gene pool as the skinny girls. Who knew how people ended up the way they did, happy or otherwise. Was it all in the genes?

Edith sang along to "We Three Kings" and "The First Noel," two carols with five verses each. Aunt Anna would never dream of cutting a verse, as they sometimes did at church to speed the service up. Edith wouldn't have minded except it was never pitched in her range; she sang too high to be comfortable with the alto part, not high enough to be a good soprano. Clayton was such a good organist it was almost worth singing at church when he played, but here, Edith felt her voice was naked and exposed.

Going through the motions. Standing between her cousin and her husband, people she'd known all or half her life, and trying to sing praises while her heart was a knot of uncertainty. Where was her son? What was the rest of the season, the rest of the school year, going to be like? How about the rest of her life? She had a memory that Joe had wanted to talk about things and that it hadn't mattered because of the broken window and the lateness of the hour. But of course it did matter. Things didn't stop mattering because you'd distracted yourself with a new problem.

Whitney, the little cousin with the peach Hi-C, came in yelling for her mama. "What is it?" Dorothy said, with a no-look pass of the sheet music to the cousin next to her.

"Jeremy done something funny with his lip."

A storm of people headed for the back porch but Edith implored them: "No. Please don't, he's sensitive. Let me take care of this." She let Whitney, already showing the missionary zeal of a Wheeler, lead her to the porch, where Jeremy sat gnashing at a bloody lip. She was struck by the incongruous calm of the rest of his body. From the neck down he was folded in an almost meditative posture, as if disconnected from the violent motion of his head and jaw.

"What are we gonna do?" Whitney asked the general gathering of adults. But Edith waved them all back into the house.

"Just leave him." She could hardly bear the little girl's voice; it was so loud. She wanted to say, "He doesn't want all this attention," but that would only compound the sin of speaking of him as if he weren't there.

She sat with Jeremy a minute, until the seizure was over and he came to. Then she said, "Jeremy, you knocked over your water glass. Would you like another glass of water?"

He didn't say anything. He almost never did. It was as if he had become mute, as well as having seizures.

"Jeremy—" She put a hand on his shoulder, which he didn't knock away. But what young man with facial hair wanted his mother babying him in the middle of a family Christmas? He'd probably rather be in the attic, listening to his music. At that moment, so would she.

Chapter 4

1989

"One boy in the war is enough," Isabella had said when Steve went to Vietnam. "Joe, you listen to your mother. You get married and have some grandchildren for me. Don't break my heart."

Her words lodged in Joe's chest, and cut deeper for not being intended that way. He'd never been the son who would break her heart; that was Steve's job. But the threat was there, and if he ever doubted his adequacy to be a father, he could not escape his obligation as a son.

In 1970 Edith and Joe both got teaching jobs in Poudre Valley. Shortly afterward they bought the house they still lived in, with its smaller neighboring house. It made no sense to Joe that Isabella should stay in the Chicago suburb of Cicero without a son to take care of her, or to take care of. Isabella came down South for the first time, with her things in a van, driven by a student coming to one of those colleges people didn't think existed in Tennessee. She moved into the little house and that's where she'd been ever since.

Steve got ownership of the house in Cicero where he and Joe had grown up. He was never in it, whoring around the ports of the world; he got a buddy to manage it for him, a handy guy who kept his eye on the tenants.

In spite of themselves, Joe and Edith became property owners. Where they bought, nineteen years before, was as rural as where Isabella had grown up in the Twenties. Land was going for, as the expression went, a song.

Edith had only been allowed to accept her scholarship and move up north because her uncle lived there. Most relatives, her Wheeler and Jones cousins, and everybody else's relatives still lived in the county, never mind the state, although a cousin or two lived over in North Carolina. But Jones, who had been given his mother's maiden name, moved north for some kind of factory job after the war, and never saw fit to return except for Christmas or the birth of a niece or nephew. Neither Pam nor Edith knew anyone else who had done this. It was still Yankee territory, in the kindest terms, and the Sixties did not soften such a view among white Southerners. Uncle Jones was a bachelor, which also made him hopelessly exotic. He dressed well, listened to music, and wore aftershave. Jones had always been a good reference for her, vouching to Aunt Anna (who would ask) and Aunt Lanie (who wouldn't) that Edith was not in any trouble, which of course she wasn't. She could not with certainty say the same for Uncle Jones.

She could talk to people, but her standard of friendship was rather high. To bare her heart and soul to someone, Edith believed, you had to share a past with them, preferably back to childhood. You had to know each other's families—it was almost like a marriage. And people in the North did not seem to want to make friendships like this. They often did not talk about, or even have, brothers and sisters, didn't know their cousins, while where Edith came from, everyone was a cousin, or a cousin of someone she knew. So when she needed to talk to someone about whether something made sense, it was still her best friend from high school, Pam, that she sought.

When Edith told Pam she'd met another student teacher named Joe Rignaldi, Pam was proud to observe that the name was Italian. She wanted to know what else was foreign. Where was Joe from? Was he Catholic?

"He's from Chicago." They were seated in Poudre Valley's only theatre, waiting for a matinee.

"So you met him in college?"

"We don't go to the same college," Edith said. "Chicago's big, Pam, a really big city. You could live there your whole life and not meet somebody who lived in a different part of town."

"But you're seeing him now?"

This was a curious expression, which Edith didn't remember Pam using before. In high school, where they'd been best friends, no one had ever talked about seeing anyone. You were dating, or you weren't dating, and there were very specific expectations (on the girls' part anyway) as to what you were supposed to do on dates and how long you were supposed to date somebody before you could do each thing. Pam, who had blonder hair and newer clothes and wore more makeup than Edith, was usually dating somebody or other, or said she was. Edie, as people called her back home, usually was not.

Now Pam was all coy and using an innocuous word like seeing when Edith was certain she was thinking of much more, of the sinful possibilities for a college boy, a man, an Italian, and a Methodist girl from the South on her own in a godless northern city. In fact Pam talked so much, and with such salacious interest, about whom she and the rest of their friends at State were "seeing" that Edith assumed they were still disappointingly virginal. By saying as little as possible about her own life and adventures, Edith herself was giving the opposite impression.

"Catholics. Don't you have to be Catholic too, to marry one?" Pam said between bites of popcorn.

"Pam, we're not getting married. I just met this guy."

"And you have to raise your kids that way, too. Yeah, I went out with a Catholic guy once."

Edith knew that this probably meant a Catholic boy had, on some occasion, held the door open for Pam, and the two of them had "gone out" through the door together.

Pam finished her popcorn and moved on to adjusting the bangles on her wrist. "What about Negroes?"

Edith looked around to see if there were any actual black people to hear this loud question, but there didn't seem to be. "What about them?"

"Aren't there a lot of Negroes in Chicago?"

"I told you, it's a big city. There are a lot of people there."

It was obvious that Pam was also proud of herself just for using the word Negroes, to which she had graduated along with her graduation from high school. Through an accident of geography, East Tennessee had been on the wrong side of the old Confederacy, which got blamed for everything bad with regard to the South and black people. Edith had read Faulkner too.

"I don't know when I'm going to get married," Pam said, moving on to the favorite subject to which all her conversations returned.

"Pam, you're not even seeing anyone right now."

"I know, I know." In Pam's lament, seeing someone was like the last piece of a puzzle you put together in order to get married, rather than a foundational building block. "But I don't know any guys."

"You know hundreds of guys."

"I know, but they're not my type. All the guys around here—" Her gesture took in the theatre and all its slack-jawed consumers of popcorn—"they don't go to school, you know, they don't have real jobs. And the college guys I know—I mean, I have friends and everything, but Edie, they're funny."

Edith felt herself wanting a cigarette, a habit Aunt Anna said she'd picked up from her "hippie" friends. They weren't hippies in any meaningful sense. They shaved and went to class; the girls returned to their dorms at night. But here at home, where she was spending the rest of the summer, Edith did not smoke cigarettes. Southern women, those who behaved themselves, were not even called women but ladies, and being a lady had little to do with one's actual social class. It had everything to do with behavior, and that didn't include smoking any more than skipping church or staying out all night.

So Edith began twisting her hair into a ponytail and said, "You mean they're funny because they don't like you?"

"Oh, they like me all right." Pam sucked her Pepsi-Cola through a straw with unseemly passion. "I mean, they're my friends. But they don't go out with girls. It's the way they talk, you know? 'Hey,'" she said, one long, drawn-out syllable. "Are there a lot of guys like that in Chicago? I hear the big cities are full of them."

Edith thought of Joe Rignaldi, the other guys she knew. "No," she said. "Not that I know anyway."

Tonight, nineteen years later, Edith stood looking at the stars, the quiet broken only by the occasional passing of a car along their road. She wondered whatever could have possessed her to think, from time to time, of moving off the land and no longer canning her own tomatoes and burying her own dead.

In the blank hell that was winter after Christmas, Dana tried as far as possible to live in her mind and its memories. At sixteen, she was convinced her memory had recorded, as if on film, everything that had ever happened to her, whether interesting or not. Sometimes she felt it too sharply, most notably when remembering the summer during winter or, almost worse, when summer had just turned to fall and all the school year lay ahead. People talked about hell being this hot place but Dana knew it was cold.

And it didn't even snow that much here. It lay on the ground for at most a few days, before melting away to reveal the brown grass. It was more depressing than snow, more depressing than Jeremy's music collection. Dana knew that in the lake, by which Rignaldis always meant Lake Michigan, up by Chicago, the water itself would freeze over in winter and you wouldn't see the ground for months. But she never went there in winter. No one wanted to go then, it was too cold; Mom shivered even at the memory of it.

Dana already felt as if she had lived a long time, long enough to be nostalgic. Ten seemed ages ago to her, when she used to swim in the lake, the waters back from the brink of chemical death and gasping for oxygen. There was no beach to speak of and no sand, just rocks, but to jump from those rocks into the lake, and what seemed to be its giant waves, was as much happiness as was vouchsafed to any child at that age.

She made the mistake of saying so once, to her mother. Who had not appreciated Dana's candor and said that if that were true, why did they spend money every summer to take the children to amusement parks and zoos if all they had to do was jump in the lake to have exquisite fun? Dana couldn't answer that. She knew if she pressed this or any other point there would be a price, probably no more amusement parks, so she kept her mouth shut as much as any highly verbal child could, which wasn't a whole lot.

"Highly verbal" was the way they put it at school, or would have, back when she was really young, like six. Now it just meant Dana was in the honors English class. "What's honors?" Isabella would ask and Dana couldn't tell her, other than it was like a regular English class only harder and you got the same grade as someone in the regular class who didn't work at all. She wished she could swim in a lake again.

There were lakes right here in Tennessee, but her family never went to any of them. Only Lake Michigan where she learned to swim because Isabella needed to go up there every summer to visit her friends, so that's where they took summer vacations. When Isabella's friends died or moved south, the family stopped going to Chicago, stopped seeing Uncle Jones, and went to the beach instead. Dana had never seen the ocean until she was a teenager.

Tennessee's lakes were fake, created in the Thirties when the Tennessee Valley Authority dammed up rivers for rural electrification. The TVA project had drowned whole communities, including the town of Butler, not far from Poudre Valley. Dana was inconsolable when she heard about Old Butler, the streets and shops just inundated where people had spent their lives. She couldn't have been sadder if the townspeople had drowned with the town; it was places she felt strongly for, more so than people. For the grass, the tender grass now waiting to grow when once the earth got warm, Dana felt a possessiveness that was as close to desire as anything she knew.

She came home from school in January clenching her hands,

feeling in them the raw, untended need for earth and clumps of grass. Needless to say she never spoke a word of this to anybody. A people who would drown Old Butler would not understand the worshipping of earth. In her sophomore year there had been some talk of Earth Day at school, but that had soon petered out. What difference did the earth make to a people waiting for God to destroy it in fire and blood? That couldn't come soon enough for Dana Rignaldi; she was itching for judgment.

Lately Dana felt angry most of the time. Enraged. She found it very difficult to keep her temper even while clenching her fists, and she couldn't believe it was all hormones or the kind of things magazines talked about. Most things nowadays seemed to require counseling or therapy, but she didn't believe in that bullshit so she knew not to say how angry she really felt. Not that it was easy to hide. Everyone just thought she had a bad temper and she did, but it wasn't like she tortured cats or anything so people usually dismissed her. Which made her even angrier.

"Styrofoam!" she exclaimed in the school cafeteria, not realizing she'd said it out loud till the girl in front of her looked up from her tray, piled with french fries. Well, at least she was using a tray. The same turquoise plastic Dana'd been eating off since kindergarten, and that was bad enough. They had Styrofoam bowls now? She just wouldn't eat soup. No telling what was in it, anyway. There was really nothing she could trust here but the salad bar.

She piled on as much cheese and dressing as her salad could hold—it had to last her hours and she was skinny enough. Then she scanned the crowd for someone she knew and liked well enough to sit with. Unlikely. Big hair to big hair they sat, all pink and fake and reeking of hairspray. Dana's stonewashed jeans would just not go.

Finally she saw Jeremy and what appeared to be an empty seat. Sitting with her brother was marginally less humiliating than what surely lay in wait with the pink fake crowd. She negotiated a path with her tray, not listening to what she was sure was talk about her.

"Hi." She plopped down, not looking at him, and stabbed

her salad with a fork that was at least metal. Take that, blue cheese.

Jeremy had eschewed the Styrofoam bowl and instead filled the entrée portion of his tray with soup beans. The meal was complemented on the one side by macaroni and cheese, on the other by a slab of salty cornbread which, if placed on a napkin, would leave a grease patch like one of Mom's classroom demonstrations. For dessert, Jeremy, like Dana, had picked up the cafeteria's approximation of a Reesey cup. How very home ec the color coordination was—all yellows and browns.

Jeremy kept chewing while Dana complained about the Styrofoam and how perverted all the adults were. By the time she stopped talking, lunch was over.

"See you on the bus?" Dana said.

He shook his head and hair fell in his eyes. "Guitar club."

Jeremy lived for guitar club. It was run by Mr. Triplett, who was a hard rock fan himself and thought some of the kids could stay out of trouble by learning to play guitar for real. He only meant guys. Dana would have been good at guitar, he figured, but she was more into jangly stuff like U2 than the classics.

Dana'd only heard him play once, other than when he'd plug in his amplifier in the attic and blast away till somebody asked him to stop. The whole guitar club had performed a chorus of "Smoke On The Water," with chords that might have been the original arrangement, for all she knew. Jeremy had felt right at home in his black everything clothes. On the bus after school Dana proclaimed the show "fucking amazing."

"Thanks."

"You're really talented," she said. "Why don't you try and do something with it?"

It was exactly like something Mom would say. Except she wouldn't say it about rock music. What could you "do" with music, anyway? They'd heard tales from Mom about men her Uncle Jones had known in Chicago, jazz musicians with junkie itch and habits like that. None of them could make a living. Dana said that might have more to do with them spending it all on drugs than with the music, but who was she, Nancy Reagan?

Jeremy didn't argue with Dana when she asked what he'd rather do. He just said, "Party with my friends." She didn't know what friends or where these parties happened. As far as she knew, he spent all his time up in the attic. He'd perfected a jump out the window to a tree limb, swing down and run half a mile over to Bear's trailer, parked on Aunt Anna's property. Bear had a truck and that, in Poudre Valley, had more value than the dollar. Mom had never woke up once.

"What colleges are you looking at, honey?"

Dana had brought her college brochures out to the kitchen table where Isabella was drinking tea. Her grandma was a gray-haired beacon of serenity while Mom fanned the flames of supper over by the stove. "It's random right now. These are all things I got in the mail since I took the SAT. I was looking through a directory in the library, but that was no help."

"Why not?" Isabella said.

"It's just statistics. I look for the highest proportion of male to female students."

"Oh, so you have more boyfriends." Isabella nodded approvingly to Mom, who was scrubbing a glass dry with a dish towel.

"No, because they're the best schools." And so she'd have friends, never mind the "boy" part. "But it doesn't matter because I could never go to them. Not without scholarship money, plus they don't want anyone from the South up there anyway."

"Dana," Mom began.

"I'm not talking about where you went, I just mean the East Coast, New England, Pennsylvania. They think it's all redneck down here. And it is. That's why I want to leave." Dana took a big swig of milk. She didn't add, for Isabella's benefit, that according to the directory certain East Coast schools had adopted non-discrimination policies on the basis of "sexual preference," and that Mom had disparaged them for this.

"Look, Grandma," she said, and waved a brochure with a picture of a tall, short-haired female student. "All this stuff is from women's colleges. I didn't think they even had women's colleges anymore."

"Let me see, honey." Isabella took the brochure. "Here's a quiz about them. True or False: Only wealthy women with horses attend women's colleges."

"Obviously they want us to say False, so it must be true." Dana took pride in her bottomless cynicism.

"Well." Isabella considered. "We had a cow fall through the septic tank that time. Does that count?" All three of them fell to laughing.

"I couldn't stand to be around nothing but girls all the time," Dana said.

"True or False," Isabella read. "Attending a women's college says something about your sexuality."

"Give me that." Mom marched over to Isabella and snatched the brochure out of her hands.

"What's the matter, honey?" Isabella was unperturbed. "We're all girls here."

"That's exactly the matter."

When Edith was in college, she'd had to wait almost till graduation for a man to call. She was in her dorm room, just drying her hair. A girl from down the hall came in and said she was wanted on the phone. So Edith wrapped a towel around her head, not bothering to change out of her robe.

"Edie?" It was her uncle's voice. "Have you heard the news?"

"What's that, Uncle Jones?"

"There's been a riot over in Ohio. Some college kids been shot."

Shot by whom? She was horrified, of course, but why was he telling her this?

"The National Guard's there," he said. "They're shooting students now."

"Oh—no," she said, hesitant after a lifetime's Christianity to take the name of the Lord in vain. "You called to tell me that?"

"To tell you for God's sake, stay out of those demonstrations. Those protest scenes. You could just be walking by and a riot break out, and what the hell would I tell Anna?"

She had not been part of any "protest scenes," in fact hadn't protested anything on her campus except maybe the atrocious scrambled eggs in the cafeteria. But she said "Yes, sir." Then she went back to her room, finished drying her hair, took out her change, and called Joe Rignaldi.

By the time he came to the phone Edith was already regretting her call. What could she say? "Have you heard the bad news?"

He had. They muttered inanities for a moment before she, perhaps insane with grief, heard herself suggesting they meet for dinner sometime.

"You mean a date?"

"I'd like you to meet someone," she said, thinking of it as she spoke. "My uncle. He—he likes music a lot, I'm sure you'd like him." What was she doing? She hadn't spoken to Joe in months, he was probably engaged or even married, and now she was taking advantage of tragedy to introduce him to her family?

"I'd love to."

When Joe met them at the Greek restaurant—anything but Italian, Edith had said—Uncle Jones rose from his seat. Edith, never quite sure what to do in these situations, did the same. Joe took her hand, smiled, then shook hands with her uncle. Jones Wheeler clapped the younger man on the forearm and smiled with a warmth she wouldn't have minded being directed at her.

Uncle Jones ordered a bottle of wine, later another, and paid for everything. Edith never drank, but Jones insisted she at least sit there and swirl her glass around, after all it was nearly graduation. "Think of it as an early celebration," he said. Where Edith came from, she didn't know any men who drank wine, though she supposed Catholics did, at communion. Drinking men she knew preferred beer, in cans. Whiskey was a rumor, something the aunts wouldn't let in the house. She was uncomfortable with drinking in general, but she couldn't think of anything Uncle Jones did as very bad.

They talked some more about the Kent State shootings. It seemed too shocking to absorb. Uncle Jones was rather liberal in his inclinations and kept shaking his head, saying "Now that white kids are involved. They've been cracking black kids' heads for years but now that white kids are involved..." Edith wasn't sure whom he meant: the blacks who had rioted? But Joe just nodded vigorously, and beamed, as if he and Jones shared some secret knowledge of black people.

"What do you think, Edie?" Uncle Jones said. He refilled his own glass and topped up the half inch she had drunk of hers.

"Edie," Joe said, and smiled. He'd never heard that name for her before, and she'd rather he hadn't, right now.

"Well—I don't know. I can't imagine rioting. But just walking to class—it makes you wonder, doesn't it?"

"What does it make you wonder?" Joe's full attention was on her now, and that felt even stranger than the way he looked at her uncle.

"What it takes, to be young in this world." She took a sip of the wine, fortifying herself. "When we're going to grow up."

"Is that why you're in teaching?"

She was in teaching because she didn't want to be in secretarial science, but that didn't sound right, with girls now getting into Yale and who knew where else. "I decided to teach science because I don't want to have to deal with those things," she said. "I don't want to teach history—I know, Joe, with elementary kids you have to teach every subject. But I don't want that. Sodium in water, it does what it does. It doesn't care if you're white or what you believe."

"What if students take things from a lab," Uncle Jones said, "and blow somebody up? Or blow up a government building, you know, as a protest. Isn't it political then?"

"What about the atomic bomb?" Joe said.

She didn't like these men challenging her. Because when they both spoke, it no longer felt to her as if she were the center of their attention, as a young lady ought to be; it felt as if they were trying to impress each other. She didn't pay a lot of attention to men, but she had noticed this about them.

"I like the answers of science," she said. "If you prove something scientifically, and it can be replicated, nobody can argue with it. They can't say, 'You're a girl, so it doesn't count.'"

Joe grinned. She could get used to seeing that grin. "Edie," he said, "I hope no one ever says that to you." And he said it with such warmth—a warmth, she supposed, he extended to all his interlocutors—that she could not even object to his adopting her family's nickname, which she had meant to leave behind.

After Kent State, newspapers displayed the photograph of a young woman, hands outstretched, crying over the body of a young man who had just been walking by when the shooting began. Edith stared at the picture, seeing something of the young woman in herself. They had the same soft build, long, dark hair that would have to be wrapped in a towel after it was washed. Edith wondered if she was capable of such an expression, of unutterable grief and outrage. Of asking "Why?" while kneeling beside a victim.

She had heard something in Uncle Jones's voice. "What would I tell Anna?" It sounded urgent, too urgent to be only an appeal to her not to get shot by the National Guard. Just for that moment, Jones sounded like a father, which he wasn't, nor could Edith picture him being one. And she, who had lost her parents, saw for a moment what it must mean to become, or not become, a parent, and what either way would cost.

On Sunday there was a Mission Moment at church, and Edith stayed afterward to talk to Eric Dufresne. The youth minister spoke of a trip he'd taken the summer before to East Africa, to visit missionaries the church was supporting there. He showed some slides of himself with Maasai people, and expressed his "passionate desire" to go back and serve as a missionary himself, once he was finished with his education. Edith wished Jeremy had a better idea what he wanted to do once he finished his education.

Edith asked her family to wait by the car, she wanted to talk to Eric for a few minutes. Dana flounced off. Lately, she'd gotten as sullen as Jeremy.

"Can I ask you about Africa?"

"Sure, Mrs. Rignaldi."

"Oh, call me Edith, everybody does." She hesitated. She wanted to say how fascinated she'd always been by Africa, how she'd always wanted to go there, even be a missionary herself. But he'd ask her why and she didn't have any good reason, like a calling from God. She couldn't say "Because I think black people are beautiful," even though she had told her relatives, when she was growing up, that Larry Doby was her favorite baseball player. Besides, you weren't supposed to have reasons like that. Black people wouldn't appreciate it either.

"Which country were you in again? Ghana?"

"Actually Kenya. Ghana is over in West Africa."

"Oh—I'm sorry."

"Don't be. A lot of these countries are fairly new, just since independence. The Maasai people live in Kenya and also in Tanzania, just to the south."

He pronounced it to rhyme with "Tasmania," and Edith had heard of it but pronounced another way. "Um—is that anywhere near Zambia?" There had been a missionary from Zambia visiting the year before.

"Yes. Tanzania borders a number of countries, but those are two of the big ones."

"Zimbabwe? Zaire?" All those Z countries.

"Actually Tanzania is across Lake Victoria from Zaire, but it borders two small countries, Burundi and Rwanda. But, I bet you've never heard of them." Edith shook her head. "Nobody has."

"Eric, just between you and me, there's so little geography teaching nowadays I doubt many people could find Africa on a map at all."

"I know, and it's a shame. Africa is a fascinating, fascinating place. So beautiful, and so much poverty, too. So much need for the Lord."

Edith wasn't sure those were quite the same thing, but she let it go. "The Maasai certainly sound fascinating."

"Oh, they are. They live just as they have for hundreds of years, on whatever land is left to them. Herding cattle and staying in dung huts."

"So...you would go back and live with them the way they do?"

"Yes. We have to meet the people where they are. If that means dung, then dung it is!" Eric clapped his hands together and smiled.

She couldn't help liking him. She didn't often see a young person this fired up about anything, despite weekly pep rallies and the cheerleaders' exhortation to "git fard up!" At the same time, she was confused. Her interest in Africa had, she feared, very little to do with the Lord. She wanted to see something different, and Africa seemed as different as any place on this earth. "What airport do you fly into, to get to where these people are? I mean, they don't live near any big city, do they?"

"Well, the capital of Kenya is Nairobi, and in Tanzania it's Dar es Salaam, which is Arabic for World of Peace. But there's actually a smaller airport in between, that tourists sometimes use. Kilimanjaro."

"Kilimanjaro? As in 'the snows of'?"

"That's right."

"Have you seen it?"

"I've been up it."

By this point, Joe had pulled the minivan up in front of the church and Dana was leaning over his shoulder, honking the horn. Edith was humiliated. "Excuse me, I have to go. Nice to talk to you, Eric."

"My pleasure. Edith."

Chapter 5

Dana and her mom still got haircuts together. Clayton Hornsby had his "shop" in a little room in his house, really a double-wide trailer that had been put on a foundation. Dana didn't like either of them very much when they were together, Mom or Clayton, but he always did a good job.

"Honey, so good to see you!" he said when they arrived, and hugged the life out of Mom. Dana wasn't a hugger. She never knew how to stand, where to put her hands, and it made it worse how Mom seemed to flirt, if moms could do that, when Clayton was around. Even him being gay—and Dana was sure Mom knew this—didn't seem to matter. Maybe it made her feel safe.

"Dana's going first," she said, before Dana could.

"Edith, have a seat, look at the magazines," he said, with what Dana imagined was a leer. To her, he said, "You going for something different?" though she never would.

"Just a trim," Mom said, for her. "But let me give you seven dollars each this time, Clayton. I've been paying you six for years."

"My, my. Flush with cash?" He laughed in that outrageous way such men had, men whose biceps, like his, strained at their sleeves in jarring contrast to the timbre of their voices.

"Well, I don't know how you stay in business," Mom said.

"Government's good to me." Clayton rolled his eyes heavenward, whipping an apron over Dana in one practiced motion. "No, I have so many regulations to comply with, you wouldn't believe. Got to have this separate entrance right here—" He pointed to a door that neither Dana nor Mom had ever used—"just so I can call it a business."

And they were off, laughing and knee-slapping, the whole time Dana was in the chair, giving each other little signals back and forth that made her feel invisible, like the least flirtworthy person on this planet. Made her want to tear her hair out in clumps.

He hardly said a word to her, except "Here's the mirror, hon," when he was finished. Dana could barely discern a change in length; it was just the ends he trimmed, where they'd lain dead against her shoulders. Her face scowled back at her, pale without makeup, though not as pale as it would be if she were used to wearing makeup and suddenly got caught without it.

Now she would have to endure the stench of Mom's perm. That would take hours. Dana wondered how old she would have to be before she had any control over her own time, before Mom would let her get her fucking driver's license. Before a guy, let alone a built guy like the basketball players, would kiss her or so much as look at her. She expected to remain unkissed for the duration of high school, at least.

How could anyone stay in this town? Least of all someone like Clayton. To spend his life flirting with ladies like her mom.

Edith flipped through a magazine. Clayton always had a few, out of date, so it would feel more like a beauty shop. She always looked at them so she wouldn't have to buy them. It wasn't the money, rather the fact that she felt defiled buying such junk, almost as if the magazines were pornographic.

She decided against a little frosting, which was more Clayton's look. It made her sad, to think of him so lonely, and such a sweetheart too. He could have run off to San Francisco or New York. God knows what would have happened to him there. But no, he stayed in Poudre Valley and she respected that. He was a good boy, playing the organ at church. It had to be hard for him and Eric, and any young man, to live without a wife (Edith could use someone to clean up after her). But she admired them, because they knew it could be done.

When she and Dana got back to the house with their new 'dos, Joe was standing in the driveway. The look on his face made Edith want to jump out without even turning off the engine.

"What? What is it? Dear Lord, is it Jeremy?" she said through the window.

"Jeremy's fine." Joe motioned for her to stop the car. "Come on inside. Dana, you too."

When they all, except Joe, were seated around the kitchen table, he put his hands to the sides of his face and said, "I got a call about Uncle Jones."

"What?" Edith felt her neck jerk. "Where is he?"

"He's gone."

"Gone? You mean dead? When? What happened to him?"

"Not sure," Joe said, rubbing one cheek again and again. "They're not sure. It was an investigator who called. He wanted to talk to you but when I told him I was your husband—"

"An investigator? Oh, no. Don't tell me he was attacked again." The kids would have no idea what she was talking about, but Edith didn't care.

"No, no. His body just gave out on him, I guess."

"Well, where? I mean when can we see him?"

"He died in Chicago. They—well, they asked permission to cremate. They want us to pay before they'll ship the ashes, though."

"Whoa. Hold on." Edith stood up, started her teacher walk around the kitchen. "They're sending us a bill? Who are these people? Where are his friends?"

Joe spoke very quietly. "Probably dead too."

Edith stared at him. "What did he die of?"

Joe didn't answer her right away, and she took a step toward him, almost menacing. “What did he die of, Joe?”

“Pneumonia,” he said.

“Why do they want to cremate?” Edith had never heard of a relative being cremated. She certainly remembered closed caskets—her father’s with an American flag draped over it—but the bodies were always there.

“Aunt Anna doesn’t believe in cremation,” Dana said.

“Aunt Anna is not in charge here,” Edith said, surprised at her own vehemence. “As a matter of fact, whatever Aunt Anna wants, let’s do the opposite.” Taking charge was the only way she knew of reacting to news like this.

“Don’t you like Aunt Anna?”

“I like Aunt Anna fine,” Edith said. “But Uncle Jones hated her.”

She could see Joe was almost smiling, and put an arm around him. “Listen, kids. Do you mind giving us a little time alone?” They were out of the kitchen so fast Edith was almost sorry she’d asked.

She sat down next to Joe and put one hand on his arm. She felt more numb than shocked, and waited until he spoke again.

“That investigator was so rude,” he said. “It was as if we sent this—this leper to die on them, or something. He made it sound like we abandoned him.”

“Well, we didn’t. He stopped calling us. What were we supposed to do?”

“I don’t know.” Joe looked at her, but his eyes were empty. “Help him out?”

“Help him out? He never asked us for anything. Never said he needed money, never said he needed help.”

“He wouldn’t have, would he? We were young, we had kids. We couldn’t have done anything.”

“That’s right. Besides, what happened to his money? He never had a wife, or kids.”

“Three guesses.”

Edith sighed. “Okay. Beer, wine or whiskey.”

“That’s not what I meant.”

“Wine, women or song.”

Joe just shook his head, as if he thought she was crazy. Well, let him. She knew perfectly well Jones had never spent a penny on women, but what was the use in talking about it? There he was, dead, with nothing, and no one else to blame.

Edith made the phone calls and all the arrangements. Turned out she was still listed as Jones's only heir, but there was nothing left to her. He'd cashed in whatever he had, even life insurance. She wasn't sure how he'd done that, but she didn't ask. Everyone in Chicago sounded so hateful.

They arranged a funeral at the Methodist church, even though Jones had been, as Aunt Lanie put it, "nondenominational" for years. Aunt Anna started once to raise an objection and Edith wanted to tell her to go to hell. Instead, she strongly suggested that Anna take a walk outside and not come back until she had thought very carefully about "let him who is without sin cast the first stone," and what that meant. Aunt Anna could always be trumped by the Bible.

Jones's obituary ran in the *Poudre Valley Crier*. Edith would have tried to get it in the Chicago papers, but she didn't know anyone there. When they got his personal effects in the mail, they were just wrapped up in a plastic bag. A comb, not even a razor. No hat. The plastic smelled old, too, like somebody had died in it. The obituary began:

> WHEELER, JONES. Died February 4, Chicago, Illinois, following a brief illness.

In Poudre Valley, there were only two ways to die: following a "brief illness" or a "lengthy illness." Lengthy was reserved for emphysema and old people's diseases, and Jones was not old. Not even seventy. It was permissible in Poudre Valley to draw the veil over an illness, so no one could raise awkward questions about how common was Kaposi's sarcoma? Or how did you accidentally shoot yourself in the mouth?

When Edith was sixteen years old and lost her parents in a car wreck, the food had started coming, Southern style. From neighbors, cousins, people from the church who were neither neighbors nor cousins. In her shock and grief, all Edith was able to register was the food. Tears failed her but her appetite never did. She ate Aunt Lanie's roast beef with carrots and potatoes on the side. She ate spaghetti with meatballs, slow-cooked by Betsy Rice, who had been bringing this same dish to every church supper for Edith's entire life, at least. Dinner rolls arrived, spread with real butter, and Edith devoured them along with fried chicken, soup beans and cornbread, biscuits piled high on plates with butter, honey and homemade jam that Hilda Reynolds had put up the year before. And canned vegetables—not from a can, nothing store-bought, but jewels of tomatoes, corn, snap beans, peas, that had been sealed in Mason jars from last summer's gardens and put away in canning rooms and basements throughout Poudre Valley. All these treasures the church women, whom Edith had only recently ceased to call Miss Betsy or Miss Hilda, took out of their storehouses with loving, knotted hands to spread before the bereaved.

And Edith, unable to cry or even to think beyond the happenings of the everyday, saw and smelled this feast of breads and vegetables and gravies and home-baked pies, and she ate and ate. She ate and absorbed into her body and soul the love of these people, women mostly, though Hank Fritts was frying sausages for breakfast the morning of the funeral.

The service itself, and the murmurs of visitors both before and after, washed over Edith like a river of words. She couldn't hear them properly, didn't know what they were saying or in many cases who they were. She developed a practice of nodding, her head slightly to one side as if inclined toward the speaker's best intentions, though nothing was going in. Had anyone asked her, she would not have remembered what a single person had said: at the house, at the church, even the assorted Jones and Wheeler relatives at the graveside. But she remembered who she'd seen, who had come, and who had not. And her mouth, the different spaces on her tongue with their appreciation of sweet, salty, bitter and sour—her mouth remembered what everyone had brought. She and Uncle Jones, while he was there, lived on those leftovers for weeks.

Now when the food came rolling in, for Jones's funeral, she could barely eat any of it. This felt more real than her parents' deaths. Maybe because she was older, and death no longer seemed quite as remote. Or maybe because she had lost her last hope of ever seeing Jones again. When she was orphaned, everyone had gathered around her, but now she was a woman and alone in the world. No matter how many people, and how many cooks, surrounded her.

She was aware of Aunt Anna avoiding her, or maybe Joe was keeping her away. She couldn't stand to speak a word to Anna right now. Lanie clucked over her and brought her cups of tea when she wouldn't eat. And Isabella took over the kitchen at home, without any resistance on Edith's part.

When Isabella cooked these days it wasn't often Italian. She had done almost too good a job of blending in, being the rare "ethnic" in this rural community. Did people even say ethnic around here? Edith could never be sure, when she used a word or expression, whether it were native to her or something she'd picked up in Chicago, or from the Rignaldis.

But even now, garlic was an exceptional ingredient in the kitchen, which Isabella graciously insisted was Edith's kitchen. On one of the first spring days in March, a Sunday, the sky was that peculiar gray that more resembled purple, a dark contrast to the green and clover on the ground below. From the kitchen window it almost looked like an otherworldly landscape, if that other world had grass. Edith turned from the sink and began peeling carrots to bake with the roast.

"Oh, good, you've got the carrots," Isabella said, coming in from the little house. She must have been back from church for a while—she usually got a ride to early Mass with one of her friends—but she took more time to dress for Sunday dinner than for church, Edith could swear it. Gay is the way people might once have described her dress; gaudy might be more accurate. An outrageous orange and pink floral pattern, it resembled some plastic tableware Edith was still using from the Seventies. Well, at least they'd match.

Isabella was preceded into the room by a cloud of old-lady perfume, like the Lord followed by Israelites. It wasn't her fault—olfactory senses dulled with age—but Edith frequently reminded herself that when she was old, the same amount of perfume would do as now. In fact Edith applied just a touch of everything in terms of toiletries: a touch of lipstick, a touch of perfume. No one could even smell it except Joe, and Isabella when she went sniffing, though how it cut through her own scent Edith didn't know.

The kitchen soon filled with much better aromas, roasting meat and vegetables and what would soon be gravy. Edith was a bit of a disgrace as a Southerner, because her gravy was so pitiful. She'd never mastered the art of keeping the flour from sticking to the bottom of the pan. In fact, whenever she was left in charge of her kitchen the most likely result was the smoke alarm going off in the hall. They'd installed it years ago when Joe found out it could keep their insurance premiums down, and it was an ugly old thing, a grubby beige, and emitted a coarse loud buzz that everyone in the family had come to associate with Edith's cooking. She should have worked for Pavlov, let that smoke alarm go off and the kids would run into the house for supper.

"You want me to help with the gravy, honey?" Isabella said, though she was already "helping." She always asked, which lessened Edith's feeling of inadequacy. "You should get a wire whisk, it makes it so easy. I have such a hard time with this fork." She didn't appear to be having a hard time at all.

"I should have asked for one at Christmas." Edith shifted past her mother-in-law and slid the carrots into the roasting pan, plunked it back in the oven. Too late, she remembered, and told Isabella, that the contact with meat meant Dana wouldn't eat the vegetables either. Oh well, there was always cottage cheese.

"I don't know how that girl does it, honey." Isabella patted her ample hip and tied a checkered apron on over the floral dress, the combination causing Edith's eyes to cross. "All the things I love to eat, oh, I couldn't live that way. I thank God every day we have more than enough to eat."

"I think she's just choosing what to eat, for health." This was vague, but Edith didn't begin to understand Dana's ways. Unlike her, Dana never had to worry about weight, so why didn't she just eat whatever she wanted?

"Eating is a blessing," Isabella pronounced. Edith

remembered that there was some verse in Paul about this, and wondered if they'd read it at St. Stephen's today. More likely it was just the fact that Isabella remembered the Depression.

Dana came into the kitchen slowly, one hand twisting her long hair into a tangle of neglect, the other clutching a magazine, from which she never lifted her eyes. Edith said, "Dana, we're having roast beef for dinner but there's some cottage cheese in the fridge, and some sunflower seeds if you want to sprinkle those on."

"Great," she said. Edith had to hand it to Dana, she didn't ever complain. "Mom, can I ask you these poll questions?"

"Edith, honey, can you stir this just for a minute?" Isabella swayed past her to the oven and popped in a tray of buttermilk biscuits—another adaptation she'd made to life in the South. It was remarkable how small this kitchen seemed when they were both in it.

"Those biscuits smell wonderful, Grandma."

"Honey, thank you. I'm sorry you won't have gravy on them. Your mom makes the best gravy."

Every once in a while Isabella would say something that could only be sarcastic, but it was so unexpected that Edith felt off-balance, as if there were something wrong with her ears. She poked the bottom of the pan with the fork. "What poll questions, Dana?"

"U.S. News." Dana sat down in the bathroom doorway, of all places. At least she was out of the way, until someone needed the bathroom. "It's all these questions about current affairs. You can see how your opinion matches those around you."

Didn't it always? "Okay."

While Isabella removed the biscuits from the oven, Dana began reading through a long list of questions, the answers to which were obviously lined up along Democratic and Republican lines. Edith was sorry about this, since she didn't consider herself a Republican, though some people at church said they were. She'd voted for Reagan in '84, of course—everyone had—but she'd liked Jimmy Carter before that, a born-again Christian and all. Supposedly Reagan was a Presbyterian, but he didn't really go to church.

“Mom,” Dana was saying.

She looked up from the gravy, which was triumphantly smooth. “Hmm?”

“‘Do you think AIDS might be a punishment for certain types of behavior?’” Dana read.

Edith returned her gaze to the pan. “‘Might be’?”

“Yeah.”

Isabella didn’t turn around.

“It might be,” Edith finally said, but she smelled something burning and before she could get a pot holder, the alarm went off. “Dana, will you go and shut that thing off, please?” She threw open the oven door and removed the smoking roasting pan, the carrots charred black. Dana stood in the hallway, fanning at the ceiling with her magazine.

Chapter 6

Only a week earlier, the teachers in the lounge had got to talking about AIDS. Someone, it was said, had died of AIDS in Poudre Valley Memorial Hospital, of all places. Of course the doctors and nurses didn't want to touch the body, living or dead. Like it was garbage.

"I don't know why," Vonda Snodgrass said, filing the side of her pointy nose with an equally pointy index finger. "But just the thought of that makes me sick, I mean somebody like that."

"Like what?" Edith said. Pam, next to her, kept scooping lunch from a square Tupperware container.

"You know, like that," Vonda said. "I had a kid in class like that once."

"With AIDS?" Even Pam was incredulous now.

"No. No, no, he committed suicide." Vonda sounded almost proud, as if she'd had a poet in her class, a real gem. Vonda taught college prep English. Dana said she was disgusting, talked about Wordsworth's Dorothy poems and everything to do with sex, but Edith just ignored Vonda most of the time.

"I'm sorry, I don't understand," Edith said. "You feel sick when you think of someone committing suicide?"

"No, Edith." Vonda looked at her the way she looked at her students, as if Edith were the dumbest thing on earth. "A homosexual. Bisexual, whatever. I can't help it, whenever I think about that, I just feel—" She put her hand over her mouth, made a heaving motion. Edith felt the same way in response to Vonda.

Later, when they were having a smoke break, Pam apologized to her. "I felt like I should have said something. I mean that was totally inappropriate of Vonda, to talk that way. About a student."

"She wasn't talking about a student."

They were back in the lounge, guilty, like students caught smoking behind the school. Edith had spent most of her life, it seemed, in this building, but she especially hated the teachers' lounge. As a kid, she'd always imagined the teachers were having fun in there. It was an ugly room, bricks painted yellow, with gray linoleum on the floor and some huge fake plants in the corner. The only light was fluorescent, somehow managing to be harsh and weak at the same time.

Pam kept tapping her nails on the Formica table. They were long, shapely nails, painted a dark pink color. Edith wondered if they were the press-on kind.

"How's Joe?" Pam finally said.

"All right. Why?"

"How long you been married now, Edie?"

"Eighteen, almost nineteen years."

"Nineteen for me and Charlie." Pam inhaled. "Seems longer, sometimes."

Edith wondered where this was going. "What do you mean?"

"You know. Same person there every day, then you wake up and you're old."

"We're not old. Pam, you look the same as you always did."

And she did. Same svelte hips, like she'd never gained a pound since high school. She said, "Edie, I feel sometimes like I'm still in school myself, like I'm still walking the halls. I imagine some guy is checking out my behind, just like they all used to. Then I think how long it's been since anyone looked at me like that."

"Even Charlie?"

"Especially Charlie." Pam shook her head. "After the second miscarriage, it was like more than a baby had died, Edie. It was—" She bit her lips.

Edith wasn't used to this much emotion from her friend. She knew about Pam's miscarriage, but they hadn't talked about it for years. She put her arm around Pam's shoulders, but discreetly, in case someone else came into the lounge.

When Pam spoke again, her voice was brittle. "Your aunt can be very hard to take."

"Who? Lanie?" Edith was surprised. "You never mentioned having trouble with Charlie's mom."

Pam waved her hand again, as if she were air-drying those nails. "I don't. Your Aunt Lanie's no trouble. I'm talking about her sister, Anna."

"Aunt Anna can say some hateful-sounding things."

"She said people who don't have children are selfish," Pam said. "Right to my face she said that."

"Does she know it's not your fault?"

Pam wiped her eyes. "It's none of her damn business, Edie. If people don't want to have children then it's best they don't. What if me and Charlie just didn't want kids?"

But Edith didn't think anybody, least of all a mother, could be fooled by that. "You and Charlie do good things," she said. "A teacher and a cop. I can't see how anybody could call you selfish."

A smile teased at the corners of Pam's mouth. "We have our moments. Charlie and me."

"Well, I'm not an expert," Edith said. "But marriage is hard, year after year. It's hard if you have kids and hard if you don't."

"God, Edie, sometimes I wonder if it's even worth it."

Edith didn't say anything. What could Pam be contemplating? Separation? Divorce? Would she have an affair, move to Kentucky? The possibilities seemed endless, and for a moment Edith was inappropriately excited about them.

"Do you love Charlie?" she finally said.

"Yes. I mean, I don't really know how I couldn't, I know him so well. He hasn't done anything wrong, Edie, never hurt me or cheated or anything. I don't think he ever would." She didn't look like someone who was pleased about this.

"Isn't that a good thing?" Edith said.

Pam wiped her eyes, looked across the room at the toaster oven as if it held the secrets of the universe. "It's why I can't leave," she said. "Don't you understand? If Charlie had done something wrong, or if he'd left me, when we couldn't have—"

The door opened. It was Bill Lowry, the vice principal. Edith couldn't think who she'd want to see less, except maybe Vonda Snodgrass. "What are you girls still doing here?" Bill said.

"We're leaving now," Edith said. "Pam just stuck herself in the eye with a fingernail."

How stupid did Mom think she was? Dana had asked her mother all those poll questions just to get to the one about AIDS. She needed to know what Mom would say. Even then she was surprised at how impassive Mom'd been, not freaking out or giving it away. Mom was cold.

Pneumonia. Obviously Uncle Jones had AIDS. Obviously that was why they'd stopped hearing from him; he must have known what a judgment Mom would pass on him, never mind if he got it from a blood transfusion. Dana sometimes wondered how life would be if Mom cared as much about common humanity as she did about church and God.

Dana couldn't wait for school to be over or, more specifically, for summer to come. She remembered the sun beating down on her as a child until she had to jump in the lake just to keep cool.

The church softball teams in and around Poudre Valley played at various parks, and tonight they were at a park in Sewer City, a bigger town with black people and bad water. Everyone at Poudre Valley High School thought they were rivals, but Dana knew no one here gave a shit about Poudre Valley. While everyone else was watching the softball game, Dana was watching the basketball court where there were some boys playing. Dana herself was awkward, too self-conscious to make much of an effort at sports, though she was tall enough and had long enough arms to play basketball. In any case, she'd spent most athletic moments of her life in the water. But now, secure behind mirrored sunglasses like the kind cousin Charlie wore, she watched the boys dash up and down the asphalt court, pouring with sweat.

One boy in particular. Dana couldn't have said what his face looked like, if he was handsome or not. All she noticed was the flashing grace of his limbs, the move of muscle under glistening dark skin. She watched him spin and leap, his large, sure hands on the ball. He wore nothing but his shorts and shoes—the boys were playing "shirts and skins." It seemed to Dana that they were moving in slow motion, the way basketball players were shown on television. She watched them as if in a dream, moving more smoothly, higher, more elaborately than she was used to seeing human movement, and thought it was the most beautiful thing she had ever seen.

If he hadn't moved to the South, Joe reflected, he'd probably never have taken up softball. He wasn't much of a sportsman, but he'd played enough baseball to know what he was doing. Everyone did, growing up a block and a half from a park with a ball field.

Edith knew more about sports than he did, though. It was like religion down here, and football, not baseball, was the Bible. The way Edith put it, you could avoid knowing about either football or the Bible if you made enough of an effort, but you risked being labeled an infidel. And there was no doubt Edith was one of the faithful. More than her son or daughter or even her husband, she was the one cheering at the Friday night football games, when the high school served as community every bit as much as the church.

But now it was spring, a time when Joe was always full of energy and appreciative of the choice he'd made. Come March, when Chicago might still be cold and snowy, the Tennessee ground was showing unmistakable signs of green. The baseball/softball season was starting; the young men formed church leagues and played each other on the ball fields around Poudre Valley, all summer long. And because the local men were raised on football, and built, at best, like football players, Joe was welcome to play the young men's game. He was slim enough, youthful enough, and he could hit and catch, throw and run.

He played first base on the softball team. The other guys, so far as he could tell throughout the league, had all spent their whole lives here. Edith's cousin Charlie was the catcher, and he looked like one. Fat as any coach Joe worked with, lumbering between bases when it came his turn to bat, Charlie looked no more lumpy in his catcher's outfit than in his police uniform. And he smoked, which irritated Joe, in that special way that people are irritated by others' enjoyment of something they've given up. He wished Edith would just quit completely, not keep sitting on the fence.

To be truthful, no one on the team was exactly handsome. Otherwise it would have been vain for Joe to compare himself favorably with them. At forty, he was in the best shape of his life, thanks to his recent resumption of swimming all year round. He'd cultivated a swimmer's build ever since he learned to swim in Lake Michigan.

Tonight they were playing Central Baptist. Edith was in the stands, such as they were, with the younger wives and girlfriends. People weren't marrying as young as they used to, not even church people. This was a cause of concern for Joe. He remembered what being a young man was like, and he worried about his children. Not just Dana, but Jeremy too, a year away from graduating and not looking like college material. Joe dreaded the day Jeremy finally found a girlfriend, dreaded what kind of girl she'd be and how fast they could get in trouble.

"Better to marry than burn," Edith would say, rolling her eyes at St. Paul. She made light of it, but wasn't it true? Wasn't there a reason to get married young? As for having kids, he and Edith had been young when they did that too, and for good reason. Who had the energy, at forty, to chase after kids?

Central Baptist's first man up hit a line drive. Joe lunged for it, but the ball shot past him and rolled to the outfield. The batter raced toward him, to chants of "C'mon Pea-Nut! C'mon

Pea-Nut!" from the women in the stands. What an unfortunate name.

Peanut made it to first with what Joe thought was too much drama for a church softball game. He also thought his pants were too tight, and that he'd forgotten his jock strap. Peanut, indeed. Obscene, with all these children around.

The Methodist supporters took up a counter-chant: "Slide right back! Slide right back!" They were making fun of the Baptists' tendency to "backslide." It seemed there was no blasphemy in sports. Joe could see Edith was eyeing first base but she wasn't looking at him, she was watching to see if Peanut would now try to steal second. That was what Joe should have been watching for, but he was looking at Edith. Story of their marriage, really. He still thought she was beautiful and she still looked out for him, everywhere he went. Except for locker rooms.

Given Joe's inattention Peanut broke for second, but the catcher had called a pitch out and threw him out easily. The Methodist crowd went silent. Joe made the mistake of looking over at the stands again. At that moment, Edith looked ready to leave him for anyone on the field, even Peanut. It was there, stalking the bases, Joe's inadequacy as a man, who could hold onto neither the ball nor the girl.

Isabella was at the end of the bleachers, smiling and talking to whoever would talk to her, but not really paying any more attention to the softball game than Dana was. Isabella nudged her, pointed out one of the shirtless young guys over on the basketball court. "He's ugly," she said, an expression that always meant the opposite when Isabella used it.

Since Dana was wearing sunglasses, nobody could see whether she was looking or not. "You think so, Grandma?"

"I know so," she said. "Edith, honey, don't you think he's ugly?"

Mom just waved her hand. "Oh, Mom." She said it in exactly the tone Dana used with her. Mom was watching the game, a form of behavior that got her all tribal, screaming at the players, and the refs, with primal rage. She was even worse during football season but at least then, she wasn't related to anyone on the field.

Dana was sure Mom wished that Jeremy played football or baseball. Or at least, if he didn't, that it was because he was such a good student, he was doing so well in school. Not guitar club. Dana knew Joe had once played guitar, in fact he still had one somewhere, but it wasn't electric, and she had the impression her parents had put their love for music behind with the Sixties, when they had kids. All they ever sang now were hymns at church, country stuff.

She didn't even realize the softball game had been lost until Mom, lightning in her eyes, jumped down from the bleachers (Dana didn't think she had it in her) and stomped over to the players leaving the field. "Joe!" she said, and Dana could see the others, Baptists and Methodists, filing by like they didn't want to witness any of this.

"Joe, don't you see anything coming right towards you?"

He put up his hands, the left one still wearing its old, cast-off glove. "Edith, don't start this."

"Well why don't you start paying attention to something once in a while?" Dana had heard this before, Mom losing her temper after a ball game that their team had lost, but tonight she seemed louder, more humiliating.

"Why're you so upset?" Joe ushered them back to the minivan.

"Because you're never paying attention," Mom said. "You don't pay attention to the ball, you don't pay attention to anything!"

"I pay attention to you, I hear every word you say."

"But you don't listen. You don't listen, Joe."

Dana didn't say a word, didn't so much as take off her sunglasses, all the way home. What were they talking about? She knew they were liars, like all parents, knew they were talking in some kind of code, and if she said a thing about it they'd say she was making the whole thing up. Well, Dana Rignaldi knew better. Better than the whole damn world. Where was that pussy, Eric Dufresne? How come he wasn't on the ball team? Probably humping some teenage girl. No way Eric, who was twenty-five, could be the saint he claimed to be.

Edith was ashamed of her outburst, but would have been more ashamed to tell Joe so. Her sorrow for Uncle Jones was breaking out. She didn't know where her tears had gone, and she was ashamed of that, too. She felt that she had already lost her uncle years ago.

The thought of Uncle Jones's death, of the illness he had been unwilling or unable to tell them about, was hard enough, but losing contact with him for years beforehand seemed even more unbearable. Edith knew what lay behind the disappearance of her uncle, his poverty, his miserable death from pneumonia, but she couldn't bear to connect it to a cold, two-dimensional news item. AIDS was a swear word in Poudre Valley, an obscene cocktail of sex and violence, two things Edith avoided in movies and in life.

She looked at her husband, at his tired, strained face over the steering wheel. They had engaged in sex to produce their children, of course. They both wanted children. Making love was the way to achieve this, but it wasn't something they repeated very often. Edith recalled the feel of Joe's long body, lean and muscled, moving over her, more aesthetically than erotically pleasing. She would will herself to relax, move gently with him, thinking of the babies they would make together.

Chapter 7

In the early days Joe had taught in a mountain school where nothing could be counted on, not the basic literacy of the parents or the most essential supplies. He developed the habit of taking two bars of soap and a couple extra rolls of toilet paper to school, one for the boys' bathroom, one for the girls'. The staff was not happy because, they said, the children could not be trusted to wipe their butts and wash their hands; they would "waste" and make a mess. They would have to make do with what the school supplied, though it always seemed to run out. Joe just smiled, offered to clean up any mess the children made, and kept supplying these things out of his own modest budget. He was never asked to clean up any mess.

Edith didn't object to Joe taking the work more personally than she did. His work day simply couldn't end when he left the school, even though that was usually several hours after the children went home. The most sacred place in the home for Joe was not his seat at the table or a chair in the living room, but his desk. It was in their bedroom—the house was not big enough to have a study or den—and the room became, in effect, his study, for stretches of every evening and weekend. They both slept there, too, but that was mostly all they did.

Being a teacher in rural Appalachia had saved Joe from Vietnam, but unlike other young men that was not why he'd entered the profession. He approached teaching as a calling. The more years he spent at it, the more likely it seemed that he would be promoted to an administrative position, being one of the only men in the school. Even when he moved to a job in the Poudre Valley City Schools, he was one of very few men teaching the elementary grades. It was a place where leadership was unquestionably male.

But Joe did not consider that a promotion. He said repeatedly to Edith, and she agreed, that he was a teacher and didn't want to do anything that would take him away from the classroom. It was one thing, and entirely enough, to be asked to motivate twenty-five or thirty first graders, but motivating adults was something he had no interest in.

"Besides," he'd say to Edith, "I don't want responsibility for anyone's livelihood but my own and my family's. I never want to be the one to have to let a teacher go or tell somebody her job is gone, or going to somebody else. I don't want to even be near that situation."

And so, year after year when the questions began, Joe would smile, and tell his superiors that all he wanted was to be left alone with the ten-and eleven-year-olds, people he understood and could help.

Dana was just like him. Joe would never say it, for fear of sending Edith down that Freudian route and putting their daughter between them, but the pattern was clear. Through the years he had sat in the sacred circle of his desk, first smoking, later just drinking in quiet moderation, not to say desperation. Never admitting that anything might be wrong. And, in a sense, there was nothing wrong. He was living the life he was born to live. They earned their living. They paid taxes and fastened the seatbelts in their cars. Joe had quit smoking, and so had Edith, if only in the house.

The principal of every school was expected both to have

a paddle and to use it, and it would not have been considered inappropriate for him to walk around with the paddle sticking out of his back pocket. Joe's principal, Mr. Tanner, loved to paddle errant schoolchildren. Some of the younger principals and teachers in the county sported new fiberglass paddles, which, according to the children, showed red steam rising off the rump of whomever was being punished. But Mr. Tanner was an old-fashioned principal, an officer of the school peace, and his chosen weapon in this war was the traditional wooden paddle. It featured a carving of a boy being hit on the backside, literally over a barrel, the paddler whaling away.

When Joe first arrived at Poudre Valley Elementary School to take up his new, "city" position, the paddle confronted him, hanging on a nail in the wall of the principal's office. Where in the world had such a thing come from? Who sold these? Joe pictured a warehouse, somewhere in Texas no doubt, supplying paddles carved with sadistic drawings to schools all over the South.

He was qualified to teach all the way up to twelfth grade, but had limited himself to fifth. He liked kids at this age. They could read well enough to pick up all kinds of things, the basics were there, but they weren't yet in junior high, ruined by puberty. And they all seemed to love Mr. Rignaldi. When the bell rang every afternoon and the children ran for the buses or their mothers' cars, Joe would sit for a moment just looking out the window, like an idle schoolboy himself. He was thankful for the privilege of working at something he truly loved, that truly mattered, and for being able to go home to Edith and his own children.

These were the things Jones Wheeler had been unable to do. He hadn't enjoyed his work, had no family, he'd died sick, poor, and alone. Joe felt that his gift for teaching elementary school was more than a living, it was life. It was what kept him from turning into some scruffy old man at a mission in downtown Chicago, someone who got beaten by rough trade, or even killed. This was why he wasn't down at the bus station, getting what he needed. It wasn't because of Edith; he had told her, he was only being honest with her. And it wasn't even because of his own kids, Jeremy and Dana. It was these kids, right here, every one of a class of twenty-six, thirteen boys and thirteen girls.

One spring morning he told them, "Today we're going to prepare for the Basic Skills tests."

A groan rolled through the classroom, like a wave at a football game. "Mr. Rignaldi, do we have to?"

"Not math again!"

"Yes, math again. We're starting the day with it so we can get it over with. Now get out a piece of paper and number it from one to ten."

Basic Skills was, truth be told, as hateful to Joe as it was to any of the fifth graders. It was rote, it was mindless, and it was a diktat of the State of Tennessee. What could be worse? But he couldn't share his displeasure with the class. If they didn't pass what the governor thought they should pass, they'd be stuck in fifth grade for the rest of their lives.

"Tell you what," he said, feeling generous. "Whoever gets finished first can come up here and do a Harry Houdini demonstration with me."

The kids loved Houdini. There was a book about him on the shelf in the back of the room, a shelf that Joe let children consult for their own reading pleasure whenever they got their schoolwork done. One girl, Emily Hines, had read every one of the books at least twice. Joe wrote a note on his doodle pad to buy more; the school would never pay for them.

It was no surprise to anyone when Emily finished the test first. She charged up to Joe's desk, all pigtails, and asked to do the demonstration. Joe shushed her until everyone was finished, a process that took so long that by the end of it, Emily was shifting from foot to foot and openly rolling her eyes.

"Okay," he said. "Emily, I'm going to tense my stomach, as hard as I can make it, and then you're going to hit me."

She looked concerned. "Mr. Rignaldi, that's how Houdini died."

"Don't worry, I'll be prepared for it." Joe prided himself on having the same tight abdominals he'd had at twenty-five, thanks to the gym. "Now everybody else, you count to three. Ready? One!"

"Two! Three!" the class shouted, and Joe tensed his abdomen.

Emily let fly a little fist that would nearly have knocked the wind out of him anyway, had it been appropriately aimed. Unfortunately, it hit him square in the nuts and he doubled over, trying to hide his agony. He heard a collective sucking in of breath from the class—or was it his life's breath?

"Mr. Rignaldi. Mr. Rignaldi, are you okay? I'm sorry."

Joe gasped that it was okay, and staggered over to lean against the edge of the desk. Maybe he wouldn't bring in any more books for Emily, after all.

Edith took the steps up to Aunt Anna's porch slowly. She hadn't been here since Christmas and hadn't missed it, though she did have to admit Anna had a lovely garden. There were always flowers everywhere, in just the right arrangement to make the whole yard look like something out of a gardening magazine. Everybody said Aunt Anna had a green thumb. Edith used to say her own thumb was black, till she realized how that sounded.

She knocked twice at the screen door and Uncle Jimmy said "Anna!" Edith could hear the TV and knew Jimmy was watching boxing or polishing one of his guns.

"Well, Edie, what a surprise. Come on in." Aunt Anna had an apron on and the house smelled of biscuits.

"You're in the middle of baking, Aunt Anna. I won't take but a minute."

"Honey, anytime is fine. You know you can always come by to see me. Jimmy!" Aunt Anna shouted into the living room. "Turn down that television."

Edith heard grumbling, but the TV stayed at a high volume. The new TV sets all had remote control now, but her aunt and uncle's set was old and huge, and Uncle Jimmy rarely felt like getting up.

Anna dusted her hands on her apron and said, "You want some coffee or tea?"

"I'm fine."

"Well now I didn't ask you if you was fine." Anna sat down, and Edith imagined that her eyes narrowed somewhat. "I know you aren't fine. You came all the way over here to admire my grape hyacinths?"

"They're lovely, Aunt Anna."

"Thank you."

The niceties of Southern conversation out of the way, Edith said, "Have you talked to Pam lately?"

"Pam? No, honey. Haven't seen her, I don't know, since whenever the last time was she came to church." Aunt Anna let her observation of Pam's sin register for a moment. "How is she?"

"She's fine. She seemed very hurt by something you said to her, that's all. I was wondering if it was recent."

"Well now what could I have said to hurt her feelings? You know I never mean to hurt anyone's feelings."

"I know." The gap between what Anna did and what she meant to do was as wide as any in Christendom. "Something about her and Charlie not having any kids."

"Honey, you know if the Lord wanted to bless them with children, he would have by now. That's up to the Lord."

"Yes, well. I don't think that sounds as kind as you mean it, to someone who doesn't have children."

"What did she say it sounded like?" Aunt Anna said.

Edith sighed. "She remembered hearing you say something about it being selfish of people not to have children. Now I told her you couldn't have meant it that way," Edith added, which was close to the truth. "But that's between her and Charlie."

"And God," Anna said. "Don't forget God."

"I never do, Aunt Anna."

"She must have misunderstood me. I wouldn't say that about people who can't help themselves. I meant people who get married, you know, or even don't, and just have a whale of a time. That's not what it's meant for." Anna had begun to speak in riddles and it was Edith's job to dance around the exact meanings of words until she got to the end, or dropped from exhaustion.

"But you don't really believe, do you, that just because someone doesn't have children, they're doing something wrong?"

"Woman is made to bear children. That's what the Bible says."

Not exactly, thought Edith, but she hadn't been exact in her recap either. "Well, I think there are some fine women and men who choose not to have children, and they're more of an asset to the world than plenty of people who do."

"Listen to you. Asset. Why'd you come in here to tell me all this? Is there something wrong between you and Joe?"

Edith's face went hot, and she caught a matching spark of triumph in the corner of Aunt Anna's eye. So this was how it was going to go. "I was hoping to just sit down and have a conversation with you," she said. "I didn't come over here to fight."

"Is there?" Anna was undeterred.

"And I didn't come over here to talk about me," Edith said. "What about you? You have plenty of children. Are you proud of them?"

"I thank the Lord every day for my children."

"I'm sure you do, but that doesn't mean you're proud."

"Pride is a sin, Edie. Why should I be proud?"

"Yeah." Edith felt her voice tighten with anger. "Why should you? Nothing too great about any of them, is there?"

"My children may not have gone to some snot-nosed rich college up north," Anna said, and Edith was surprised at how angry Anna had gotten but also pleased that she'd riled her up. "But every one of them is born again. The boys make an honest living, the girls are good mothers and wives."

"They'd make a lot better living if they hadn't dropped out of school."

"Wayne is a teacher," Aunt Anna shot back. "Every bit as good a man as Joe." In Anna's world, the fact that Edith was also a teacher didn't count.

"Wayne is a coach. And if he weren't a coach he would not be allowed within a mile of a school 'cause he can barely read. And he isn't even that good a coach. When was the last time Sewer City won anything?"

"He doesn't smoke. He doesn't drink," Aunt Anna said. "Which is more than I can say for some people."

"I don't drink," Edith said.

"No. But your precious Uncle Jones did nothing else. Oh—

forgive me—he did something else. But I won't have talk of that in my house. This is a Christian home."

"Yes." Edith stood up. "Well, I'm sorry you brought up Uncle Jones, Aunt Anna. You never liked him when he was alive and I would have hoped you could leave him in peace now that he's dead."

"Well. That's hardly in my hands. If Jones had wanted peace after death, he should have lived a very different life."

"Shut up!" Edith clenched her hands, not caring if Uncle Jimmy heard; he was too fat to stand anyway. "Shut up about Uncle Jones. You don't know anything about his life."

"And you don't know much about life at all," Aunt Anna said, almost serene now. "It's a wonder to me you have two children, with the husband you have."

About to shout at Anna to get out of her house, Edith remembered she was in Aunt Anna's house. She stomped to the screen door and slammed it on her way out.

"Nice seeing you," Aunt Anna called through the door.

Edith was so mad she almost ran into Bear, the young man who lived (actually squatted) on Aunt Anna's property. "Oh, excuse me," she said, and kept walking.

"Ma'am." She knew Bear would be tipping his greasy baseball cap, but she didn't wait to see it.

Bear was a good-works project of Aunt Anna's. He was a high school student, and Jeremy had ridden the bus with him until Bear acquired a truck. Edith had no idea how, since he seemed to have no job and never did anything but chew tobacco and spit it into a Dr. Pepper can. But somehow he had conned Aunt Anna and Uncle Jimmy into letting him stay in a trailer on their property, because his parents were dead and he'd taken to coming to their church, looking for redemption. Looking for a handout, Edith suspected, and maybe a church girl to deflower in the bushes, but if her aunt was that stupid...She wouldn't mind so much if Anna were less judgmental about everybody else.

Chapter 8

"Billy!"

Even Billy looked up at her this time. Edith didn't care to yell at kids, but she was on her last nerve. Just having other people around, even one, disturbed her, and there were so many of them. She swore there were more every day.

"Billy. Where is your assignment? I asked you all to hand your assignments in."

To her astonishment, Billy reached inside his worn-out book and produced a single sheet of notebook paper, folded over in neat vertical halves. "Thank you," she said, smoothing it flat on her desk. "Next time, you don't have to fold it this way."

"But Miz Bailiff told us to—"

"This is not Mrs. Bailiff's class."

The sharp tone shut him up. Edith was sorry, but it was the only way to quiet the pounding in her head. She and Pam were friends, and family. That was all the more reason not to act, in front of the students, as if they liked each other.

In the teachers' lounge Edith must have been puffing more

frantically than usual, because Pam came over to her, stirring something awful-smelling in a Styrofoam cup. "Heard you got into it with Billy Lowry today." Pam set her thin frame down on the rubbery couch and spoke delicately, since Bill Sr. could walk in again at any moment.

"What else is new? Hey, Pam, tell me something."

"Penney's," Pam said.

"What?"

"This lip gloss. I bought it at JCPenney's." Pam smiled. "Isn't that what you were going to ask me?"

"Oh. No, but it looks real nice." Pam was obviously back to her even-keeled self, for whom the protocol for asking a real question was like haggling in a Middle Eastern bazaar. "You know how you ask all the kids in your class to fold the paper in half lengthwise?"

"Yes. It fits better in my bag that way."

"Well, nobody else does that. Every year I have to start off getting people to stop folding papers that way. In Billy's case, it just happened today because this is the first assignment he's done."

Pam's eyebrows went up. "Did you look at it yet?"

"No."

"Might want to have a look, Edie. Based on my experience, could be a design for a paper airplane."

"At least he'd be doing physics then." Edith lit another cigarette, offered Pam one. "Honestly, how do you stand it?"

"How do I stand what?"

"This. This whole thing. Every day, stand up there and might as well be talking to a brick wall."

Pam looked at her curiously. "You get paid this month, Edie?"

"Of course."

"Your checks from the school system ever bounce?"

"No. You think I'd be sitting here if they did?"

"So what's the problem?"

Edith waited, but Pam seemed to have made her point. "You're just doing it for the money."

"It's either that, or stay home and watch *The Guiding Light* every day." Pam dragged on her cigarette. "I'm not that into soaps, though, never have been. I like reading, you know."

"What, Harlequin romances?"

"What's wrong with them? They're books. They have stories. Things happen in them."

"Guess things haven't picked up with Charlie," Edith said.

"Oh, Edie." Pam let out a smoky laugh. If she took some of that makeup off, she'd have been a fine-looking woman. She waved her hand in the air like their previous, heavy conversation was nothing. "You and I've been married women a long time. I'd be bored to death without my romances."

That was so typical. Everything was always more work for women. Men could just look at their pornographic magazines, but women had to read a whole book. "Your romances," Edith repeated.

"Honey, I've told you about my romances since Day One. Besides," Pam whispered, "I don't mean to insult your family, but Charlie is not overly endowed. More like training wheels."

"Pam!" Edith laughed in spite of herself.

"I mean it! He drives that big cop car and you know what they say about men and big cars." Pam narrowed her eyes. "Is there anything to the fact that Joe has a minivan?"

In the garden, Edith snapped on her gloves. Not for her the polka-dot cloth type that Isabella wore. The gloves she wore for gardening were proper work gloves, toughened leather—as tough as the glove Joe wore for playing softball. But she could catch better with hers.

It bothered her that Joe was so uncompetitive. Maybe she should be grateful he even played. Neither Jeremy nor Dana showed the least interest in sports. She (not Joe) had tried to get them involved, at least recreationally, when they were younger, but it took up too much time, driving them around. In the end she was as happy as anyone when they wanted to quit. Why did it have to be so organized? What happened to good old-fashioned slugging it out with the neighbors? They didn't have neighbors to speak of anyway, but kids were getting fatter and lazier every year. Edith saw it in the classroom and she was not going to see it happen at home.

"As long as they get their exercise," Joe would say. It didn't matter to him if they competed at anything or if anyone even saw them do it. She figured he was talking about himself. She was a wife and mother; she belonged in the stands, or here, with her mother-in-law, wearing gardening gloves. But neither she nor Joe could afford him staying away from the ball field. If he couldn't coach, or match his fellow teachers as a roaring fan, he could show up each week with the other churchmen and do his duty to God and his country. It was absolutely crucial that he play softball with them, not just swim at the Y and read books. And every time he dropped the ball or was looking everywhere but at the action on the field, Edith felt a knot of fire tighten around her heart.

"Edith, honey," Isabella said, her face partially concealed by an enormous collapsible hat of bright lavender. "You're ripping up half the ground."

Edith realized she had a fistful of weeds by the roots and was clenching them, her knuckles white. She released the earth and knelt further down, poking in vain with her trowel.

"Are you all right?"

Edith looked up. "It's hopeless, Mom."

"What is?"

What wasn't? "It's no use me trying to help you with this garden. I can't grow anything but weeds." She made another stab with the trowel and winced, killing a marigold.

Isabella didn't stop moving, her hands more dextrous and graceful in those gloves than Edith's had been patting her newborn children. She remembered the feel of Jeremy's incredible skin, could sense it now, under her hands. Giving birth to a son had been, for Edith, a thumb in the eye of the universe, a rebuke, through happy tears, of a world that had orphaned her. For the price of a long night of labor she had, as she saw it, made Joe a father, and deepened her connection with his mother and with every woman who had mothered before. Finding this aspect of herself, seeing the child of her body and knowing she would die for him if necessary, came as more relief than success. The relief of belonging, again, to a family, with a mother and father. Even if the father was Joe.

"What do you want to know how to do, sweetie?" Isabella scooped the earth around the area Edith had just devastated, patted it into a mound.

Raise children, live with a man for the rest of our lives. Worship God and still have energy left in my body to eat and laugh and love life like you do. "You can start by showing me how to weed without killing everything, please." Edith slapped at a sweat bee.

"Okay." Isabella scooted over, grass staining the polyester covering her knees. "Now in the garden, remember, everything lives there together for a reason. You don't want to think of it as killing the weeds or tearing out everything—"

"My hair."

"Right. Look at your hair, honey." Isabella removed a glove and ran her hand through Edith's perm, encountering considerable resistance. "Now why cook your hair in those stinky chemicals, when it's so beautiful? You hardly have a bit of gray."

"Look closer," Edith said, and couldn't help laughing when Isabella moved in, intent on finding whatever gray there was. "Not too close."

"Well, that Clayton did a nice job but you don't have to get it permed like that. I never even let him cut mine. Just trim it, you know."

"But you wear it up anyway, Mom."

Isabella sat back, removed the lavender hat, and untied the bun at the back of her head. Her silver-white hair tumbled down like in a Breck commercial, longer than Edith ever remembered wearing hers. It was quite a contrast. Isabella in bright colors, the flowers healthy around her, like a picture in a stained glass window. And Edith with her Methodist sobriety, a life without incense or wine.

"Why do you think Joe missed that catch?" she asked Isabella.

"What, sweetie?"

"That catch the other night. He's caught balls like that a hundred thousand times," Edith said. "Why'd he stop paying attention?"

"I don't know." Isabella slapped her hat back on. "Maybe he was paying attention. You know, thinking about it too much."

"I doubt that."

"No, look." Isabella stabbed her trowel into the dirt, Edith-like. "I've been planting gardens all my life. When I was growing up and in my house with Stefano, and now here. I don't remember learning, it's something I just do. But now you ask me to show you something, how to weed, and I start thinking about it. I get all awkward, I can't feel right in my hands doing it. So how can I explain it to you?"

Edith wasn't even pretending to garden anymore. "I tell my students, if they can't put something into words, they don't really know it."

"Oh, honey." Isabella laughed, held up her blue-veined hands. "You shouldn't say that. I mean it's your hands that know how to do some things, and your body. You start thinking about it, using words, you're going to mess up."

"So you think Joe was thinking too hard about how to catch the ball?"

"I don't know what he was thinking, but I know you were telling him to think about it." Isabella plunged several fingers into a mound of earth. "Why are you asking me?"

Edith pulled off her gloves and stared at them. Oh, she didn't even know how to put it in words. Her gloves were brown, the earth was brown, the grass on its surface still showed traces of brown, and everything she wore was earth tones. "You gardened with your husband?"

"Oh, Stefano was never in the garden. Never wanted to be outside at all, if he didn't have to be. Bad for the skin, he thought." Isabella patted her hat. "That's why I wear these things."

From pictures, and from his son, Edith thought her father-in-law had been swarthy. "He was worried about getting sunburned?"

"Oh, no. It was bugs that bothered him. He was always troubled by mosquitoes." Isabella shook her head. "They don't bother me, I don't even notice them, but he would step outside for half a minute and the mosquitoes would be all over him.

I told him I would have been, too, it was 'cause he tasted so sweet."

Edith didn't rise to this lip-licking occasion. "Was he allergic?"

"Honey, it was all to do with the war," Isabella said. "He was in Italy, you know, with the army. When Stefano Jr. was a little boy, before Giuseppe was born—see, I still call them by their baby names, Stefano always did. Anyway, I guess he got stung by some bad mosquitoes over there, and got very sick."

"Malaria?"

"I reckon," Isabella said, and this Southernism in her mother-in-law's mouth made Edith laugh.

"I'm sorry," Edith said quickly. "Did he tell you about it?"

"Honey, he didn't tell me a darn thing."

Edith had heard this about veterans of World War II—it was true of her uncles, Claude and Jimmy—but she thought of it as some kind of cliché. "What, not ever?"

"When he got back to Chicago," Isabella said, "he put his feet on the ground—" she emphasized with the trowel— "and he said, 'I am never, ever going on a goddamn ship again.' I'm sorry but that's what he said. 'Or a goddamn plane either. And I'm not gonna set one goddamn—'"

"Okay, Mom, I've got it." It wasn't even hot but Edith was flushed.

"So that's what he said, when he got home. And he took me in that bedroom, never mind little Stefano was still crawling around on the living room floor, and he made up for all that time he was away overseas. And I never heard another word about it."

"Well," Edith said with some difficulty, "he'd been away from women all that time."

"Sweetie," Isabella said, and looked at Edith like she was a girl. "Don't you think a soldier knows where to find women when he wants them?"

"Mom!"

"I'm just saying, when he came back, I came back to him too, and he was mine again. And I was glad to have him back."

"I'm sure." Edith looked around, suddenly desperate to find

a weed.

"Listen to what I'm telling you, honey. It's right for a man and a woman to live together. Otherwise your life is not complete." Isabella waited until she had Edith's full attention. "But what you do and how you do it, that's nobody's business but God's."

"You're right, Mom. I won't talk about it anymore."

"Now sweetie, that's not what I'm saying. You talk to me any time you want. But I know my son."

She was ahead of Edith, then. "Yeah, he doesn't talk about anything."

"He talks," Isabella said.

Edith didn't know whether she knew about their Christmas conversation—the last time Joe had "talked"—or if she was just being cryptic. "You mean, he talks with his hands or something?"

"Well, we are Italian, honey." Isabella made flamboyant gestures with her still-gloved hands, embarrassing Edith even further. "My son is like me. Both of us, what we hate is conflict in the family. We don't like fighting. We'll change the rules before we go and break them."

"As opposed to me and your husband," Edith said, but soft enough that Isabella didn't hear.

"Look at you," Isabella said, and she'd returned to her garden work so Edith figured she'd given up on teaching her anything. "You're beautiful people. You've got beautiful children. It's a good family, Edith."

She thought of her son, his future, and how she felt powerless to affect it. "I worry about Jeremy."

"He's doing all right, honey," Isabella said. "His medicine seems to be working."

Yes, the epilepsy they managed. But what about when he was on his own? "He doesn't want to go to college."

"But he's a beautiful boy." Edith wondered how anyone, even his grandmother, could describe Jeremy as beautiful at this particular stage of his life, though he had been once. "And he works hard."

"What does he work at, Mom?"

"That guitar, honey. He's good with his hands. Why don't you apprentice him to a trade?"

"I don't think they have apprentices anymore," Edith said, though she didn't really know. Dana had said the same thing about women's colleges.

"I know you think I'm ignorant because I never went to college." Edith started to disagree, but Isabella waved that basil-garlic trowel at her to shut up. "It was the Depression; we all had to work. There's no shame in working for a living."

"Teachers work."

"Oh yes, yes you do. And I'm so proud of you both for teaching. But there's other jobs in the world."

Edith felt sweat trickling down her face and neck and pooling in her A-cup bra. They'd gotten nothing done—well, she hadn't, anyway. Isabella was gardening up a storm. She noticed her mother-in-law's body, big-breasted, a figure of fertility dressed in a citrus palette. She thought of Joe, her handsome Joe, the product of this stunning old woman and a long-dead G.I. Edith wondered whether more than looks had attracted Isabella to her own husband. Whether it really was true, in the Forties, that a young Catholic couple could agree to move in together and "do their own thing." Well, they did only have two children.

"What about your other son, Mom?" she said, not meaning to be cruel. "Do you ever hear from Steve?"

"Honey, Steve doesn't write. He's alive, or the navy would tell me." Isabella was busy with a basil plant that seemed to be taking over the yard. "That's why I don't call him Steve, I've hardly talked to him since he started calling himself that name. But some boys do that."

Do what? Go by Steve? Join the navy? Not call their mothers? "Don't you miss him?"

"Oh my God, yes. When you only have two—well, you know, you just have the two."

"How—" But Edith could never ask that. She didn't want to ask about Isabella's love life, because heaven knew, she'd tell her.

"You remember," Isabella said, "he wouldn't even come to your wedding. That war changed him. That's why I came down here. I mean, how could you get married up in Chicago, with all your family here and I didn't have any family to give you?"

What a peculiar expression. "I thought we decided to do it here because we couldn't get married in a Catholic church," Edith said. "Without me becoming Catholic."

"Well, you did what you had to do, honey. We all did."

Chapter 9

There was a certain lilt, or otherwise unidentifiable sound, in Mom's voice when she mentioned Eric Dufresne. It was Wednesday and she was talking about the church supper. What she was usually talking about, in relation to Dana and church, was how Dana should become more involved with the youth group. Dana felt that she went to quite enough church as it was for someone her age, and Joe seemed to agree, so Mom never pushed too hard. The youth group, in Dana's very limited experience, was not a particularly nice group of young people who talked or acted in particularly nice ways.

"New" Eric, the second youth minister of that name, said nice was not the point. "We think Christians are supposed to be nice, and say and do nicer things than everybody else," he had exhorted them once, when Mom persuaded Dana to give him a try. "But what about the true needs of the world? The world is crying out for the love of God. People are starving and dying of preventable diseases—are we going to save their lives with nice words? We have to be the love of God to these people. We have to be God's love in the world."

At first, Dana was attracted to this message, if not to Eric and his hippie hair. She didn't mind that Bibles remained closed at youth group meetings while Eric talked about mission, their mission on earth, to be God's love to other people. She adjusted easily enough to the absence of the word mankind, and was open to Eric's eager intellectual approach, which involved references to the original Greek of the New Testament. Eric, like other youth ministers they'd had, was a divinity student, doing his M.Div. or "getting his preacher's license," as Mom put it when she first met him. Mom didn't seem all that impressed with Eric at that stage, so when, after an appropriate trial period, Dana expressed the desire not to go every week anymore, Mom didn't object.

Eric, it turned out, had a mission to go to Africa. Only he didn't see his "mission" in quite the same traditional way as other missionaries Dana had heard of. "We all have a mission," he said. "We are all called to be missionaries of the gospel. Not all of us are called to go to Africa, and not all of us are called to preach. But we are all called to our mission."

This idea appealed to Dana, but she couldn't quite identify what it was that Eric meant was his own mission. He wanted to go to Africa in the name of Christ, but he didn't want to "feed people's souls without feeding their bodies—just send them on their way with a 'Be warmed and filled,' when they're sick or hungry right in front of me." He said some highly critical things about "some old-fashioned missionaries" who were not sensitive to the culture they were visiting, had a "neo-colonial" attitude to the people they were missionaries to, treating them as little more than "heathens." All these words were new to Dana, or at any rate the criticisms were.

But after a while she stopped going to the youth group, and soon she forgot about neo-colonial and everything else Eric had said, and thought only of how turned on Mom seemed by the whole Africa thing, and how Eric must have the hots for somebody.

Tonight she was going, along with Jeremy, who didn't want to attend either. Mom had volunteered him to help out with the little kids. It would not have occurred to their parents to give Dana or Jeremy freedom of choice in this matter. Dana and Jeremy would go to church, in the same way that they would go to college and get jobs doing something worthy in the world, like teaching. The Rignaldis knew of people to whom these things did not apply, but they didn't aspire to be such people.

Dana rode along in the backseat of the minivan, hating both backseat and minivan and wishing she could stay home with Isabella. She'd become Catholic if that's what it took, though she'd never so much as been to a Catholic service. "We're not welcome there," Mom had said, and Dana refrained from asking how welcome Grandma felt at a Methodist church. Dana thought the idea of real wine, which she'd never tasted, at weekly communion services was exotic. She'd occasionally sat in the back pew of St. Stephen's when there was no one else in the church, overcome not just by the incense but by the novelty of having a church open on a regular weekday at all.

Sneaking over to St. Stephen's, one of the few places she could walk to from the high school, was a kind of anti-vice Dana had taken up in the last year. The saints, the Catholicism of it all was a delightful contamination, like the residue of incense in her pores. If the church hadn't abandoned Latin, the whole foreignness of the experience would have had Dana in fits of alienated glee.

But now only the nauseating fumes of minivan exhaust filled the air. Damn, you were not supposed to have to smell this in a moving vehicle. "Dad, are these back windows supposed to be open?" she said, unheard over the rush of air and particulate. "I think I'm gonna be sick."

Mom sang, "I think I'm gonna be sick" to the tune of "Ticket To Ride." She sang it in that Karen Carpenter croon Dana hated, not like a Beatle. Not the way Dana would serenade her dresser mirror (and God help anyone who ever found out about that). The selfsame mirror in which Mom expected her to apply makeup and "make your hair look nice." This, when at sixteen she still lacked any real need for a bra.

Mom stopped the singing and said, "Jeremy, what are you going to play tonight?"

"I don't have my guitar."

"Well now, of course you can't play the electric guitar in a church," she said, though Dana knew there were churches where you could. "Eric said he'd let you use his. He plays it too, you know."

"Yeah." Jeremy threw his arms across the back of the bench seat, taking up acres of space. "Hippie stuff."

Mom craned her head around and frowned at him. "Don't make fun of Eric. He's got a lot of young people interested in the church again."

"Not me."

"Jeremy, don't be ugly."

It was the worst thing a Southerner could be, ugly, a step beyond nasty and even hateful in the lexicon of bad behavior. There were not really any ethics, only aesthetics, which is what Dana was convinced had tamed the worst excesses of Southern evil in the past. It was the ugliness, of black children being beaten and spat upon or fire hoses and dogs being turned on protesters, that had undone the defensive posture of her native land.

"Eric doesn't have young people interested in the church," Dana said to Jeremy when they were out of the minivan and their parents' earshot. "He's got their mothers interested. Why'd you let Mom talk you into coming anyway?"

Jeremy shrugged, the way he did when she asked him anything, like what he was going to do with his life. "You're here."

"I don't have to be," she said. "I want to hear you play."

He didn't say anything, but made a face like he was smarter than all these people, which she didn't doubt he was.

They got to the church basement and found Eric's guitar, though not Eric. Jeremy picked it up and immediately began twanging a folk tune:

"This land is my land/ And it ain't your land/ I got a shotgun/ And you ain't got one/ If you don't get off/ I'll blow your head off/ This land was made for only me."

The kids laughed until they saw that Eric had slid the door open. He had this look on his face, a look Dana called Stupid Male. As if he didn't know whether to chastise Jeremy for irreverence, in his capacity as youth minister, or to succumb to the guffawing humor that males up to an astonishing age were reduced to.

Dana'd found a copy of *The Autobiography of Malcolm X* on Joe's bookshelf and read it—it was the first time she'd even heard of Malcolm X. It pleased her, in a teenage self-flagellating way, to read his incendiary comments on the white race, and in particular the white man. Oh, she agreed, when she looked at the so-called young men around her—all white, all straining to grow a disgusting bit of fuzz above the lip or, even worse, on the chin—that those of European origin had only just stopped swinging from trees.

"Dana," Eric was saying. She blinked, and gathered from the snickering around her that this was not his first effort at getting her attention.

"What?" Damned if she'd "Sir" someone barely older than she was. Fucking goatee.

"What do you know about Ethiopia?"

She exchanged insolent glances with Jeremy, who still held Eric's acoustic guitar. "Famine, right?"

"A few years ago, yes. What else do you know?"

"It's in Africa."

"Where in Africa?"

"I don't know." She tried to think of another African country. "Near South Africa?"

"Dana, pay attention, please. There are Ethiopians coming here to church, refugees, and you don't even know where they're from. And famine is only one problem. Africa is a continent with many problems. There's malaria—"

"I know about malaria, I read the Little House books," Dana said. "I thought we were talking about missions."

"Look at you," Eric continued, and marched over to her. If she stood up she'd be taller than he was. "Ripping your jeans. You rip them on purpose, don't you?"

"They're old jeans."

"What are you trying to look like, Dana? Are you trying to imitate poverty? Because poverty doesn't work like that. Poverty is starving to death—"

“You self-righteous jerk,” she said, and Jeremy was setting the guitar down and coming over to her. “Don’t shut me up, Jeremy, I won’t shut up.”

“What do you know? Self-righteous!” And Eric trembled, from that very quality, or maybe with lust for her torn jeans or from his own inadequacy. “You think being a Christian has to do with being smart and knowing the Bible better than everybody else and—”

“You know why you’re so hung up on poverty, Eric?” she said. “Because you’re a fucking hypocrite.”

The sudden silence in that basement room, separated from the next, adult class only by a foldable wooden partition, resounded with the violated firstness of that fucking, a word that had never before been uttered within it.

“No, really,” she said, “I’m sorry I said fucking in church. But it’s not as bad as doing it, is it?”

“Dana!” Eric started snapping his fingers at her like she was maybe somebody’s dog.

She pressed on. “Who are you fucking, anyway, Eric?” Snap. “Why won’t you tell us?”

“Dana—”

“Is she my age?”

“Okay, Dana.” Jeremy’s arms were around her from behind, and he heaved her out of her chair and toward the opening in the hinged partition. She was aware of the carpet beneath their feet, an orange-gold shag, discolored with years of spilled Kool-Aid and communion grape juice.

They were silent till they got to the minivan. Dana had to get out the keys. Mom wouldn’t let Jeremy drive on account of his epilepsy.

When they were inside with the door shut, all Jeremy said was, “What the fuck?”

Dana grabbed onto his denim jacket and made sobbing sounds, but no tears came out.

Chapter 10

When she went to a special night service, like midnight Mass on Christmas Eve, Isabella would get a ride with Joe. But when she went to Sunday Mass she insisted on riding her bicycle. It was one of the things Dana had always loved most about her grandmother, a reliable hit with the kids at school. "My grandma rides a bicycle." Because their grandmas, or mammaws as they were more likely to call them, all sat on porches, rocking back and forth and dipping snuff. At least that was how Dana pictured them.

Serving not only Poudre Valley but the surrounding community, there not being a large number of the faithful in this Baptist county, St. Stephen's Catholic Church sat along Mountain Highway into town, just before one got to the high school.

It was therefore within three miles of their house, and quite accessible by bike, but Dana herself wouldn't chance it. There was no space to ride along the side of the road, not even a shoulder. And people didn't confine their dogs, big or small, which meant that if they chased you you were at their mercy on a bicycle.

Still Isabella rode. It stretched her legs, she said. In her Sunday finest, collapsible hat snug on her head, a purse—containing what?—in her bicycle basket, she would set out early on Sunday morning. Joe and Mom had talked about it, right there in the kitchen. Dana thought that was rude since Isabella wasn't even there.

"She doesn't want me driving her," Joe said. "It's daytime, she can see as well as I can. She likes her independence, Edith."

For Isabella had never learned to drive. Why should she? Didn't need it, growing up in the city; the bus was always there. By the time she moved south with Dana's parents, she'd been in her fifties, an age at which Dana couldn't imagine learning anything new.

But riding a bike was that archetypal thing that, once you learned, you always knew how to do. They sometimes met in the driveway, Dana and her grandmother, as the latter set off for Mass and Joe was letting Dana practice driving to church. "If you can drive these country roads," Joe reasoned, "you can drive safely anywhere in the state of Tennessee."

"Chicago too, honey," Isabella said. "Oh, those city streets aren't like these, they're so straight and flat."

"At least there's room for a bicycle, in your old neighborhood," Edith said.

"Well, they've yet to paint a line down the middle of this road," Isabella said. "What do you think, Dana? Maybe after you learn to drive, they'll paint a line? You won't need it anymore, then."

Dana, rueful, rarely said much in these encounters. It was stressful enough, driving with a permit. Joe always had to be the one to sit up front with her, because Mom was a nervous wreck. You'd think Dana was a hellcat, the way Mom'd clutch at the car seat, sucking air through her teeth every time she rounded a bend. Mind you it was Mom, not her, who had once taken a bend so fast she went clean off the road.

Anyway the last place Dana wanted to go this Sunday morning was church. It was already hot at eight o'clock, a sultry June day. She'd have to avoid the basement, and Eric; she wouldn't go to youth group again if Mom tried to drag her in by the heels.

Jeremy hadn't said a word about Dana's outburst, to her or to their parents. Which wasn't unusual, but neither had Joe or Mom said anything to her. Was it possible they didn't know? And if they did, and didn't say anything, that was even weirder. It seemed so wrong Dana feared she would have difficulty keeping silent again.

She pulled carefully into the gravel parking lot, as she always did, Mom hissing all the while. Jeremy slid the door open and skedaddled even before Dana put on the emergency brake. By the time Dana got inside, escorted by her parents, she could see through the glass Jeremy already in the junior church room, playing Eric's guitar as if nothing had happened. They were singing about the Acts of the Apostles:

"Ananias and Sapphira/ Got together to conspire a/ Plot—to cheat/ the church and get ahead/ They knew God's power but did not fear it/ Tried to cheat the Holy Spirit/ Peter prophesied it and they both dropped dead/ Unh!"

"That is so irreverent," Mom tut-tutted, and Dana took quicker steps, keen to find a space in a pew far enough from her so-called peers that she wouldn't have to answer any questions.

When they returned home, Dana heard the phone ringing in the kitchen before they were able to get in the door. Mom heard it too, and glared at Joe, her fingers spread on her thighs as though she were wiping them. She was always so impatient, especially on a Sunday, and Joe was so impervious, taking his time, finding his key, turning it in the lock.

Mom was the first through the door and raced to the phone, but the person had hung up. Dana knew this because Mom said "Great. Just great," in the same tone a normal person would say "Shit," or something similar.

"Why don't we get an answering machine?" Dana said.

"For what? I don't want some salesman to know we're not home," Mom said. "Besides, I don't think it would even work with a party line."

Ah yes, the party line. Other households, within the city

limits, had answering machines and phones in the teenagers' rooms, but out here the Rignaldis had a party line. And no cable and no line down the middle of the fucking road.

Five minutes later the phone rang. Mom snatched it from the hook. "Hello?" she said in her phone voice. Then her tone changed altogether, enough to make Dana shut the refrigerator and turn toward her. "Oh my Lord. Oh, Lord."

This was not a phrase Mom used lightly (unlike nearly every other Christian in Dana's experience). "What's going on?" she said, but Mom flipped her hand savagely in Dana's direction.

Dana went to her room and shut the door, only a moment later to hear Mom shouting "Joe. Joe!" Then came the slow steps; Joe was never in a hurry. "You'll be late to your own funeral," Mom would say.

But Dana would not go out. Let them come to her, if they would.

And in the end it was Jeremy who came to the door, which never happened, and summoned Dana. She saw his eyes, bright and red around the rims. "What?" she said, crossness covering her own shock.

"They found Grandma," he said in a very low voice.

"What do you mean, found her?" She stormed into the kitchen where both their parents sat at the table, holding hands, a stricken look on their faces. "What's going on?"

"Grandma was in an accident," Joe said with apparent difficulty. "She died, Dana."

Dana didn't know what to do, so she jerked her thumb at Jeremy. "And you told him first?"

"We wanted to tell you one at a time," Joe said. "Jeremy's the oldest—"

"Oh yeah, by ten months."

"Dana, please," Mom said, and her voice, choked with tears, upset Dana so much she thought she'd explode. She threw the screen door open and headed outside. "This is not about you," she heard Mom cry.

She knew it wasn't about her. How stupid did they think she was? It was about her grandma—her brilliant and beautiful grandma, whom Dana had not sat with often enough, whose stories she had barely begun to hear. A presence in her life, and she'd always imagined that grandmothers slowly faded away into great old age, with plenty of time to rock on a porch somewhere with their grandchildren. But she should have known that was not how Isabella would go. Her grandma rode a bicycle and no one's grandma, mammaw, granny rode a bike. She'd ridden that bicycle right off the road, just like—this was the worst part—just like Mom said she would, even if it wasn't a question of being run over, just a massive heart attack brought on by a lifetime of Ricotta cheese and Alfredo sauce. Dana would hear it soon enough, all this bullshit, but like everything else she heard it would go right in one ear and out the other because all that mattered, the only thing that mattered in the world right now was that Isabella, the person she loved most on this earth if she loved anyone at all, was dead.

Edith had heard of bicycle helmets, though she'd never seen anyone wearing one. She didn't know where they were sold. Maybe in Knoxville, but she wouldn't drive a hundred miles to buy anything; she wasn't much of a shopper. Of course she thought about a helmet now. She always thought of the risks after taking them, of protection after she'd failed to protect someone she loved.

Going to the funeral home, she felt as if she were gliding out of the minivan, up the sidewalk, into the parlor where more people than she'd realized knew Isabella had gathered to view the body. It was, in hideous reverse, like the kind of gliding she'd done up the aisle on her wedding day. She had a bizarre vision of Isabella, all done up in gaudy purple like a grape Popsicle, gliding up the aisle to join some heavenly choir, though in Edith's confused imagination she wasn't sure what color the choir members would be, only the color of their robes. Could Isabella even sing? Surely everybody would have to be black in heaven, to sing and never get tired, like that.

The funeral home was Protestant. There would be a Mass at St. Stephen's, but here the wider Wheeler clan could gather, along with people who knew Joe or Edith or the kids from school. It was a tradition Edith didn't much care for, the viewing of the body, and she'd avoided it in the case of her own parents. She could remember her great-uncle's visitation, Aunt Anna just petting his head the whole time, wailing away. It gave Edith a queer feeling that she didn't look forward to tonight.

She wanted to cuss Isabella. I told you not to go riding a bike all over those hilly roads, you silly, stupid old woman. Rather die than lose her independence, that's what Joe said. Well, that was what a young, healthy person would say. Was it true?

She didn't realize how hard she was crying till Aunt Lanie put an arm around her and handed her a lavender handkerchief, which was too nice to smear makeup and snot on.

"Honey, it's okay," Lanie said, ushering her forward. "Go ahead and cry."

"But—" Edith started to say, though it came out more like "Bwaahh."

"We know how much you loved her."

Hypocritical though she felt, Edith nodded, and then Uncle Claude was at her other side and they were leading her, against her will, to the casket as people called it now. She remembered Jesus' words to Simon Peter: When thou wast young, thou girdedst thyself, and walkedst whither thou wouldest: but when thou shalt be old, thou shalt stretch forth thy hands, and another shall gird thee, and carry thee whither thou wouldest not. Maybe if she cried hard enough she wouldn't have to see.

But when she reached the casket, the body lying there was not Isabella's. It wasn't anyone else's, either, but it looked nothing like Isabella Rignaldi. For one thing, it was too small. Isabella had been big somehow, loud and life-giving. You could hear her from another room, smell her perfume. For another thing, her face was all wrong. Her nose was at a different angle, Edith was sure of it. It was all waxen and, well, just wrong.

And her hair! Where was the wild flowing hair, like a halo, encasing the head that had not been hard enough to resist the side of the road? Where was the ubiquitous hat? The hair was done nicely, everyone would be saying so, but it wasn't Isabella. Edith had an incongruous thought, something a student had told her, that the hair continued to grow after death. She wondered who might know if this were true, and when might be an appropriate time to ask.

Aunt Lanie was still standing there, holding her while she cried. "It's okay," she was saying. "You can touch her if you want to."

Edith just shook her head. What could she say to make this moment pass? "Who did her hair?"

"Clayton, honey."

"Clayton works for the funeral home?"

"He does everybody's hair," Aunt Lanie said. "When Jeannie had her cancer last year it was so hard for her to keep her hair clean, you know. She had to wear a baseball cap, poor girl. Anyway, when she died Clayton done her hair up so nice, honey, you'd never know she was sick."

Edith felt an urge to bust out laughing; it was the hysteria kicking in. To stifle it, she said, "How come he couldn't do it for her while she was alive?" As soon as she asked the question, she no longer wanted to laugh. "Huh?" she choked, and tried to repeat herself but Lanie shushed her.

"Come on over and sit down for a little while."

Edith gave up and went toward a folding chair, still shaking her head. There was no way that was Isabella in there. The crazy dumb woman, getting run off the road.

She sat and shook to herself for a while, only looking up to take offered hands and say "Thank you" to people. She didn't know Clayton did hair for the dead.

But Joe did. It was Joe, after all, who had to make the arrangements this time. The country Methodist get-together for Isabella's body, Mass for her soul. Most of the time his mother and wife carried on, perfectly capable of taking care of their own affairs and his too, but at crucial moments they became women. He became the man, at any rate, and as in so many other areas of his life, his role as a man had to be carefully learned.

He knew not to cry openly or lose it, and for the most part he was calm in a crisis—calm all the time, but especially in a crisis. So he called people: the preacher who directed him to the funeral home, the funeral director, this and that relative (though they were Edith's), and, at the recommendation of the funeral director, strongly seconded by Aunt Lanie, Clayton to do his mother's hair.

This is where a woman would have been handy, but the only woman he could think to ask was Isabella. He didn't feel right asking Edith about getting his dead mother's hair done. Edith went to Clayton for her hair too; how would she feel, thinking of his hands in her hair just like they'd been in Isabella's, both before and after death? No, Joe was a man, and men were practical. They didn't care whose hands touched whose hair. Men were grateful to have any hair at all.

He knew who Clayton was. Clayton looked like what he was, a hairdresser—a buff, butch hairdresser with highly developed pectorals and biceps that could crack a nut. Joe had learned the language of the gym, like other languages of males, by observation and practice, memorizing pecs and lats and abs like road signs in a foreign language.

But losing a parent rocked him, unmoored him. He remembered losing his father and how it had left him and his mother and brother at sea, literally in Steve's case. It left them free to imagine a world in which Stefano Rignaldi had never been, and they felt guilty about that even as they mourned his passing. He thought he'd known how Edith felt, an orphan at sixteen, but he had not known. Her loss was simultaneously greater and less than his, for it had happened all at once. No one expected a child—and his children were still children at that age—no one expected children to bury their parents with equanimity, but he was a man, in his forty-second year, and he felt as alone and grief-stricken on the phone with this stranger, Clayton, as if he were five years old and abandoned in a suburban mall.

And Clayton soothed him. It was that easy hairdresser's voice that must lull all the ladies into telling him their secrets. Edith joked that if anybody ever wanted to take over the county, or the state for that matter, all they'd have to do was talk to Clayton Hornsby, he knew everything about everyone.

"Clayton?" Joe said on the phone. "It's Joe Rignaldi. We've spoken at the gym—"

"Oh, hey Joe," Clayton said, as smooth as caramel sauce on ice cream. "I know who you are. I cut your wife's hair."

"Yeah." Joe cleared his throat. "Well, my mother passed away—"

"I'm sorry to hear that," Clayton said, with a little gasp of recognition. "That's Isabella. Oh, my God."

"I was told you did hair. You know, for burial—I don't know anything about this stuff," Joe finished, remembering he was supposed to be a man.

"Of course you don't," Clayton said, as though that were the thing being talked about. "Of course you don't. I would be honored. Honored, to do your mother's hair. Oh, I'm going to miss Isabella." Clayton kept talking, telling Joe all about his mother as if the two of them had never had the pleasure of meeting. Joe got the feeling he could put the phone down, go away and make a Dagwood sandwich, come back, and Clayton would never realize he'd been gone, but he could not take that liquid voice away from his ear. Next thing you know Clayton had invited him to the funeral home on Monday evening, the day before the viewing, saying he'd like a family member to be there, that it helped to remember the person the way she'd been in life. Joe knew a cock-and-bull story when he heard one, but the hairdresser had cast his spell and he could not resist.

He told Edith he was going to the home, but not for what. Edith was in no position to question his arrangements, since she didn't have to make them.

Clayton met him at the home. "Hey, Joe." He briefly clasped Joe's hand in both of his, then pulled him in for a hug. Joe stood straight, as if he could tower over a man of equal height by sheer willpower. Clayton released him in a moment, appearing not to notice.

"You're a swimmer," he said, and Joe could not be sure but he seemed to be appraising his body, his build. "I've seen you in the pool," Clayton added quickly. "I usually swim a few laps myself, after I'm done with my workout." He snapped his shoulders back, an automatic movement, in response to Joe's stiffening posture.

Joe still did not say anything. Clayton would think he was weighed down by grief.

"Do you want to see her?" Clayton asked, gently.

They went into a room and there was his mother. This was a bizarre ritual. Clayton had done hair for so many women, and Isabella's many times, but the silence, the absence of chatter appeared to invest this last time with something sacramental. A sacrament like the Mass itself, which Joe would attend with his brother, whom he hadn't seen in years, and whatever Catholic friends his mother had, all of which would seem remote in both time and significance. There was no remoteness here. There was an intimacy, the silence between them, neither he nor the hairdresser saying a word more than the dead woman.

He could not take his eyes off Clayton's hands. The arms he had noticed, and the chest, that ropy torso that tapered down into—he didn't know what kind of legs they were or how you got them, but not by swimming. He had noticed that, and how Clayton was always talking and his voice did some weird, high-pitched thing, a thing the unselfconsciousness of which astonished Joe even as he admired it. He would never have dared talk like that. He supposed, from a hairdresser, it was expected, along with the loose dangle of the wrist, a certain hippy posture Joe was not accustomed to in other men. Indeed, he could barely acknowledge to himself that he noticed their hips.

But he had never seen Clayton at work and this was not the same, this was silent work. His hands, fine and soft as you would expect from a man who had his hands in hair care products all day, were pale white, the only color Joe could see being the tiny tufts of hair on the back of each knuckle, which was easily distinguished from the silver-white of Isabella's hair. Clayton washed her hair gently, dried it, "did" it, and Joe could not help thinking that his mother must be soothed by such ministrations, the tangles of her hair unknotted effortlessly by Clayton's expert fingers.

Joe had never had so long and such ease to watch another person before, for Clayton worked solemnly, lovingly, as if he were the only one there. Joe had never been in the presence of anyone like that, who appeared to have lost all sense of time or place. Edith, or any woman, even the men Joe knew, would have looked up long before now and said "What?" People didn't like to be watched. Joe didn't; every morning of his working life he went and stood in front of a bunch of kids who were watching him to see what he would do next or what they should do, and still he wasn't used to it, it was his least favorite part. But Clayton ignored him, in a benign way. The three of them, Joe, Isabella and Clayton, in silent communion.

Edith talked to Joe later about how many people had gone to the funeral home and viewed the body, and said how nice Isabella's hair looked. She said it with distaste, as if she were ashamed to be part of this tradition. She remarked also on how good his brother Steve looked, compared to the last time she'd seen him. Steve had been at Mass, flew in the night before, late, insisted on staying at the Ramada because he didn't want to put them out, he'd told Edith on the phone. Left the same evening, not even a bite to eat.

Joe must have said something to his brother, must at least have exchanged a manly handshake, no tears, on the occasion of their mother's death. He remembered none of it. He didn't remember the priest, what anybody said, or even who was there. The whole week, in fact, dissolved into a watery blur for him, his grief like drunkenness although he didn't recall drinking either. Or eating, or sleeping. Or even drawing breath. All he remembered, all he ever remembered from the week his mother died was shaking his head and surfacing to see Clayton Hornsby at work, his fingers along Isabella's scalp, and something like a smile on his face.

Chapter 11

After they buried their mother, after Steve had jetted out to his ship or base or wherever, it was as if Joe had buried a part of himself that had been holding him together all these years. It was a grievous loss and, at the same time, a loosening, an opening up. It felt as if he'd been constrained, by always knowing who he was and how he should behave, and now when he got up in the mornings and engaged in his bathroom ritual, it didn't seem like himself that he saw in the mirror.

He and Edith didn't talk about it. Not Isabella, and not what they had discussed earlier: themselves and how they would arrange things. It was difficult for him to be the one to bring things up, though he'd tried at Christmas. He had the sense that if Edith wasn't talking about something herself, then she didn't think it was important. At any rate that's how things were for him. Once something had been said, it was decided, and he didn't feel the need constantly to apprise Edith of the situation. It was like his love for her and like his commitment to stay: there it was, every morning, staring back at him in the bathroom, a fact of life.

In school, he had been a very good dancer, a habit he lost in college as he and the times slipped further away from the kind of music you could dance to. He was always happiest dancing with his girlfriend Diane. She never expected him to talk much. He just kept moving, leading, although Diane said it was the girl who did the hard parts. He felt good dancing with her and it was because he was so comfortable. She let him be himself and all he had to do was relax. For so much of his life, he was unable to relax, to let go of that stiffness he always felt in his body, the tension of not knowing where to look or in what way it was safe to move. Diane was someone it was okay to follow with his eyes, and the more fluid his motions when they danced, the more likely they were to win the school contests.

He missed that. He missed just dancing. He had dated Diane because she was a good girl who would resist sexual overtures, and so he wouldn't have to find someone else.

Now he swam more, longer sessions. It eased his stiffness, and if his eyes welled up with unmanly tears, no one could tell in the chlorinated water. He watched for Clayton Hornsby but only behind the safety of his goggles. When he saw Clayton, he would swim harder, faster, occasionally splashing the other man in his wake. He would continue swimming until long after Clayton's exit from the pool, avoiding any conversation in the locker room. What had been an after-school workout from four to five o'clock began stretching closer to six, as Clayton tended to go later in the afternoon. They never spoke, but Joe had to see him and would swim until he did. On the odd day that Clayton didn't show, because his appointments were late or for whatever reason, Joe would towel off, crestfallen, feeling bereft as Isabella's death had not made him feel.

Edith started to complain. "Joe, I have supper ready at six. I make the kids sit down at the table and then we're waiting for you. It isn't fair."

It was an article of faith with them, as much from the Rignaldi side as the Wheeler, that a family should sit down together for supper each evening, the TV off. It made them freaks in this age, though their freakishness was cushioned somewhat by the families around them who also kept the faith. For Joe to be swimming at the Y at that hour was a shirking of his responsibilities as a family man. He realized how much he had depended on the gravity of Isabella to keep them in her orbit.

Another article of faith was that they did not have these conversations openly, as in the kitchen where, in the unlikely event the kids weren't in their rooms, they would hear the argument. The bedroom was the place for conversation, argument or otherwise. It had become less and less the place for anything. But that was not a conversation they had, or that Joe felt like having.

About six weeks after his mother's death, Joe was swimming hard one afternoon, aware of Clayton in the next lane but ignoring him, hiding in the wake. But Clayton was not swimming at his ordinary, cool-down pace. He was plowing through the water and Joe, frightened of a confrontation, was forced to swim faster to keep ahead of him. At the end of the lane he touched the side and pushed off, racing back, but Clayton executed an Olympic flip-turn and coasted what seemed like half the length of the pool.

An unaccustomed fire crept into Joe Rignaldi's belly, something he'd felt as a child when Steve would bully him and he'd be forced to fight back, to compete. He felt his hands, which he knew were bigger than Clayton's, become slicing blades in the water, his legs kicking in rhythm, pouring on the speed. He pushed off from the other end but Clayton was right behind him and adjacent. Down the pool they scythed, the water foaming around them, and there might have been crowds of other people there or none at all, Joe neither knew nor cared.

They had swum far more than Clayton's usual three or four laps; it might have been fourteen. Joe's lungs were burning and the blood was pounding in his head, in his eyes. He tore down the lane and back again, gasping at each breath, gulping air through the side of his mouth. At the next turn he felt a hand grab his foot and tried to kick free. The hand would not let go and Joe flailed for the surface, finally resting his hand on the rope that divided the lanes. A lifeguard, who until that moment hadn't shown any interest in what was going on in the pool for as long as Joe'd been coming here, blew his whistle and said, "No horseplay."

Joe heard a low voice next to his ear. "He don't know the half of it."

Joe was glad he was in water. He wanted so badly to keep swimming, away from Clayton and his terrible energy, but exhaustion had caught up with him. He allowed Clayton to tow him to the end of the pool, then just hung there till he had the strength to make his way across the outside lane to the ladder. He didn't look to see where Clayton had gone, or at the lifeguard, though he imagined everyone in the pool area could see his discomfort.

In the locker room Joe was peeling his ancient swimming trunks down to his ankles when there was a knock on the side of his locker. He tripped getting out of the trunks and braced himself on the rough gunmetal.

"Whoa, big boy," Clayton said, and Joe could only pray no one was around because discretion did not seem to be in Clayton's vocabulary. "I just wanted to give you my card."

Joe noticed, as the auditory signals fought their way into his brain past competing stimuli, that Clayton had lowered his voice in pitch, though not in volume. Maybe other men were used to back-slapping and exchanging business cards in the nude, but Joe was intensely embarrassed. He somehow managed to accept the card with one hand while maneuvering the locker door, to hide the lower half of his body, with the other. "Thanks," he said, attempting a gruff, masculine voice.

Clayton disappeared into the shower but there was no way Joe was following him in there. He hurried into his pants and stuffed the card in the back pocket, but not without reading it first. It said:

GLAMOR SHACK

CLAYTON HORNSBY, Proprietor

Clayton had crossed out his address in slightly smeared felt-tip pen, and written:

The Cooking Club

ASAP

Joe had heard of the Cooking Club. It was an establishment that had opened on the east side of Mountain Highway, a building that had been quite a number of things, most recently a Chinese restaurant that had gone out of business only a few months earlier. Joe put it down to the building being concrete, cavernous, a place with no windows. Who wanted to sit down and eat in a place where you'd never seen other people eating?

He looked at his watch—a fine, though not too expensive model with an accordion band. He thought of the watch Jones Wheeler had worn, which was expensive, valuable enough at any rate to have been ripped from his wrist. Or maybe they'd fought over it, Jones and his...It was after five now. If Joe drove straight to the Cooking Club, met Clayton, and drove straight home without dawdling or chitchat, he should be home by six. There was no reason to call Edith or upset her by being late.

As he drove down Mountain Highway—just far enough, like so many places one drove in Poudre Valley, to make walking an impossibility—he wondered if there had come a particular point when he and Edith had become troublesome to one another. It was not his nature to analyze so he didn't, just wondered abstractly whether he had ever, in fact, been free to go where he chose and not answer to wife or children or parents or teacher or boss. What would it feel like? Sunlight touched the tobacco leaves by the side of the road. He suddenly craved tobacco.

In the entrance of the Cooking Club, formerly Hong's restaurant, was a wall that screened the inside and added to the dark atmosphere. There was a woman behind the bar, watching a big TV. Joe saw that it was tuned to a cooking channel, but there was no other evidence of food.

She waved to someone behind him and there was Clayton, offering a cigarette, which Joe took, and holding the flame, his hand cupping it as though there were a wind in the building. Joe inhaled the smoke and felt his legs almost buckle with a feeling he recognized. It was desire, but it had been a long time since he felt it like this, the object of attention.

"Would you like a drink?" Clayton said. His eyes seemed to give off sparks, though it could have been a reflection of the TV, or the lighter. In the shadows Joe felt somewhat safe addressing his face, the neat mustache, the clean-shaven planes.

"A Sprite, please," Joe said. "No ice." He figured Clayton would remark about the hard stuff but he only ordered a shot, something clear, from the bored-looking woman who silently filled their glasses. Then Joe started worrying what the protocol was. The only man he could remember buying him drinks was Jones.

Clayton handed him the Sprite and they each drew on their cigarettes. Joe thought of saying he'd never been here before, but wasn't that obvious?

"I figured," Clayton said, "I ought to ask you here. You seem too classy for the bus station."

Joe was so startled he spit Sprite. Clayton laughed. "Honey, relax. I just meant, I know you're clean."

"I can't stay." Joe fought the rising tide of panic and a more elemental urgency. Edith would not leave his mind and truthfully, why should she?

"I know that." Clayton drained his glass and jerked his head toward the back of the large room, where it was even darker.

Down a corridor they went, turned once, and they were in a tiny claustrophobic hall lit by a single bulb. Two doors appeared to open off it but Joe didn't know to what. He felt Clayton turn and pin him gently against the wall. It was clear to him that they were equal in physical strength and that he was free to flee Clayton or to fight him, but it was equally clear that Clayton was not afraid.

Joe was. He was terrified, and it made him more afraid that Clayton wasn't. He had never known that there were men like this, men who not only picked one another up but wore their—Joe didn't even want to call it anything—who would bring each other here in daylight, knowing each other's names and knowing they'd recognize each other on the street the next day, that they'd have to. It was not that big a town.

It was impossible to hide his fear, or the heightening effect that fear was having. It was worse than in the locker room. But Clayton didn't laugh, though Joe did see something crease his young face, which the light didn't flatter. He sank to his knees, unzipped Joe, and had him in his mouth before Joe could react or even think. Joe closed his eyes, a vestige of the childhood belief that if you couldn't see others, they couldn't see you. His fingers felt in vain for a hold on the cinder block wall, and his head knocked in a way that would've been uncomfortable, had he cared.

All smooth and fluid and over in probably less than sixty seconds, not that he was counting. He knelt when Clayton released him, eyes still closed, the fear of discovery rising with the fading erection. He opened his eyes and stood up in a hurry, stuffing himself back in his pants. Clayton had produced a red handkerchief and was wiping his mouth.

"You see," Clayton said, "that didn't take long."

They stared at each other for a minute. Joe had barely spoken since asking for a Sprite. This struck him as so ridiculous that his mouth spread in a grin, he couldn't help it.

"You have my number," Clayton said, and kissed him on the cheek.

This had more of an effect on Joe than the sex. He pushed back on Clayton's shoulders and saw startled eyes. He leaned in and kissed him, feeling unimaginable tensions explode like fireworks in his middle. They leaned there, kissing, for what in any event was longer than a minute. When Joe stepped back, Clayton let out a sigh that sounded spontaneous, though it was beyond him what was practiced at this point.

Don't think about it, just do it. Joe bent his knees, purposefully. Clayton was all ready for him when he lowered his lips.

Ten minutes later, Joe raced home in the minivan. He'd tell Edith he'd hit every red light on the way, which was true—all three of them. He could think of nothing but Edith, not so much the conversation they'd had, but the one they had not had. The things Edith had every right to say, but hadn't said.

He couldn't remember either the last time he'd made love to her or the last time he'd wanted to, or which was longer ago. This was no surprise but she hadn't complained, had never said anything about it to him.

And Edith was the talker. If she had a problem with something she would say. He had only been honest. He had only told her the truth up to today, and he would tell her the truth now. There was no reason to doubt she'd do the same.

"Didn't you believe me?" Joe said.

They were in their bedroom. Edith sat on the bed, the edge of the yellow blanket in her hands. She was fully dressed, cross-legged, and she worried the blanket like a dog with its teeth. Not for the first time, she wished there was someplace besides the bedroom, somewhere in the house or on the acres around it, that she felt was truly private.

Yes, she'd heard the words. Joe had said them and she'd not only heard, but accepted them, agreed to them. The terms. The terms and conditions of their partnership—oh, it sounded like a legal agreement, and marriage was more than that. She'd heard the words but believing them, that was another matter.

He sat down beside her, touched her shoulder; she shrank away. "I told you the truth," he said. "Edith, I've only ever told you what was true."

"I didn't think—" But it wasn't true that she didn't think he'd really do it. If he'd changed his mind, he would have said. She felt so raw, so hopelessly naïve. She'd insisted he tell her the truth, the truth at every stage. But when he said it, she didn't want to hear it, after all.

"Why him?" she finally said.

Joe stood up, went to the front window. From the corner of her eye she could see him finger the curtain. Was this how it went, he met a hairdresser and was now taking an interest in interior decorating?

"He's my hairdresser, Joe," she said, and her voice sounded thick, like something Isabella would stir. "I've sat there, with his fingers in my hair."

"And you never had any inkling about him, all this time?"

"That's not it." She sounded angry, though the anger was far below the surface of her feelings, clawing for air. "I never thought about it. Him. Not with my husband, anyway."

"Would you rather it was someone you didn't know?"

He might as well have been talking to the curtain. These questions didn't make any sense. She tried to imagine anyone she'd ever met asking such a question. Who would you rather your husband see, Edith? Your hairdresser, or a total stranger? By night or by day? By land or by sea? She must be losing her mind, she felt as if she were in the Paul Revere poem.

She looked down at her hands, clutching the blanket. She didn't know why it was hands, the thought of her hairdresser's—no, that hairdresser's hands, that bothered her. She didn't know what to think of his hands doing. Joe had spared her that much detail.

She knew what was involved, of course. She'd read Genesis without believing that men and dinosaurs walked the earth at the same time, and she'd read about Sodom, she hoped, with the same God-given mind. She could picture even more disgusting things, but chose not to. It was jealousy—an awkward feeling, since she neither remembered, nor cared, when Joe had last touched her like that. Oh yes, somewhere in the last twenty years the church had decided that sex was important after all, though only in Christian marriage. But what was a Christian marriage? Two Christians who married each other, that's all. Nobody could make them love each other, let alone have good sex.

"What do you want me to say, Joe?"

"I asked you," he said. "Would you rather—"

"I'd rather you didn't. It doesn't matter what I'd rather. It never did. That's what I have to live with."

"It goes both ways, Edith."

"Oh yeah," she said. "Thanks. I'll just go hitchhike the highway and get picked up by some trucker, I'll just go prostitute myself. Or I'll have an affair with your principal, Mr. Tanner. That's fair, and exactly what I have on my mind right now."

"You don't want me either."

"No." She turned to face him but he still looked away. "You don't want me. You never have, and—"

"Do you want me not to see him again?"

"What difference would that make?"

"If you ask me not to, I won't." He looked up. "You know that."

She did know that. It was maddening, and she didn't feel like giving Joe credit right now. "I repeat, what difference would it make? You wouldn't stop thinking about it. You always did, didn't you? Probably when we were conceiving our children." How else could he have gone through with it?

"I've never lied to you."

"Yes, honesty's very sexy, Joe. Women love that in a man. It's rare. But it doesn't make up for everything else."

And yet it wasn't Joe who had lied. It was she herself, saying she understood when she didn't, saying she would help him when she didn't want to. The vows, the children—the things that held other couples together were what held them, not each other in the night. No, she was only fooling herself.

She felt flayed in the ensuing days, as if everyone could see her preoccupation, that layers of her had been stripped away and what she found beneath was inadequate. She went to work each day with the "I'm over it" feeling of a much older teacher, wondering if she would make it through the day without throwing her chalk down and telling a full classroom that she just didn't care, nothing she could teach them was important, they were just going to have to figure it out on their own because she needed all her energy for herself. Duty, of course, prevailed.

On Friday, which she had gotten to, she supposed, by sheer nail-digging will, she was writing on the blackboard, really a green board but at least they hadn't made her switch to an overhead projector. She wrote the possessive form of it in a sentence, and used an apostrophe. She knew that its was spelled without an apostrophe; it was a slip of the hand, a hand she was lucky was not shaking so hard the chalk fell out of it, if anybody wanted to know.

But she was unaware of having made this mistake until Wayne, a smart boy who sat in the back because he was too cool to care about being smart, said, "Miz Rignaldi."

She turned, chalk still in hand. "Yes, Wayne?"

"It's spelled wrong."

She scanned the blackboard but her eyes had been bothering her all morning. A film of tears—allergies, perhaps, or chalk dust. "What?"

"It's spelled wrong."

She shook her head. "I'm sorry, what is?"

"Its," he said, and now the rest of the class was catching on, snickering, and he smirked, or that was how Edith perceived it.

"I don't see—"

Wayne dropped his hands to his side, as though exasperated by her stupidity. "Its doesn't have an apostrophe when it's used like that, Miz Rignaldi. Only when it means 'it is.'"

Finally, she saw what he was talking about. She took one of the big erasers and slowly wiped the apostrophe out with a precise edge. She should thank Wayne, but do so while making clear that she did know this rule, that anyone could make a mistake.

Before she could think of a way to do this, Wayne said, "See, in English class they tell us spelling is not just for English. I mean, we're supposed to be graded for correct spelling in science class too."

"That's right," she said, trying to control her voice.

But he wasn't finished. "That's not really fair though, is it? I mean, we don't have to know science in English class. Or history. We don't have to know science for history."

"Oh, I'm sure you've read about scientists in history," Edith said, thinking how far they may have gotten in an American history class that might only reach the Civil War. "What about Benjamin Franklin?"

Wayne shook his head, and Edith felt the heat in her face. She could not get visions of what men might do to each other out of her mind; it was making her crazy. "I mean the rules of science," Wayne said. "The rules of English, well, they're important everywhere, right? I mean you're supposed to know how to spell. Just because you're the science teacher doesn't mean it's okay to be illiterate."

She hated Wayne. The class knew it, and they held their collective breath, sure that illiterate was a terrible thing to be though unsure exactly what it was.

Then Wayne threw down the gauntlet. "I'll bet Miz Snodgrass doesn't even care about the laws of physics."

The eraser flew out of her hand and hit Wayne smack in the face with a puff of chalk dust. A body in motion...He began to cough and Edith, who had not thrown anything for a number of years, said, "Get out of my class."

Wayne was covered with dust where the eraser had tumbled down his body. "Did you hear me?" Edith said, her hands stiff at her sides. "Get out of here."

It was the closest she'd ever come to physically punishing a student, and this made her crazy too. She didn't see how she could come back in Monday, stand in front of students let alone talk to the principal, while always on the verge.

Maybe a haircut would help, she thought after school. If she left these long curls in she'd tear it all out anyway, the way she was feeling. She could not, needless to say, go to the Glamor Shack anymore so she booked an appointment at a shop across town, where she paid a woman twice as much to feather her hair in a short cut.

Chapter 12

1990

"Dana, you might as well have told him to go to hell."

Edith was furious. She had not raised her children to speak disrespectfully to anyone, and had never, in fact, heard them swear. There were gradations of disrespect in the Rignaldi household, from the most strictly forbidden (the taking of the Lord's name in vain) down through ordinary profanity and such expressions as "stuff it," which Dana had just directed loudly at her brother. There was no place for any of these under Edith's roof, though she excepted Yiddishisms she'd picked up in Chicago, like "putzing around."

Dana looked at her with something like hatred in her eyes. Edith wasn't sure she'd ever felt before what it was like to be hated by another person. What bothered her, even more than being hated by her daughter, was that she couldn't link this emotional outburst to Jeremy or to any specific action of her own.

"Where's Dad?" Dana demanded, her fists clenching impotently.

Putzing around.

Edith didn't know what to say to Dana. At least with Joe she could always think of something.

"Your dad and I both love you, you know that," Edith said in a softened tone. There. She had said something TV-movie correct, without answering Dana's question about the whereabouts of her father. Instead, she'd told Dana what she ought to need to know. How parental of her. Edith was vaguely disgusted with herself.

Edith had just spent a long time with Joe at the bar and grill that had been their favorite dinner spot since they got married. The two of them going out to dinner together and without their children, which Edith understood to be uncommon among couples who'd been married for almost twenty years.

They'd ordered salads and lasagna, and Edith helped herself to most of the bread basket, though normally garlic bread wasn't a favorite of hers. She stuck to iced water with lemon, while Joe had his inevitable wine, which he drank anytime and with any kind of food. Normally he took a long time getting through a glass, but tonight he went through several and all his food as well. His gaze was steady, just below the level of her eyes, barely responding when she tried to converse. The effect was that he seemed to stare at her without ever making eye contact, and it made her crazy.

She didn't say much, and Joe said less, pretty much the pattern of their lives writ large. Of course, she would have had more to say if she'd been trying to defend herself. But she had little or nothing to say on her own behalf, so she just kept eating.

At one point, still not exactly looking at her, Joe asked, "Do you want to leave?"

Edith didn't know if he was talking about the restaurant, or their marriage. "Yes," she said.

"Are you going to?" he said, without surprise or expectation.

"Probably not."

"So," Joe said, looking past his fork. "If you're not leaving, then what are we going to do?"

"What are we going to do?" Edith repeated, Joe-like.

"How is it going to be different?"

The words sounded heavy and difficult. Clearly it was taking a great deal of effort for Joe to produce them at all. Edith felt she should reward this. "It's entirely up to you, Joe."

How dare Mom talk to her like some character played by Meredith Baxter Birney? What was Dana supposed to do now, smoke something or go make herself throw up? Parents never said shit like this unless they were on the brink of divorce; everyone knew that. Well, she'd seen it coming.

All the years they'd lived in this house together, every evening was the same. Joe sat at his desk, studying, sometimes pecking away at his typewriter, which he would never trade in for an electric, let alone a computer. Mom stayed in the kitchen, washing dishes, wiping up the inevitable spills for which she always blamed Dana or Jeremy, although they were just as likely to be Joe's.

The only variation in Mom's—indeed, the family's—daily or weekly routine involved church. Sunday mornings they all got up, forced themselves or were forced into nicer clothes than usual, hurried through something of a breakfast compromise that no one objected to much but that wasn't exactly what any of them liked to eat, and piled into the minivan together. Dana just shook her head when she heard of other young people who didn't go to church, or who argued with their parents about going. Like divorce, it was all around her, yet unimaginable in her own home.

But Dana wasn't stupid. She knew when Mom told her they were no longer going to the Glamor Shack, as if Dana wasn't old enough to choose where to get her hair cut. She didn't know what it had to do with Mom throwing an eraser at a kid, but that was all over the school system. Dana wanted to throw things at somebody nearly every day of the year, but could she get away with it? No.

She saw fakeness everywhere, but she also believed she was being lied to by omission: by the teachers, the government, the church, above all by her parents. They wouldn't tell her what was going on, while she had to put up with her mother's behavior and bizarre things like crossing town to get to the hairdresser's. The fucking hairdresser's. She'd taken to cussing a lot, at school with her friends, or what passed for friends, and fucking was her favorite word now. She thought about fucking a lot.

The worst thing was, as close as parents were to a kid, living in the same house, you had no more control over what they said or did than over a total stranger, even though it affected every aspect of your life. She wasn't a child anymore, yet she was still under the control of Mom and Joe. She didn't want to go to this new hairdresser, or church, or anywhere with her mother. When you were an adult you could control others' behavior, but a kid was helpless.

She had started getting a magazine, a highly liberal, even left-wing publication, which she'd heard of through the mail. She got a lot of mail from progressive organizations since joining a human rights group she'd learned about from the liner notes of one of Jeremy's rock albums. Dana wasn't much interested in the type of men her grandmother, whom she could only think of with a spasm of grief, had ironically called "ugly," but she did have a soft spot for thin-lipped Christ figures who played guitar. They reminded her of her brother.

Her bottom dresser drawer was stuffed with these magazines and brochures, from everyone except the National Abortion Rights Action League, whose direct mail Dana had torn up and thrown away. All she needed was Mom finding that. In fact, the thought of abortion made Dana feel sick in the gut, but then so did the thought of being pregnant. She wondered if joining one group, with the seemingly unarguable goal of stopping torture, meant you had to join a whole new religion.

It was starting to feel that way. She'd saved an old copy of U.S. News in which a homosexual had been profiled—literally; his face could not be shown in the magazine, for his protection. For he was not only a homosexual, but a man dying of AIDS. His community treated him horribly, spreading rumors that he spit in salad bars and so forth. Dana felt sorry for him. They'd only just gotten their first salad bar in Poudre Valley, and why couldn't people just enjoy it?

Her leftist magazine was more sympathetic. It told her that homosexuals were actually "gay" and even profiled gay "kids"—faces showing—though she was dismayed to find that the youngest was twenty-one. No doubt that was for their protection.

Finally, Dana decided that she was called to act in solidarity, and she took the minivan, the only car she was allowed to drive, and defied Mom by going to the Glamor Shack. Clayton seemed surprised to see her, but he was quickly back to his old self. "How you doing?"

Dana observed him carefully while getting her trim. He certainly didn't avoid the gestures and vocalizations that were associated with homosexuals. Dana knew the rumors, but so did Mom, and long before she stopped going to him for her haircuts. What was this new paranoia about AIDS? Did Mom really believe, as she'd said in response to the poll question, that AIDS was God's judgment?

"How's business, Clayton?"

"Oh...you know." He shook his wrist, dipped into the Barbicide.

A picture of the "kids" from her magazine flashed into memory, and Dana was seized by something wild. "Cut it really short, please."

He looked at her. "Honey, are you sure? You've been growing your hair out, what, since you were eight, nine years old?"

"No, cut it off."

"It's your funeral," he tsk'ed, and though she knew he was talking about Mom's reaction, Dana imagined something darker in his voice.

As he moved from the shears down to the clippers and she enjoyed the buzzing sensation along the back of her neck, Dana felt her solidarity with the persecuted growing. Clayton was not afraid to work each day, and look what people said about him! She knew homosexuals were the most despised people in the world and therefore had some empathy with them, but she didn't think about what such identification meant. She might as well be shaving her head in solidarity with a Tibetan monk, or a chemo patient.

Finally, he straightened her hairline with a razor. It was a straight razor and reminded Dana of a story she'd read, translated from Spanish, about a barber who thought about assassinating someone in his chair. She tried not to breathe audibly.

He picked up the mirror with his other hand. "Here you go, hon."

She regarded herself and saw Clayton nodding with approval. "Mmm. Fierce."

As he unwrapped the gown from around her newly shaved neck, he nicked himself. Dana jumped from the chair, towel askew. What was in that blood? Power in the blood, AIDS in the blood...

"Where you going?" Clayton said, and Dana remembered so she threw a ten-dollar bill on his counter. Then she fled.

Mom had her own new hairstyle, and seemed not to want to discuss what Dana had done—"At least it's not a tattoo, it'll grow back." The idea of getting a tattoo, especially after seeing Clayton cut himself, made Dana feel faint, but she let Mom think (from the shrug) that it might just as easily have been a tattoo.

But the danger Dana faced was not from a razor or from blood. It was waiting for her at school in the person of Tracy, a girl who had been in Dana's grade from the first, though if ever there was an example of social promotion, Tracy was it. Dana figured her Jordache jeans were tight enough to constrict whatever brains she had, since they were surely in her ass. Tracy had a worn circle on her back pocket, like the one Bear and his friends had from carrying a can of Skoal. Rumor was this was her birth control pills.

Dana hadn't thought faggot was commonly used to abuse girls, but it was probably one of the few words Tracy knew. She turned around slowly. "Who're you talking to, Tracy? Your john?"

Tracy grinned, in the way that stupid people do when they think they're being clever. "No," she said, "you must be John. I'm sorry, I thought you was a girl who used to go here."

Dana felt her hands tense. "What girl?"

"A faggot girl. Like you."

Dana's fist shot out before she even knew it had clenched. It connected with Tracy's nose and Tracy grabbed at her face, slumping against a locker in disbelief. The light-speed telegraph that was the high school halls began to buzz, "Girl fight. Girl fight" and more students surrounded Tracy and her gang, who were discreetly backing away.

Dana felt the adrenalin and put up her fists, as she'd seen boxers do on TV at Uncle Jimmy's house. "That it, Tracy?" she said, while Tracy pulled her long-nailed fingers away from her bloody nose. "What about that slap you gave me in first grade? I never forgot it." Tracy made a cat-like sound, but Dana socked her in the jaw and a crunch reverberated down through eleven years of school. Tracy crumpled to the floor.

The crowd murmured, not having gotten their money's worth. Some teacher had summoned the vice principal. He stepped toward Dana, saw the blood on her hands, and reconsidered. "Wash up and be at my office in two minutes."

She had never been in trouble before. She'd never sat here, across from the vice principal's halitotic gut. Why wasn't Tracy in his office?

"You want to tell me why I shouldn't suspend you?" he said.

She swallowed. "Tracy called me a name."

A grin, the same grin Tracy had. "What name?"

"Faggot."

"But you're not a faggot."

"No," she said, "that's why—"

"We won't have talk like that in my school," he said, his grin disappearing. "I'm calling your mother."

Mom was not amused to be summoned at school. That afternoon she let Dana have it. "Fighting, Dana? Suspended? You are going to college next year. What is wrong with you?"

Same thing that was wrong with her. But Dana couldn't tell Mom the reason for the fight, and the vice principal had been enjoying it too much to bring it up.

Mom shook her head. "As if one of you isn't bad enough."

"What?"

"I mean," she said, "Jeremy isn't doing anything; you're who we're counting on."

"That's ridiculous, Mom. I've been suspended, not Jeremy."

She didn't think that was what Mom meant, but neither of them elaborated now. As if Jeremy was a failure just for not being academically gifted. As if everybody had to be a fucking teacher. She was glad to be out of school for a few days.

Chapter 13

Joe had never had so little idea of what to do. It had been such a long time since he'd had sex with anyone but himself, and doing it with a new person was a sensation so rare that he had difficulty absorbing the impact. To risk everything for such release—he had resisted because he knew, or thought he knew, how men were: they did not take sex very seriously; a blow job didn't count as sex anyway; they did not even have to know the person they were with, let alone get emotional about it. In this respect, Joe knew no distinction between the darker reputation of heterosexual and homosexual men, and so he had resisted it. They were pigs, the kind he would warn his daughter against, if he only knew how. They refused to control their overpowering drives. Joe knew, and God, he had tried.

But try explaining all this to a woman. He didn't know how women felt, but he had gathered that Edith, at least, did not think sex was very important, as long as it was between him and her. On the other hand, this did not mean she could countenance it when it involved someone else, least of all one of those types, those young men she'd read about in magazines, who were so bitter. She badly wanted him never to see Clayton Hornsby again, but she wouldn't say so.

And he couldn't stop, because he was drawn to the younger man, and he didn't want to be one of those men for whom touching had nothing at all to do with a person you knew. He had waited, fought off being touched by a man, and it had cost him most of his own personality.

Yet he loved Edith, and she'd known about him since he asked her to marry him. She had guarded his life. It awed him now, his inner destructive power.

Clayton seemed surprised, but not displeased, to hear from him again. They skipped the gym and went directly to the Cooking Club, but afterwards Joe asked if he had some time to talk.

"You're like a woman." Clayton lit a post-coital cigarette for each of them. "You want to talk, better buy me a drink so I still know who's in charge."

Joe ordered a screwdriver for Clayton and a Sprite for himself, which made Clayton laugh. They sat in the light from the bar, and Joe wrapped his hands around the glass. For a moment, he could hardly speak for the beauty he saw in front of him. Looking at Clayton's body in a Speedo was one thing; gazing into his face was another.

"Aren't you afraid?" Joe finally said.

Clayton smoked, never took his eyes off Joe. "Of what?"

"Of—being here, in the light of day," Joe said. "Of going back to your place without getting beat to death. Of everyone in Poudre Valley knowing you're a—"

"Faggot?" Clayton said. "Cocksucker?"

"Please," Joe said, glancing away toward the bored woman in front.

"I'll take that as an invitation." Clayton lit a second cigarette from the smoldering stub. "No, I'm not afraid. You know why? Because there's no fucking point. I've been a faggot, called a faggot all my life, before I knew what one was. For me to pretend not to be a fag—"

"Do you have to keep using that word?"

Clayton's eyes were unkind, but his voice soft. "Oh, get used to it, big boy," he said. "You may as well get used to hearing it from me."

Joe started to say, "I'm not—"

"Now I love to see your mouth open," Clayton interrupted, "but shut it now. Let me tell you how it is. I'm a cocksucker from way back, and it takes one to know one."

Joe stood up slowly, but Clayton was fast on his feet, a hunk of sinew on the other side of the table. "You see these muscles, big boy? You know how long I been building them? Eighteen years, 'cause I got sick of getting beat up. I got all the beating up I ever need in that junior high school where Edith teaches."

"Let's not talk about her."

"Why not? You feeling sorry? You think maybe I'll go home to my wife and be a straight man for a while? It ain't like going on vacation."

Joe shook his head. "You don't understand," he said. "She knows."

Clayton put his cigarette in his mouth, took a long drag. "Why don't we sit back down and finish our drinks."

They talked then: about how he had never been dishonest with Edith, from the time he proposed to her, though even now she didn't really want to know; about how angry she was but how she wouldn't ask him to stop, maybe because she doubted that he could. Clayton seemed to doubt it too. Joe realized that this was a new situation for him as well, to be dating someone, actually to spend more time talking than the other stuff they did.

The drives home from the Cooking Club, or from the gym on days Joe didn't have time—for he made it a point of honor still to be home for supper at six—became perplexing. He felt that Clayton was drawn to him for more than sex. That Clayton needed him to listen to his angry stories, about being called names, beaten, the horror and the fear of what he insisted on calling "faggots." Joe also felt that this had begun out of some perverse respect for Edith, who stayed away from her rival's hairdressing shop but would not make her husband stay at home.

At the gym, Joe told Clayton, "It's spring break next week, I won't be able to meet for workouts." He said this for anyone else in the locker room to deduce that he and Clayton were workout buddies.

"I need to pick up something for supper," Clayton said, without looking at him.

Joe dressed and went to his car, drove to the parking lot of the Piggly Wiggly, and waited there. Clayton parked several spaces away and rapped on his window.

"I'm going in the grocery store," Clayton said when Joe rolled the window down. "You go to my trailer, wait for me. It's not a trailer park, it's behind some woods. You'll be all right unless people see us here. Now get."

Joe drove to the Glamor Shack, a place he'd never been. His anticipation swelled and with it the guilt. There was something about going to this guy's home, even if it was his shop. A line had been crossed somewhere. What if he lost track of time?

But when he got there, and Clayton arrived and let him in, the scene was not as he imagined. There was no rush to satisfy the lust of an afternoon. Instead, Clayton thrust a newspaper in Joe's face. "Did you see this?"

Joe took his eyes from the immaculate, though sparsely decorated living room, which smelled cleaner than any man's room he'd ever been in. "That today's *Crier*? No, I never look at it till the evening."

Clayton jabbed his finger at an article. "AIDS. We all have AIDS, it says. Where do they get this shit?"

Joe scanned the article. It was a vocabulary unfamiliar to him as to most readers of the *Crier*: HIV, T cells, Kaposi's sarcoma.

"Do they have any idea?" Clayton said. "Do you have any idea what it's like to have a friend with this invisible disease?"

"I—" Joe closed his mouth, realizing he didn't.

"You know how many friends I have? More than friends. You know what it's like to see them dying before your eyes? One young guy went blind before his mama came and took him home to Georgia. Sometimes I bring them here."

Joe felt compassion, and confusion. He reached for Clayton but Clayton pushed him away. "Did you know your daughter was still coming here?"

"Dana?" he said, as though he might have another daughter. "I don't know anything about Dana."

"No, you don't. And I'm not worried about her, she's like me, not scared of anybody anyway. She's a lezzie but she doesn't know it yet."

"Don't say that," Joe said in a sharp tone.

"Why not? Scared you might've spilled your seed?"

"You think that about everybody."

Clayton eyed Joe lewdly. "Shut up and take your belt off."

Joe could not react before Clayton had his arms pinned and was kissing his mouth. For some reason it was harder to adjust to a man's kiss, that rough face. Joe fumbled with his belt buckle but Clayton urged him on, yanked his pants down, then shoved him over the couch. Joe smelled it, a clean fabric smell. He stifled a squeal as Clayton took hold of his jockey shorts and ripped.

"Don't worry, big boy. I play safe."

Joe didn't resist; he couldn't. Clayton stood where Joe could see him, naked, stroking his magnificent sex several times before pulling on a condom. He bent toward Joe's ear. "Breathe deep."

When it first went in it hurt Joe more than he'd ever been hurt. He kept breathing, breathed Clayton into him. It was slow strokes at first, but as sounds began escaping from Joe, Clayton took hold of his ass cheeks with both hands and pumped him, harder and harder, until Joe let out a cry and came all over the until-then spotless couch. Still erect, Clayton pulled out, whipped the condom off with one practiced hand while offering his sex to Joe with the other. Joe barely had it in his mouth before Clayton threw back his head and came with a holler.

"You're bleeding, teacher."

Joe felt the sky open and the earth swallow him up.

Long ago, Edith had found Joe not a bad-looking young man. He'd really looked at her in those days—not at her chest or legs, as other young men did quite openly, but her eyes, as if he could see something in them he liked even better. One June night they were on the lakefront in Chicago. It was after dark, but the lights were on, and she felt safe with Joe there, his large hand around her fingers. They walked around a bend in the shore and he said, “There’s something I want to ask you, Edith.”

“Should we stop walking?”

He smiled, but didn’t stop. “Your relatives in Tennessee. What do they think of Catholics?”

“Not much.”

“Oh, boy.”

“No, I don’t mean they think Catholics are terrible,” she said. Wrong, yes. Terrible, no. “I mean they don’t think about them much. I went to school with a few Catholics, you know. We had fish for school lunch on Fridays.”

“If I were in Tennessee, visiting you,” he said, “could I go to your church?”

“I don’t see any reason why not.”

“Wouldn’t I have to be baptized again?”

“Just to go to our church? No,” she said. “Some of the Baptists are like that, but I wouldn’t worry about it. Why?”

Joe strode along forward, but she noticed sweat in his palm. “I’m thinking of applying for a teaching job down there.”

“In Tennessee?”

“Well, where are you planning to be?”

“Back home, I guess. But you’ve lived here all your life; you’ve never even been there.”

He stopped, and a breeze from the lake fluffed his fine brown hair. “I know we haven’t been going out for very long. You’re not dating anyone else, are you?”

Didn’t he know this? “No. What about you?”

“No,” he said. “Not anymore. I don’t know if you’ve given any thought to—Well, we’ve both graduated now.”

“Yes.”

“I’d like to keep seeing you, I’d like to be with you. I—I’d like to marry you, Edith.”

This was it? He was still standing up. “Are you proposing, Joe?”

“The thing is—” He spotted a rock ledge big enough to sit on, pulled her over to rest on it. “The thing is, I do love you, but—"

"But?" She withdrew her hand. "This is the first I've heard about love, Joe, and you're telling me 'but'? But what?"

All the air seemed to have gone out of him. He looked out across the water. It was very quiet, just the underlying hum of traffic that was inevitable in Chicago, like crickets at home. Edith had a pang of missing summer there.

"You see," Joe said. "You see, I feel so at home with you, Edith. I want a wife, I want to have children. Isn't that what everybody wants?" He looked at her. "Is that what you want?"

"I don't want a wife." She laughed and slapped his knee, but he looked at her, stricken. Oh, brother. Was he choosing this moment to lose his sense of humor?

"Don't you want kids?"

"Well, yes. But Joe, we haven't even talked about this. It seems—why are we talking about kids, we haven't even talked about marriage."

"I just asked you."

She took his hand again. "This does feel comfortable, doesn't it?"

They sat there for a long time. From her limited experience of dating, she was sure he should at least kiss her at this point, but there was no movement from his side. She had the strange sensation that theirs were negotiating positions, that he was not making his move because she hadn't said yes. Nor had she said no.

"Edith," he said, "I know we haven't had a very physical relationship."

"I appreciate your respect. I don't know many ladies and gentlemen up here, but you know my religious beliefs."

"That's what I was trying to ask you about. See, Catholics—I don't know what your folks believe, but in marriage, we're only supposed to have relations, you know, to have children."

"Joe, I'm not sure I want to talk about this."

"I'm sorry." He was silent again for a long time. "I just—Well, most guys probably don't believe that, and you may not believe me when I tell you this, but that is what I believe."

She shook her head. There was a bug of confusion in there;

it wouldn't go away. "I don't understand what you're saying. You want to marry me, but you don't want me to think you're only trying to get me in bed, or—?"

"No—"

"You're so romantic, Joe."

"I thought this was important to you."

"What, marriage? This is the first I've heard about it."

"No, your religion. I mean, not religion. Listen—if you'll marry me I'll move down with you, I'll go to your church, it doesn't matter to me. I don't want to stay in the city."

"Why not?" She looked at him, unbelieving. "Why do you not?"

"Because," and it appeared to take him concentrated effort to get out every word, "I don't want to end up like your Uncle Jones."

"Oh." She sat back, the flats of her hands on the rock beside her.

"I don't mean anything by that," he said. "I like him a lot. It's just—well, he never had children of his own, I think he regrets it."

"He could still get married. He's only in his forties, Joe. For a man that's nothing."

"He's not going to get married."

Edith became conscious of Lake Michigan's fingers touching the shore. They seemed louder than the traffic, louder all the time. "Could I have one of your cigarettes?"

"Sure." He nearly fell over, lighting it for her. She inhaled, flicked the ash away in a practiced fashion.

"I didn't know you smoked," he said.

"Well, I didn't know you wanted to get married." She gave a little, harsh-lunged laugh. "So we're even."

"You're telling me no, aren't you?"

"I haven't told you anything yet. I asked for a cigarette, that's all."

They smoked for a minute or two. "What do you think?" he said, in a very soft voice.

"I think you want a wife and kids. I don't know why you're asking me, and I don't know how you think you're helping by insulting the only family of mine you know."

"Edith, I'm not insulting him."

"Well, you're implying things."

"Edith." He placed one hand on her knee. "I like Jones, I was talking to him about us. You and me. I was asking him for—well, his blessing, I guess."

"For my hand in marriage?" She stubbed her cigarette out on the rock beside her. "It's 1970, Joe."

"Well, I don't know. I've never been in love with a Southern girl before."

"You've never been in love with a girl before."

A look passed between them. It was freighted with an understanding deeper than they had the words for. It was also a look of love, but just at that moment, a kiss was not what either of them wanted.

"Give me another cigarette, please," Edith said.

Again, he lit it for her. "Does it being 1970 mean anything else to you?"

"Meaning what?"

"Well, you smoke, and I shouldn't ask your uncle for permission to marry you."

"Most things are still the same."

"What, for example?"

She blew more smoke out toward the poor polluted lake. "Men marry women. Women are teachers. Men are teachers, too, but you'll always make more money than I do." He looked as uncomfortable at her mentioning money as she'd felt at his mentioning sex. "You will."

"Okay," he said. "Now let me tell you something. I believe money should be shared. You work, I work, and it all goes into the pot together. We save, we get a little house, have kids—"

"How little is this house?"

"A big house, then." He chuckled, for the first time all evening. "How much does a house cost in Poudre Valley?"

"I have no idea." She looked at him, and this time, they did kiss, tongues wreathed in the same smoke.

"Does that mean yes?"

"What did Uncle Jones say?"

"It's fine with him," Joe said, "if it's fine with you."

She kissed him again, a brief clinging of the lips. "Then let's go buy some rice."

Chapter 14

When Joe came home from Clayton's, he could tell Edith knew. Not exactly what she knew, but that something was different. He was on time for dinner, so she didn't overtly complain, just slammed things and was short-tempered with the kids, and who could blame her? Sex was powerful and jealousy too, although he wasn't sure it was so much jealousy she was feeling, as envy. She wasn't interested in his body, less so since a man had touched it. But now that Joe knew, for the first time in his life, how good it felt to be touched, he thought she must miss it. How could she not want it too?

He wanted to reach her, but was overwhelmed. What could he do for her? To stop now would solve nothing; she knew what he was, knew much better than anyone else, perhaps even more than he did. He was beginning to understand why homosexuals were supposed to feel so guilty, though he still didn't call himself one, except in the darkest reaches of his own mind. To embrace that part of himself, to be, unapologetically, what Clayton was, would be to negate his marriage and family, and he'd given up too much for that.

So what was he doing? Giving it up. Risking his ass, quite literally, for what he'd waited twenty years for. Wasn't half his life enough?

The more he saw of Clayton the more urgent sex became, not less. When Clayton allowed Joe to fuck him for the first time, he did so with a fury. Mostly, though, it was the other way around. It was as if there were this yawning hungry space and in the time they spent together he had to fill it up. When they were smoking or at the Cooking Club, which took less time than going to Clay's trailer, Joe would ask about his boyfriends, other friends, and he knew Clayton thought he was jealous. He was not. It was anthropology, the study of a whole new country.

"Joe, I don't ask you about who else you've had sex with."

Joe didn't say he never really had, before.

"But I'm the one who should be jealous," Clayton continued. "You go home to your wife. Now I don't want to hear about you two, you know I don't. But I've been single for a long time, and friends—well, they're my family, aren't they? If I love somebody and he's dying on my couch, I'm not thinking about whether I fucked him or not."

"Couch—"

Clayton waved his cigarette, wiped his mustache. "Don't worry, big boy, it's been cleaned. Professionally cleaned."

An alarm went off that had not penetrated the latex barrier of Joe's mind before. "Have you been tested?"

"What am I, a dog?"

"Clay—" Joe wanted to put out his hand, touch him like he might have touched Edith, but the muscles wouldn't work. "What about your friends?"

"Listen, big boy. I use rubbers and I expect everybody else to. I assume they're all positive, but I don't really want to know. Not enough to let some fucking Christian doctor come near me, wrapped in Saran Wrap, and tell my business to the fucking world. You think I need that kind of hassle? They'd run me out of town on a rail. Run a broomstick right up my faggot ass."

Joe shook his head, as if to clear it. They had safe sex, it was true, but what about all those others? And what, for God's sake, did Clayton mean by love?

"I didn't mean to pick on Christians, by the way," Clayton said. "Do you still go to church?"

Joe nodded.

"I haven't been to church in I don't know how long. Unless you count funerals. They want us to do their hair, play the organ or conduct the choir or decorate with flowers. But they still hate fags."

It was getting close to six, but for some reason Clay was waxing loquacious. "God hates fags. That's what they put on their signs, they've put them in my yard, held them up when my buddy Ronnie went home to die. I've seen them at a goddamn funeral. Well, fuck them and their goddamn God."

"Clay," Joe said. "Please."

Clayton lit another cigarette, smiled at Joe's franticness. "Oh, you think he's listening. Well, never mind. If the worst sin on earth is for men to love each other, then goddamn me, I'm guilty as charged."

Joe had to go, but he had to stay and know what Clay meant. "Love?" He loved Edith, and he guessed he loved Clay too, but how could that be? And what was he supposed to do about it?

Clayton blew smoke toward the ceiling. Though he was only thirty there were faint rings around his eyes that never went away. "I've fucked a lot of men in my life," he said, "and loved a lot and hated a lot. Sometimes all the same people, sometimes not. Ronnie I loved. We were friends, mostly. Sometimes more. But the most we were was right before he died. See, it's one thing to suck each other or jerk each other off. You can do that and not think you're a faggot at all. But you hold somebody's hand, you hug a guy in front of other people—you cross a line, then, and you can't ever go back."

Joe looked at Clayton. And beholding him, he loved him. Joe reproached himself for the biblical thought, but there it was.

Clayton said, "You have a son, don't you?"

"Yes. Jeremy."

"How come I never hear about him?"

Joe said, "You never hear about anybody from me. Why would Jeremy come to the Glamor Shack? I don't know the last time he even cut his hair."

Clayton stubbed the cigarette out. "You want to go to North Carolina with me this weekend?"

"What for?"

"I buy all my cigarettes in North Carolina. Don't you? How can a teacher afford to pay twice as much tax?"

"I don't normally smoke this much," Joe said.

"You don't normally fuck this much, either."

But sex with Clayton, Joe thought, was not so different from sex with himself. It was the only kind he had ever really enjoyed, and how could he change now? When he was with the younger man he had difficulty thinking of anything but himself. He'd always been so aware of other people before: Jeremy's hair, Dana's maturing appearance, Edith's warm body in bed. He'd been as attentive as a mother, even more so. When they were little the kids always wanted Daddy to wash their hair, because he took his time and was gentle with his hands, not like Mommy, always rushing. He never hurt Dana's tangles, and when Jeremy was a little boy Joe cut his hair himself, never took him to a barber. At some point, he stopped, and that might explain why his son was now a shabby mess. Could Jeremy find his way to a barbershop? What would Joe's own redneck barber have to say about his Glamor Shack colleague?

Edith didn't say a word on Saturday morning when Joe said he and Clayton were going to North Carolina for cigarettes. Not "Your son needs a haircut," though he obviously did, and not "I didn't think you smoked anymore," because Joe could have said the same to her.

"I'll pick you up a carton," he said.

Joe and Clayton had crossed the French Broad River before they exchanged more than a nod. "How's Edith?" Clayton said.

"I told you I didn't want to talk about her."

"I meant as a customer. You know, Edith used to be friendly with me. I'm sorry."

"Sorry for what?"

"Sorry about this. She never had to know this, Joe. You think I've never been the other woman before?" Clayton flipped his finger out from the steering wheel in an exaggerated motion.

"She did have to know," Joe said quietly. "I wouldn't have done it otherwise." He kept looking straight out through the windshield.

"Oh, right. She's been putting up with this for twenty years."

"I haven't been with anybody in twenty years."

Clayton laughed uncertainly. "Oh, now you're scaring me, Joe. You're not going to fall in love now, are you, and fuck it all up?"

Joe felt suddenly bold. "I've already fucked it all up," he said. "The question is, are you going to fall in love?"

Clayton didn't say anything, but Joe already knew. He felt elation and terror. He had never properly loved and had it returned to him. He loved Edith, but not like this.

They went all the way to Charlotte before stopping for cigarettes. Then Clayton drove to a little brick building with a small parking lot behind it. "You want to get tested, don't you?" he said. "Why'd you think I drove you clear across the state? They'll do it anonymously here. This far from Tennessee, they'll never know you even drew blood."

Joe's eyes widened. "What about the results?"

"They make you come in. You have to drive back so they can tell you in person."

"You've been here before."

"And I'll be here again when you get your results. They want you to have somebody with you. Believe me, I've been through this."

Joe looked at him. For the first time he saw something soft, like compassion, in Clay's eyes. "You got your results?"

"Today," Clayton said. "That's why you're here."

Edith's principal hadn't been overly concerned with the eraser-throwing incident. It was not as if it was a ruler, or she had been in the habit of assaulting students before. Edith explained to him, because it was bound to be talked about anyway, that she was having difficulties at home, but that nothing like this would happen again. The principal was gratified, in that way people are when you tell them your bad news.

Of course Edith didn't understand what Joe was going through. Why should she? What she got out of their "arrangement" was obvious—a man's salary, two children. Of one thing she was sure: it was nobody else's business. She could look the other way, but it hadn't been her idea to do it this way, with somebody not only that she knew, but who everybody else in town knew was—like that.

She felt so stupid. She'd never taken it seriously, never imagined that love would be involved. She didn't know who loved whom, but something had changed. She had been sure, as everyone else was, that men like that would just do anything with anybody and it didn't mean a thing. You read about young men, like in the paper, dying, but they were always alone, like Jones...Edith was more sad than alarmed; there was no question of Joe touching her now.

When he'd suggested moving next door for a while, she surprised herself by crying with relief. A bed to herself! She couldn't believe how well she'd slept that night. She'd always suspected he slept with her because he thought that's what she wanted. She was actually happier being friends.

Outside that bedroom, though, everybody from their kids to church to school to the wider world knew them as husband and wife. Here Joe was letting her down. He'd strayed and now she could no longer protect him from what he was. Dana had already had a run-in with her miserable fool of a vice principal. Edith foresaw a slipping away of everything.

One afternoon about a week after Joe moved his things into what had been Isabella's house, she felt hot. She couldn't stop feeling flushed although she'd never experienced a hot flash before. Perfect, menopause was just what she needed right now.

There had been a certain amount of snickering all day, but Edith had been a classroom teacher long enough to tune that out. She only turned around when the Lowry kid would not shut up. "What is it, Billy?"

"Nothing, Miz Rignaldi," he said, his eyes an expression of mock surprise.

She turned back to the board, scanned it for errors. She heard that whiny voice again. "What you keep these gerbils in the classroom for, Miz Rignaldi?" he said. "Experiments?"

"No, Billy," she said without looking back at him.

"Does Mr. Rignaldi like gerbils too?"

Edith set the chalk down, narrowed her eyes at him. "What?"

"Does Mr. Rignaldi like gerbils?"

She walked toward him, wanting to hit the boy as she had never hit a child. "Say that again, Billy."

He hadn't expected this tactic. "Ma'am?"

"Say that again," she said. "About gerbils. I know what you're thinking, Billy Lowry. You're the kind that sticks a firecracker up the backside of a gerbil to watch it run around and explode. You'd probably do it to a cat or dog if anybody was fool enough to let you near one. Don't you know it's perverted to do that to a helpless animal?"

"I'm not perverted," he said. "Sticking things up backsides—I—"

"Don't lie to me. I know the things you get up to, Billy, and it really makes me wonder about you. Why you'd hurt something, want to destroy something, that never had anything to do with you at all."

Edith had reached his desk and stood there, fists clenched. He looked intimidated, and she thought he was until he straightened in his chair and announced, "Mr. Rignaldi's got hisself in trouble. My daddy says he's a faggot."

She felt the air go out of her. "Who is? Your daddy?"

A flash, and Billy was on his feet. "Don't you talk about him, Miz Rignaldi. Your husband's a faggot pervert, he sticks things, gerbils—"

"You son of a bitch," Edith said, and Billy lunged for her but she knocked an empty chair over in his way. He went sprawling. The class erupted into confusion. Billy freed himself from the desk and Edith had a vision of being thrashed, like a teacher in a one-room schoolhouse on the prairie. She abandoned the classroom, took off down the hall to the office and shut the door, still shaking.

Rhonda, the school secretary, looked up from polishing her nails. "Edith, are you okay?"

"I need to talk to my husband," Edith said, leaning back against the door.

But when Rhonda tried a person-to-person call, Edith couldn't get through. "Mr. Rignaldi left early today," said the ditz who answered the elementary school phone.

Quickly, Edith motioned Rhonda away from the office phone to use it herself, an unheard-of imposition. Oh well, the students would already think she'd had a nervous breakdown or something.

The phone in the little house rang several times before Joe picked it up. "What happened?" Edith said.

"They fired me."

Chapter 15

It was like swimming underwater. Edith saw Isabella's house as if it were behind glass in an aquarium. Joe had done it up neatly already, plants, the big speakers from their old stereo playing classical music. Handel. Trying to cheer himself up with the Baroque.

He was sitting in an ancient, burlap-covered armchair that had been Isabella's. Edith couldn't imagine anyone had ever been comfortable in it; it was like sitting on a hair shirt.

"Don't tell me," he said. "I'm an idiot."

Of course, that was exactly what she was thinking. "No."

"You know what happened?" he said. "Tanner came to my classroom at eleven o'clock this morning, asked me to come to the office. Right in the middle of math. Said he'd take care of the class. I get there and there's a police officer there with Emily Hines."

"Why wasn't she in your class?"

Joe shrugged. Always that shrug. "Her mother said she was sick. I just marked her absent. Anyway, Emily's crying, saying

'I'm sorry, Mr. Rignaldi,' over and over and over. The policeman wants to know what I'm doing making little girls touch me inappropriately. I didn't know what he was talking about until Mrs. Hines said Emily told her she hit me in the crotch that time." Joe refreshed Edith's memory of the Houdini incident.

"So then what?" she said. "Who fired you?"

"Tanner comes back, I don't know, maybe he sent the class home. Says there's no reason for me to stay for the rest of the day, I'm on leave until all this is cleared up. Unpaid leave." Joe sighed. "That's why I'm such an idiot."

"So you haven't been fired."

Joe looked at her, put his hands on his temples. "Edith. By five o'clock every hysterical parent in Poudre Valley will think I'm a pedophile. I'll never get my job back."

"You sound awfully calm about it."

"So do you."

Edith flopped down next to him on Isabella's couch. She tried not to wonder if Joe had been consoled on this couch. "I don't see the point in panicking, Joe. Our private lives are private, but our jobs are very important. Mine could be in trouble, after today." And she told him about Billy Lowry.

Joe's face went pale. "They know."

"They know nothing," she said fiercely. "Talking about some little girl. You wouldn't touch a child in your life." She rubbed her forehead like it was Aladdin's lamp. "I could kill you, Joe, but it's nobody else's place."

"Don't you see? They're the same to these people. A pervert is a—"

"Please, Joe. I don't want to hear that word one more time today."

He sat for a minute. Then, to Edith's astonishment, he made a sound like a desperate little laugh. "Well, you certainly like to take it out on junior high boys," he said. "We're the Macbeths."

Edith tried to process some of this, any of it, but her mind was shooting blanks. "Joe," she said. "Do you have any wine?"

He poured it, two neat glasses. Had he thought of everything? "You're quite the housekeeper, Joe."

"Please."

The wine tasted good. Since she didn't normally drink at all, she felt the first sip. She had visions of her new single life, surviving on Hungry Man dinners and drinking all the time.

"The way I see it," she said, "we're allies here. You and me."

"I don't—"

"Shut up, Joe." And she'd never said that before, either. "Listen to me. This is our life. Your job, my job, our family is on the line here. It's not right for somebody to take it, over something that isn't even true."

She didn't know where these words were coming from, and wasn't sure she meant them. But there was no time to worry about that now. She needed all her strength, for the fight ahead.

When Dana got home both her parents were sitting at the kitchen table. Something was up; they always stayed an hour or so after school. "What's going on?"

Mom looked hard at Joe. He put up his hands, then dropped them weakly. Mom despised him. Nothing got past Dana.

"Let's talk about this when Jeremy gets home," he said.

But Jeremy was late, and when he came to Dana's room, where she was shut up with a mix of worry and her usual rage, she was shocked to see his cheeks bruised. "What happened to you?"

"What the fuck's going on?" he said. "Please tell me why three guys jumped me by the flagpole yelling 'faggot.'"

"Sounds familiar."

"This isn't funny."

They went into the kitchen. Joe started. "Your mother and I—"

"Oh, please," Dana said. "Please. If you're splitting up, just tell us, before everybody else in town knows anyway."

"We're not—"

"Yes we are," Mom said. "Living separately, as you very well know. Your father lost his job today."

Dana spluttered, "And you're leaving him? Oh, great timing, Mom."

"I'm not going anywhere," she flashed, and her tone told Dana to be quiet. "Your dad needs to take some time, needs to think about some things."

Jeremy's eyes narrowed. "What things?"

Both their parents looked at Jeremy, just noticing the bruises. "What happened?" Joe said.

"Never mind. What happened to you?"

"I lost my job."

"And Mom's kicked you out of the house," Dana said.

"Shut up, Dana," Mom said.

"Okay," Jeremy said. "I'll tell you what happened to me, then maybe you can tell me why. Three guys jumped me at the flagpole, called me a faggot. They said you were a faggot—" He pointed to Joe—"and you—" he pointed to Dana. "All of us. All faggots. And before I fought all three of them, you want to know what I said?"

"What?"

"'A girl can't be a faggot.' That goes for Dana and that goes for you too, Dad."

"Jeremy!" Dana said.

"No, I'm sick of it. You're all pussies. I have to fight this whole county and sister, you're as fucked up as I am." Dana saw Mom recoil from the *fuck*. "I don't even want to know what's wrong with you. Sick puppies. You're a bunch of sick puppies, not even worth drowning." And with that, he took off.

Dana looked at her parents accusingly. "You want to explain this?"

"Is that what your fight was about?"

"Oh, Mom. Don't make this about me."

"Okay," Mom said. "Your father was suspended because somebody made a false accusation—"

"Edith, I'm right here!" he said, as if he'd been waiting all his life to blow up like this.

"So speak for yourself," Mom said. Dana had never seen her so angry. She could tell, because Mom was speaking quietly and Joe was not.

"I was put on unpaid leave," Joe said to his hands, "because of a rumor of something inappropriate."

"With a student?" Dana said, calm only because the question was rhetorical.

"Yes."

"A little girl?"

"Yes. But—"

"It's not true," Mom said. "Do you understand me, Dana? It didn't happen."

It was the humiliation Joe hadn't counted on. Sex might have been humiliating, but he didn't experience it that way. It wasn't Clay who humiliated him but everyone else: his principal, Tanner; that cretin Bill Lowry; his wife when he had to tell her, not that he was queer because she knew that, but that he had been fired, emasculated, that he couldn't support his family the way they needed him to. Watching his own son, with whom he'd barely exchanged a word all year, walk out of the house, carrying only a guitar case and contempt.

Edith assured him that she wasn't thinking of divorce, that they hadn't really even separated; after all he was only living next door. Joe tried to think of something that would somehow make it better but she just looked at him, her face in this twisted expression, like her mouth was frozen from dental work.

He went to Clayton's trailer Saturday night, when he couldn't stand to be alone. Clay wasn't home. Joe parked, sat in the minivan and wondered how he had come to trade a lifetime of teaching kids and a wife who loved him and a family, all he'd worked for for twenty years, for wonderful, amazing sex such as he'd never had before in his life. Maybe it was worth it.

The Glamor Shack sat up on a hill through some woods. It was probably pretty in the fall; right now the branches were so thick with green Joe couldn't see if there were neighbors. Just as well.

Clayton showed up late, must have been working out. Joe was still sitting in the driver's seat, the sky dimming around him. A sharp rap at the window. "What're you doing here?"

"I lost my job."

Clayton seemed unsurprised. "So, it begins."

"My son walked out."

"I'm not surprised. You're a bastard."

Joe shut the car door and stood in the driveway, arms crossed.

"Okay," he said. "I get it. You're a bitter queen who's hard done by, you're still healthy but the virus is in your body so you know you're going to die." Saying it out loud made Joe's voice shake, but he kept going. "Anything that happens to me, I deserve it, and besides worse has happened to you. You get off on fucking the teacher and now everybody's fucked the teacher. What did I expect? Did I leave out anything?"

"Honest to God, Joe, that's the most you've ever said at one time."

"Oh, I'm not done," Joe said. "Now see, you thought if you told me you were HIV, I'd run screaming. But I didn't. You thought I'd go back to my wife, to whom I've been unfaithful, and not tell her, and hide in my job and my family and not risk anything, while you paid the death penalty. I wasn't man enough to be a 'faggot.' That's what you thought, right?"

Clayton went to unlock the trailer door. "You staying the night?"

When Joe came in, Clayton looked surprised. "What you bring that for?"

Joe looked at his ball bat, tucked through the handles of a duffel bag. He laughed. "So Edith won't bust the window with it."

Clayton looked at him through narrowed eyes. "Is it yours?"

"Yeah. The church ball team." Joe realized that's why he'd picked it up; he could never face those guys again. "Do you work Sundays?"

"No. Why?"

Joe smiled painfully. "I don't remember the last time I slept in on a Sunday morning."

Clay stepped toward him. "You got a lot to learn."

Joe shook his head. "I can't right now. I'm drained." He thought of Jeremy, kept looking at that stupid bat. "Jeremy left when I told him. Only had his guitar."

"You told him what?"

"That I'd lost my job."

"Oh, that." Clayton took his hand, held it; it was a new sensation, like a first date. "Well, worse things happen every day, big boy. Let's get you in the shower."

Joe's spirit was unwilling, but he could not control the flesh. The bathroom was neat, polished; the porcelain sparkled white and the bottles were all in rows. He undressed, shy and virginal, while Clayton ran the shower, so hot the room filled with steam. When Joe got in all his muscles seemed to melt with relaxation, and he only tensed up slightly when he saw that Clay was stripping too and climbing into the tub. Joe lathered shampoo into his hair and closed his eyes, feeling Clayton's fingers slide into place behind his, massaging his temples until a hot wire ran down the length of Joe's body. Clayton slipped a hand around and jerked him off smoothly. Joe reciprocated. Their kiss was slow, come and shampoo flowing down the drain.

All the time now Edith felt like there was something wrong in her stomach, like any minute she might just double over and puke. She felt trapped, not having anyone to talk to, no one who could possibly understand. There it had been, in the bed between them, where it belonged, like other secrets of a marriage.

She'd never talked about it, hardly even to Joe. Who would understand? The preacher who'd married them? Isabella? Some counselor? Either a Christian one who wouldn't be able to get past sin, or the other kind who would probably help even less because as Edith understood it, they didn't even believe in sin. Nobody could know because nobody outside a marriage understood how it held together anyway. Even the people in it barely understood.

These were the things Edith knew: You got married and from then on, you were happy or unhappy, you moved or you didn't move, had kids or didn't, saw your family or didn't. You worked and saved or you struggled with money, had sex too often or not often enough. Everybody on the outside kept changing the rules. Edith remembered when sex had gone from a sin, which Christians were not even supposed to talk about, to a divinely ordered pleasure. God had evidently ordained this during the Ford administration, by which time everything else had gone to hell.

But it was too late for Edith and Joe. They had already

committed themselves, unaware of their right to enjoy, and all she knew was that you hung together somehow and it didn't matter if you had to pray or stick pins in voodoo dolls, you just did it.

This had worked as long as Joe was equally willing to live with more commitment than pleasure. It wasn't that there was nothing there. There was the warm companionship of a bedmate, not a small part of guarding against loneliness. And being an eighth-grade teacher, she was skeptical of any talk about sex. Every survey, everything said people were having all this sex, or thinking about it whenever they weren't actually having it.

Who were they kidding? Nobody had that much sex. She had two kids, all right, and there they were now, walking around making her life miserable.

"Where's Jeremy?" she asked Dana when he failed to come home that night.

"Don't worry about him, Mom."

"You know where he is, don't you?"

"Trust me, Mom, he's okay."

But Jeremy didn't show up for school the next day. Edith was as enraged as worried but couldn't report him truant; he was eighteen, he didn't have to finish school. "Mom, leave him alone," Dana said.

"He won't graduate, Dana."

She shrugged—just like her dad. Edith could've slapped her. "He wouldn't anyway, Mom, he was failing. He can hardly even read."

"Don't make excuses for him. Your brother's not stupid."

Dana's eyes were not as wide as other girls', since she didn't paint her face over tight with makeup. "I didn't say he was."

So Jeremy was gone, and Dana said they shouldn't try to find him. Meanwhile Joe, who had married her and raised these ungrateful children with her precisely because he wanted to be a father and a teacher, because he loved kids, wanted to sit in church with his wife and be irreproachable—this man, this deacon of the Methodists, had thrown away everything since his mother died. His livelihood, his reputation, not to mention his pact with Edith. For a desire she could barely think about. And when she'd asked why, he said, "It's more than that now."

"You were honest about that too. At Christmas. I told you how I felt then," she said.

"But you don't feel that way anymore."

"I never imagined this, Joe."

"Neither did I." And he caught his breath, like some schoolgirl.

"That people would know. Talk. That the kids would hear. That Tanner would fire you. I thought you could be...more discreet."

"That I wouldn't fall in love."

It felt to Edith like it had when, as a young girl, she had crawled under some farmer's electric fence into an old cow pasture to play, and accidentally touched the fence. The jolt of electricity wasn't a "shock" at all; it felled her to the ground like timber, like a blow from something extremely heavy.

She felt stunned now. Under the circumstances, she deserved monumental credit just for standing upright, never mind doing the work she had to do.

The last place she wanted to be anymore was the teachers' lounge, but she couldn't survive without cigarettes. She couldn't go and "hang out" behind the vocational building, with the delinquent students. That left the lounge.

People stopped talking when she came in. It was like wearing the scarlet letter. Then she heard Pam. "Edie," she said in a steady voice, "how're you doing?"

Edith hadn't even talked to Pam in a while. She gave her a guarded hello, so brittle she could crack.

The people around them, perhaps realizing they wouldn't be missing a public execution after all, went back to their lunch conversations. Pam motioned for Edith to sit down in her corner. Edith wasn't hungry, but sure, she'd take a smoke break.

"You know," Pam said, digging something out of an I Can't Believe It's Not Butter container, "people ask us sometimes why we don't have kids. Charlie and me."

Edith nodded.

"You know what I tell them?"

"That it's your choice?"

"No," Pam said, and Edith didn't know if she meant it wasn't their choice, or it wasn't what she said. Pam leaned in closer. "I tell them to mind their own business."

She said it in a soft voice, and the impact was not lost on Edith, who was so raw and exposed. In a culture of courtesy, where everyone was ma'am or sir, "mind your own business" was a curse. That you could have your own business to mind, in a town the size of Poudre Valley, seemed contrary to the laws of Aunt Anna and God.

"What are you telling me?"

Pam never stopped digging with the plastic fork. "People ask you what your husband does," she said. "You think they mean is he a policeman, teacher, or what, but it's just a way of getting in your business. They're really asking about you."

Edith's cigarette was burning out. She reached for another one.

"Edie—don't take this the wrong way, but I know we don't have much in common anymore." There it was, the crush of isolation. "But you'll get through it, okay?"

Edith couldn't help asking, "How?"

Pam said, "Any way you can."

Edith thought of this in the days ahead, when she heard Bill Lowry say, loudly, so she could hear, "If I knew a faggot with AIDS I'd kill him myself," when Julie, the girl on the school paper that Edith sponsored, came to tell her she was quitting and just kept saying "I'm sorry," again and again, like little Emily Hines. When Edith's own principal told her that she had no more chances after cussing Billy Lowry and the only reason he wasn't firing her was because he felt sorry for her kids, they needed to eat after all. She thought of this when Pam herself couldn't seem to think of anything to say to her, when she was ignored by all her fellow teachers, except Vonda Snodgrass who salivated at her misfortune like a dog over hamburger.

And she concentrated on it, like some Protestant rosary, in an attempt to take her mind off Jeremy being gone. She had never experienced, only read about, the pang of hollowness felt by childless women when everywhere around them were women having babies, baby carriages, baby clothes. Now, Jeremy's absence bit into her, as if someone had snatched him from her, not yet grown. Not seeing him and not knowing what to do about it trapped Edith, crushed the part of her that nurtured, so she was no longer very good at taking care of anyone. Not even herself.

She got one card, from Aunt Anna. The card had a picture of the Good Shepherd bearing home a lost sheep. In her flowery, roller-ball penmanship, Aunt Anna had written:

Dear Edie,

I want you to know I do not listen to gossip. I only know because of something Charlie told me.

Although I cannot condone Joe's lifestyle, I still care about you all because you are part of the family of God. I am praying for you.

She signed it with love. Edith wadded up the card and envelope, but didn't throw them in the trash. She put the ball of paper next to her address book, by the phone.

Chapter 16

Edith thought the porch would be better to smoke on. She was not used to the smell of smoke on the furniture, didn't feel like spraying stuff everywhere, even though Joe was just visiting and it was her house now. So when she saw him pat his pockets and look up, questioning, she opened the screen door and they went outside.

They avoided the swing, which had not held the weight of two people in some time. They sat in scrapy metal chairs at opposite corners of the porch and let the smoke and tension drift and dissipate between them. Edith kept looking at Isabella's rose bush, which gave no sign of giving up. Well, it was only Labor Day.

"Who do you like for the World Series?" Joe said.

Edith tapped her cigarette into a cracked Melmac saucer the color of butterscotch pudding. "You know I can't watch baseball on TV."

"Been to any of the church games this year?"

She thought she heard a note of wistfulness in his voice.

"No. You?"

"No." He paused, tried again. "Heard from Jeremy?"

"Joe, I promise you, I hear anything and I will let you know."

"I just thought—you might not want to—"

"I'll find you." She leaned forward, hands on knees, into the path of his smoke. "I'm crazy worrying about Jeremy. I don't know how I'm going to get through another school year." It was meant as a rebuke and she watched it hit its mark. "The only reason I can go in to work is Dana's in touch with him, and she swears he's okay."

"And you can't get her to tell you?" Joe said.

"You want to put your daughter in thumbscrews, you go right ahead. She'll have Amnesty International over here, I have no doubt."

Joe shook his head. "You're not going to believe me, I know, but—"

"Save it, Joe."

They finished their cigarettes. Joe's pack came up empty. "You want to try my brand?" she said, and couldn't resist, "or is it too girly for you?"

He took the cigarette, lit it. The way he took it away from his mouth, blew smoke—had he always been so, well, faggy? She half expected to see lipstick on the filter tip.

He said, "Do you want a divorce?"

"Do you?"

"Now Edith." He almost smiled. "Don't make this my decision too."

"Well, let's see," she said, the nicotine kicking her heart rate up a notch. "We decided to get married because you wanted to be celibate. We decided not to be celibate, once in a while—kids, you know. You decided not to be celibate at all, and like a fool, I said Sure, date my hairdresser. You decided to get yourself fired, and it's just a matter of time before you decide to get run out of town, tarred and feathered. Why on earth would I want a divorce?"

"You don't need to be sarcastic."

"Oh, honey, I do," she said. "Please don't take away my

pleasure and survival."

"Have you been talking to Pam?" he said.

"Why?"

"I—I think Charlie knows about this."

She let out a bark of laughter; it appeared to strike him like a physical blow. "Everybody knows, Joe."

He was trying to say something, but Edith let him struggle. Why should she make this easier? Finally he said, "Clay thinks we should move away to Florida."

"Before you get run out of town?"

"It's true," he said. "It's not safe."

"Pardon me, Joe, but that's the least of my concerns."

"Well, what do you want? You don't want a divorce?"

"Do you?"

"No."

"Why not?"

"Because you haven't betrayed me," he said. "It's you who should want to get rid of me."

"Yes, I should. But I don't."

"And why not?"

This was getting ridiculous. So much of what people called love was just trying to make something work. "Would you mind if I brought out the whiskey?"

He nodded, wide-eyed. They had almost forgotten the whiskey was there, a half-empty bottle in the ancient drum table, who knew how long ago he'd bought it. It smelled like Listerine, but it seemed right.

She poured them each what she thought was a small glass. "Joe," she said, "I don't know where my son is. My daughter—and please remember these are also your children—is about to go off to college, six hundred miles away. Your relatives are gone. Mine aren't speaking to me. As loath as I am to admit it, you're all I have left."

"What about church?"

Edith snorted. "I'm not talking to anyone but God at church these days."

"Why don't you just tell them you're divorcing me? We're not Catholic—wouldn't they understand?"

"Joe." She shook ashes into the saucer. "I am not divorcing you. I married you. If the price was too high, that's nobody else's fault."

"Is it too high?"

She watched the alpenglow, the dusky rose of the sky, backdrop to that oblivious bush. "Well, I am in the habit of paying our monthly bills," she said. "I don't know how I'm going to do that on my salary, but then there's only two of us here now, not four." Sip. "And Dana is going off to school. Thank goodness they gave her a scholarship. So when you think about it, it's a question of me supporting myself." She blew smoke at him, just to be hateful. "You know what a liberated woman I am, I shouldn't have any problem doing that."

Joe knocked back his whiskey, poured himself another. In the time it took for him to say anything, Edith counted seven lightning bugs blinking in what was still the summer of their front yard. She had never drunk whiskey; it swam in her head.

"You seem to have this all figured out," he said.

"Someone has to think things through, Joe." Bull's-eye. She actually felt a pinch of regret. "Besides, what else should I do all night here? I've got no one to talk to."

Joe swirled his glass, as though his life depended on something at the bottom of it. "We could talk to some counselor."

"We?"

"Okay, you."

"I don't think so. I don't think I could even begin to explain how I feel about this and how complicated it all is."

"What's complicated? Your husband's an adulterer and an asshole, he's lost his job and can't even contribute his earnings anymore. Your kids can't stand to be around him. Seems to me you have everything coming to you."

"What's complicated is that I still love you." She tried the fit of the word in her mouth. "Asshole."

"Isn't that something," he said. "I love you too."

"Explain that one." She still was in no mood to go easy on him.

"I don't trust anybody but you," he said.

"Is that love?"

He'd gotten all talky lately. "It lasts longer than sex."

"With you, yeah." Edith gave a sharp and mirthless laugh. She held up her hand, the one without the cigarette. "You know what, don't try to explain anymore. I don't want to talk about sex with you, I mean you're only my husband." She laughed again—short, like Sarah's laugh in the Bible, when angels tell her she's going to get pregnant by Abraham and him a hundred years old. "I know you men, you can't help yourselves. I mean you can help what you do but not how you feel about it. I don't judge you for that, I never have."

"I know."

"I want my family, that's all I've got now. I want Jeremy to come home and to have somebody to come home to. And if it's just me, then it's just me." Her voice was breaking and she hated the sound of it.

Joe looked like he was internally hemorrhaging. She could see him trying to control the twitch of every tiny muscle in his face, as if inside he was being torn apart, fiber by fiber, by a microscopic army of ax-wielding maniacs. Edith turned the porch light on, that filthy buggy thing with its yellow bulb, so she could watch every minute and every motion of the torture. Good.

"I tried to..." he whispered finally, gripping the rusty arms of the chair. "I never thought it would go like this."

"Save it."

It was the second time she'd said that to him and she felt inspired, as if the Holy Ghost were giving her the words in her hour of need. No—that was blasphemous. Forgive me. It was like the guardian angel of wives of queer husbands who had tried to be faithful but in the end just couldn't live without sex. She didn't know why; she'd gotten quite used to it.

"I'll leave him," he said.

"I didn't ask you to." Damned if she was taking the blame for anything.

"I'll tell him I can't. I'll find another job, I'll send money home if I have to." He drained his glass. "Maybe I will go to Florida."

"Yeah, well, you let me know." She stood up, waited for him.

He looked at her in that tormented way, like he didn't know what to do with his hands and feet. She wouldn't move. "Goodnight, Joe."

It was late for Edith but early for the Cooking Club, and Joe took his time getting there. He was pleased, if he could use such a word tonight, with the amount he had managed to say, yet he knew their conversation had been anything but complete.

It hadn't ended the way he'd intended at all. It was true he didn't want a divorce, but he hadn't intended to agree not to get one, let alone to leave Clay. He was surprised how much Edith still directed all interaction between them, considering he was no longer living there. If only he'd been able to tell her what he needed to say to her, she would have little problem agreeing to the divorce.

It'd been six months since that trip to Charlotte. Six months to the nearest Saturday and Joe had headed back to the clinic alone, without telling Clayton, without telling anybody, even though the clinic discouraged this. For he was not altogether ignorant. He'd taught science, he knew about the incubation period of a virus. His knowledge had the effect of foreshortening his entire life's perspective, making the loss of livelihood and the diminishing of his family's prospects move into the shadows.

When the diagnosis was positive this time, he came right home and told Clay. He expected Clay to get upset, to react with grief or anger, smashing things, but he did not. He didn't say anything, didn't do anything, just sat there on that couch, stroking its arm, not Joe's, and staring fixedly ahead. Joe imagined that his stare said So, faggot, it's got you too.

But love, or whatever it was, didn't come and go so quickly, and anyway Joe was still stunned from his drive back. After all they'd been having safe sex. Was he really going to die for some blow jobs without condoms? Joe was still not used to thinking this way; he'd let his pornographic imagination come out into the main room of his life, and the consequences were as disastrous as anyone had ever warned, for all of them. And as exhilarating as they were unable to admit.

Clay wanted him to leave, wanted him to go to Florida,

grow a mustache and live out his days in some Hawaiian-shirted idyll. Joe felt it when Clay could not hold back from fucking hard and fast. He tried not to dwell on what fantasies of bully-revenge were playing behind Clayton's eyelids. He couldn't see his face anyway. For his part, after waiting so many years for the sex he wanted, Joe didn't think about anything during it; it was pure sensation, the state of thoughtless ecstasy that Zen or something taught, the mind at rest. Empty.

But they hadn't made love this time, Clay hadn't made a move or said a word, and Joe knew he had to go to the big house (he still thought of it as their house, after all his name was on the mortgage and he'd paid most of it) and talk to Edith right away. It almost made him laugh, as loopy as he was from his long drive across the varied landscape of North Carolina, not even stopping to pick up cartons of cigarettes. Low tax, low tar, low pressure. Clouds had rolled across the highway on his drive back and no doubt they were still there now, though the tinge of the sun was gone, dark on dark invisible.

He pulled into the parking lot behind the Cooking Club. His was not the only car there; it was nearly eleven and people would be filling up the small dance floor, under cover of night and disco balls. Joe didn't care much for the music they played, but couldn't be picky; at least he and Clayton could dance together.

He had never danced with Edith anywhere, as she did not come from a tradition that smiled on dancing. It would be even stranger to dance with a woman now. He hadn't since Diane, and they had just been kids. He thought he'd have a smoke by himself before he went in there to face Clay, resentful of mortality, and whatever conversation he was having with his bitchy-queen friends.

But halfway through the cigarette Joe saw Clayton come out and motion him round the corner, to a narrow passageway where the Club threw trash. As Joe stepped forward, he felt Clayton's hands, rougher than usual, shoving him into the alley. He inhaled a sweet drunken smell before being rocked by a blow to the kidneys.

It seemed longer than twenty-five years ago, Cicero. No

smoking, no drinking anything stronger than Coke. And as he fell, he saw Diane, still a girl to him though somewhere she might be fat with middle age, twirling across a dance floor, luminous in his mind.

Chapter 17

It was trash day. Edith woke before dawn to the sound of the truck. Memory of the whiskey scared her. Where was her judgment? Out with her marriage by the side of the road.

The phone was ringing and ringing. How many times had Dana said, "Mom, get an answering machine!" It seemed so unnecessary, as if she were a business taking fifty calls a day. A machine would have picked up by now, but on it rang, until Edith stumbled out of bed and answered it with the only voice she could muster this morning.

"Mrs. Rignaldi?"

"Yes." She gripped the phone tighter, remembering that crazy call.

"This is David, Charlie Bailiff's partner on the police force. Charlie asked if I could give you a call. You need to come down to the hospital right away. Your husband's in the emergency room."

She opened her mouth and closed it, like a fish at the surface. The standard questions came to her: what, where, how. None of them came out.

"Mrs. Rignaldi?"

"Yes," she said, a long, slow diphthong. "Thank you, David. I'll be right there."

She went to get her robe from the back of the kitchen chair. Dana emerged, rubbing her head. "What's going on?"

"Dad's in the emergency room."

"What happened to him?" Dana's voice was so sharp, Edith knew she must be frightened.

"I don't know." She decided the robe was pointless. Might as well just get dressed.

"Do you want me to come with you?" Dana said.

Yes. No. She wanted to smoke. "Would you mind staying here? I'd feel better if there were someone at home."

"No problem." Back to teen-speak.

The whole drive to the hospital, Edith smoked, the window rolled down a crack. Since Joe had moved next door she kept a stash of cigarettes in the glove compartment. Did he want to kill her? Did she have to get cancer too?

When she arrived, a young policeman met her; he looked about Jeremy's age. She remembered the last time they were here, Jeremy with his seizure. It was too much, to expect that she would be able to handle everything. She should have brought Dana. Even Dana would have been more comfort than a cigarette.

"I'm David, Mrs. Rignaldi." He extended his hand.

"Call me Edith." She didn't remember meeting Charlie's partner before but who knew how long this one'd been out of school?

"It wasn't us that found him," David said. "But Charlie wanted me to call you."

"Found him? What happened?"

"Blow to the head, ma'am."

Edith felt eighty years old. "What kind of blow?"

"Ma'am—Edith," he said, and didn't sound like a cop. "He's dead."

She laid her hand blindly on some kind of ledge. "Why didn't you tell me?"

"I didn't want to tell you on the phone." David took her arm, guided her to a seat. "Somebody hit him. Crushed his skull."

"Who..."

"Lady at the Cooking Club reported it," he said. "There was—Somebody found him, she doesn't—"

"Who did this? Somebody murdered him? What?"

"Ma'am," he said. "Nobody will talk to us."

"Why not?" Moths, satanically angry, buzzed in her head.

"This—restaurant," he said. "It's—"

"It's what?" she said. "A club for homosexuals? I know that. Everyone in Poudre Valley knows that. You can talk to me about murder but not about where?"

He put his hands up, as if surrendering. "I just wasn't sure you knew."

She supposed she should ask to see Joe. What should she do, identify the body? She barely recognized the living man.

She did not want to tell Dana over the phone either so she asked for a cup of coffee, which seemed like the next best thing to the whiskey bottle. She'd like to take that bottle herself and smash it over Joe's head. Was he on drugs? She'd heard they pumped themselves full of all kinds of stuff, so they could dance and do whatever else.

It was light out by the time she got home. Dana was in the living room, watching the news, of all things. "Is Dad okay?"

Edith sat down beside Dana on the couch, put her hand on hers. "No, he's not," she said. "He was killed, Dana."

Edith felt all the life and strength draining out through Dana's fingertips, and she prayed that some of it at least would leak right over into her because God knew how she was going to get through this. What could Pam have been thinking when she said "Get through it?" Pam didn't know what she was talking about. Nobody did. Nobody ever understood what someone else was going through.

"What happened?" Dana said in a dull voice.

Edith kept stroking Dana's fingers back and forth with her thumb, a little motorized gesture like a purr. "He was at a restaurant—"

"A restaurant?"

"In the parking lot," she clarified. "It was late, and somebody attacked him."

"Where at? The Waffle House?"

Her daughter sounded like such a hick at times. "It's called the Cooking Club."

"Oh," Dana said. "Oh. I know where that is. It used to be Hong's."

"Yes." Had she heard about it? Well, of course, she must have. She lived here. She wasn't stupid.

"Oh," Dana kept saying, and Edith sensed deflation, all the air going out of Dana's lungs, out of the room.

"They can't tell me why."

"Was it a robbery? Was Dad robbed?"

"What would they take, Dana?"

"Then it was a murder," Dana said, and for the first time she looked at Edith and her eyes, no less than her voice, were shrill. "He was murdered!"

Edith shook her head. She wanted to bang her hand on the side of it, to get the moths out, then bang it against the wall.

"Don't you get it, Mom? Don't you get it? Someone killed him because—because they thought he was—"

"It certainly seems that way."

"Well what are they going to do?" Dana said. "The cops?"

"It was Charlie's partner that told me."

"Rednecks."

"I'll talk to Charlie."

"I mean all of them. Oh, come on, Mom. You know how they are. They just sit around, fatsos, they're never going to— It's true!"

Edith put her hand over her eyes. "Look, Dana, I don't know what I'm going to do. First Jeremy and now this. Have you talked to him?"

"He's fine." Dana's voice went dull again. "Do you want me to get in touch with him?"

Even through the moths, Edith was beginning to realize how it might not be a good idea to talk to her son right now. What would she say? "Yes, please."

"Should I tell him there'll be a funeral?"

The cold click of reality, like a trigger. The church? Her relatives? Steve?

"We'll talk about it later, Dana," she said. "I can't deal with this right now."

She had a memory that suicides could not have a Christian funeral, that they were buried somewhere far away and dark, perhaps with a stake through the heart. She could not remember reading about this anywhere in the Bible, however.

But what about the other suicides? Not those who actually did the deed but those who practically did, who volunteered out of their chosen lives to court death somewhere on the dark sidelines, in the shadow of death? She knew that was biblical, but she couldn't reconcile it. "Yea, though I walk through the valley..." It was as if death and evil were not, in fact, entirely apart from God, and this she couldn't reconcile with the God of light, in whom was no darkness at all.

It was not the Bible but an Edna St. Vincent Millay poem that came to her mind. The thinking now, Edith had been shocked to read, was that Miss Millay had been crazy, depressed, when she wrote those poems. Or having a fit or something. Edith had always loved them, especially "Renascence," which struck her as an exact expression of ecstasy in life. All the more since ecstasy had so far eluded Edith and, she supposed now, always would. If only she could say the same for agony. Well, maybe that's what being crazy meant. Maybe "Renascence" described something that was never real.

"We'll get through it," she said to Dana.

The funeral was furtive, like an elopement with death. Only the two of them from the immediate family, not even Charlie or Pam. That was how Edith wanted it. There was no proper way to say goodbye, to a violated body and an end of life that had not been resolved.

"Charlie, I want to talk to you."

The phone line crackled, which Edith knew it didn't have any reason to do. Maybe Charlie was crumpling paper—some investigative report, no doubt.

"Sure. We can talk now."

"No, I mean sit down and talk. They let you take lunch, don't they?"

"Well..." Like he had to look at his incredibly busy schedule. "Tomorrow I have time."

"Let's meet at the Quilting Bee."

"Downtown?"

"Yes, 314 Main."

It was the last place anyone would look for either of them—a fabric and sewing shop, with a tiny lunchroom in the back. Edith could barely sew on a button, and she doubted he could either. Pam must do all that. She'd always been good at home ec.

Charlie looked so ridiculous amid all those quilts and yarn, even though he wasn't wearing his uniform but some pullover sweater that he would probably deny was pink. Filled it out nicely, too; he looked more built, less fat, than the last time Edith saw him. Would fit in better at the Cooking Club than here.

They ordered tuna fish sandwiches and coffee. Edith fantasized about dumping a flask into hers.

Charlie's chin jutted like he was wearing his police face. "I know what this is about, Edie."

"Ooh, you're a smart man."

"And I can't help you," he said. "I wish I could."

"Now Charlie," she said, "you and I both know that's a lie. You don't want any part of this."

"Edie, I know how bad you feel. Believe me. You're not the first relative I've ever had to break news to."

"You didn't break anything to me, you had your buddy do it. Were you there? Did you see Joe?"

Charlie rubbed his chin. He hadn't touched his sandwich, and Edith imagined that must be quite a challenge for him.

"I talked to everybody who was there. Me and David did, or tried to. Nobody would tell us anything. It must have been somebody there that night, someone they all knew—"

"Who all?"

His face reddened. "The—gays," he said. "It had to be one of them."

"How the hell do you know that?" He looked surprised she'd

even cuss. Well, if that's what it took. "No, how the hell do you know? Why wouldn't it be one of those rednecks you just know goes looking for somebody to beat up on a Saturday night?"

"Because they won't talk to us there," he said. "If it was someone attacking them, they'd want to tell."

"Charlie." She spoke before she could suck the words back in. "I always thought you were stupid but I didn't know just how stupid you were."

"Thanks."

"Oh, come on. You think if somebody's at this club and the cops come in, they're going to trust you?"

"No, they don't, Edie. No one will talk to us. They're afraid of being exposed."

She allowed herself a small, rueful laugh. "As if they aren't exposed. Everybody in Poudre Valley knows what Joe was up to, or thinks they do, and probably they know about everybody else who was there. What more do they have to lose?"

"If they're breaking the law, they're no different than everybody else," he said.

"Do you really believe that?"

He stabbed his pickle with a fork; Edith had an obscene thought. "Listen," he said. "I don't understand it, and I feel terrible for you. I felt terrible for you before. It's just asking for trouble, hanging out with them." His jaws worked in his ruddy face. "But if there's a crime, then I'm going to investigate it, it doesn't matter if he's kin to you, or them, or not. That's my job."

"Right. Like it's my job to teach the kids even if they're stupid, or some redneck's son like that Lowry. Why aren't you talking to Lowry?"

"Edie, what are you talking about? There's no reason to think he was anywhere near the Cooking Club that night. He was probably at home in bed. Like you were, and I wish I'd been."

"And Joe. Just eat your sandwich."

She waited till he had his mouth full and lettuce sticking out before she said, "Didn't you find any blood?"

Charlie chewed; she didn't know what his look of distaste

was directed at, Joe's death, the mention of blood, or the tuna fish. All of equal importance, probably.

"Only his," he said.

"So there's no evidence and no witnesses. You're just giving up."

"Until somebody will tell us something, it's unsolvable."

She looked at him and despised him. Always knew he was a stupid redneck. There may have been a moment of hope, when they were children together; there may have been a chance, as there still was for the kids in her class, but he had not taken it.

Edith pushed herself back from the table, leaving her sandwich hardly touched. Let him pay for it and eat it too. She turned her back on Charlie, made her way through the quilting displays, the hanging swaths of fabric, every one of them impugning her femininity. She had never been a customer of the Quilting Bee but the others probably knew her as an impostor, not only in the world of crafts and sewing but as a wife, a widow. Somehow, whatever happened to her, she was both more wronged and more deserving of it than other women.

Chapter 18

As Edith had walked out of the Quilting Bee, so she moved through the winter, feeling older (well, at least thinner), the cascades of humiliation giving way ever so gradually to lapping waves of grief. She felt more and more removed from people around her, all of whom knew of her misfortune but none of whom had a damn thing to say about it.

She went to church late and left early. She still felt the need to turn up, not because other people looked for her there—in fact, they looked away—but for God. Amazing how large God loomed when your family'd been taken away from you.

She had Dana, of course. Dana did what she was supposed to do, as did Edith, though no one had written rules for this. They each went to their respective schools, so inured to the repetition of scandal that in the end people just left them alone. Edith could hardly bear not to smoke during the day, but she didn't, just to avoid the teachers' lounge. The students were, if anything, more subdued in her classes. It was as if she were the murderer, not a victim.

She became one of those zombie teachers who pulled out a file folder for the lesson she'd taught at that time last year—not just sodium before Christmas, but every day. Well, what was the point of teaching the same dadgum things for twenty years if you couldn't coast when you needed to? And Lord knew, she needed to. There were drugs and alcohol for things like this but it seemed safer to rely on the Lord.

She'd been taught to do so by her family, and she couldn't talk to them either. She hadn't, other than bumping into them in the Piggly Wiggly or somewhere, since Joe had lost his job. It was funny how, without an answering machine, you could communicate so seldom with relatives only a few miles away—if you wanted to.

Edith wasn't sure wanted was the word. She missed Isabella in her kitchen, puttering around. She would eat Kraft Dinner for supper, or even popcorn if Dana was doing something else, and she missed church suppers and Aunt Lanie's deviled eggs, Aunt Anna's ham.

Aunt Anna would never approve of watching television during supper. Things had definitely slipped around Edith's house. She and Dana took to watching game shows, *Wheel of Fortune*, everything but crime shows which did not hold any interest. The two of them and Vanna, every night, alphabet soup and vowels.

The only person with whom Edith could identify—though not relate—was Clayton Hornsby. She would never talk to him, of course. How do you talk to your own husband's survivor? Could they both be widows of the same man?

She heard in the spring that Clayton had moved to Florida, just packed up his trailer and left. Who knows, maybe they'd burned him out. She couldn't blame him, wanted to pack up herself.

Through the dull of her pain she blinked at Dana, at her new hairdresser, the fellow zombies at school, and almost envied Clayton, as evil as the situation was. He could just take his scissors, set up shop somewhere else, leave it all behind. And here she was, like some knocked-up pregnant girl, holding the bag as usual.

Eric Dufresne finally went off to Africa, sent little aerogrammes back to the church. Edith knew Dana was relieved not to have to go to youth group anymore. She wondered what she should do with the little house next door. Joe's life insurance had paid off their mortgage, but it was like blood money. She spent a lot of time in the garden, wished she could let it grow over the house and cover it up.

She thought about Jeremy every day, though she tried not to think about him too much. On days when he wouldn't leave her mind easily, she tended to work outside more. Kneeling, digging, working with her hands and hand tools were meditative for her.

Today, however, it was raining, a hard, surprisingly cool rain interspersed with low heavy clouds. The weather forecast had been for warm sunny days both yesterday and today, but it couldn't have been more wrong, and though she knew the rain would do a lot of good for seeds that were already in the ground, she was impatient to glove up, take her trowel, and get to work weeding and digging men out of her mind.

She wondered why it was so hard for weather forecasters to get it right, despite all their modern equipment. Isabella would always say, "Honey, he said..." He being the weatherman, as if there were just one in the world. Maybe that was why he was wrong so often, just too busy.

Years before, Edith had fantasized about packing a suitcase and buying a ticket to Los Angeles—just flying there, no plan or destination other than what was now the second biggest city in America. Chicago had been the second biggest, when she lived there, and now both the World Almanac and she had changed.

But she had never been able to get past that fantasy of just landing at the airport—she didn't even know its name—in LA, setting down her suitcase, and thinking "I've arrived." She imagined the moving walkway rolling by her, and Californian-looking people regarding her briefly, in recognition that she was now one of them. But she couldn't imagine what she'd do next—go out and buy a whole new set of pink and purple clothes, or hit the beach, or take her and Joe's credit cards and just live off them as long as they lasted, figuring it would be months before he'd realize she was no longer opening the bills.

Now Edith wished she'd done it. Without a plan or a warning, like Jeremy, who she was not convinced could live on his own anywhere. She smoked cigarettes on the porch these days, crushing them neatly in a silver ashtray—she'd dug that up at least, no sense sticking to the Melmac. Jeremy's leaving now seemed like a rebuke to her, as if to say, "You never had the guts to live your dream life. I'm living mine instead."

Jeremy shouldn't have been driving. But he'd only had the one grand mal seizure, and he could tell when a petit mal was coming on. He wasn't going to kill anybody.

The sweetest sight was an empty left lane late at night. He was on I-75 just past Chattanooga, hoping to make it to a gas station in Georgia where the prices were lower. He had Bear's truck, the price he'd asked to not tell the police that Bear had once made a threatening phone call to his house. Jeremy knew well enough Bear didn't have anything to do with his dad getting killed, but he needed wheels. And Bear couldn't argue with him. Didn't have the sense.

He thought it might be the fumes, then maybe a seizure so he changed lanes, pulled over to the shoulder just in case. But it was more like an aura, the way he'd heard a migraine described. People thought he didn't know jack, that he could barely read, but he could find out stuff when he wanted to.

He turned off the engine but not the radio. "Stairway To Heaven." You couldn't often find a station that would play that whole song through. Jeremy set his forehead against the wheel and just listened. He remembered Eric Dufresne, that freak youth minister, saying that Led Zeppelin was demonic or something, but Eric was a guitarist too and Jeremy was sure he'd sell his soul to play like Jimmy Page.

He thought he heard somebody, jerked up in his seat. He checked, but the doors were locked. Great, what a time for ghosts to come out of the stereo. Maybe Eric had been right.

But when he heard his name the voice was more familiar than Robert Plant's.

"Daddy?" Jeremy whispered.

He hadn't called his father Daddy in years, and even then only when they were alone. It was the Southern way but always made Jeremy feel weird. Yet this was his daddy's voice and he answered instinctively.

The ghost didn't say anything else. Jeremy looked out the corner of his eye at the passenger seat, but nobody was there. Fuck, maybe it was sleep deprivation. He wasn't drunk or high.

The electric solo had begun but for once Jeremy didn't feel like head-banging or playing air guitar. He turned the volume down and spoke, quietly, like maybe somebody outside could hear him. "Man, you got something to tell me, say it. You're making me a crazy person."

No one spoke. A big rig thundered past and rattled the windows. Jeremy saw stars over the open highway.

He shook his head, rubbed the side of it with his palm. He'd get some gas station coffee and call Dana.

Before pulling back into the lane, he fiddled with the radio, no longer in the mood for songs about ghosts and shit. He found a station playing Simon and fucking Garfunkel. Whatever. He left it on. Something about a boxer and whores.

"How's it going, Jeremy?"

"Hey, Dana." He was chewing something, sounded like the phone was only halfway to his mouth.

They didn't talk very often. He would call her, give her a number where she could call him, and she would use that next time and until it didn't work. It had worked when Joe died. She hadn't cried till her brother came on the line, then she started crying and just couldn't stop. "What's wrong?" he kept asking. It took forever to get the words out. But Jeremy was the only one who did ask about Joe, his death, or funeral.

"Still working on your music?" she said now.

"Yeah." Pause. Chew. "I have an idea."

"What's that?"

"About Dad."

"You have an idea about Dad?"

"Yeah. Don't worry," he said, chewed some more. "Tell Mom not to worry."

He always said that. And Dana always told Mom not to worry. She didn't tell her Jeremy was working in bars, playing places where people crowd-surfed. Like she'd even know what that was.

"I will," Dana said. "I love you, big brother."

He called after Mom was in bed, which was by ten o'clock. Mom had taken to turning the ringer off on the phone outside her bedroom door. She turned it off at night and frequently didn't remember to turn it back on in the daytime either. She said she never wanted to be wakened in the middle of the night again. If Jeremy called, the phone in Dana's room would ring and he only wanted to talk to Dana anyway.

No one else ever called. Dana was a senior and could hardly wait to get the hell out of Poudre Valley.

There were now strange rituals in the house. The TV was on a lot, flipped on uncritically by Mom, who had also taken to assembling a mountain of objects in the living room. The living room was where the TV used to be, but it had been moved to the eat-in kitchen, where TV had always been forbidden before. The mountain of objects included things like clothes hangers and a huge steam iron, an old one that weighed forty pounds or something. All this was supposed to accompany Dana to college, where Mom seemed to believe students dressed in ball gowns. Dana called the pile Mom's sculpture.

"I'm moving to Chicago, Mom, not Mars."

"It might as well be." Mom wound an exceedingly long extension cord into an expert coil, though Dana doubted her whole dorm room would be big enough to need it.

Dana wanted to tell her mother that there was more than enough drama in their lives, without grieving over what was essentially a good thing. It was a wonder she had even survived school, what with the vicious rumors and her dad dying and nobody even raising their eyes to say sorry about it. The idea that her enrollment in a university, on a full scholarship so they didn't have to worry about paying for it, was the cause of Mom's sorrow made Dana deeply resentful. And if resentful, sullen. And if sullen, then even less inclined to talk, which they so seldom did anyway.

Dana wished she were going to Mars. She couldn't get far enough away from this town, with its small minds and smaller hearts. She'd gotten used to people talking, not even behind her back, just talking right there in the halls. She'd been warned by that prick of a vice principal that one more attempt to jump somebody (that was his version of her fight with Tracy) and she'd be expelled, would not graduate and her life would be over. She could tell he was just daring her to do something, that the thought of ruining her life made him drip. It was not giving him that satisfaction that got her through.

At least she had someplace to go. She didn't often regard life from her mother's perspective, as it seemed to Dana that Mom was all about overdramatizing things. But she was going to a place Mom had gone, when she was young. To where her parents had met, where Joe was from. There would be no relatives to meet her but still, she would be escaping. What's keeping you, when the only place you've ever lived has never felt like home?

Chapter 19

1991

When Edith cooked now, the kitchen smelled of despair. She mostly confined herself to the one pot, of beans or whatever. Why bother? She would come home from school and promptly change into a green sweat suit, something she'd never want another adult to see her wear but that was oh, so comfortable. As soon as she was out of her teacher's outfit—she still wore a skirt, and dress shoes, every day, didn't care and couldn't afford to do what the women's libbers did—she would turn on the television in the kitchen, no matter what was on, and empty a can into that little saucepan with its insulated handle. Then it was just her and the TV for the rest of the night, crying into her white trash cooking.

She'd never eaten like this when she had a family to take care of. There hadn't been TV dinners. There had been no Kraft Dinner; she was a Southerner and made macaroni and cheese from scratch. She had bought spaghetti sauce in jars but still, you boiled spaghetti yourself. She'd never before eaten that red-staining sugared stuff out of cans. Something that sweet, it had to be Yankee.

Now she stood in the yellow glow of her disinfected kitchen, stirring SpaghettiOs with, of all things, a wooden spaghetti spoon, and listening to Pat whoever yammering on the TV. She could hardly wait till *Jeopardy!* came on; it was the highlight of her evening, of her life. No one would call. Dana called, religiously, as it were, every Sunday. Her pattern never varied. Jeremy never called.

Whenever Edith asked Dana on the phone about Jeremy she was always told not to worry, which so enraged her each time that she nearly hung up. How could Dana patronize her that way, how could she possibly know what trouble, or not, her brother was in? Their talks, hers and Dana's, became shorter, as Edith wanted to avoid the topic yet kept coming back to it, like a sore in her mouth.

She had those, too. It was November and already she was being afflicted by winter bugs, things that hadn't affected her before. When she was a young teacher, at first she caught everything, every cold and flu, every viral or bacterial infection known to the public schools and their snotty inmates. She thought she'd built up a cast-iron immunity, but the last year's trauma must have worn down her resistance. She took vitamin C pills and prayed a lot.

She did pray. She prayed while stirring SpaghettiOs, that the Lord would take her burden and put it wherever it was he put burdens that were too great even for him to bear; that he would forgive her selfishness and weakness for thinking her burden was worse than that of starving Africans or people who were in constant physical pain. That he would comfort her in her tears. "Blessed are they that mourn," the Beatitudes said. She'd tried to read the Bible in Today's English Version for a while, but she knew it would be of no further use to her when she saw that verse translated as "Happy." What was that? Edith wasn't sure what blessed meant in this context, but she was certain it didn't mean happy.

She wished there were someone she could ask about these things.

She'd gone to the Religious Book Store, not far from the

Quilting Bee, and looked for one of those books by authors who'd helped women in the Seventies lead godly lives. There was a whole rack of them. She'd tried to find one that wasn't about dirty diapers but dealt with absolute despair, when every moment of life was a struggle to bear the weight of grief. She found a book about a woman who'd lost the use of all her limbs, but Edith couldn't read that, it made her feel guilty because there was nothing wrong with her. She found another book about a woman who'd lost her husband to an excruciating death, by cancer; it had gone on and on. The only reference she could find to her own problem was a mention of someone's son, who had been "lost to the homosexual lifestyle." Edith got the impression that the less said, the better. "Lost" in the Christian tradition she knew generally meant roasting on a spit for all eternity.

So, nothing to help her there. Bereft of faith, she would rely on facts to get her through. After all, she was a science teacher. But she wasn't having much luck finding facts, either.

Every week or two she called Charlie and was told how terribly sorry he was, but there was no cause to pursue the case further; they couldn't even find the weapon. Edith had no time for her redneck cousin except that she knew it would be even more useless to try anyone else. You talked to who you knew; there was no appeal.

They had done an autopsy and determined death by a blow from a blunt instrument. Edith had found this inadequate, and she insisted on the full details of the medical examination, which it was taking months to obtain. She'd called everyone she knew, plus a few she didn't know. No one wanted to touch it. She wasn't sure what it was she wanted to know, but she thought maybe, at least, she could find out if Joe had died instantly, had not been in pain.

But wasn't he in pain now? she would torment herself by asking. Wasn't he burning in hell? It's one thing to be a homosexual, people can't help themselves, but not to fight it, to leave your wife whom you love, or say you love; to leave your family...

But he hadn't been leaving, Edith would argue back to

herself. He was going to come back. That very night, he was going to come back, only somebody bashed his head in. Wasn't murder enough?

But…neither fornicators, nor idolaters, nor adulterers, nor effeminate, nor abusers of themselves with mankind...

"Shall inherit the kingdom of God," Edith said, right out loud to the SpaghettiOs can.

She was losing it. She dropped the can in the trash, then remembered the Piggly Wiggly now had a box for recycling. She made a face and fished among old coffee grounds for the can. Dana would be outraged: "You're contributing to the landfill, Mom." Edith wished she could just lay her body down in the landfill and contribute that way.

It was a sinful thought. She finished warming up her SpaghettiOs just as Alex Trebek was coming on television. A Canadian. When she'd met Joe, they'd talked a little bit about Canada. Neither had ever been there, but Joe knew young men who had gone, to get out of fighting in Vietnam. He was not prepared to do that but wondered what he should do if he was drafted. Edith didn't want him to go to Vietnam, didn't want him to go to Canada either, or to jail. In the end, he was lucky. He was teaching and never had to go.

She wondered then what their lives might have been like if he'd gone to Canada and she'd gone with him. They could certainly never have moved back here, pardon or no. Her relatives, and those around them, had never forgiven the draft dodgers, or the Vietnamese, or President Carter.

But she'd voted for Carter because he was a born-again Christian. Didn't that count?

It was enough to make your head hurt. Reagan and Carter, Canada and Vietnam, fornicators and adulterers. Maybe something she remembered would be in the history category on *Jeopardy!* tonight. It shocked her suddenly, to think that times she remembered living through were history.

When the phone rang Edith considered not picking it up, but it was that boring part of the show when Alex was talking to the contestants about their mother-in-law's pets. She wondered, sometimes, what she would say if she were ever on *Jeopardy!*

"Edith Rignaldi," Alex would read from his note card, mispronouncing her name. "It says here that you're a physical science teacher in Poudre Valley, Tennessee." (He'd mispronounce that too.)

"That's right, Alex. My husband was a teacher too, before his skull was smashed in. They say homosexuals did it but I don't believe them."

"Why would homosexuals smash your husband's skull?" Alex would say, in that humorous, slightly condescending tone he always used.

"Oh, they wouldn't, Alex." She'd laugh. "You see, he was one of them. It will have been some redneck from the hills who still says gook and nigger."

"Gook? Well, we don't have anyone fitting that description here on *Jeopardy!* Imagine your chances then, eh?"

"I'm coming," Edith called to the phone, as if it could hear her. She answered with the sweet Southern lilt that she expected to use until her own death.

"Mrs. Rignaldi?"

"Yes."

"It's Naomi over at the hospital." Naomi did not speak like anyone else Edith knew in Poudre Valley. She had a brisk, get-things-done approach that was also unique. When Edith's persistence had led her to Naomi, she'd liked her immediately.

"Call me Edith, please."

"I've got the information you wanted, Edith." Naomi paused. "You sitting down?"

People always asked this. Must be regulations or something. Edith plunked herself down in the floor. "Go on."

"I'm sorry this took so long, it took a lot of paperwork to get it...bottom line, your husband's blood showed antibodies for HIV."

HIV. "He had AIDS?"

"He was HIV-positive, Edith. Not showing symptoms of any AIDS-related illness."

"But he would have." Edith spat the information back out as quickly as she could absorb it. "If he'd lived, he would have gotten AIDS and died anyway."

"Eventually. Yes."

Just for a second, before reproaching herself, Edith hoped that whoever'd killed Joe had been spattered with his blood, and had plenty of open cuts to get infected.

"Thank you, Naomi," she said, though she didn't feel thankful at all.

"Edith, I'm sorry."

"Nothing for you to be sorry about."

"For your loss."

Edith made some kind of sound. Then she sat, receiver in her hand, staring at it like maybe it would answer her for a change. She was glad Naomi'd asked if she was sitting down. She didn't want to bob and sway, maybe fall and hit her head on something, lie there, paralyzed or dead, till somebody came by and who would that be? They used to know their neighbors, the lovely old couple from across the road, but they were no longer living and their son, who now owned the house, just came by every couple weeks in the summer to mow the lawn.

No wonder nobody wanted to touch Joe. She resented everyone, Joe, Isabella, the neighbors, for dying and leaving her alone. But especially Joe, who had not only died in a way that was as unnecessary as it was hideous, but who, it turned out, had been at fault, would have died because of who he had been while he was alive. A person whom she'd thought she knew. A person she had lost.

Along with her memory of him. Who, after all, had Joe been? When he'd called her on this phone, not in his last year but for years before that, when she'd stood (or sat) talking to him on this very phone, this very green phone, had he been lying after all? Was it indeed impossible for men to keep their pants on, was he promiscuous...because it wasn't possible he had just gotten sick like that...was it?

She remembered when the actor in *Chariots of Fire* had died, the one who played the Christian runner. She'd heard that it was AIDS, and so all her illusions were shattered. She knew he was an actor, not the character, and yet somehow she'd been under his spell, as it seemed she'd been under her husband's as well. All these years she thought that Joe was different, he wasn't like those other men; even when he left her it wasn't for nothing, he had fallen in love, though she still didn't understand how men could fall in love.

She wished she'd killed him herself.

Edith felt her certainties, the myths she'd lived by, slipping away like an ebbing tide. First she was married, then she was married to a homosexual, then she was widowed. She'd kept revising her perception of herself and now these successive stages were no use to her anymore, now she was at sea. She'd known Joe was a different man than anyone else perceived but it had made him special in some way, it had made him hers. Now she had been cheated on, lied to.

Oh. God. What if he'd given it to her? They hadn't made love in so long, but how did she know what was safe? How long had he known, if he'd known? How did you get AIDS anyway? She didn't really know, it wasn't something that came up at Women's Council. Where could she go? How could she find out?

"Edith!" She finally heard the screaming from the phone. Hadn't Naomi hung up?

She put the receiver to her ear carefully, as if it were a gun that might go off. "Yes?"

"Are you all right?" Naomi said. "I thought I'd lost you."

"I'm here."

"Edith, please come down to the hospital. We need to do some tests."

"Dana, it's Mom."

This couldn't be good. Mom never called during the week. In fact, Mom never called, because she didn't know Dana's schedule. Didn't want to know was more like it. Dana was careful to call Mom every Sunday night, whether or not she had anything to say. Which she mostly didn't.

"Hi, Mom. Are you okay?"

"Yes. I'm fine. That's what I'm calling to tell you. It's about Dad."

"Did they find out who killed him?"

"No. I got someone at the hospital to help me, finally." Mom cleared her throat; Dana hoped she wasn't going to cry. "Your dad had the AIDS virus."

"What?"

"But I don't, Dana. I'm fine. I'm fine."

"Mom, I'm real, real glad to hear that," she said, "but it doesn't make sense. Dad was killed, he didn't die of a disease." Dana was aware of her roommate, Tomas, sitting on the other bed. They'd separated the bunk beds their first day in the dorm, as a result of which they didn't have any space to go in and out now. Tomas was listening quite openly, eyes bright in her beautiful dark face.

"Dana. Dana, did you hear what I said?"

"Sorry. What?"

"He would have, Dana. He would have gotten sick and died of AIDS."

"But he didn't. Mom, this is really hard to talk about right now."

"Oh, I'm sorry, honey. You must be getting ready for exams."

"December, yeah." Dana put a hand over the receiver and mouthed, "Do you mind?" at Tomas, who closed her book and left the room.

"Dana, I want to see you, at Christmas. But I don't—Have you heard from Jeremy?"

"A few weeks ago. He's fine. He said—"

"Not to worry, I know, I know. I don't know what he's scared of, I'm not going to hurt him." Mom started sounding choked up. "What does he think I'm going to make him do?"

"I came home last Christmas," Dana said.

"So you're not coming home this year at all?"

"No, I'm not saying that." She twisted her long hair around her fingers. It had grown out and she wondered if she should shave her head. After all, she was a sophomore. "I just remember how it was last year."

"How was it?"

"We had nothing to say to each other."

"So we'll rent movies. Dana, please. Do you want to go somewhere?"

"Go where?"

"I don't know. Myrtle Beach." Mom was now giggling and Dana thought she must be hysterical.

"You want to go to Myrtle Beach with me for Christmas?"

"Well, I'm not going to Aunt Anna's. We'll do whatever you want, I just can't stand being alone here. Were you planning to do something else?"

"No," Dana admitted.

"You don't know how sick I've been, worrying."

"About Jeremy?"

"About AIDS. What if—what if I'd gotten it too?"

Dana pondered this. Her mom? She tried to connect this with the news, with Freddie Mercury; it didn't compute. "Mom, do you have anybody you can talk to about this stuff?"

Dana heard a little snort. "I'm talking to you."

"I mean—I don't know, a counselor or something."

"Dana, I wouldn't even know how to begin to talk about this to a counselor."

"Well, everybody isn't as—fundamentalist—I mean, isn't there some nice Jewish person you could drive to?"

"The woman at the hospital, Naomi. She did the test without putting it on my records. I think Naomi's Jewish."

"What? Mom—"

"Oh, even if there was someone who didn't care, how could I talk to them? They don't understand where I come from. What I did, or why."

Neither did Dana. "I'm sorry, Mom."

"Do you think—is there any way you could get hold of Jeremy?" Dana started to answer but Mom cut her off. "I know, he doesn't have to come, I don't have to see him. I just want him to know."

"About Dad?"

Mom paused. "It's a reason to talk to him, isn't it?"

"I'll try."

"Thanks. I love you, Dana."

"I love you too," Dana said, hanging up as Tomas walked back into the room. Tomas always had this expression on her face, like whatever Dana was doing or saying was slightly crazy.

“You all right?” Tomas looked at her, hard, then rummaged through a shelf of dried food. Whatever time of the day or night, Tomas would eat whenever she was hungry; she rarely ate in the cafeteria. Who knew how much money was going to waste on her meal plan?

“Shit,” Tomas said. “These noodles are busted open.”

“We probably have mice,” Dana said. “We should set a trap.”

Those wide eyes. “No, I couldn’t do that! Do you really think it’s mice? We should tell the resident manager.”

“So she’ll set a trap.” Dana felt her shoulders sag. The disconnect between what Mom had told her, and Tomas’s concern over some ramen noodles, was so vast a gulf that she laughed at the absurdity of it.

“What’s funny?”

“Nothing’s funny. That was my mom.”

Tomas sat down on the bed next to Dana, put a hand on the small of her back. A flash of heat. “How long since your dad passed on?”

Tomas knew only that Joe was dead, not the rest of it. Hell, Dana didn’t even know the whole story, and it sounded like Mom didn’t either. “A year ago,” she said. “Just before I came up here.”

“That’s rough,” Tomas said, and for once sounded as if she meant it. “No wonder you were so wild last year.”

Dana had only gotten to know Tomasina Jefferson, the preppy pre-med, in the spring, when Tomas had come to what she claimed was her first and only fraternity party. It was being held on the front lawn of the frat house, so technically it was outdoors. Tomas would only go to outdoor events because she could not abide, in fact was allergic to, cigarette smoke, and “everyone smoked” at these parties, to which she’d never gone.

Dana had gone to them, and smoked at them. It was difficult now for her to remember what else she had spent her freshman year doing. She’d gone to some classes, just enough to stay off academic probation. Even that was touch and go until the academic dean got a good look down Dana’s strategically unbuttoned blouse. Dana had discovered that she was beautiful, and that her lack of particular interest in the frat boys made them ply her with even more alcohol at their parties. They probably hoped she'd fall face down in a punch bowl and be at their mercy. She did drink a lot, but managed never to pass out.

It was early morning by the time she ran into Tomas at the party. The Phi Delts had removed some red paint from the front of their house, which had been sprayed there in an anti-Gulf war protest. The frat had had the temerity to fly an American flag.

Dana was getting herself a seventh drink—she was fine as long as she was counting—and this immaculate young black woman was talking to a bearded white guy. "The fact is, this wasn't a war," she said. "It was a conflict. War can only be declared by an act of Congress. Read the Constitution."

"Why are you supporting it?" said the guy, whom Dana knew to be a socialist. "It's people of color, like you, who are disproportionately fighting this war against other people of color."

"Save it for the Black Students' Union," Tomas said. "I'm no more colored than you are."

"It's all about oil," the guy tried again.

"Enough politics," Dana interrupted, simultaneously offending them both.

The bearded guy said, "Whatever, slut," and moved on, while Dana steadied herself on the edge of the snack table.

Tomas rested a hand on her arm. "What are you doing? You're going to be so sick in the morning."

"It is morning," Dana said. She dug a cigarette out of her pocket and lit it, just to annoy Tomas.

Dana didn't feel like moving, so they ended up sitting on the lawn till the sun came up over the grass. By then, they'd decided they had so little in common that they would never bother each other, and ought to room together next year. Dana would probably have forgotten all about it later, but Tomas didn't.

She had breezed onto campus that winter like a Caribbean wind. That was what Dana thought, anyway, since she spent most of her own time listening to old Bob Dylan recordings and thought of everything in those terms. Tomas had arrived with her car that was too nice to park on the South Side, and moved into an apartment down the hall which could be a double or a triple residence and already had two students living in it. They were all biology majors, all groaned through the winter term of organic chemistry together, and listened to Pink Floyd and The Doors.

But when she met Dana in the hallway Tomas would smile, and flash a set of pearly but not unnaturally white teeth, in contrast to her gums which Dana was sure was a horribly politically incorrect observation. She had not met that many black students before and she certainly didn't know any like Tomas, who did not congregate with the other black students and thereby risked being called an "Oreo" or worse. The Oreo remarks, or prospect of them, was something Tomas told her about, along with the expression "politically correct."

Although it seemed that spring would never come, this year as well as last, mind-expanding music made the world seem brighter. Jim Morrison singing about LA women all the time gave her the impression that it had always been summer in the late Sixties, always the summer of love, and Dana began to identify with this period even though Jim Morrison had died in Paris before she was old enough to remember anything.

Paris was a place she wanted to go someday. In fact she had never been outside the United States before, not even across to Canada to see Niagara Falls. She liked the idea of going abroad and this would have meant Europe to her, but it made sense that Tomas would see things differently.

When Tomas first talked of going to Africa Dana thought perhaps Egypt, as she'd always wanted to see the pyramids. She hadn't grown up thinking of Egypt as part of Africa, just as she hadn't thought of Mesopotamia being the same place as what was now called Iraq. Iraq, as far as Dana knew in the 1980s, was just a Middle Eastern country at war with Iran, and therefore "good" by the standards of the U.S., which was also an enemy of Iran.

Tomas had raised Dana's consciousness. She pointed out things which later, it seemed to Dana, ought to have been obvious, such as the origins of civilization in Africa, or the fact that the dictator of Iraq had been financed by what Dana discovered were called "Western" governments. In fact, it was largely thanks to Tomas that Dana realized there was such a thing as Western civilization, distinct from the world at large.

But this was not what endeared her to Tomas. Dana was reminded how much she enjoyed the sight of rippling muscles under dark skin that seemed to carry the strength of the sun even through winter days. She was further illicitly delighted by the sparkle of teeth and of bright eyes, their whites as dazzling as the snow outside that would not melt through all the months till March, at least. And when, over coffee, Tomas would question, say, Dana's remark that she admired the Israelis for making a democratic home for Jews in the Holy Land, Dana's world would shift to one side, her notions of left and right, not to mention black and white, edging ever so slightly towards a new angle.

Chapter 20

1992

Dana was home from college for the summer. Like her daughter, Edith was not used to being the age she was, or to her place in life. She didn't feel old enough to be without a husband, although having one hadn't really suited her either. Dana was almost twenty but still seemed awkward, like a girl. They each expressed a vague need to make the most of the summer, Dana because she was young and it came naturally to her, Edith because she was no longer young and life was feeling precious. While Dana listened to new albums on her newly acquired CD player, took a desultory interest in her lifeguard job, and spent as much time as possible in the sun, Edith structured her summer with projects. It was what she and Joe had always done, getting the garden harvested or the porch painted in those months between school years, but it took on an urgency now with the need to stay alive. It was the only way Edith knew to make the most of her time. To make it count.

As the garden started coming in and she emerged from the hibernation of grief, she wondered what to do about church.

She believed, had always believed, that the spiritual was the foundational aspect of life, even though there were few spiritual or other truths of which she had always been sure. The end of Joe had made the neat Methodist parameters of their church life together impossible, and eventually she'd stopped going altogether. She wanted to go back, but to a church she could think in, a liturgy different from what she'd been praying for forty years. A church that centered its services on sacrament rather than sermon, that served communion every blessed week. Even if, God help her, it meant drinking real wine.

This, and a long-suppressed and hidden taste for incense, robes and kneelers was what led Edith Rignaldi downtown to the Episcopal church, named after that most difficult of apostles, St. Paul. Edith had always had a bit of a secret argument going with Paul, though it remained in the religious closet of her mind, along with the desire to kneel. She wondered about the apostle's "thorn in the flesh" and why—in her perhaps preoccupied reading—he seemed so preoccupied with sex. Were Christians, let alone apostles, really supposed to think about sex that much? Edith knew of no healthy precedent for this in the Protestant tradition, the only one she knew. The church history she'd studied began with the Reformation, with Martin Luther marrying a nun. As far as Edith remembered, the Church of England originated because Henry VIII wanted a divorce. Maybe Anglicanism, this vague, liberal space between Catholicism and Protestantism, could be a fresh start for her.

She was not encouraged on the first Sunday to find that the sermon was about the prophet Nahum. Edith was ashamed never to have read Nahum. But at least the sermon wasn't about Paul. Edith was further encouraged by its brevity (what could even the most ardent Hebraist say about Nahum?) and the service's climax in what these Episcopalians called the Eucharist. But afterward, something happened which, in all her years in church, Edith had never experienced or imagined. Church let out and the congregation poured into the "foyer," and there was a coffee machine set up. One of those giant percolators—not in the church basement or even in a fellowship hall, but right in church, practically in the sanctuary. And everyone gravitated toward the tables and had coffee in a kind of brown paper cup, not Styrofoam (Dana would be pleased). They were a white bunch, casually dressed, like this one lady in a blouse and black slacks who, horror of horrors, was headed straight for her.

"Good morning," the lady said, flashing all her teeth. She was the same height, and Edith looked straight into light brown eyes. "You visiting with us today?"

Her accent was Georgian, deep and rich. "Yes, ma'am," Edith said.

"I'm Linda Nye."

Of course you are. Every other woman their age was named Linda. "Nice to meet you, Linda. I'm Edith Rignaldi." She gripped the outstretched hand, and Linda pumped it vigorously.

"Good to have you here today, Edith."

She looked at Linda more closely. Linda appeared older, or at least her hair was grayer than Edith's: shoulder-length, silvery. She had trim nails, a politician's handshake and, Edith could not help but observe, little of that telltale flab on her upper arms. Maybe she had a job all day pumping people's arms up and down, alternating hands.

Linda had said something. "I beg your pardon?"

"We're getting together, a group of us, to study the role of women in the Bible." Linda smiled very broadly again, which somewhat unnerved Edith. "You're more than welcome to join us this evening," she said. "It's potluck."

Potluck did not sound very Episcopalian, as Edith had imagined it. And the last thing she needed right now was an intimate, chatty gathering of earnest feminists who all read New Testament Greek. On the other hand, she was looking for projects this summer, and it wouldn't hurt to make one of them social. "I'd love to," she said.

When Edith got home Dana was lying on the floor of her bedroom, head near the speakers of the infamous CD player. "Hi, Mom. How was church?"

"Fine." Edith judged the volume less than dangerous to young ears, and didn't move to turn it down. "I wish you'd come too, Dana."

"I told you, I'm not going to some church where I don't know anybody. What's the point, just for a few months?"

"You could have gone to church with your friends," Edith said. "I just don't feel comfortable going there myself."

"What friends?" Dana rolled her eyes. "I don't want to talk to anybody there. What would I say?"

"You don't have to say anything, Dana. It's none of their business."

Edith knew how hollow these words sounded. Dana said, "So, you want me to help with lunch?"

"Yes, please."

Edith wondered what state the kitchen would be in if Dana were left to make herself supper. "I was invited to a potluck study group tonight. Will you be okay here?"

Dana looked curious. "Sure. I picked up a new CD. We usually just have sandwiches on Sunday nights anyway."

Edith felt a sharp, unreasonable pang of maternal guilt, as she did almost every time she looked at her daughter these days. "I don't know what to do for lunch," she said.

"Why don't we just use some of this squash?" Dana said, picking up one of the yellow vegetables covering every inch of counter space. "It's coming out of our ears."

The potluck/Bible study was being held in the church basement. So they did have a basement. Edith left Dana to the accompaniment of some unintelligible rock song, which made her miss Jeremy. She arrived at the church, Corningware dish in hand. She'd baked the squash this time, little squashes cut lengthwise, stuffed with breadcrumbs, chopped tomatoes (those, too, fresh from the garden), sunflower seeds and only a sprinkling of cheddar cheese. It was the Nineties now, and cheese-and-sour-cream concoctions were things of the past.

When Edith got to the basement kitchen several ladies were removing foil wrap. "Glad you could come," Linda said. "Everybody, this is Edith. This is Nancy, Judy..." Edith smiled at each, still holding her own hot dish. "We're taking the food into that room," Linda said, gesturing.

"Yeah, don't want the men to smell it and come poking around," said Judy. Or was it Nancy?

Edith laughed a little, though her heart wasn't in it. She saw Linda give her a little smile, as if they were in on something together.

A few more ladies—women—arrived. One of them, Pat, who was leading the group, asked everyone to turn to the last chapter of Paul's letter to the Romans. A groan went up as those who were able to turn the pages faster (their Bibles were marked with special thumb tabs for this purpose) saw that the final chapter was essentially a list of names, Paul's thank-you list to those who had made this divinely inspired Oscar speech possible. "Oh, Pat," said one of the women whose name Edith didn't remember, "you said there wouldn't be any more begats."

"There aren't," Pat said. "In fact, unless someone here is still using the King James Version, the word begat shouldn't appear in your Bibles at all. And as I said the first week, the King James is an unreliable translation, riddled with—"

"May I interrupt for a second?" Linda said more quietly. "Sorry, Pat, but for Edith's benefit, I wonder if you could summarize a little of what we've talked about so far."

"Oh yes, of course." Pat turned and beamed at Edith through a pair of glasses attached to a chain around her neck. She didn't look old enough to be wearing them. "What we went over the first week was just a little of the history of the Bible, the merits of the various modern translations, and so forth. And the way the Bible has been read, in the past, and how women have been sort of left out of discussions of the Scriptures. And then last week, as Judy mentioned—" Pat gave Judy a well-bred nod—"we looked at the genealogy of Jesus, as given in the Gospels of Matthew and Luke. And we talked about the women mentioned there, like Ruth, whom we'll be talking about later. And also the women who aren't mentioned. For instance, in Luke, a totally different list of ancestors is given for Jesus' father—"

"His earthly father," Judy clarified.

"Yes, his earthly father, Joseph. Which has led to the conclusion that these are actually Mary's ancestors. Mary, the mother of Jesus," Pat concluded, as though Edith didn't know who Mary was.

She figured they'd get to Mary soon enough. You can take the church out of Rome, but..."I see. Thank you."

Pat began the discussion of Romans 16. As she went through it, woman by woman, Edith couldn't help but think that Pat spoke in the cadence of the King James she had criticized, beginning nearly every sentence with "And." She almost expected Pat to intone, "And it came to pass that Junia, the only known name close to this 'Junias,' is a female name…"

"What do you think, Edith?"

"I beg your pardon?"

Pat looked at her intently. Perhaps she was gathering prophetic force. "Why do you suppose this name has been mistranslated 'Junias' when the only known name is feminine?"

Edith looked in her King James, where it was Junia. She felt out of her depth. "A typo?"

Someone twittered. "A fault of the nib, perhaps," Pat allowed. "Judy?"

"Because it was assumed that people like these, Paul's 'kinsmen,' had to be male."

Edith looked back at her Bible. "But then why are all these other women's names here?" She ran her finger up the page, searching. "You know, Phebe—and Priscilla and Aquila, not the other way around. They're all in here before Junia or whoever it is. Why leave them in?"

"We're talking about the original Greek," Pat said, a little condescendingly. "What translation do you have there, Edith?"

Out of the corner of her eye Edith saw Linda, again with a little smile playing at the corners of her lips. "Edie," she said. "Call me Edie."

Dana had come home from her year with Tomas more sober than her freshman year, in every sense. Last summer her image had been rage, ripped jeans—she'd even told her mother people called her Dane now, though Mom had dismissed the nickname as something out of Hagar the Horrible.

This summer was altogether quieter. Dana figured it would

be her last one at home; she couldn't imagine spending her twenties in Poudre Valley. So she looked at it now as something receding into her past. She noticed the quality of the sunshine, something you never saw in Chicago, smelled the honeysuckle as though it had never bloomed before. She now wore her ripped jeans only for black raspberry picking, since the thorns would tear at her clothes anyway. It was a summer for letting go, and to someone who rarely felt release of any kind, it felt so good.

Mom had started going to the Episcopal church and her Sunday night women's group. This suited Dana, because it meant the summer squash was getting used up on someone other than her. It also gave her precious time alone, when she could turn her music up and dance through the house if she wanted. Mom wouldn't have minded, might have joined her in fact, who knows, but Dana was too self-conscious for that.

She noticed that Mom came home Sundays with a certain lifting of her spirits, which might or might not have been attributable to one Spirit in particular. Dana was fairly certain that Episcopalians did believe in the Holy Spirit, since they spoke of the Trinity and all. She herself was not so sure, but she knew that it would be unforgivable to say anything against the Holy Ghost, as she'd been taught to refer to that being.

Mom would come in now of a Sunday and prepare a big dinner, though it was just the two of them. She seemed happy that her teenage daughter, rather than worrying how her belly looked hanging over the waist of tight jeans, ate like a wolf. Often Dana would come to breakfast (which she wouldn't think of missing) to find sweet rolls on the table and Edith already busy with the Crock-Pot, making beef stew or something, for Dana had taken to eating meat again. Dana wondered if this was part of her mother's hearty sendoff to the fall and whatever they served in a college dining hall. It made her feel like a turkey being stuffed.

Mom seemed to have an abnormal interest in the Sunday night Bible study. Mom, who eschewed modern versions and appeared to fetishize her King James for literary rather than theological reasons. For her to come home all excited about women of the Bible, talking about prophetesses (or "women prophets") and Deborah the judge, noting the names of female disciples in the New Testament, was very disconcerting.

It was August, a few weeks before Dana's return to college, and they were picking black raspberries around the edge of the property where the honeysuckle hadn't choked them. Mom had taken to doing these things, which Joe had always done before, as a way of bonding or something. She was all got up in a plaid flannel shirt and a hat Dana had never seen before this summer. And the whole time she was explaining her discoveries in a way that sounded to Dana dangerously like a questioning of biblical authority—something Dana had been taught was unthinkable, like the sin of not going to church, though she did both herself.

"Wait a minute," she said. "Don't modern scholars also say that Paul couldn't have written most of those letters, and all kinds of other stuff?"

"I'm not talking about that kind of scholarship, Dana. You know we don't believe that. I'm talking about Christian scholars. Men, and women, of God."

Dana shook her head. "Mom, I've never heard you talk like this. You sound so feminist."

"I don't think it's so bad to be feminist," Mom said. "You're a bright young woman, Dana. Surely you believe that men and women are equal."

Dana didn't know which was more surprising, Mom's remark about feminism, or being called a woman instead of a girl. "I don't see why that's so feminist. It just seems humanist to me. I'm not interested in women, any more than men." This was not in every respect true, but she couldn't contemplate that now.

"I don't like that word," Edith said. "Humanist. It means putting human beings at the center of things, rather than God."

"Don't you mean putting 'man' at the center of things?" Dana didn't dare to joke about Goddess. "Anyway, that's secular humanism, like they're always saying in the news. I don't see why humanism has to be secular. Didn't God create man to be the pinnacle of all creation?"

"'Male and female created he them.'" Mom untangled

herself from a berry vine. "But that 'pinnacle of creation' idea is dangerous, Dana. It makes people reckless with their responsibilities to the earth God created. They should be stewards of creation, not just dominate it."

Dana shook her head. "I'm not believing this. Are you an environmentalist now too?"

"Well, I've never believed in waste," Mom said. "Why do you think I started taking Chinet to the potluck supper? It's better than Styrofoam."

Chapter 21

When Dana returned to school in the fall, the house became quiet again. Edith tried hard not to slip into the depression that so easily came with the season. Aunt Anna had always complained of nostalgia in the fall, then reminded her listeners that it was a sin to give in to it. Edith made a point of playing records again, and going to the high school football games. She usually sat with Pam, and cheering gave them something to do, where they didn't have to think of things to say.

Things had returned to normal at school, in the way the whole family had pretended life was normal after Jeremy's diagnosis with epilepsy. People talked to her, all on exactly the same level of superficiality as Pam. No one ever mentioned Joe. It was as if all Poudre Valley had by unspoken agreement put the memory of one resident behind them. Well, him and Clayton, and anyone with AIDS. Thinking about it only made Edith hate them, so she tried not to think.

Of course, she continued with the women's study group. One Saturday morning, while she was doing her breakfast dishes, Linda Nye phoned. "This is the most gorgeous October I ever remember. Let's go to the lake."

Resisting the instinct to hide, Edith said, "Okay. Do you want me to meet you?"

"I'll pick you up. Half an hour?"

She gave Linda directions to her house—Mountain Highway, turn left and watch your odometer. Then Edith returned to the sink. Even with four people she'd never been able to justify buying a dishwasher, yet she was amazed by the number of dishes even one person went through. The only thing keeping her from leaving them was the knowledge that the sink wouldn't hold another meal's worth. That, and a lifetime's habit, which seemed to be her reason for doing everything.

Linda was right; it was unbelievably warm for this time of year. Maybe they'd be able to dip their toes in the lake. Edith switched her long sleeves for a T-shirt and put on sandals. She wasn't quite sure why, but they'd never taken the kids to Unaka Lake, not even once. Their lives were always pointed west, toward what passed for town, never east toward North Carolina.

An old station wagon with fake wood paneling on the sides pulled into the driveway. Right on time. Edith rushed to the door, comb in hair. Joe had never been right on time for anything, and it astounded her that anyone was. That someone would do what she said, when she said she was going to do it.

Not to be outdone, Linda wore a white sleeveless shirt that showed off her lightly tanned arms. And she had that grin on her face that she wore for study group. For a moment Edith was nervous, lest she be required to keep up with Linda's wisecracking for an entire day. But Linda sounded almost shy. "Sorry about the car. I just threw everything in back."

She had, too. It was the kind of station wagon some of the other mothers used to drive when Edith's kids were in kindergarten, with the third backseat actually facing backwards. It was supposed to be safer, but Edith didn't think she could have stood having the kids that far back and not even looking at her. In Linda's case, the backseat was barely perceptible under piles of—not exactly trash, just paper bags that couldn't be told one from another, containing what looked to be paper, mostly. Construction paper? Not wanting to make her curiosity too obvious, she just climbed into the passenger seat. But Linda had noticed.

"It's my office," she said once they were both in the car. "I don't really want to keep carting this stuff in and out of my house, so I just keep it all in the car. I work at a day care."

So that explained the construction paper. Possibly the station wagon as well. "How long have you been doing that?"

"Twenty years," Linda said. "It's Central Baptist, where you can drop your kids off for the day, you don't have to sign them up for a regular class. It's always someone different."

The Rignaldis' driveway was not easy to get out of. You had to go in reverse uphill, and there was a big tree in the line of sight that had grown bigger since Joe's death but that Edith had never gotten cut. But Linda managed with no hesitation, shifting gears without even a break in the conversation.

"You didn't have any trouble getting here, I guess," Edith said. One of the kids' friends had been coming over once, and the mother must have been looking only at the odometer, not the houses, because when she finally got there she complained that Edith's directions had only been accurate to one decimal place. Edith was just grateful the woman hadn't plowed into anyone, or run off the road into a ditch.

"No, I know this road," Linda said. "Sometimes I give kids rides home—not so much now, but we used to do that, you know. One of the girls I worked with years ago lived out this way." She gestured to a subdivision that had been built in the Eighties. "Right after this, there's a little road, I think it's called Jeff Hyder." Edith nodded; roads here often had first and last names. "You go down that a little ways and it's a whole different world, I mean those little houses and trailers on foundations, with laundry strung over the porch."

"There's houses on Jeff Hyder that've been abandoned my whole life." Edith used to go poking around in there when she was a kid, found old wallpaper and everything. It was a wonder she hadn't picked up lockjaw. There was even a bathtub in one of the houses, one of the old kind, claw foot. All rust.

Linda turned down Jeff Hyder, as if she'd always meant to. Edith didn't ask for an explanation. They had to pull over into the ditch to allow a pickup truck to get through, since the road wasn't wide enough for two vehicles. The driver wore a John Deere cap, the type with foam in front and mesh in back, but he waved nicely enough, and the back of the truck was full of barking dogs. Linda smiled, waved as though she knew the man, but by the time Edith waved, it was strictly to the dogs.

"Do you know him?"

"I don't think so." Linda looked amused. "I just wave at everybody. It's not like they think I'm trying to pick them up; I'm almost sixty."

They pulled back onto the road and Edith wondered why everything Linda said made her feel odd. After all, she'd lived here all her life, and Linda was from Georgia. These were Edith's roads, even if she never walked anywhere—not all the dogs were friendly and fencing them in was unheard of. Not to mention what had happened to Isabella.

"So what made you go into day care?"

Linda looked straight in front of her, one hand on the wheel, but her eyes flicked back and forth to the side and rear view mirrors automatically, like blinking. "It was the best way I could think of to spend a whole lot of time with kids."

"You like kids."

"Love them. But you know, when they're not yours, you can just send them home at the end of the day."

"Or drive them." Edith wondered if Linda had wanted kids of her own, but it wasn't a question she could imagine asking. Linda wasn't married, said she never had been, and this wasn't Murphy Brown country. Whether and why—you just didn't ask someone questions that personal about kids. Well, Aunt Anna would.

Linda turned on the radio at one point—it was an old car radio and she turned an actual knob, not those preset buttons you just hit in the newer cars. Both the dashboard and the sunlight falling across it were a golden color, and the dashboard had a crack running through it from just above the glove compartment almost to the steering column. Edith rested her eyes along the crack, feeling a strange affection for it.

The radio was tuned to a country station. Glen Campbell singing "Rhinestone Cowboy." Edith vaguely remembered liking his other hit song but wasn't crazy about this one. It was followed by Willie Nelson's "On The Road Again," which she did like. She had a lot of respect for Willie Nelson, the work he did for farmers. People didn't take him seriously, or realize the length of time he'd been writing songs.

"He wrote one of Patsy Cline's hits, you know," she said.

Linda looked over at her for the first time in a while. "'Crazy.'"

"That's right," Edith said. "I don't really like country music, but—"

"I didn't think so."

Edith smiled a little. "So why'd you turn it on?"

"I don't know. I mean I just didn't—Let me change the station." Edith wondered why Linda was so flustered, not leaving the knob alone until Nat "King" Cole crooned "Unforgettable" out of the crackly speakers.

They ended up at Unaka Lake and the sun was brilliant, but there was no one around. Slaves of the calendar, thinking summer was long over despite what it felt like outside. For some reason, Edith was glad. She had all the solitude she wanted at home, and yet it was nice to be in another environment, outside but not parading the grounds of her own house. The edge of the lake was sand and Georgia clay and she took off her tennis shoes and walked barefoot, carrying the shoes by their laces around her wrist. Linda walked behind her, and every so often Edith would glance back and Linda was always looking, smiling only when she caught her glance.

Edith wished they'd brought a Frisbee or something. It had been years since she even ran, but this weather brought the ghost of athleticism to her body memory. There was that sense of trying to cheat winter; a fall day like this was handed to her like a gift.

These were not things one said aloud. But Edith found herself doing so, a bit later when they'd found a sandbank tucked behind some scraggly things that had once been bushes, and

Linda asked if she'd like to sit down. They hadn't been walking for long and it didn't seem necessary to rest, but for once Edith wasn't in a hurry. Nothing felt worth rushing back to.

She couldn't remember a day like this one since she and Pam were in school together. In their teenage years they'd had everything in common and would just talk, it didn't matter about what, just run their mouths as girls did. Pam had been her best friend, something she hadn't thought of in some time, and it pained her now to remember that she didn't have a best friend anymore.

"We should have brought lunch," she said.

"Are you hungry?"

"No." It wasn't even noon. "But it's nice here, it'd be nice to sit here and eat."

Linda was looking at her, a little too closely if she wasn't mistaken. "Do you still eat meals at the same time? Now that nobody's in the house with you?"

"Usually. It's a habit."

"What else do you do out of habit?"

Edith stared back. People didn't ask questions like this, they just didn't. It thrilled her. "Most things. I get up the same time every morning."

"What time?"

"Six. And I've been doing it for all the years I've been teaching school and all the years my kids were in school, but I hate it, every day I hate it. I always pack my lunch then because I can never stand to do it the night before, and then in the morning I have to and just the thought of lunch food at that time makes me sick. Of course at school, we have to eat at the same time every day, it's the only time we have. And I can't stand up in front of a classroom and snack, so that's it." It was unaccountable why Linda should be interested in listening to these details. "You work with kids, you must know."

Linda shook her head. "Not about you."

It continued like that, Linda asking things that seemed inconsequential and Edith finding what an astonishing amount she had to say in response. She half sensed that Linda was circling around something, that there was something deeper at the heart of this Socratic method, and she found it when Linda said, "I don't reckon you want to talk about your husband, do you."

"He was killed."

"I know that."

"He was bashed."

Linda raised one eyebrow at her. Edith found herself, irrelevantly, wishing she knew how to do that.

"These bashers," she said with some effort, "I don't know who they are, these guys, you've heard of them. They just go looking for someone and when they find him, they put him in the hospital. Well, Joe never came home from the hospital."

Her throat was very dry. She was aware of saying things aloud she hadn't before, and they sounded distant and passionless. Linda said, "They didn't catch anybody."

"No, they did not. My cousin Charlie's with the police, but he's a disgrace. He couldn't find his way out of a burlap bag. It could've been anybody, even cops."

"Doesn't sound like you have much hope for an answer."

Edith felt she sounded more bitter than angry. She didn't want Linda to think she was without emotion. "All rednecks are the same," she said. "Even if they knew, they'd protect each other over something like this. They're just one step removed from the Klan."

"Why aren't you scared of them?"

"I don't think I have any ability left to be scared," she said. "I was scared before it happened and then it did."

"Before it happened?"

Edith closed her eyes. "Few years ago, somebody called me, I don't know who. Said I should watch my husband too, around this guy. Said the guy was—you know." She blinked. "It could have been anybody. Why should they be after me though?"

Linda's eyes were on her, the color of hazelnut. "Why should they have been after Joe?"

She felt her husband's name strike her, like a sharp drop of sleet. "Because he was a homosexual," she said, but quietly, as if someone might hear. "I knew it, I knew when he married me."

"But that's not why he was killed."

Edith made a harsh sound. “I don’t know how you know so much. It was a bashing, I said—”

They say with age you get the face you deserve, and Linda’s shone with perception. “A fag-bashing, yes. Believe me, I know what you’re talking about. But they don’t bash people because they are homosexuals, just because they think they are.”

“Okay. Why are we talking about this? Are you the private eye that’s going to solve all this for me? Or the bodyguard that’s going to protect me? If they were going to come after me, they’d have done it by now.”

“I’m sorry, I truly am, not to be either of those things,” Linda said. “I’d do anything to help you and I’d do it for free. Then I’d be broke and have to get a second job.”

Edith caught herself about to laugh. What was this woman doing to her? “You have to remember, Joe died two years ago. It’s not that I’m over it, it’s just—I’m beyond certain feelings. Part of me died and was buried. So in a way, they got me, too.”

“And you hate them.”

“We can’t hate,” Edith said, feeling like they were back in Sunday school. “We’re called to forgive, I know that, but—”

“Whoa.” Linda put her hands up as though reining her in. “Forgive whom? You don’t even know who these people are.”

“You don’t have to keep at it.”

“No—this is important, Edie. Even if you knew these—murderers, how are you supposed to forgive them? It’s not like they’ve apologized to you.”

“It wouldn’t be for them.”

“We are not called to forgive,” Linda said, “until someone repents. Even then, we can only forgive something done to us. Not to somebody else.”

Edith didn’t have the Gospels open in front of her, but this put her on guard. Because when someone corrected her about something biblical, it always sounded like trying to justify sin.

The next thing Linda said surprised her. “Were you angry at Joe?”

“For getting killed? Yes.”

“For everything else.”

“I wasn’t angry because of who he was. And I couldn’t be

angry at him for lying, because he was always honest with me." No need to talk about the other stuff now. "I chose to do what I did, to stay."

"Were you always honest?"

It suddenly infuriated Edith, being looked at like that out of the corners of someone's eyes. It felt like she was being cut into. "It's not dishonest not to tell someone everything. And why should I tell you?"

Linda didn't reply. The two of them looked out on the lake, in the fall light that made you squint and wonder where your sunglasses were. Well, Edith knew where hers were. They were always in the glove compartment, in her own car, which she was used to having wherever she went. It was strange, this feeling of being out for the day, she wasn't quite sure why, with someone she was only beginning to know. It was an experience grownups, people past their school or college years, didn't seem to have. With a date, maybe, if they were at that point again, but not with a friend. Grownups, if they went out for a day with anybody not related to them, it was an old friend, someone they knew like a sister. Edith felt as if she'd been grown up for a very long time.

They stopped talking about Joe but there were other topics, wide-ranging like the arc of birds in flight over Unaka Lake, and through the afternoon a thread of light, glinting gold in the corners of Linda's eyes. She had crow's-feet so deep it sometimes looked as if they were ready to walk away. Edith hoped she would look that wise in fifteen years.

"How many times have you been in love?" Linda asked. Her voice was so quiet, with the depth of still waters, that Edith looked over at her, startled. But there was no eye contact. Linda just gazed across the lake, as if Edith's answer could be read there.

"Once," she said. "I guess."

"And how many times have you been in love," Linda said, "and then later decided that you hadn't really, because it fit the narrative of your life better to believe that?"

Edith was astonished. "People don't talk this way, Linda."

"I do." She said it with the solemnity of the wedding vow.

Chapter 22

1993

Tomas Jefferson was everything that no friend of Dana's had ever been before: black, regally intelligent and attractive. This last confused Dana a bit since she had long prided herself on being above all that, unlike everyone else in Poudre Valley and, especially, her parents. In fact she had announced, upon her arrival at the university, that she was asexual. Just in case anybody assumed.

"I think you've got something there," was Tomas's comment on asexuality.

They were out for a Saturday night pizza. The cafeteria was closed and, since Tomas always seemed to be on the studying clock, she could not fit in a long social evening. Hence, their ritual dinner, an hour and a half out from their time for studying, no more.

"Did you always want to be a doctor?" Dana said.

Tomas looked at her watch; they'd ordered the pizza five minutes ago. "Yeah, I did. My parents encouraged me. They're both doctors."

"Sort of the family business."

"Sort of. But I wanted to for myself as well. It seems like the ultimate profession."

Dana raised her eyebrows, knowing Tomas would mistake this for an expression of awe.

"No, really," Tomas said. "It's the hardest to get into, I mean of real professions, not like playing for the Bulls. If you're smart, if you want to study the hardest subjects—"

"And help people."

"Yeah, sure. That too." Tomas put a hand on the back of her chair, shifted around. The waitress was nowhere in sight.

"So, will you be a surgeon, or—"

"I haven't decided on a specialty yet. You don't even have to be a bio major to get into med school."

"But you've known all your life," Dana said. "I mean, weren't you pre-med in prep school or something?"

"It wasn't 'prep school.' The public schools are just shitty where I'm from."

Dana doubted that any school was "shitty" in a suburb as wealthy as Tomas's, but she knew better than to say so. Tomas wore her privilege as lightly as the name of a slave-owning Founding Father. She would have mocked any student, black, white, or otherwise, who questioned her. There was no sense of irony but there was a great sense of being chosen, of having been given great gifts with which she was in turn to bless the world. It was an utterly unfamiliar combination to Dana, and an intoxicating one.

When they'd first roomed together the only black musician in Dana's music collection was Tracy Chapman. The tape had a song about Nelson Mandela and was vaguely folk. Tomas laughed at this, and said if Dana was into that kind of thing why didn't she just play Marvin Gaye?

"Oh—was he the one that did 'I Heard It Through The Grapevine'?" she said, thinking of the raisin commercial.

Tomas just shook her head and pulled *What's Going On* from an impressive and alphabetically ordered collection of CDs. Dana's education proceeded apace, with Tomas slipping in Sly and the Family Stone and En Vogue, bending her ebony neck as she fiddled with the settings on a compact but overly elaborate stereo.

It turned out Tomas was rather idealistic, she just didn't like to say. She had emerged from a demographic Dana wasn't aware existed outside *The Cosby Show*. She hadn't qualified for a dollar's worth of need-based financial aid, though she did tell Dana she thought she should have gotten some scholarship on the grounds of pure merit. Dana was shocked by this. It had never occurred to her that there were people who could afford a college education on their own. She wondered what interest Tomas had in her.

It seemed her Southernness provided a certain connection. Tomas had relatives in Tennessee, though she rarely saw them. "Most black folks have family down South," Tomas said. "That's where our roots are. Although I would like to go to Africa."

"Me too," Dana said.

"What, as a missionary?" Tomas was always poking fun at Dana's church background. Dana had thought all black people went to church.

"No. Just to explore." That wasn't the right word either. "I'd like to see the snows of Kilimanjaro."

Tomas snorted. "Before global warming melts it all."

Edith often talked to Linda extensively after Bible study. She was the first friend she'd made in ages. When, in early January, Edith was ready to have someone in her home again, Linda was the only person she wanted to invite.

Over chicken enchiladas, Linda mentioned that what they were doing was in itself subversive. "Like Anne Hutchinson, the early American who was thrown out of her church for discussing the sermons."

"And for saying Indians shouldn't be slaves. I know who Anne Hutchinson was."

Edith loved their discussions but she was defensive too, and never more than at her own kitchen table. If she thought the living room would be more relaxing, it wasn't. Linda went straight for the picture on the mantel. "Dana's graduation from high school," Edith explained. "That's Jeremy next to her."

Linda quirked an eyebrow. She noticed the fine lines, decades of laughter around the light brown eyes. "How come you never talk about them?"

There Linda went again, starting a conversation in a way she didn't expect. Anybody else would ask "How old are they now?" or "Are they in school?" But Linda only seemed to be interested in her.

"I don't care to be one of those women who's forever talking about her kids. Or her grandkids," she added, mindful that Linda was older, not knowing whether that made it better or worse.

Linda laughed out loud. She had a beautiful smile; her teeth looked almost too perfect, except they weren't unnaturally white. "Well, no danger of that from me. You are a mother. Stands to reason you'd want to talk about your kids."

But that would mean I'd have to talk about their father. "Dana's up in Chicago," she said. "It's a long ways away. But I went to college there too."

Linda nodded. "And how about Jeremy? What's he doing?"

"I don't know," Edith said, her misery bubbling to the surface.

"Isn't he in touch with you?"

"Jeremy had a hard time when his daddy—with everything that happened to Joe. He'd been through a lot himself. He has epilepsy, you know."

"No," Linda said with a gentle smile, "I don't know. You never told me anything about him, Edie."

"I hardly know him." It was a sad truth, which she had certainly never spoken aloud before. "I never understood Jeremy, even though he was my son. Is my son. All he ever cared about was music—"

"Is he talented?"

"What?" She swiped at her eyes.

"Is Jeremy a talented musician?"

"I suppose so."

"But you wanted him to care about something else."

"Anything else! School, girls—I mean I didn't want him getting in trouble, but Linda, what if he was like Joe?"

"Or like me." Linda squared her strong shoulders.

Edith didn't know where to put herself. "I'm sorry. That was an awful thing to say."

They sat down on the couch. "So what, he just disappeared?"

"He calls Dana once in a while. He doesn't want to talk to me. I must have been a terrible mom, for him to hurt me so."

"Oh, Edie." Linda rested a warm hand on the back of her neck. "It sounds like he has a lot to work out. Besides making a living, that takes up most of everybody's time. And epilepsy is serious. How did you react when you all found out about it?"

Edith swallowed. "I tried to act like nothing had changed."

"But it was a big change."

She wanted to lean into that warmth, but Linda had taken her hand away. Too quickly. "I wanted Jeremy to feel normal. Like he could still do anything, be anything. He was already having trouble in school, he didn't need any more pressure."

Linda's face was so expressive Edith felt as if she could see little thoughts forming along the nerves, under the skin. She wanted to stroke her cheek, but did not.

"It must seem like you've been waiting forever," Linda finally said, "but it takes time to get over the loss of a father."

"I know."

After a moment's silence Linda asked, "What about Joe? Do you believe he was wrong, Edie?"

"To do what he did? Yes, of course. He ruined his life." She would have said "our lives," but her own life wasn't feeling quite as ruined lately.

"But to be who he was," Linda said. "Was that wrong?"

"I don't know." Everything in Edith's life went against this. Not just the religious teaching but her entire life's experience. She'd been married to a homosexual all those years, she'd had every chance to think it through. "I married the wrong man."

"Oh no, Edie," Linda said, and there was that glint in her eyes. "You married exactly the right man."

"I can't imagine what you mean by that."

"The right man to love and take care of. The right man to learn with, grow with, have children with. The right man to love and take care of you. At least—"

"Please," Edith said. She couldn't bear to hear this now.

"I was going to say, not that you need anyone to take care of you. Edie, listen. Is this really about the Bible?"

"You know it is."

"I mean is it about the Bible? Or is it about the church, and what the church has said?" Edith started to speak, but Linda held up her hand and continued. "I don't just mean your church, our church, I mean the church, everybody, historically. Everybody has told you it's wrong, but is it them you believe? Or the Bible?"

"The Bible does say it's wrong, Linda."

"Who in the Bible? The Book of Leviticus?"

"Yes, and Paul."

"Our old friend St. Paul." Linda smiled; it looked almost derisive. "Paul said a lot of things, Edie. Do you believe in slavery too?"

"That's not relevant."

"Oh, yes it is."

"Slaves—back then it was different." They'd had this conversation before, about wine versus grape juice. "It's not like racist slavery, the way—"

"Okay, women then." Linda didn't hesitate to interrupt. Joe never used to interrupt her. "You think what Paul says about women is irrelevant? Hell, what's the point in even talking?"

Edith's cheeks colored; she would have to speak quickly to keep up. "I'm not sure I see your point. Are you saying we can disregard biblical teaching because there are things in the Bible we don't like? You're acknowledging it, then. You're saying it is against the Bible and you just don't like it. The entire culture may be that way, Linda," she said, knowing how much like Aunt Anna she sounded. "But I don't believe it. And I didn't think you believed it either."

Linda closed her eyes briefly. Oh, she's handsome. Edith squelched the thought in an instant.

"These passages. Supposing they apply to modern homosexual people—though we could argue about that, too. More than about slavery, for heaven's sake." Linda took a breath. "What did Jesus say on the subject?"

"In the Gospels?"

"In the Gospels, Edie. Did Jesus ever mention it in the Bible?" Linda didn't wait for an answer. "Not a word. Didn't say anything about masturbation, either. Hey, that one's free, I read it in James Dobson before he got all political."

Edith was too shocked to say anything. Linda went on. "Now see, Dr. Dobson didn't point out what else Jesus never mentioned. But I know. Do you know how many chapters there are in the New Testament?"

"Chapters? No."

"Two hundred and sixty. That's five for each week of the year. I've been reading them since I was a girl—one time through every year. Now I'm not saying that makes me a better Christian or anything else. It doesn't make me better, but it makes me better informed. Nobody can tell me what the Bible says, because I know."

Edith spoke, almost in a whisper. "'It is impossible but that offences will come: but woe unto him through whom they come! It were better for him that a millstone were hanged about his neck, and he cast into the sea.'"

Linda recoiled as if she had been slapped. "Is that what you think I am? A stumbling block?"

"Jesus said that, Linda."

"Let me tell you what I think," Linda said, her eyes narrowed. "There are a lot of things written under Paul's name and none by Jesus. Paul was an apostle." She paused, looked as if she were about to give a testimonial in Edith's former church. "But Jesus is Lord."

The impact of this statement was not lost on Edith; it was the confession of faith. "You're going to sit here," she said, "and say that Jesus is your Lord and Savior like—like you're being born again right here in my living room?"

"I'm telling you what I believe, Edie." All the energy appeared to have gone out of Linda. "I'm not telling you what you should believe."

"Well, that makes a change," she said, and forced a smile. "I mean, not for you—I mean a change from people who are always trying to convert—you know."

"I'm not trying to convert you to anything." It astonished Edith how age and weariness could flash into Linda's face, almost as if she were willing them there. "I'm talking about me, not about you. Nobody knows you. Not even you."

Edith stared at her. At that moment, she wanted with everything in her to touch this woman, but she resisted the impulse. "I appreciate your confidence in me."

Linda put her hands on the table and raised herself up by it. "I'll take that as my cue to leave," she said. "Will I see you Sunday?"

Edith forced a smile, though the last thing she wanted to think about now was going to church. "Sure."

Linda left, without their hug at the door. The customary Christian greeting no longer felt right. Everything was awkward now, and Edith felt a surge of anger, mixed with something else. What she most needed now was to be alone. Alone with her thoughts, her nightly bathroom rituals, the cotton nightgown that connected her to an innocent time in her life.

In bed, Edith could not calm down. What had this woman done to her? She was forty-four years old and had never been comfortable touching herself, it had never brought her pleasure. So little had, sexually anyway. Damn you, Linda, she thought, and felt even guiltier. Well, if Jesus never mentioned it in the Bible...God, how big an issue could it be, a woman alone, just trying to get to sleep. She stroked more firmly, more quickly, allowed herself a little gasp. She wanted a cigarette but it was foolish to smoke in bed, so she just slid into sleep.

Chapter 23

Edith didn't have Linda over to the house again, but she kept going on Sundays. The women fascinated her, not just Linda but all of them, staking their claim on the Bible and talking about everything, as if there were nothing in life unrelated and unconnected to it. They didn't talk about *that*, however.

During Lent, when Edith was accustomed to the church turning inward and urging her to reflect on her own soul and her own sins, the women's study group turned outward. Pat had heard of an opportunity to go as witnesses to Africa—not Christian witnesses as Edith was used to the term, but to bear witness to some kind of peacemaking in a country Edith had never heard of. "I think Christian witnesses should be in Arusha while these peace talks are going on," Pat said. "To show that we're not all missionaries."

Edith was going to ask what was wrong with missionaries, but Linda spoke up first. "There's nothing wrong with mission, Pat."

"Well, no. In the sense that a mission means you're being

sent by somebody, but I don't know who would send, in this instance. The church won't pay for it."

Linda shrugged. "God."

"Are you going to go, Pat?" Nancy asked, reaching for another of the flaky pastries that someone had brought in.

"Oh—I can't," Pat said, and sat up straight in her chair. "The kids, you know. But someone should go."

They all looked around the table, waiting for an anointing of some kind. Finally, Judy said, "Linda, you don't have kids."

"No, I don't." Linda's voice was tight. Edith was tempted to reach for her hand, but knew how ridiculous that would be.

"You could go."

"Excuse me," Edith said, her voice sounding loud and high as it always did in that room, with all these women who spoke Aramaic or something. "Can someone explain where and what this is? Is Arusha in South Africa?" She had, at least, heard about the changes that were going on there.

"This is East Africa," Pat said. "Tanzania." Something Eric Dufresne had once said came back to Edith. "They're meeting in Arusha to make peace in the region. It's a time of great hope on the continent."

"Who is meeting? I mean, if these are politicians, then what difference—"

"We can't leave governing to the politicians," Nancy said. "We have to bear witness."

Edith resisted saying "To whom?" Instead, she asked what exactly this trip would involve. A flurry of brochures soon made it clear that what Pat had found out about was a kind of safari, with game-viewing drives. There was a lunch in Arusha one day, in the same hotel where the peace talks were going on. Edith wanted to know how that was witnessing or a mission, but she didn't say anything.

"The best deal is if four people go," Pat was saying. "Of course, we could add a fifth person if she was willing to pay the single supplement."

"And how do we decide who's the fifth?" Linda said, but Judy was already waving her hand.

"Whoa whoa whoa whoa whoa," she said. "I can't go."

"Why not?"

"Kids," Judy said, although even Edith knew Judy's kids were thirty years old. "Besides, there's no way Robert would—"

"Let you?" Nancy snorted. "There's no way Robert would what? Judy, I'm surprised at you."

Judy's face reddened. "There's no way Robert would ever understand my spending all that money," she said, "to go somewhere without him. We haven't been anywhere for years."

"Oh, well, if you have to go everywhere with your husband—"

"Yes." Edith surprised herself by standing up. "Go places with your husband. While you still have a husband. You too," she said to Nancy. "I know you've got better things to do than go to Africa. You know, just because you all are Episcopalians I'm tired of acting like everybody is filthy, stinking rich. You think three thousand dollars is a deal? We paid that for a car. New. It's sixteen years old now. Maybe I can drive it to Africa." She was suddenly very tired, and pushed back from the table; her cup was knocked over but it was empty anyway. "I have to go." She grabbed Joe's trench coat from the closet and opened the door.

"Edie," she heard behind her in the parking lot. "Edie, wait."

She turned around and said, "Don't do this. Don't make this into a spectacle."

"Let's go on this trip," Linda said. "Everybody else is bailing out. Haven't you always wanted to go to Africa? I'll go with you."

"Yeah, well, I'll call you when I have three thousand dollars."

"Edie." Linda took her arm; it was the first time they'd touched since..."I'm asking you to go. I can't spend all my money on construction paper."

Edith looked at her. Then she said very softly, "I won't be at church next week. I'm visiting Dana on my spring break."

The thing Dana noticed most that spring, when it finally came, was how much seemed to have changed since she was a kid. She was scarcely an adult but childhood seemed hundreds of years ago. On this particular afternoon what threw her off was the sight of a little kid walking with her father, and him pulling an even smaller child behind them in a wagon. Or what looked like a wagon. In fact, Dana noted with alarm, this contraption was plastic and turquoise, and had high walls like a box. For safety, she supposed. It bore no resemblance to what Dana thought of as a wagon, which was necessarily red, and metal, and shallow enough that a child could easily topple out.

When had she last seen a little red wagon? Did they even make them out of metal anymore? The possibility that they didn't bothered her intensely. It was busy on the street but she still heard, cutting through the din of shopping, the alien sound of plastic wheels and the muffled babble of helmet-wearing children.

She shielded her own eyes from the sun, pausing in front of a large stone church before continuing further east toward the restaurant where she was meeting Mom for lunch. Mom would be coming from that direction, driving down along the lake, and at the moment Dana wished she could just continue walking, let Mom drive by without noticing, and walk right down to the lake, if not into it. It seemed, on a day like today, more important to see the lake and to spend time with it than to waste time on something as plain as eating, or talking to her mother.

It wasn't that Dana didn't want to see her. She just had nothing to say to her today. Mom could never understand that, and neither could anyone else. Dana talked a lot, everybody said so, so no one could believe that there were times when she didn't have anything to say. Or did, and didn't want to say it. That probably seemed even stranger.

Driving south along the lake toward where she was to meet Dana, Edith felt that she was going the wrong way. In the mornings hordes of people would be stuck on Lake Shore Drive, commuting north into the downtown, and back the other way after work. But she had the quiet side of the road. She never wanted to come down here in the evenings. She didn't think she was afraid of the city after dark, but no one would blame her if she were.

She'd rather be at home today, working in her garden, not in Chicago at all. It was such a sunny day and spring here didn't compare. That, however, did not seem like something she could say on the phone to Dana and have her understand. Even to Edith, it didn't seem justifiable for a still young, healthy woman to want to spend all her time at home or pottering around outdoors. That was something older women did. Edith wasn't sure at what age a woman was really old; she kept pushing the idea of old forward as she herself got older, and now it had to be older than sixty, older than Linda at least.

Dana could see her mom walking up the sidewalk. Late, as usual, but then so was she. All their lives the Rignaldis had worked at the art of being just a little bit late for every appointment, ten minutes or less, not quite late enough to have to call but just enough for the other party to have to wait, and sigh, and check their watch, and shuffle their feet, all of which Dana had done discreetly before Mom came into view. As it was still morning the sun threw Mom's shadow just slightly to the west, the direction in which she was walking, and Dana had the feeling of being approached first by the shadow and then (only reluctantly) by her mother.

"Hi, Dana," Mom said in what Dana always heard as a slightly clipped tone.

"Hi." She pointed to the restaurant. "This still okay with you?" Mom nodded. Dana's asking was a reflexive politeness, no doubt acquired from her mother, because she wouldn't have considered meeting anywhere else.

They went inside. There was never a wait here. The walls were still yellowish-brown, a kind of tobacco-stain color that somehow, in all this sunlight from the south-facing front windows, looked cheerful. The windows were large, letting in the maximum amount of sunshine. Dana found seats where she always sat, right in front.

Soup arrived and they scooped it to their mouths silently, mother and daughter almost a mirror image of each other's restrained movements. Edith wondered whether Dana—or

"Dane"—were too thin, mentally compared Dana to even thinner women she knew who truly were too thin, decided that there was nothing wrong with the way her daughter was eating.

"So Mom," Dana said between spoonfuls, "how's it going? What have you been up to at home?"

Edith thought of the women's study group, and described for Dana the trip Linda wanted her to go on. To her surprise, Dana was very excited. "That's great, Mom! When?"

"Well, of course we're not going," Edith said, her tone suddenly less bright, appropriate for the indoors.

"What? Why not?"

"It's way too expensive."

"I thought it was some kind of mission trip," Dana said with her mouth full.

"Not exactly. Sounds more like tourism."

"So you contribute economically. Come on, Mom, when are you ever going to get a chance like this again? Me and Tomas would go if we could, we were just talking about it the other day."

Yes, Tomas. Tomas and Dane. Did anyone go by a normal name anymore?

Dana glanced at the card on the table illustrating desserts. "I'm going to get some bread pudding."

"I don't think I'll have any. It looks nice, but I'm too full."

When they had finished, Edith touched up her lipstick and smacked her lips together in an automatic motion she had performed thousands, if not tens of thousands of times. She put the lipstick back in her clutch and, also automatically, pulled out money to pay for their lunch.

"Thanks, Mom."

"I know you have class this afternoon," Edith said. "But let's go to a ball game while I'm up here. Tomas too."

"Sure," Dana said.

Dana didn't want Tomas to think her mother was ignorant, so before she brought up baseball, she mentioned the trip to Africa, implying that Mom was actually going.

"With her church? Is she a missionary?"

Dana made a face. "I wouldn't say that. I mean they're not going to convert the natives or anything."

"Sub-Saharan, though, that's exciting," Tomas said, unwittingly teaching Dana another new word. "I'd love to do development work. What I'd really like to be part of is something on the ground, like working with AIDS patients. Not that I could do much until I'm a doctor."

"Right." Dana had been so fixated on the problems of her own family it had never occurred to her that AIDS was in Africa, too. "Do a lot of Africans have AIDS?"

Tomas stared at her. "Unbelievable numbers. But nobody famous. Well, unless you count Freddie Mercury; he was born in Zanzibar, you know."

"No kidding. Where exactly is Zanzibar?"

"Jesus, Dana." She winced but Tomas didn't notice. "It's part of Tanzania, the country your mom and her friends are going to. There's fantastic scuba diving. I'd like to do that too."

"Wow, Freddie Mercury," Dana said. "I didn't know he was from Africa."

"There are a lot of folks from that part of the world who aren't African. Europeans, people of Indian origin."

"But if they live in Africa, aren't they all African?" Tomas looked skeptical. "Guess it's a minefield, huh?"

"I wouldn't use that word, either." Tomas fished in her satchel for a magazine, something serious and important, all black-and-white pictures. "Here." The article had a picture of a black African child, a little girl bent intently over some string she was winding.

"What's she doing, making a friendship bracelet?"

Tomas looked vastly annoyed. "Playing, I guess. It's not child labor."

"I wasn't even thinking about that," said Dana, who indeed had never given child labor a thought in her life.

"This is *The Economist*," Tomas said. "It's great but I never have time to read it. I bet you would. You can't have more studying than I do."

Choosing to overlook this last remark, Dana said, "I was

thinking of majoring in economics."

"Why?"

"Why not? It's one of the best departments we have here. It's probably the only practical major there is, for a non-scientist."

"I don't know why there's such an anti-science prejudice," Tomas said, warming up to one of her favorite complaints. "What are we all supposed to study—classics? Don't people know all those great scientists used Latin? They were humanists too."

"I don't have an anti-science prejudice," Dana said. "It's not as if I try to avoid science. I came to this university on purpose, and I have to take two years of science no matter what I major in."

"Econ. Who are you going to work for, Arthur Andersen?"

"They recruit here a lot. It's probably a great place to get a job. Somebody told me about a girl who graduated a few years ago and started at fifty thousand dollars a year or something."

Tomas said, "Do you even know what she did?"

"I don't care. My parents are teachers. I've never known anybody who made that much money in my life."

"Money isn't everything," Tomas intoned, in the manner of someone who had never lacked for money.

"It's different for you," Dana said. "You've always known you wanted to go into medicine."

"Well, if you don't work for Arthur Andersen," Tomas went on with a curl of her lip, "maybe you can work for a pharmaceuticals company."

"Yeah. They're great for researching cholesterol. But how much money is there for AIDS and stuff in the developing world?"

Tomas winked satanically, lifted her cup. "The markets are efficient."

It was comforting to be going to a baseball game again. Edith hadn't been to this kind of sporting event since Joe left the church ball team. They climbed to their seats, high in the stands of the new Comiskey Park, and then Dana went to get hot dogs and drinks.

Tomas wasted no time in getting acquainted. "So, I hear you're going to Africa."

"Oh," Edith said. "Well, a friend of mine was interested in going. But it's a package trip for four people, and no one else seems to be able to go. I—"

"That's no problem," Tomas said. "We'd love to go."

"We?"

"Dana and I."

Edith would need to ask Dana about this when she got back, but the game was about to begin. "Are you a baseball fan?" she asked Tomas.

"Not really. I don't have a lot of hobbies, I'm afraid."

"Yes, Dana tells me you're planning to go to medical school."

"That's right."

Well, what was there to say about that? What did you go to medical school for, other than to be a doctor? "You know, I saw Larry Doby here in 1959."

"Who's Larry Doby?" Tomas said.

Edith tried not to show surprise; after all, Tomas said she wasn't a baseball fan. "He was the first black player in the American League."

"What about Jackie Robinson?"

"Oh yes, he was the first in the major leagues. But Larry Doby helped the Cleveland Indians win the pennant." The year she was born.

"Oh, the Indians." Tomas rolled her eyes till all Edith could see was white. "Real P. C."

"We came up to Chicago just that once," she said. "I was ten years old...no, it was summer, I must have been eleven. My parents brought me to see the big city. The only time I was ever up here." Edith felt she was already talking too much, and talked faster. "Anyway I always loved baseball, and I begged to be taken to a baseball game, so my Uncle Jones brought me here. I brought my glove—"

She stopped her story when Dana returned with the hot dogs. She had to unwrap each one to check, because Tomas hated onions and Dana couldn't stand relish. Edith wondered what had become of the vegetarianism. In high school, it seemed, Dana would only eat green things. But then she'd gone through that "Dane" phase too. Only waited the exact amount of time it would take to get used to the new name before she switched back.

Before Edith could ask what Dana had said to Tomas about the trip, Dana said, "So how is everybody, Mom?"

"Who?"

"The relatives." Dana said to Tomas, "My mom has about a million aunts and uncles and cousins."

"Well, you know, I don't see them that much, since they all go to the Methodists." She hoped she didn't have to explain everything to Dana's friend; on the other hand, she dreaded the thought that Tomas already knew.

"Have you been back at all?"

"Only for Uncle Claude's funeral."

Dana's eyes went wider. "I didn't even know he died."

"Yeah, you did, Dana. I know I told you that. The funeral was just after the last time you were home; there was no way you could have been there."

"It's creepy, anyway, with the body laid out." Dana spoke again to Tomas, a hand to one side of her mouth (Edith figured she wasn't worthy of having food blocked from her view). "In the South, funerals are really gross. They lay the body out for everyone to touch it."

"I know," Tomas said. "We have them too."

Neither of them was watching the game. Edith turned her eyes toward the field, tired of Dana's chewed-up hot dog and the looks those two kept giving each other, like a secret code.

She watched the players but her mind was still on Uncle Claude and the last time she'd seen him alive, slumped back in a chair, as waxen as in death. Really, he'd looked better at the funeral. She'd only come by to visit because Aunt Lanie had called and insisted that Uncle Claude specifically wanted to see her. Edith could never refuse Aunt Lanie. She hadn't heard from her in so long.

They'd sat on either side of Claude's armchair, Lanie holding one hand, but he only groaned in response. The two women talked to each other, though, and his presence made that possible where it hadn't been for some time. After all you had to overlook things when someone was dying, didn't you?

"We sang some Fanny J. Crosby this morning," Aunt Lanie said. "'All The Way My Savior Leads Me.'"

"I do miss her hymns."

Edith waited for her to ask why she'd left the church, but Lanie put it this way: "How can you stand them Episcopalians?"

"They can stand me," Edith said.

"So, I told your mom we were going with her to Tanzania," Tomas said.

Dana glanced at her mom but she was completely absorbed in the baseball game. "What?"

"It'll be great. I've always wanted to go, see Africa for myself. You can get a load of the developing world before you get snagged by Arthur Andersen."

"Ssh, you'll jinx me." Dana sure hoped that wasn't a politically incorrect word. "What are you talking about, 'we're' going to Tanzania?"

Tomas shook her head like Dana was slow. "Look. I know what I want to be, a doctor. But you don't have any idea. You might want to save the world or you might just want to make money, I don't know. You can't pass up an opportunity like this."

"Tomas, you're crazy. You know I can't afford anything like that."

"That's no problem, I'll pay."

"You can't do that!"

"Sure I can. Call it my contribution to your education."

"What are you talking about?"

Tomas spread her hands on her knees. "You have got to start seizing opportunities if you're ever going to be happy," she said, in a paternal tone she must have learned in prep school. "You know what you say when somebody offers you something? Thank you."

"I appreciate it," Dana said. "But—"

"You'll be happy," Tomas said. Dana wasn't sure if she meant happy to go on the trip, or happy otherwise, and if that were a threat.

She tried to recollect being happy. She'd been angry for years but even before that, when did she feel really happy? Perhaps not since swimming in the lake. Well, maybe miserable African villages and the melting snows of Kilimanjaro would melt her confused and calloused heart. Even she was starting to get a little sick of it.

Although Edith hadn't said yes to Linda's offer of a trip to Africa, she was aware that she hadn't said no either. That would leave Linda continuing to try and persuade. Mentioning it to Dana had somewhat complicated things. Tomas had declared they would like to go, and offered to pay Dana's way as if she had the money sitting right there in her Coke cup. Edith didn't remember knowing anyone who splashed money around that way since Uncle Jones, and she doubted there was anyone else like this in Dana's life. She wondered how Dana and Tomas had become friends. And she wondered, although she didn't want to, if Dana had simply collected Tomas because it was her first opportunity to meet a lot of black people. On the other hand, Tomas seemed unselfconscious about it.

When she went to Bible study group the next Sunday, Linda was waiting for her in the parking lot. "You're early," she said. "Thought I'd wait for you to have a cigarette."

"I don't feel like smoking." Linda looked at her that curious way she had, one eyebrow raised. "I haven't been smoking as much this week. My daughter doesn't like it."

"Your daughter sounds very smart."

"She is."

"When will I have the pleasure of meeting her?" Linda said.

Edith was surprised by Linda's directness, though she shouldn't have been. "This summer, I'm sure. I mean, I'm sure she'll visit this summer, at least." She realized she couldn't assume Dana would move back in with her.

"Have you thought any more about that trip to Tanzania?"

Edith exhaled. Now she wished she did have a cigarette, but

she'd deliberately left them at home. "I mentioned it to Dana."

Linda brightened. "Great! So you're going."

"Well, Dana also has a good friend, her roommate, Tomas. Anyway, Tomas said right away they'd love to go on a trip like that, and she even offered to pay for Dana to go too."

"She offered to pay Dana's way?" Edith saw traces of amusement around Linda's jaw. "Mighty generous of a roommate."

"I don't see how it's different from you offering to pay mine." Edith crossed her arms and shuddered, though it was warm out.

"But they're college students."

"You work at a nursery school. I know how much that pays."

Linda's mouth was a tight line. "It's amazing how little it takes to live on when you've never had anyone to support. No big house, no new car. The only money I ever spend is to go somewhere and I always go alone. It would be nice to go somewhere with a friend, that's all."

"Well, that's not the group Pat had in mind. I mean none of you all know each other."

"It's just the four people we need."

Edith shook her head. "So you think you, and I, and Dana and Tomas should all go to Africa together? And this will help Africans in what way? Are we going to take them communion wine? Maybe swap them some beads?"

"Edie—"

She didn't know why she was so upset. "It's just tourism, Linda. I know your do-good friends would love to go throw a quilting bee in Guatemala or something, but really, what good does it do? We're just more white people spending money. Yours, in this case."

"And Tomas's."

"Well actually, Tomas is black."

"Wonderful!" Linda said this in the way Edith imagined Dana had experienced it, like she'd won a prize, a stuffed animal you shot for at the fair. A real live African. Edith felt very weary, and leaned against the car.

"Linda, we better go in now."

"Okay." She hesitated. "Come over to my apartment afterward."

"I'm pretty tired."

"I promise I won't—"

"I know you won't."

Linda looked so eager that Edith smiled. "Just for a few minutes. I'd like to see your place. Sure."

She knew that even in Poudre Valley some people lived in apartments, but she'd never been in one before. Linda's apartment was actually half of a small house, a narrow, shotgun space, wood-paneled like a rec room from a decade earlier, with green carpet that looked even older. The couch, when Edith sat on it, was very soft, with worn-out springs.

"You need the Jaws of Life to get out of there," Linda said, in a tone of joking or apology. "Get you anything to drink?"

She wasn't thirsty, but you never refused Southern hospitality. "Some water, please."

"Ice?"

"No, thank you."

Linda got two glasses from the kitchen and went to the bathroom to fill them. "I find the water is always colder from the bathroom faucet," she said. "Do you mind?"

"That's fine."

Linda was standing; there didn't appear to be a chair. To break the awkwardness, Edith heaved herself off the couch and walked over to the bookshelf that stood opposite, where a television would normally be. "You like reading, obviously."

"All I do. My TV finally stopped working—old black-and-white—and I never did have cable, so I don't even miss it. Well, football." Linda laughed a little. She seemed rooted to one spot on the floor.

Edith ran a finger along the spines of the books. "Football fan?"

"Used to be."

"What do you do now, on Sunday afternoons?"

Instead of answering, Linda set her glass down on the coffee table, a lovely, glass-topped thing, came over, and picked up a paperback from the shelf. Edith had the strange feeling she was trying to protect the books.

She stood very near and Edith could see that, yes, she did have breasts, though at first it hadn't appeared so. Never having nursed children would do that. Linda's shirt was open at the neck but she wore no jewelry; there were fine freckles on her skin. Edith realized she was looking and moved her glance to Linda's hair, took it in at once, every strand silver. She'd had no idea how good gray hair could look on some people.

"I'd give you the tour," Linda said, "but..." She gestured at the almost-bare paneled walls, a little hallway that must have led to the bedroom, which Edith was determined to avoid. "This is pretty much it."

"Thanks." Edith felt very hot. "I don't see any pictures."

"My family isn't close."

Hers wasn't anymore, either, but Edith hadn't meant to pry. "I'm sorry. I thought you might have—oh—pictures of your class or something."

Linda shook her head. "It's just a drop-off center. Not really a school. I've always been a helper, you know, never had a class of my own."

She said it as if she meant more, somehow. Edith thought of her own young children, missed having them. The loss of Jeremy wounded her afresh. She picked up her pocketbook and held it with both hands close to her chest.

"You don't have to go," Linda said. "Here, I'll get a chair."

But Edith couldn't stay. "I'll see you next Sunday," she said. "Thanks so much."

For what? she asked herself angrily after the door was shut behind her and she'd started up the car. For the water? She hadn't drunk it. Tears came and she wiped them away with the back of her hand.

There was no way she could take Linda up on her offer of Africa. She would have to phone Dana and explain. She couldn't even fake normality sitting in a room with Linda Nye.

But when Linda called to ask, again, if she would like to go on the trip, Edith said yes.

Chapter 24

For the first leg of their journey to Tanzania, Edith and Linda had to fly through Charlotte, which Edith knew was several hours' drive away but hardly seemed worth flying to. Hub system. It had annoyed Edith on the way to Chicago and it annoyed her now. They were going through New York, but Dana and Tomas would meet them in Amsterdam, from where they would all fly to Kilimanjaro.

So although she was already tired from the transatlantic flight, Edith didn't feel the trip had really begun till they got to Holland, and as if by a miracle, there were the girls, having already arrived from Chicago. It was different being in Amsterdam. The airport seemed not to have restricted smoking areas, and the gift shops were full of Dutch cheese. Edith didn't remember ever seeing anything fresh in an American airport. She'd bought milk once, against her better judgment, and had to throw it out; it tasted like gasoline smelled.

"Not smoking, Mom?" Dana said. She probably wasn't being insolent but everything she said sounded that way, and she wasn't even a teenager anymore.

Edith did crave a cigarette, since everyone around had one, but she shook her head. "I didn't bring cigarettes." Out of the corner of her eye she was aware of Linda looking at her sharply.

"Well, you can have this secondhand smoke." Tomas was fanning herself. "You could cut it."

"I'm sorry," Edith said, realizing she hadn't introduced them after their initial hugs. "Linda—this is my daughter, Dana, and her friend Tomas."

"How do you do?" Linda took each young woman's hand for a moment and held it. Edith felt an inexplicable pang. The only way she could describe it to herself, and this made no sense, was that she wished for the moment when she had first met Linda, missed holding that hand.

They had to board the plane for Tanzania right away, because their plane from New York had been so late. It was a very big airplane, but when they got on board it was only about half full. Edith had never been on an international flight until today, and the earlier one had been packed. Was she actually going to be able to stretch out?

As if reading her mind, Linda said, "We don't have to sit all jammed up to each other this time." Edith perceived a note of regret.

They sat on the right side of the aisle, leaving a seat between them for bags. Tomas and Dana, having booked from Chicago, were seated in another part of the plane. Edith wanted them to switch, since there was so much room, but when they made no move to do so she figured it must be illegal.

A black woman sat across the aisle. By her headdress, Edith guessed that she really was African, but she couldn't ask.

The moment the plane was airborne, the seat belt sign went off and people got up and started milling around as if the cabin were a lobby. Edith had never seen anything like it. One man a couple rows ahead of them spread himself the length of three seats and wrapped up in a blanket. When the refreshments came around, the African woman took a bottle of red wine and clamped the headphones over her ears for the rest of the long flight south.

Edith was crossing the Atlantic and the equator for the first time, both within twenty-four hours. She'd looked at a map, after being embarrassed about geography, and been surprised by how close Tanzania was to the equator. She'd also bought a travel guide and read a bit of history. Although it said Tanzania was a poor country—was there another kind in Africa?—it was multiethnic, not that she would be able to tell, and run with somewhat less corruption than some of the others. No wonder, as Linda pointed out, the region's leaders had chosen Arusha for their conflict-resolution meetings. And no wonder Edith had never heard of it.

Linda gallantly offered Edith the window seat, so she spent most of the trip looking out and insisting that Linda look too. Although tired, she was far too restless to read. At takeoff, the Dutch landscape was gray and green. Then some beautiful snowy peaks came into view, which must have been the Alps. When all the clouds disappeared from below them and Edith could see straight down to the sand, she drew in a sharp breath. The Sahara Desert. It was beautiful; it was desolate; it was endless. What if they crashed and died here, like Antoine de Saint Exupéry? Could anyone ever find them?

Dana had remarked that it was a long journey and Tomas had told her it wasn't, that it was nothing to go to Africa in a day and a half by jet while a hundred years ago it would have taken a month or more by treacherous sea journey. So Dana said, "Think of all the energy it takes for all these plane trips, all this fuel, now that so many more people can afford to travel. Isn't that a source of pollution?"

To which Tomas responded, "Well, what do you want? People burn fuel in their car engines all the time anyway. It depends what they're going to do. A lot of tourism is destructive, but if you're making a contribution to the country..."

"To the economy, you mean."

"I mean like what we're going to do."

They hadn't stopped over in Amsterdam, just spent a few hours waiting in the smoky Schiphol airport, where Dana noticed the smoking but thought the people around her didn't seem to be nervous, which she associated with cigarette smoking. This being her first experience of Holland she didn't want to jump to any conclusions, but people did seem more relaxed. Were they all here for the famed legal tolerance, the red-light district, or were they earnest visitors to the Anne Frank house? Was one a more sincere objective than the other? She could have asked Tomas for a snap judgment, but Tomas was dozing in a visibly uncomfortable chair, and seemed to surface from sleep only to meet Linda and then board the plane.

It was an odd way to begin her first trip abroad. She saw Europe only out a plane window, but didn't want to ask Tomas what she was seeing for fear of sounding stupid. Tall Dutchwomen served in the aisles. Dana tried not to make up amusing stories in her head about what they did on their days off in Amsterdam.

She felt about the Sahara the way she felt about the pyramids, or Rome. They were ancient, mysterious places that she only half imagined visiting someday. Crossing the Sahara from the relatively safe height of a very fast plane, Dana imagined the dangers it presented and thought about "sub-Saharan:" what it meant to cross this desert and what lay to the south of it.

Most of the plane's passengers were oblivious, not just Tomas. Perhaps they lived in Tanzania, or in any case had been there before. Dana could not stop looking, and she wondered how she was going to get any sleep on this trip at all, with such wonderfully different things to look at. The weeks of preparation, getting vaccinated, packing repellent, fumbling through a Swahili phrase book, had not prepared her for so much as the journey, let alone the destination.

When they disembarked the air felt different, more southern. Dana imagined that it had to do with crossing the equator. There was a dampness in the air, humidity, but not a hot or heavy humidity, because the season was different here. "Rainy," they said. She couldn't remember getting out of a plane outdoors before, walking down steps from a big aircraft and into the terminal, such as it was. Being mostly made of wood and with a small straight desk for the lone official, it reminded her of an old-fashioned classroom. Nonetheless it was formal; Dana was allowed to approach the desk with her mother, since they were family, but Mom spoke in her clipped Midwestern voice, precisely answering only the questions that were asked.

It seemed to take a very long time for all of them to get their visas inspected, their passports stamped, and their luggage into a white Toyota Hiace driven by a man who introduced himself as Lazarus. He wore a white golf shirt and blue jeans held up with a belt of gorgeous multicolored beads. Dana made a mental note to ask him about it when she didn't feel so tired.

Lazarus didn't speak further as they wound their way along deceptively smooth roads to Arusha. That was the name of the nearest town. Dana had heard from Mom that some kind of peace talks were going on here, having to do with a small country that bordered Tanzania, but well on the other side of the country. Right now, Dana was too tired from back-to-back plane journeys to give much thought to Rwanda.

As they checked into the lodge where they were staying, she did notice the scent of strange vegetation, the fresh open air that came in and out of the rooms. She hit the mattress under the mosquito net thinking only of sleep, but first-time jet lag was powerful, and at three o'clock in the morning local time she woke, almost violently, and with such a compulsion to be touched that she was almost ready to wake Tomas in the other bed, never mind the reaction she would get. But she couldn't quite dare to get up, or move at all, for fear of ruining the fantasy.

She had rarely felt this way before, even in the spring when the city was starting to get hot. So randy and raw. She had the feeling that Tomas didn't matter, that anybody could come in here right now and she'd be happy to see them. Well, almost anybody. For all she thought about it (and she thought about it a lot, especially when she woke up at three in the morning), there had never been a long line of people waiting to touch her.

There had been opportunities, which she carefully missed. There were summer festivals when the city came alive, and people lost their ordinary inhibitions in the sun and heat. If you paid attention and had less to drink than everybody else, you could get hugs and kisses, possibly more if you were into that kind of anonymous groping. Dana didn't think she'd mind or feel weird about it.

But the Africa trip had pre-empted all that. Now here they were, thousands of miles from anybody they knew, with unfamiliar (and, Dana thought, wild) sounds filling the night around them. The air was heavy with moisture, and she could feel it in her bones, the climate entirely in contrast to the American Midwest, wide and continental. She could almost taste the sex.

She turned on her side, afraid of disturbing or waking Tomas just by making a sound in the room. She regarded Tomas's sleeping form, the way her head rested in the crook of her arm, so that the arm itself would probably be asleep by morning and Tomas would have to shake it out, cursing the pins and needles.

Dana knew she wanted to touch, but she could only imagine how. The fine, silken dark skin of a neck was just a tantalizing surface to behold. Sometimes she felt, for all her misdirected and frustrated desire, that she was looking at art, at the abstract beauty of a sculpted human form rather than flesh and blood. The way she might look at a man.

This jet lag was fucking her up. She lay staring at the ceiling, trying not to think. It seemed like hours before she slept.

Their first safari, they drove out of Arusha and into a muddy road where they needed the four-wheel drive. Never had Edith found the Southern expression "in the road" more appropriate. The road in from the airport had been paved, in the same way that country roads back home were paved, but she suspected she wouldn't have such a smooth ride again for a week. The horizon was so far, and so wide, she kept feeling her eyes adjust, as if she'd gotten new lenses.

In the game park baboons hopped around, and Edith was the first to spy a giraffe. She could not imagine a more stunning thing than giraffes in the wild, striding along with that peculiar gait that looked straight out of the Garden of Eden (the notion of creation clashing with evolution somehow fell apart for her, especially today). It was hard for her to remember sensing this before, magnificence, something so big and grand, and wild, there for her theoretically to touch. She spent more time than not standing up with her head out the roof that Lazarus had opened for them. Linda sat in the back where there was more room. Much of the time, she was silent under her pith helmet, her face a white mask of intent observation.

A pair of smaller, deer-like animals appeared, with bay coats and glossy eyelashes. "What are those cute things?" Dana asked, and to Edith she sounded endearing, like a child applauding a cartoon.

"The dik-dik," Lazarus said. "They mate for life."

When they left the park and were heading down a rough road, Lazarus said, "If you want to give the kids something, give everyone something. You don't want to give one little kid something because the bigger kids will beat him."

"Like back home," Dana said, and Edith laughed sharply, but she noticed Lazarus did not.

"What, like candy?" Tomas said. "Real nice. Rot their teeth out. We should have brought them toothbrushes."

"I got some ball caps," Edith said, pulling out a Hefty bag she'd filled with White Sox gear on her trip to Chicago. At the last minute she'd found a souvenir shop, one of those sports stores right on Michigan Avenue, and swept the shelves clean. She figured she'd been ripped off, but when were these little Tanzanian kids going to have anything nice?

They slowed down, a bunch of boys (Edith didn't know where they kept the girls) waving at them. She began handing caps out to the eager hands. "Help me, Dana."

There were exclamations of "Chicago!" and "Ah, Michael Jordan!"

Edith was startled. "How do they know Michael Jordan?"

"Everyone in the world knows Michael Jordan," Dana said. "He's like Muhammad Ali."

"Didn't Michael retire?" Edith said. A sharp bump in the road caused Lazarus to swerve, and even Linda made a grunting sound.

"His father died," Dana said.

"Oh. Did he?" Edith didn't much follow basketball. She didn't think any of these caps had the Bulls logo.

"He was murdered."

Edith's stomach dropped, as if the Hiace had lurched over a steep hill. "Oh."

On the outskirts of Arusha, there, at last, were some women, balancing incredible quantities of bananas on their heads as they walked to market. Lazarus told his passengers that in the region around Kilimanjaro—he pronounced it "Kilimankyaro"—bananas were made into beer. When Dana asked if they could try some, Lazarus made a face and said he didn't recommend it.

"What are all these Xs, on the houses?" Edith said.

"That means the houses are illegal," Lazarus said. "They are too close to the road."

"So what? Are they just going to be torn down?"

"Yes."

Edith looked at the houses more carefully. There were dozens, even hundreds of them, almost all marked with an X. But houses may not have been the best word. There were walls, four if the people were lucky, rarely any roof at all, or doors or windows. She wondered how long it would be before this destruction would happen, and where the people would go. It seemed unfair, for the sake of what only the magnanimous would call a road, to take away what little they must have. Where were they to sleep? In a malarial swamp?

She was there to see animals, and in the game parks Edith forgot about everything but the wildlife, which truly was amazing. But outside, she was aware of poverty, on a public, naked scale, that she had never imagined before in her life. There was no famine here; the children looked healthy enough, not like the pictures of Ethiopian children that had constituted her previous knowledge of Africa. But they had nothing, and as far as Edith could see nobody had anything. Here was an entire country, at peace, lush and green, food growing everywhere, and people basically living in the dirt.

She knew there was poverty in Poudre Valley. She'd had students who qualified for reduced or free lunch, free breakfast, kids with head lice, kids whose parents couldn't read. But it was invisible there. In Tanzania, she couldn't see the structure that would allow people not to be poor. She wondered if the violence in the region, and the disease that was also present here, had something to do with poverty too. It felt disturbingly communistic even to wonder such things.

"Do these people actually want to meet us?" Dana said. They were bouncing along a dirt road, or rather through the dirt. Four-wheel drive had been designed just for this.

"Well, we're paying them, of course." Tomas swatted at a fly, put on some more insect repellent.

"Do they use money?" Dana said.

"The tribe does. They must buy books or something. I don't really know."

They were on their way to a Maasai village, to meet some of the people whom Dana had only hitherto heard of as the objects of mission. She was beginning to appreciate, in this very remote spot, the lengths to which missionaries would go to adapt and live with people. She also marveled that any of them, goat-eating or not, would be welcome if they were as white as she was and attracted the attention of young Africans like the flashing of a neon sign.

Lazarus introduced them to the son of the village chief, a beautiful shaven-headed man wearing scarlet robes. The two men engaged in some kind of negotiation but Dana couldn't tell how real this was, if it was a fixed-price formality that drivers did every day. She didn't even know how to tell. Lazarus was the only Swahili speaker of their group, and it was in that language that he and the chief's son communicated, though when the chief appeared, he spoke flawless English.

Dana's main observation was that this man, who lived in a dung hut and told them he had ten wives, was at least trilingual. The Maasai women did not seem happy, moving back or to the side at a gesture of the chief's hand. Were they all married to him? But the children were lovely, and like their mothers and fathers they all wore bright red, and no hair on their heads.

When they were back on the road, or trail, Lazarus said that "the Maasai women do what the men tell them, because sometimes the men will beat the women."

Tomas snorted. “Same as back home.”

“Yes?” Lazarus seemed surprised.

Dana didn’t want to continue this conversation, so she took the opportunity to ask Lazarus about his belt.

“Maasai,” he said. He looked proud of the belt, hitched it up and smiled. Before they got to the Maasai village, it had been the most colorful thing she’d seen since their arrival in Tanzania.

“Can I buy one?”

“Last day,” he said. “Before we return to Arusha.”

She asked Lazarus what languages he spoke.

“I don’t speak the Maasai language, just KiSwahili,” he said. “I speak the Chagga language, my people’s. And some Italian.”

Tomas clapped her hands and said something to Lazarus in Italian. Dana felt inadequate enough next to a Tanzanian driver who spoke four languages, but Tomas was almost more than Dana could bear. She had joined the Italian club because the language classes weren’t advanced enough to help her with anything, and she didn’t have time in her schedule. Tomas came back from meetings with the club full of wine and in good spirits. She joked that the later it got and the more she imbibed, the better her Italian. And here Dana had a dead Italian-American grandmother, and not a word to show for it.

Acclimation to the country so far had been literal for her. It was wet and the sun set sooner, as it was approaching winter in this hemisphere. She wasn’t getting much of a sense of what it was like to live in rural Tanzania. They saw these condemned houses, four walls with no roof, while the lodge’s roof had been a beautiful design of wooden beams and thatch. She had no idea what the local people ate, but their group had been eating extremely well. Better than a college student was accustomed to, at least.

That night, their second, they were staying at a coffee plantation some distance from Arusha. It was hard to get to, and as Lazarus had driven over more and more difficult terrain, a civilization receded that was strange enough in itself. So to Dana, brushing her hair in the dimly-lit concrete bathroom, the lodge seemed opulent and otherworldly in equal measure.

Tomas said, “Coming to bed, Dana?”

She was so startled she let the hairbrush slip from her hand. It clattered to the tile floor. The fact she was using a hairbrush was startling enough, even though her hair had been growing back for over a year now.

She rubbed lotion between her hands, bug-repellent lotion; it wasn't necessary to moisturize the skin in a climate this humid. There could be mosquitoes buzzing around, though. Dana didn't need another virology lecture from Tomas Jefferson.

"So what's going on with your mom?"

Dana got into bed. "What's the matter with her?"

"Nothing, I guess. She seems kind of jumpy around her friend."

"I never met Linda before. They're in that study group together, but I don't know if they have anything else in common."

Tomas looked at her this funny way. "That all your mom's been doing since your dad died?"

"You make it sound so natural. So normal, 'died.'"

"Natural and normal are your words. You want to turn off the light?"

Dana slid under the sheet. She missed the comfort of a teddy bear, anything to hold at night. She hadn't had one for years, had taken no comforting stuffed animal away to college, and now she felt deprived. In the dark she lay, blinking at the ceiling, while Tomas shifted into sleep.

Dana didn't sleep this night either. Outside there were lions; they would trot along beside the safari vehicle like cats. Dana wished she had a cat, wished to sink her fingers into its deep, soft fur.

They got up in the early morning for a drive before dawn. Lazarus took them out before breakfast. Linda was barely conscious in back, though she sat up when Lazarus turned off the motor and pointed out lionesses hunting for their morning meal. Dana saw one look back at her, with nothing between them but an open window; she was sure the lion could jump her if she wanted to.

"The female does all the work," Lazarus said. "She brings back the kill, then the male will eat first."

"The lion's share," Mom said.

"Like back home," Dana said. Everything Lazarus told them, men beating women or lions taking advantage of their mates—it reminded her of men and women in America, there was nothing new under the African sun. Not that Dana knew anything about male-female relationships firsthand. Joe had worried that she would end up with some boyfriend, get into some kind of mess on account of some man. Ha. She should have been warning him.

"Ssh," said Tomas, and Dana realized she had laughed out loud and her laugh cut through the silence of the morning hunt.

Chapter 25

Edith dozed in the Hiace with Dana while Lazarus took the others to exchange some money in Arusha. She woke when they hit a rut; must have gone off road again. Tomas was scolding Linda. "What exactly do you mean by the 'inferior man'?"

"I was quoting Confucius," Linda said, gilding her voice with just a touch more twang for effect.

"You can't put 'his or her' in the mouth of Confucius," Dana said to Tomas.

"Smart-ass. I bet you felt so white out there you went blank."

Edith raised herself to look at her daughter's face. It did seem strikingly pale. Maybe it was contrast, or the sun.

"You've never been to Africa either," Dana said. "Compared to those kids, you're white."

"Them's fighting words," Tomas said, and Edith hoped Tomas was kidding because she didn't want a race war in the backseat.

She asked Lazarus about his name because she'd never met

anyone before named after that particular character. "It's from the Bible," he said.

"Oh yes, I know who Lazarus was. He was raised from the dead."

"Yes."

"I don't know anyone named Lazarus in America," she said.

"You are Christian?"

"Yes, but—it's a little like naming someone Jesus, isn't it? We don't seem to do that in English."

"Yes." Lazarus's smile was brilliant in the rearview mirror. She wondered how he kept his teeth so sound and white. It made her feel better about herself, that he was paid well enough and got dental care. "But Jesus raised Lazarus from the dead," he was saying. "Lazarus did not rise himself."

Why was she not surprised? Everywhere she went in the world, someone had a Sunday school lesson for her. She saw that Linda was listening.

By now they had bumped and swerved miles from Arusha. She said to Linda, "This witnessing thing. We're miles away from the peace talks, from anywhere. What can we possibly be bearing witness to?"

"I think Pat said that just to get us over here," Linda said wryly.

"So what? We see people, how they live. How does that change things for them?"

"Maybe it'll change things for us."

Linda had that look again, like she knew more than she was letting on. It could have been those extra years of living but if it was, Edith found it incredibly attractive. She wanted to know what made Linda so at ease in her amazingly youthful looking skin.

"How do you keep your skin so soft?"

Linda's hazelnut eyes sparkled with amusement, and something more. "How do you know? You've never touched it."

But I want to. Linda was right. Witnessing meant seeing, and she saw everything.

By the time they got to the coffee plantation where they

were staying, that endless sky had grown dark, closing in on the land like a drawn curtain. Edith had long since given up on knowing what time it was. She hadn't changed her watch since Amsterdam and, given the amount of time they'd been traveling and the fact it was fall in this hemisphere, there was no telling. The bucolic luxury of their surroundings, the fact she could smell fresh coffee in the air—not coffee freshly brewed but fresh coffee beans, growing right on the trees—contrasted with the tortuous muddy route they'd taken to get there. Why would anyone drive a white vehicle here? Her mind was fuzzy and thoughts drifted peacefully over the surface of it like insects skimming water, and she felt neither the ability nor the inclination to take hold of any of them.

The four retired to their two separate cabins on either side of the main lodge, at a point when Edith feared she could no longer command her legs. Even in college she'd never pulled an "all-nighter," never remembered going morning to morning without ever going to bed. She'd always been too disciplined for that, too much a creature of habit. Linda would probably have found her boring in those days. They'd never talked about their respective youths, and it was hard for Edith to picture Linda as a partying drunk, but you never knew with Episcopalians.

"At least you have a functioning mosquito net," Linda said as Edith struggled to get it down around her bed. "Mine has a hole in it."

"Are there likely to be mosquitoes in here?"

"Honey, there could be anything in here." Linda gave her own net a yank and the whole apparatus came down from the ceiling. "Best check for bedbugs first."

The bathroom reminded Edith of long-ago church camps, just a concrete floor with a showerhead and a sink with water they weren't supposed to use. Sounds from outside the window were familiar too, the chirp and hum of woods, such as she might have heard growing up. But there was the odd reminder that they were very far from church camp. This was where missionaries went. The mosquitoes were bigger and carried deadly diseases, and from time to time, over the sound of bottled water on her toothbrush, she heard a roar that was not from any animal she'd see at home.

Linda was in bed when she finished. Edith lay down quietly in her cotton nightgown and pulled the string extinguishing the single bulb that hung, like the mosquito nets (well, hers) from the ceiling. She'd expected to drop right off to sleep from exhaustion, but her body felt rigid and her eyes wide open, as if she could gain insight from the dark.

"Are you going to be all right over there?" she said after a moment.

"Yeah, I'll just keep slapping."

Edith waited for the sound of two slaps, some time apart. "I could share with you, if you want."

Linda grunted. "Be awful tight."

"We'll manage." She shifted her weight, thankful that neither of them had put on much with age. "Come on."

It seemed to Edith that an enormous number of minutes passed before Linda joined her, easing onto the edge of the bed as if terrified of their bodies touching. She herself was giddy from lack of sleep and didn't much care what she said or did. "Relax." She poked Linda in the shoulder. "I've had all my shots."

"Me too. That arm was so sore for a week afterward, I didn't think I'd be able to lift my suitcase." Linda rubbed the spot Edith had touched. "Tetanus."

"You didn't have an up-to-date tetanus shot?"

"I'd let it lapse." She squinted at Edith, though their faces were inches apart.

"Sorry, I'm a mother."

They lay there, unmoving and unblinking, while any number of malaria-ridden mosquitoes buzzed around their one intact net. Any lapse in turgor and she knew they would make contact with one another. She could not remember the last time she'd attempted to sleep in a single bed with anybody, probably Pam or a cousin staying overnight.

It must have been the humidity, the rush of rainy season combined with early darkness, a confusion of the southern hemisphere. Edith had never felt so alert in her life. It was as if her mind were ever so slightly separated from her body, floating at a remove, like the mosquito net. Like the lightheadedness the first time she'd had a glass of wine. The Rignaldis had taught her everything she knew about drinking.

She was forty-four years old and this was the first time she'd ever felt drunk.

"What's the matter?" she said, knowing it was a question Linda would deflect.

"Do you know a Bob Marley song about a single bed?"

Edith shook her head, a gesture Linda could feel, if not see. "I don't know any Bob Marley, I'm afraid."

"That's what's the matter," Linda said after a minute. "You're a mother, and I don't need a mother."

Edith felt a pang of anger. "You can go back to your own bed anytime you feel like it," she said. "Don't let me mother you."

"That's not what I meant."

"Well, what did you mean?" Edith said, turning on one elbow so she could see Linda's face.

But Linda wasn't looking at her. "I mean, you're somebody's mother. You have grown children, you have a daughter staying just next door."

"What do you think they're doing over there?"

"Sleeping, by the look of them," Linda said. "Dana may have a crush, but Tomas doesn't have a clue."

"How do you know?"

Even in the dark, Edith saw a questioning look on Linda's face. "What?"

"You heard what I said."

She was astonished at the words coming out of her mouth. She'd never talked this way to children, let alone to another adult. It was as if she were daring Linda, trying to get her riled up.

Linda turned her face to the ceiling. When she spoke, her voice was so quiet Edith strained to hear. "I know."

Their kiss, when it came, was soft, no more than a brush of the lips. It was a motion Edith was not fully conscious of making, but there was no doubt who was responsible. She peered down into Linda's face, which was full of something—fear? wonder? She couldn't be sure, and did not find the distinction particularly useful.

"'Is This Love,'" Linda said.

"What?"

"The Bob Marley song."

"Oh," Edith said, and "I don't know," and then they were upon each other, skin and nails and awkward cotton nightclothes and the one good mosquito net flapping loosely against the side of the bed. Linda's side, although there was no more reason for taking sides on this than between fear and wonder, or any other emotions playing across Linda's face. It didn't matter, nothing conscious any longer mattered. She had not felt this way for more than twenty years, or perhaps she'd never felt this. Teeth tugged at lips, a thread of fluid connected them like the gossamer of a spider's web. Linda's fingertips left bruises between her shoulder blades. Edith was glad Linda cut her nails so short, then found herself wishing she hadn't. She wanted to feel what she was making Linda feel along the length of her now-naked back. What she hoped she was making her feel.

Neither said a word until Edith, on her knees in what passed for the middle of the bed, ran out of actions to perform. Linda noticed her hesitation. "What, what is it?"

Edith had not known it was possible to whisper and cry out at the same time. "I want to—but I don't know—"

"It's all right, you don't have to."

"It isn't all right!" Edith whispered so fiercely that the tears came. How could she be forty-four and not know what she was doing? She'd never really known with Joe.

Linda put a hand on the back of her head, threading fingers through her hair. She kissed her. "What do you want to do?"

"I want to...touch you."

"Do you touch yourself?" Linda's voice was gentle.

Yes I do, yes it's the only way I can get to sleep at night and every night, I do and it's all because of you. She nodded.

"Then do the same thing."

But Edith couldn't move. "What if...you don't like it?"

"Darling, at this point I promise, I'll like anything." Linda exhaled with some difficulty. "Just do something soon."

There was no awareness of time now. Edith had passed from the state of sleepiness or even the ability to feel tired, and was rapidly passing from the awareness of her brain commanding bodily actions. Her hands were warm and they slipped along flesh as they had never slipped so easily before. She moved into recklessness, closing her eyes, letting herself try things, her fingers go wherever they found to go. Linda sighed and didn't speak anymore. Her body seemed to tremble, almost vibrate under Edith's touch, and it made her feel powerful, incredible. She took them both to the edge of collapse and then relief clung to them as a thin film of sweat in the humid air.

Edith pulled up the sheet, careful to tuck it around and not between them. She did not want anything between them. There was barely room in the bed as it was.

Some time after dawn, but before they had to get up for breakfast, she heard Linda say, "Did you sleep at all?"

"I don't remember," Edith said. And she couldn't.

"There's an advantage," Linda said after a moment. "You don't have to guess about a woman. It's not a mystery."

Oh, but it was. "Is that how you think of men? As mysteries?"

"Not men. Just their bodies." In the early morning light Linda's silver hair looked soft, her face etched with fine wrinkles. "What about you?"

Edith didn't know how much effort she'd actually made to understand the only man's body she'd ever been well acquainted with. There hadn't been much motivation, which she'd always thought was because he wasn't interested in women. "My husband tried to—he tried with me," she said. "Harder than a lot of men, probably."

"He had reason to."

"Yeah, I know. I was just thinking, he must have wanted to do his best, to live the life he'd chosen—I mean, that we'd chosen—"

"That's not what I meant." Linda's eyes were upon her. "He had every reason to love you. Didn't he?"

"Yes, he loved me." There was no other reason for him to stay so long. "Why are we talking about him?"

"We aren't."

Little arrows of ardor were flying from Linda and hitting her all around her body and up and down her spine. It was light now and she wanted that cotton between them. Yet she was afraid to move, and startle the wild and exotic creature they had invited into the cabin. Nothing on the Serengeti, Edith was certain, could scare her the way this was scaring her now.

Linda, not so constrained, laid a hand on her shoulder. "Are you all right?"

No, she was not all right. She wasn't all anything. She was rich, she was crazy, sky high and in the pits of despair. There was nothing in all the world, at that moment, she wasn't feeling. Sleep deprived, for one thing. How could she stand up today, let alone react intelligently to what they would see and to her fellow travelers—oh, Dana. Dana would see something in her face, Dana would sniff it out somehow. She let out a small groan.

"Where have I heard that before?"

Edith put her hand over her eyes. "We have to spend the day with Dana. We have to spend a whole week with other people. What are we going to say to them?"

"Nothing."

"But Dana, she'll know."

Linda turned, a motion Edith now realized must be intensely uncomfortable. "Can I ask you something?"

"What?"

"Why are we talking about your family? I thought you didn't want to."

"I didn't want to talk about my husband, no." Edith tried to keep the hostility from her voice. "Not here."

"Here, in Tanzania?"

Edith slammed down her right hand; it hit the side of the bed away from Linda. "Here, in bed. In bed with you. All right? Look, I haven't slept in a bed with anyone for years. I've certainly never—" She stopped, because that was obvious.

Linda took her hand away, eyes still on her. Edith felt appreciated by those eyes, and she didn't relish the appreciation. It seemed wanton. Had no one taught this woman, or the girl she once had been, not to stare?

"You're so beautiful," Linda said.

Edith tugged at the sheet, making little effort and achieving no effect. Part of her wanted to kiss Linda but she feared if she did, she wouldn't be able to stop and the whole thing would go on, through breakfast and the rest of the day. The fear won out. In the daylight, she felt pale and shy.

She sat up and was pulling on her nightgown before she realized she hadn't replied to the compliment. "Thank you."

It took a minute for her to get the nightgown on, and she peered between the buttons. Linda was stretched out, one elbow crooked to show that remarkably un-flabby bicep. Edith remembered the arms and the feel of skin against hers. She struggled the rest of the way into the garment.

"Edie."

"Yes?"

"Why are you putting that on now? Are you wearing it to breakfast?"

She hesitated a moment before letting a laugh escape. Then the laughter became hard and fast, and the tears, and she stayed like that but on the edge of the bed, unable to do anything but shake. She didn't think she'd shed so many tears since Joe died.

Linda seemed unable or unwilling to move, just watched her. "You didn't sleep at all, did you?"

Edith shook her head and struggled back out of the nightgown. She didn't look at Linda again but got up and searched for her clothes. She could hear Linda doing the same on the other side of the room.

Breakfast was on the terrace of the lodge and rather elaborate, with English things like tomatoes and beans. Edith was ravenous and it was all she could do to resist eating with two fists. Dana and Tomas still looked sleepy, but to make sure they didn't pick up on anything, she sat diagonally across from Linda. Too far away for any accidental little touches, but not opposite either, so she couldn't watch the sparks from her eyes.

They spent the day on the Serengeti. It was wildebeest migration season, and endless herds went by. Pairs of zebra mingled with them, neck to neck, as if dancing.

"The zebra stay with the wildebeest," Lazarus said, "for cooperation. The zebra can see well, and the wildebeest can smell well. Together, they help avoid predators."

"Why do the zebra stand that way?" Edith asked.

"For protection also. One looks in one direction, one in another."

A day before, she could not have imagined anything more stunning. But she had glimpsed something, right next to her in the seat, and she was careful not to touch, not even to think about that now.

They stopped for lunch and Edith wished she'd said she was a vegetarian. The girls, who had, dug into box lunches so full of bananas she would have made a monkey joke if it hadn't been for Tomas, and she and Linda struggled through the piles of meat some caterer obviously believed was the way Westerners liked every meal. The sun set early, since it wasn't spring here, and they watched it from the bar of a somewhat opulent lodge. Edith felt privileged and guilty and romantic beyond compare.

She had avoided Linda's eyes all day, spoken only of wildlife, and as supper was ending announced that she was going for a walk. She meant alone. Edith feared the girls would start to puzzle it out, and she didn't need that.

But Dana only said, "You better take lots of bug spray, Mom. We don't need you getting malaria."

"Wouldn't that be awful?" Tomas said, and launched into one of the gory medical monologues she liked to have at mealtime. Edith excused herself.

On the path around the lodge, dusk was gathering, along with a hiss of insect life. It sounded more ominous than Tennessee crickets. She had put on bug spray, but just to be sure, she bent to pull her socks up and roll her pant legs down around her ankles.

"Hey," Linda said as she caught up with her.

Edith feigned indifference. "I didn't know you were coming."

"You seemed to know last night."

She resumed walking. "I don't think I'm really up for this kind of double entendre right now."

"I'm sorry."

Edith's pace was brisk, and Linda took long strides to keep up with her. They had completed one circumnavigation of the grounds when Linda said "Hey" again.

For the first time, Edith looked at her. "Hey, what?"

"Aren't we going to talk at all?"

She turned back into the path and began walking again. "You decided to come along. I was just going to walk."

"All right," Linda said.

Edith could tell she was hurt. Damn it. This was what she hated, what she had never wanted to happen and now it had. She hated that you couldn't be alone. When someone—man, woman or child—loved you, it was a promise, a threat. They were a demand upon you and reserved a never-expiring claim on your attention. If you were there, you were available. Edith could understand having to respond to children's needs, when they were still living at home, but a grown woman?

Joe had not been like this. Joe had always been off in his own space somewhere, and expected her to be the same. The more she thought about it, the more she realized her marriage had worked only because it had scarcely been a marriage at all. It hadn't demanded the work that five minutes with Linda seemed to. She and Joe had an understanding. He never shuffled along after her, sounding hurt.

"If you want me just to go away," Linda said, "I will. But we're staying in the same room again tonight. You'll have to see me again eventually."

There it was, the threat. But the thought of all this coming out with Linda in four walls was too claustrophobic for Edith to bear. "All right," she said. "Talk."

"What do you want to talk about?"

"You're the one who wanted to talk," she said, trying to contain her temper.

"How do you feel?"

"Why are you asking me about my feelings? This is about you feeling hurt because I wanted a minute of privacy."

Linda shook her head. "I'm not hurt, I just want to spend every minute with you."

This was sounding more and more horrible. Edith tried to be gracious. "Tell me why, please."

There was a pause while Linda drew several breaths. "Ever

since I saw you in church that first Sunday, I've wanted to spend more time with you." She waited, but Edith didn't reply. "And now there's this—bond between us, and I have reason to be with you, I would like to—I could spend the rest of my life with you."

Edith inhaled sharply, stopped in her tracks. "Wait a minute. Wait just one cotton-picking minute. What exactly is this 'bond' between us?" She didn't give Linda a chance to respond. "Am I yours now? Because I was married for twenty years and my kids have left home and frankly, I'd like to try life on my own for a little longer. Just try it. I never lived on my own before," she said, and it dawned on her, just then, that it was true. She never had lived alone, before Dana went to college. From her family home to Aunt Anna's to her college dorm to Joe and the children. It was like the women they talked about in Bible study, passed like property from father to husband to son.

"I'm not asking for us to live together, Edie," Linda said. "But what happened last night—"

"What happened last night was wonderful." Her tone softened. "And strange. I don't even know how to comprehend that right now."

"Hadn't you thought about it? You don't seem like the kind of person who spontaneously combusts."

Edith closed her eyes while an elderly couple, British, who'd been sitting near them in the bar, walked between them on the path. She opened her eyes after they'd passed and saw they weren't touching, but keeping a gentle pace with one another. He was much taller than she was and kept bending his head in her direction, as if to bring his old ear closer to her words. "Yes," Edith said. "I had thought about it."

"I'm not asking you to marry me." A note of humor had crept back into Linda's voice. "But you don't believe in premarital sex, do you?"

Edith was not in the mood. "I believe in it. Happens all the time."

"For God's sake," Linda said.

"See, that's what's wrong here." She turned back into the path. "This God talk. It's making me really uncomfortable."

Linda didn't say anything else, and they returned to the lodge in silence. Edith had an impulse to go back to the bar and have a drink, or several, but a lifetime's habit wasn't broken that easily.

Who was she kidding? Sure it was. It had been one thing to compromise with Joe; marriage was compromise, no matter whose. She'd believed she was helping him, and who knew, maybe she was. She'd believed that these feelings belonged to other people and that it was their responsibility to control them. She'd even had the sneaking, unworthy thought that she could have lost her husband to something worse. Killing was something someone did to you, but AIDS was something you did to yourself.

And yes, she would have said the same thing about lung cancer. She'd bought a pack of cigarettes to smoke in the bar. The irony was just too rich. Thank goodness Dana and Tomas had retired for the night. She had cut back on smoking, was thinking of quitting, but this was not the day.

She and Linda were lovers. She tried out that word—she'd never liked it, it was against everything she believed, for herself, Joe, the kids. An "affair" sounded so cheap and tawdry, like nothing she would ever do. She didn't believe Joe had had an affair. He'd had something, all right, but it was allowed. It was no one's business what married people did.

So what was this? If he hadn't been cheating on her, then what was she doing wrong? She had the feeling it was not last night that had formed a bond between her and Linda. That had happened much longer ago. That afternoon at Unaka Lake.

Chapter 26

At great expense, Tomas had arranged for a day of scuba diving with some dicey operator on the coast. Like everywhere else in Tanzania, it was further than it looked on the map. Dana went along for the ride. Sitting in the boat with a crowd of multilingual tourists, all European, and the captain, Jeremiah, gave a whole new meaning to being a fish out of water.

They were rewarded on the way out with a school of porpoises surfacing joyfully near the boat. In a week of travel Dana had almost become used to spectacular wildlife a couple of arms' length away, but in this new context of the sea, she was startled again by the beauty of movement. Things in their natural environment, like (and she rapidly squashed this thought) the boys playing basketball, the curve of an ebony neck.

Only after they had reached the dive site and everybody else had tipped over the side and submerged did Jeremiah turn to her and say in English, "You are American?"

"Yes," Dana said, with a mixture of surprise and the shame she had learned a good American should always express.

"You are not a diver," Jeremiah said.

She was squinting against the sun and he was a black silhouette in the stern of the gently rocking boat. “No,” she said. “My friend is.”

“African?”

“We’re both Americans. We’ve never been to Africa before.”

He had a tool chest open and was holding a small object, Dana couldn’t tell what, in one hand, and polishing it with a cloth. The sea felt very wide and she tried to remember how long the dive party would be under water. How much English did Jeremiah know?

“Your name,” she said. “It’s like my brother’s name.”

“Yes?” He kept polishing, but didn’t seem to be looking at his hands.

“I haven’t seen my brother,” she continued, not knowing why but feeling compelled to keep talking. “We just talk on the phone. For years now.”

He seemed to nod. “Many people here do not see their brothers.”

He was probably referring to Africans who traveled far from home to work—perhaps even himself—but in the salt sea air Dana chose to hear something deeper. “Us too,” she said. “I mean Americans—I mean Westerners. We hear about Africa, on the news, but we don’t really know what’s going on.”

A small wave washed under the boat and Jeremiah turned slightly, not looking at Dana but so that she could see his face. “Here, we hear all about what happens in America,” he said. “What do you hear?”

“Not much,” she said. “I know they’re having peace talks in Arusha—”

His hands stopped moving. “Peace,” he said.

“You know about this?”

He moved one thumb over the web between his other thumb and forefinger. “We hear the radio,” he said. “Do you know a Tutsi, Hutu? If you see them?”

“No.”

“Tutsis are tall,” he said. “We hear of the killings of Tutsis that have been going on this year. They want to drive them into

Ethiopia. And all this time the peace talks have been going on."

Dana felt for the ledge of the boat behind her, smelled the lingering fumes of gas. "They mustn't be working very well."

Jeremiah replaced what he had taken from the chest, closed it. "On the radio in Rwanda," he said, "someone said 'Cut the tall trees.' But if you heard that, maybe you would only think of trees."

Dana did think of trees—of beautiful elms felled by disease in Illinois, of trees submerged forever in Old Butler, trees stripped from the earth. At the same time she feared she did understand what he was saying.

"It is not the words," Jeremiah said. "It is who is hearing them."

Soon the first of the dive party surfaced, the boat was washed with piss from the wet suits and Jeremiah did not speak another word in English.

Other than about animals, Edith had barely spoken to Dana in days. In fact, she didn't seem to be having ordinary conversations with anyone. It was difficult for her to remember what her life was like before.

The lack of ordinariness began first thing each morning, with the amazing breakfast buffet the lodge spread out for them. It was the most beautiful thing in the world to Edith: a whole cooked breakfast and she hadn't had anything to do with it. She finally caught up with Dana when they were each waiting for an omelet, being cooked right in front of them. "Are you having a good time?"

Dana looked at her before answering and Edith wished she wouldn't do that, always suspicious. "I'm having a wonderful time, Mom. Thanks so much for inviting us."

"Oh, it wasn't me," Edith said. "We can thank Linda for all of this."

"Yeah." Dana was still looking at her, and Edith busied herself with examining the pepper mill, although her omelet wasn't ready yet. "You having a good time?"

"Oh, yes. Yes." Edith startled herself with a giggling sound she didn't usually make. "I never imagined anything like this."

"You're cheery." Dana took the omelet, thanked the cook with a big smile Edith hadn't seen for years.

"So are you." She didn't know if she should say anything further, but was afraid Dana would head back to the table and she'd miss her chance. "You're very close to Tomas, aren't you?"

"I was thinking that about you and Linda," Dana said.

Edith dropped her plate. People looked up from the dining room and, habit of a lifetime, she bent to clean it up herself, though she had nothing to clean it with. A Tanzanian woman came up silently and cleared it away. Edith felt so white and exposed, being waited on by black people, something she'd avoided her entire Southern life.

That day they went into the Ngorongoro Crater. She felt less guilty after using the bush toilet; there could be no modern sanitation of any kind in the crater. She felt less privileged, more like she was truly in Africa.

Lazarus named the ubiquitous yellow plant (bides), the crowned cranes and vultures. He said the Ngorongoro Crater was a caldera, a collapsed volcano that had blown up ages ago.

Like sodium before Christmas. Dana was right; she was giddy. Lack of sleep and what substituted for it. The four-wheel drive rounded a bend in the forest growth and there was a herd of buffalo, arranging themselves as if for a photo shoot. She felt that they were looking into her eyes, that they knew her, as by some animal smell. There was an elephant standing with its gleaming tusks, ivory as it was meant to be seen, and Edith thought she would weep with the beauty of it.

Their last day they went back into Arusha. She felt so strange, no longer bumping over ground or unpaved roads. She and Linda had lain together the night before, trying not to touch, then wrapped around each other in the sticky heat of bugs and other things.

Tomas had been full of tales of the deep, a fish that had swum right into her hand, the heedless destruction of the marine environment by less thoughtful divers. She complained that her ears refused to equalize, still felt stopped up. Dana also felt like this after her conversation on the boat. Jeremiah's words had stuck in her ears and altered her sense of the Africa around her.

As promised, they ate lunch on their last day at the hotel in Arusha. While they sat on the terrace, sipping fresh carrot juice, Dana looked at the pictures of dignitaries on the walls. A small number of equally impressive-looking people, some in army dress uniforms, filled the gold-toned lobby, which was done up in gleaming tiles.

One in particular, a senior officer, had his luggage with him and stood near the elevator. But he didn't appear to be either checking out or going into meetings. Throughout the meal Dana would glance up and there he would be, sometimes talking on the lobby telephone, loudly enough so she could hear him, though not what he said.

"Tomas," she said, "can you tell what language he's speaking?"

Tomas inclined her ear to the cadence of unintelligible words. "Probably French," she said with her mouth full.

"Come with me to the restroom," Dana said, and without waiting for a response from Mom or Linda she marched Tomas into the lobby. At the elevator she stopped, motioning to Tomas, who was still chewing, to tell her what the officer was saying. Two men in suits stepped in front of them, wanting to use the elevator.

"I can barely understand African French," Tomas said. "Something about blood. 'How did my people's blood get mixed up with yours?'"

Dana heard it too: sangre, sangre. She moved toward the phone and waved one arm in the officer's face; Tomas grabbed the other. "Sangre? Whose blood are you talking about?"

"Dana," Tomas hissed, "he might understand English."

But the officer, still holding the receiver, just looked at them, no longer talking. Dana was emboldened by adrenalin, but reverted to the niceties of Southspeak. "Sir. I don't know who you're talking to, but I heard what you said about blood. Are you in the army? Because you must know about blood. How mixed up it can get. Do you know how many people in your country have AIDS?"

He seemed to stiffen his posture. She went on, "You get a bad batch of blood and down you go. What kind of blood is your people's, anyway? Who are your people? I don't see that much difference between, say, you and my friend here. Or you and me. Suppose we could tell the difference, if you and I both drew blood?"

"Dana, please," Tomas whispered, in a voice Dana had never heard before.

"You're a military man. Did you know back in World War II the Red Cross used to separate the blood of white and black people? Yes, sir. My grandfathers, if they needed blood back then, well, they were out of luck if it was 'Negro blood.' Does that make sense to you? Sir?"

He drew himself up, all five feet and something, and spoke so forcefully that the plosive formed drops of spittle in the air before him. "Je ne comprend rien." Then he put the phone to his mouth and spoke again to whomever had been waiting all this time.

"What'd he say?" Dana asked Tomas, finally allowing herself to be led back to the table.

"'I don't understand anything.'"

Dana was shaking when she sat down, though she tried not to let on. "Find the restroom?" Linda said.

"Oh. Yes," Dana said, though Mom and Linda must have seen everything.

"Dana, are you all right?" Mom said. "What on earth possessed you to talk to that man? We could get in real trouble."

"Not unless we take his picture," Linda said, and tapped her watch. "Come on, ladies. We have to get out of here."

They found Lazarus waiting in the vehicle and took off for the airport, going faster than they had the entire trip. As they left Arusha Dana was very quiet. She didn't want to explain herself to her mother, her mother's friend, not even Tomas. She felt something growing inside her, something like rage but fuller and more purposeful than the rage she'd been feeling for the past five years. It wasn't happiness, as Tomas had promised, but it had direction.

Chapter 27

On the flight back to Amsterdam Linda suggested Edith and Dana sit together, because Edith was quite concerned about Dana. On the flight she asked Dana about her outburst in the hotel lobby. Dana, struggling to contain her own emotions, told her what she'd said, about AIDS, the human rights situation, and that she wanted to do something with her life, "not just keep using up resources." Edith had been looking around ever since the hotel, worried that they were going to be stopped by someone official. But the only things they were asked for were their grubby Tanzanian shillings.

They left the girls by the luggage carousel at Schiphol. There was a significant delay in Atlanta, where they were routed on the way back. Linda, who had flown to Atlanta many times, said there was always a significant delay. By the time they got back to their home airport, retrieved Linda's car from long-term parking, and drove back to her house, Edith was fighting to keep her eyes open. She knew Linda had another half hour of night driving ahead of her, and she wouldn't be there to help keep her awake.

"You want to come in?" Edith held the car door open.

"Do you want me to?"

Edith tried to smile. "I'm falling asleep here in the driveway. I don't want you falling asleep at the wheel."

Linda looked hesitant, then got out, shut the door. The stars were shining in the northern sky.

Edith unlocked the house. There was a familiar smell she noticed only in this house, and only in this house when she unlocked it after an absence of days or weeks. It enveloped her in its familiarity. She heard Linda gently shut and lock the door behind her, as if aware of the quiet. They didn't touch.

In the bedroom, Edith fell lengthwise on the bed, letting her shoes drop to the floor. She felt Linda climb onto the bed beside her, but she was so tired she didn't care about removing her clothes or even covering herself with a sheet. In the last moments of dim awareness, she felt Linda rustling something, but she couldn't even open one eye to see.

They had never spent a night together in America, and this one passed in oblivion. When Edith awoke the next morning, she felt like her mouth was full of mud. She vaguely remembered brushing her teeth in an airplane bathroom, but that had been over the Atlantic. Every wrinkle in her clothing dug into her skin.

She drew herself up into a sitting position, every part of her body stiff. Mercifully, Linda was still asleep. The sun was bright and hot; the clock said eleven. Even at her most depressed, Edith had never slept this late any morning in her life.

She was revolted by herself in the bathroom: her face in the mirror, her body as she undressed. She felt filthy and unattractive. Normally, she preferred a bath, but she needed to wash her hair and didn't want to lie down anymore. Her entire middle felt crushed in the shape of a plane seat.

The shower took a while to get really hot. She let it pound into her skin and rubbed herself red. She felt unable to get all the dust of Africa, all the nastiness of the plane air and the kinks out of her body. Her hair felt thinner and looked grayer; she hadn't been in bright artificial light for a week. Altogether, she felt old.

She took time to pat down with talcum powder and wrap

herself in a fresh towel, since all her clothes were in the bedroom. When she stepped back into the kitchen, she could hear that Linda was up and moving around. Should she return to the bedroom and risk undressing? She couldn't stay out here in a towel and anyway, there was nothing to eat.

Linda smiled when she came in. Her eyes were tired; it was just as well Edith hadn't let her drive home last night.

"Morning," she said in a deep soft voice, and the love in it threatened to break Edith's heart.

"I'm afraid there's not much for breakfast—tea, if you want it." Edith looked at the closet, willing Linda to leave the room so she could dress. "You're welcome to have a shower, though."

"Thank you, ma'am." Linda shuffled off to the bathroom. Edith's arms ached to hold her and she bit her lips to stop them yearning for Linda's. She couldn't, not here, in the bedroom she'd shared with a dead man.

Later, dressed and with cups of tea, they sat across from one another. Linda spoke first. "So, I guess we're back then."

"It's strange," Edith said, and she meant everything between them but she didn't want Linda to know that. "Compared to the Tanzanians, we're so rich. Things here don't seem to matter very much."

Linda put a hand on hers. The skin on it was loose, warm, a large vein prominent and blue. The hand was beautiful enough to make Edith cry, but that was tiredness. "They matter to me."

Slowly, and as painfully as she'd arisen, Edith pulled her hand away. "I can't do this, Linda."

Linda just looked at her, waiting to hear what she would say.

"I can't do it. Not here."

"Here, in your house?"

"Here in America. I'm sorry." Edith started to cry, and she hated that, hated that womanly weakness. Joe's death had never made her cry like this woman did. She wondered how old these tears were.

"I'm sorry, too." Linda stood up; she hadn't touched her tea. "It's okay, I understand."

"But you don't," Edith said, her hands on the edge of the

table. She wanted to explain, to tell Linda that she was confused, she just needed time, but her mind was full of fabric and her tongue too thick to speak. And Linda was speaking.

"I've lived sixty years. You think I don't know what 'here in America' means?"

"Linda—"

"I'll see you in church."

Linda shut the door and it seemed to Edith that she shut it unnecessarily hard, though everything sounded so loud now, in the quiet in the house in the country. Something had gone, so quickly that Edith wasn't even sure what it was. Arusha was like a dream, a place she'd imagined that had once become real, but now, in her memory, was imaginary again.

She knew there were people living in Arusha, in Tanzania, all over East Africa, and that every day they got up and worked, just as she did in Poudre Valley, each oblivious to the other's daily existence. That there were women whose job was to cart bananas to town on their heads, as remote from her own life as anything else that had happened in Africa. And that was where it had to stay. "See you in church." Was Linda kidding? She could no more see Linda in church now than she could go back to the Methodists.

In fact, as the summer wore on Edith left home very little. She went outside, walked a lot in the sun, forced herself to mow the lawn, as she had in the summers since Joe's death, although she couldn't care less if the grass grew over the entire county. She was depressed, but that was nothing new. She'd been depressed since Joe was killed, and it seemed an entirely reasonable reaction to her. It didn't stop her from doing everything, just non-essential things. She understood that people were not supposed to be able to do things normally, essential things, in the midst of depression, that depression was different from profound grief, that depression was something for which one turned to drugs. Prozac, marijuana. It sounded like something a celebrity would do.

She did at last find a counselor, the only one she could stand to talk to because, unlike everyone else, he didn't assume her refusal to succumb to medical depression was just another sign of denial. Instead, he asked her how she was doing. An anodyne question, meaningless in a day-to-day context, but it was remarkable how few people asked it. Nobody really wanted to ask the widow of a murdered pervert how she was doing. What if she answered?

And when she told him that she was holding herself upright for as long as it took to get through grocery shopping and then collapsing on the couch, and she'd become one of those teachers she'd despised from the time she herself had been in school, but did not mention Linda, the counselor said, "And your Christian faith really seems to be helping you too."

Edith couldn't believe it. She had picked this man because he didn't advertise as a Christian; she couldn't bear to be judged by her own. And they never talked about faith. He knew she went to church, or used to, but that hardly made her exceptional. She'd assumed he would dismiss going to church as one more hypocritical thing people did. That was what everyone outside the church—if indeed he was outside—cited as the problem with churches: hypocrites inside.

Was that it? she wondered. She was in the Piggly Wiggly, looking for the aisle staffed by Gary, the young man with Down syndrome, because he was the only person who would smile and say hello to her. What could sustain her now that even church was no longer an option? She'd stopped reading the Bible, too, convinced that the women's group was just wasting their time on Paul's letters. Paul wasn't interested in women, and look what it said right there in Romans, about women and that which was against nature. Maybe Linda Nye could ignore something like that, say it didn't matter because Jesus never mentioned it. But Edith couldn't.

"Hi, ma'am."

"Hi, Gary." She froze. There on the magazine stands was a copy of *Newsweek—Newsweek*!—and the cover story was about LESBIANS. Right there in the checkout, in Poudre Valley. There were middle-aged women, wearing more clothes than the women on any other magazine cover, and they were embracing. All Edith could think of was "Turn, Turn, Turn" and that line from Ecclesiastes: "A time to embrace, a time to refrain from embracing." God only knew what Linda would say the Hebrew meant.

Grinning at Gary as though this were a normal purchase, she bought the magazine.

Thursday of finals week Tomas left to go to her art history exam early, at eight a.m.; it was her last final. Dana had already finished and was packing to fly to Tennessee for Christmas, having learned to book early flights out of Chicago because you never knew when a snowstorm might blow in and your schedule be thrown off for the rest of the day.

She counted pairs of socks, hearing rain pelt her window. She thought of the basketball-playing boys, long ago by the lake, remembering how she felt when she first saw Tomas, who was not a basketball player but whose physique reminded her in almost every way of the boys she had watched play. It confused Dana and she tried not to think about it any further.

Tomas thought it was "ludicrous" that someone who already knew she was pre-med had to waste time fulfilling an arts requirement. She'd spent a lot of time cross-legged on her bed with an expensive art book, staring at reproductions of paintings and questioning what anyone could say about "another fat baby in first-century Palestine—yeah, real authentic." Finally, Dana suggested she prepare for the final by going to the art library.

The truth was, the exchange of ideas with Tomas had become more one-sided than ever. Over the summer, Tomas had shared a sublet with other pre-med students, and now her future career was all she could talk about.

Like Joe, Tomas had perfected the art of being just late enough, and Dana had gotten used to waiting for her. So she was still in her oversized nightshirt and sweatpants at eight thirty a.m. when Tomas returned, walking slowly and with a dazed look on her face. "What are you doing back here?" Dana said.

Tomas shook her head back and forth. "It was yesterday."

"What?"

"The exam. The fucking exam was yesterday." She looked at Dana for the first time. "I missed it."

"Why did you think it was today?"

"Because it's a Tuesday-fucking-Thursday class," Tomas said with what Dana was proud to recognize as tmesis. "Why the fuck would it be scheduled for a Wednesday?"

Feeling blamed, Dana thought it best not to ask if Tomas had checked the timetable beforehand. Tomas was saying, "I don't know how I'm going to tell my parents."

"Why don't you talk to the professor?"

"Oh, I already did. I went straight to her office. She wasn't very sympathetic. She doesn't much like science types."

Yeah, that must be it. "I wouldn't worry about your parents," Dana said. "You can work something out after Christmas."

Tomas shook her head. "You don't understand," she said. "I've never done anything like this. In my whole life I've never gotten less than a B on anything. My parents won't believe me."

"Believe you?"

"That I just forgot. They'll think I'm on something, or I've been partying too hard."

Dana knew how much Tomas partied. "I could tell them, all you've done for the past month is study for that final."

"Thanks, but I don't think that would help."

"Why not?"

Tomas smiled, an apologetic smile, so Dana knew right away it was fake. "Well, they know I met you at a frat party."

Dana was about to retort, hand on hip like one of the "sisters" whose company Tomas shunned, but the phone jangled unhappily. Who called college students at nine a.m.? "I'll get it." Tomas lunged.

It was for Dana. Her brother. "Jeremy, I haven't heard from you in months. Where are you?"

"I'm in Florida," he said. "Man on a mission, Dana. You wouldn't believe where I've been."

This was a long string of words in a row for Jeremy. "Where have you been?"

"Hanging around gay bars. Southern fags, man. It's freaky."

Dana sat down heavily on the edge of her bed. "You're not bashing them, are you?"

"No. And I'm not fucking them either."

She wasn't sure if she wanted to hear that. "What are you doing?"

"Making music. Listen, Dana. I need a favor."

"You want to tell Mom something? I'm flying home tomorrow."

"Yeah. Tell her not to worry. What I need is some relatives' contact info. You got all that stuff written down, don't you?"

"Yeah, mostly. Why?"

"Christmas cards." He gave a snort of laughter. "Seriously, though. I want you to come visit me."

"Come visit? Jeremy, it's Christmas. Why don't you come see us?"

"Not right now. I've got to finish up some stuff. Spring break, okay?"

"Okay what?"

"Come see me spring break. I expect I'll be here a while."

"Jeremy—"

"Goodbye, Dana."

She sat there with the dead receiver, looking at Tomas, who didn't even pretend not to be listening. "You think you've got things you can't tell your parents," Dana said.

Edith had never thought she would become one of those Christians who went to church only at Christmas and Easter, but returning to services was out of the question. She saw her life now divided into two parts that were anything but equal: before Africa and after Africa. Before she had thought of Africa as a distant place, hadn't even known the names of distinct countries; she hadn't known a Maasai village from Dar es Salaam, but regarded the continent as a basket case where missionaries went. She'd never heard of Julius Nyerere, let alone realized that the founder of Tanzania knew Shakespeare better than she did.

Now, the world looked totally different. The Serengeti, endless earth and sky stretched out "in the glance of the Lord" had altered her perception, literally the way she saw. She who had spent her whole life between the southern Appalachian Mountains and the tall buildings of Chicago now saw with a wider perspective. She had seen faces of humanity she'd never expected to see: along dusty Arusha roads, in her bed, and in herself. She had experienced things she'd never thought of and she did not know how to carry them home.

So her only trip to church this year was the late Christmas Eve service at St. Paul's Episcopal, because she knew Linda was an early riser and would be at the early service. The carols were bowdlerized, no reference to Son or Him. Edith wondered why she'd bothered. Even Linda had contended with the Bible as it was.

She might not have gone at all except that Dana was home and, while acknowledging she hadn't been to church herself all semester, insisted she wanted to go on Christmas Eve. And what kind of example would Edith set if she didn't go? She limited herself to one further question about Jeremy, beyond whether he was all right to which the answer was always the same. Dana indicated she might see him sometime in the spring.

Edith grieved for her family. True to her word, Linda had left her alone, and Edith felt twice widowed, having sacrificed first love and then pleasure. She had taken out a subscription after that first *Newsweek*, and read each issue faithfully. She knew *Newsweek* must be liberal because it was published by the *Washington Post*, and hadn't they broken the Watergate story? Edith would go to her grave proud of not having voted for Nixon. She'd had to wait till the age of twenty-four to vote in a presidential election, and at least she'd had the sense to vote for McGovern, though it had been as futile a gesture as her young marriage now seemed.

Even without the lesbians, the magazine still seemed forbidden. She didn't know what to think about foreign countries, whether Tanzania or her own sexuality. She did not, *pace* Linda, believe in sex outside of marriage, what had once been called "living in sin," but equally she could not imagine, here in America, in Tennessee, what it would mean to be married to the person she loved. Because she had loved Joe, and he'd loved her, and she still believed that, in spite of everything. And although she was willing, not to say eager, to acknowledge that she now loved a woman, she could not be with her.

Had she been like this "all her life"? This was the thought that bothered Edith, when she skulked through Gary's line at the Piggly Wiggly, or on Sunday mornings when she sat up in bed and read *Newsweek*, because she could not face real women and men. It seemed that gay people—Edith was only now getting acquainted with that word—were "always that way"; they had memories, some of them since they were four years old, of being spat upon as sissies or whatever. Even Joe claimed to have been different and to have fought it. It was this that had cost him his life.

What would it cost her? What was her excuse? Would the right man have solved all her problems? She doubted it, but even more, she now doubted whether she'd married the wrong man at all. Maybe Linda was right. Joe might not have been the right man to make her happy, though he sometimes had, but he was surely the right man to make her reach into herself, to dig out what she was truly capable of, not to stand on ceremony but before God and witnesses, till death did them part.

She rolled up the *Newsweek* and stuffed it under the bed, though no one would be in the house with her for months.

Chapter 28

1994

In her senior year of college, Dana had enrolled in a French class and joined all the groups she should have joined freshman year, when they were all soliciting members. She sat cross-legged on wooden floors and wrote letters on behalf of prisoners of conscience. She spent Saturdays in Pilsen, now a Mexican neighborhood, getting her country hands dirty, building houses with Habitat for Humanity. And, one Wednesday in January, she walked into a meeting of the engagingly named Friends of University Queers (FUQ), a group that proclaimed itself open to people of all sexual orientations and genders, some of which Dana had never heard of.

The male co-chair of FUQ introduced himself as Elijah, and sidestepped the question of his sexuality: "You can consider me gay." Dana didn't know how that was different from being gay, or if he just didn't care. She found herself looking at his chin beard throughout the meeting, strangely attracted to the set of his jaw. What did this mean? Was she attracted to gay guys? Was Joe to blame for this?

After the meeting, whose topic was lost on Dana, she approached Elijah. She wanted to ask this stranger something she'd been ashamed to articulate for four years: "Do you believe people are born gay?" As it left her mouth she realized it sounded like a question of faith, as if she'd asked this nice Jewish boy if he believed in Jesus.

Elijah smiled. "What do you think?"

"I don't know." Not what she thought, nor what she was. Je ne comprend rien.

"People think, if we're born gay" (Dana noted his use of we) "then it's not okay to discriminate against us. Like being black." What would Tomas say on this topic? "But it's not like being black. You can see that every day; you don't have a choice."

"So it's a choice?"

He parried. "It's not supposed to be a choice because it's as if no one in their right mind would choose to be gay."

"Where I come from," Dana said, "that's true."

"And where might that be?"

She put on her long-mothballed accent for the occasion. "Tennessee."

"Tennessee," he repeated, stressing the first syllable as she had. "What do you do, if you're gay in Tennessee?"

She thought for a moment. In the whirlpool of desire there was only celibacy to cling to. How many before Joe had foundered on that rock? "I don't know," she said again.

"Would you like to go for coffee?"

Coffee wouldn't keep her awake at three a.m.; she drank nine cups a day. "Okay."

They went to the same yellow-brown place where Dana had eaten with Mom on her visit to Chicago, but it was dark outside now, and frigid. Dana hadn't gotten used to it in four years, at the same time vowing never to move back South. She'd mentioned spring break in Florida to Tomas, who rolled her eyes so far back in her head they could have stuck there.

She and Elijah both ordered coffee. The waitress, a dark-haired, masculine woman, bore some resemblance to Elijah (no beard though). Dana found them both cute, wondered if the waitress knew Elijah, or if she thought they were a couple, before deciding the waitress wasn't thinking about them at all.

Elijah cradled the white ceramic cup in both thin hands as if to warm them. "What's your story, Dana?"

That could take all night. "My dad," she said, to tell someone. "He liked men but he tried to stay married to my mom but it didn't work so he moved out then he got HIV then he died. Was murdered." She closed her eyes. "That's what you do if you're gay in Tennessee."

He looked at her, unblinking. He was like a doctor who had heard everything before. "You're not in Tennessee now."

"I'm not gay either. But I'm not straight. I don't know," she said, impatient with herself.

"Are you bisexual?"

"I'm not—" What was she trying to get out of this guy? "If my dad is, was—then am I? I mean, I can't see marrying someone I wasn't attracted to, but then again, I can."

He nodded. "I've thought that, too."

Having no experience beyond occasional frat-party gropings, Dana wondered if there might be a safe way to experiment, just to find out what a good kiss might be, for fuck's sake. A sober kiss. Lust was so frightening. A guy could be a decent roommate, maybe; he wouldn't tell her to get her underwear off the floor or that she had to eat out of a dish, like Ms. Virology. Yet she could hardly propose cohabitation to a man she'd just met.

"I thought I was attracted to my roommate. A girl," she said before Elijah could ask. "But now I'm not sure. Maybe I just thought that because everybody in my family's doing it."

He motioned the waitress over and for a moment Dana was terrified he was going to consult with her, but he just ordered fries. "How about you?" the waitress said, and put a hand on Dana's tense shoulder.

"I don't know," she said miserably.

"Hey, it's a big basket of fries. You can share." The waitress hurried away.

"I'm sorry," Dana said when she'd left. "I feel like a fool."

"Oh, don't worry about Barbara. We go way back."

Dana drew her finger along a deep groove carved in the table top. Elijah said, "You said 'everybody' in your family was doing it?"

"Yeah, well. I've wondered if my mom could be in love with her friend. A woman. I mean maybe she doesn't even know, but why the fuck would she marry a gay guy, you know?"

"What about your roommate?"

Dana explained that she felt she owed Tomas for the money she'd spent on the Africa trip, which had changed Dana's life, but now all Tomas talked about was medicine and besides, they had roomed together too long, it was getting irritating. "I guess we can make it a few months till graduation, though."

He twirled a fry in ketchup, with what Dana thought was a very gay motion. "Tell me this," he said. "If somebody thought you were gay, would that bother you?"

"No. I figure everybody does think so."

"Why?"

She hesitated. "Because I've never had a boyfriend."

"Neither have I."

In the four years of his own education Jeremy had come to understand a few things about his father. He knew that Joe's liking guys had been no better and no worse than his own desire not to attend college. It was what he had to do, and other people might have preferred otherwise but it couldn't be helped. He knew, as everyone in Poudre Valley knew, that his father had loved Clayton Hornsby and had been at the Cooking Club the night he died. It had been Jeremy's intention, years before any of this had happened, to keep that fairy out of his family's lives, but he had failed in that task.

At first, he blamed Bear, but the use of Bear's truck had made up for whatever part Bear had played. Probably no more than one botched phone call. For sure not a murder; he didn't have a truck to run off in.

Cousin Charlie, the cop, had talked to Jeremy—not saying anything to his mom—but Jeremy was ruled out as a suspect pretty quick too. For one thing, he hadn't been anywhere near the area. After Charlie dropped it, Jeremy started forming his own suspicions. He only called Dana when he felt sure. He asked her to meet him in Florida.

She said she'd never liked Florida, growing up in Tennessee—it was where everyone went. But how could she say no to Florida in March, when Chicago was covered with snow?

It was hot in Tampa. Used to the sun, he was surprised how pale she looked. "Like your shirt," she said.

"Thanks." The shirt was real Hawaiian, with wooden buttons. She didn't comment on the beard he'd grown. "This the only bag you got?"

"I don't like to check luggage. They're liable to bust it."

He was glad to hear she still sounded Southern. "Thanks for coming down."

"No problem."

They were both in the car, seat belts buckled, and Jeremy had started the car before Dana said quietly, "You okay to drive?"

He looked at her, shrugged, got out of the car. Dana scooted over. He'd let her drive the rest of the week.

The road hugged the Gulf Coast. She said, "What are we going to do?"

"Beach. Whatever you want. Only, I have to be somewhere tomorrow night. And if you could come with me, that would be great."

For an afternoon and a day they hung out on the beach, like regular kids. Dana asked once if the Howard Johnson was expensive. He said it was but no use getting a lease on an apartment when he didn't know how long he'd be there. Anyway, musicians had no credit.

On the second afternoon he told her they were going to O'Reilly's. "I know some guys, made some friends. We play in bars."

"I know."

"There's kind of a drug scene around here," he said. They were drinking Negra Modelo on the balcony. "But I'm not involved in that. Just want you to know, so you don't misjudge something."

"Okay." She swallowed beer. "So are you playing tonight, or what?"

"No." He drained his bottle, then said, "It's a gay bar."

"Cool."

"Ever been in one?"

"No," she said, not too fast or too slow.

They got to O'Reilly's about ten. People were just starting to come in. Mostly men, a few women, all wearing similar clothes. Those sport sandals. The women had mullets. Dana commented on them, touching her own hair.

Jeremy didn't say much to any of the guys who talked to him. He kept his eye on the door. Dana seemed buzzed. Maybe she wasn't used to drinking beer all day.

At a quarter to twelve he showed her his cellular phone. "Lord, Jeremy, it's like a brick."

"If you don't mind, when I tell you, just stay here and hit this button. It's speed dial. Okay?"

"What—"

He laid a hand on her arm, slid off the stool. In the green light of the bar sign he could see who he was waiting for, though it was hard to recognize the guy. Only good thing was there was no way he would recognize Jeremy.

He approached the skinny man, one hand on his wallet. The guy turned his thin face toward where Dana was sitting. Jeremy heard her say, "Clayton?"

Clayton lunged, but Jeremy grabbed him from behind and bent him over a bar stool. "Now!" Clayton was still struggling so he banged his head against the bar.

Dana was holding the phone to Jeremy's ear. A voice said, "Charlie Bailiff."

"Charlie, it's Jeremy. Are you in Tampa?"

"I'll be right over."

Edith opened her mail right at the mailbox, out beside the road. This day, in April, she received a graduation announcement from Dana. She was touched, somehow, that Dana had gone to the trouble of ordering them herself, and sent one to her mom. She went to the wall calendar to write the date down, realized that she'd already done that months ago. So she circled it instead. Then she sat at the table and felt a little sad. This was it, all her (and Joe's) hopes and dreams building in one crescendo to their daughter's graduation. She wished Jeremy were doing the same, and wondered if Dana had sent him an announcement too.

Then she turned to *Newsweek* and was shocked beyond measure.

Mass slaughter in Rwanda. Hutus, Tutsis. People, kids, hacked to death with machetes, pieces missing. Thousands of them.

She was sickened by what she read. The result of the failure of the Arusha Accords of 1993—the peace talks Pat had said they were going to witness. Edith had been present at a moment in history and had missed again.

Who could she talk to about this? Surely Linda had heard the news already. She wouldn't, like Edith, rely on a weekly magazine for all her news. Edith remembered that Linda didn't have a television, but she must at least get the *Crier.*

Edith got up to call Linda, who would—wouldn't she?—be gracious even after all this time, such a tragic day. She sat back down at least ten times, went to the refrigerator, got a Coke. Now she was really going to do it. Her hand was on the receiver.

The phone ringing almost shook her out of her skin. She half expected it would be Linda. But of course Linda didn't read minds.

In fact it was Charlie, whom Edith hadn't seen or spoken to in even longer. She tried to hide her disappointment. "Everything all right? How's Pam and Aunt Lanie?" Oh no, what if something had happened, and here Edith hadn't seen any of them for months. Guilt washed over her like nausea.

"They're fine, Edie. Everybody's fine up our way."

"So." She tried to think of a polite way to ask why he was calling. Her mind and tongue were thick like cotton balls. She felt as if she hadn't slept for a hundred years.

"Well. Edie." Charlie sounded thick, too, but then he always did. "It's about Joe."

"What?" Edith leaned against the counter so hard it made a ridge across her palm. She stared at Dana's graduation announcement, propped there.

"Someone's confessed," Charlie said.

This made no sense. "What, you found some junkie to pin it on? Some homeless guy, let me guess, a black, right, Charlie? Or don't you call them blacks in the police department?"

"None of those. And that's not fair, Edie. We have black guys on the force now. I got no problem with them."

"So who is it?"

"Clayton Hornsby."

She saw a tiny light start up at the corner of her eye, like a pinwheel in the sun. It spun wilder and wilder till she could see nothing and thought she might fall and crack her head against the floor. She pictured herself lying there, peaceful.

"Edie. Are you all right?"

"Fine." She heard herself say it, way up high behind her somewhere.

"Clayton was picked up for selling drugs in Tampa. Now we've got him back in Tennessee to face murder charges," Charlie said. "He's confessed, Edie."

"Okay." She let go of the counter and slid her back along the lower cabinet, sat on the floor. The linoleum was so cool.

"He's in the jail now. I thought you'd want to know."

She'd want to know. Did she want to know that Charlie was right, that a gay man had killed her husband? Did she want to know that it was his lover, who had no doubt given him AIDS too? Did she want to know it was the man who used to cut her hair? "Thank you, Charlie."

"I'm not happy about this." Charlie was now speaking faster than she'd ever heard him, almost like a Yankee, or maybe her mind was slow. "I'd much rather have arrested a stranger. I mean I'm glad we finally got the guy, but I'm sorry it was somebody you knew."

"He's gay, Charlie." Edith almost laughed as she said it. "What do you care?"

"I've got nothing against them. Listen, Edie. I'm sorry about Joe, I can't even tell you."

"That he died? Or that he was gay too? Charlie, you don't know half the things to be sorry for about Joe."

"I told you, I wish it was somebody else. Just because I don't understand homosexuals doesn't—"

"And you think I do?" Edith didn't understand homosexuals. Or regular folks either. Edith Rignaldi, at this moment, understood no one at all.

"I mean," Charlie said, "I just don't understand why anybody would not want kids." He cleared his throat. "If they could have them."

Only then did the full horror of what Charlie was saying rush in, behind images of machetes. "Joe wanted kids." It was as if, in saying it out loud for the first time, she was realizing it herself. "That's why we got married."

"Me and Pam too. Isn't that funny?"

He didn't sound like he thought it was funny at all. Edith had never heard for sure, until now, that he and Pam couldn't have kids. She should have known that too.

"Let me come over and see you, Charlie."

Charlie let her into the jail. There was a jailer, with keys, but he didn't get up from his desk when Edith came in. The place seemed pretty quiet, like a school building on a day off.

When Clayton came in the room he wasn't handcuffed or anything. Probably couldn't find any to fit him. He was much skinnier than Edith remembered. His face somehow managed to be dark in patches and pale at the same time. Must have been the shadows of his bones. She had a hard time imagining him bludgeoning anyone to death. Which was just as well, since she didn't want to imagine it.

"Why'd you want to see me?" he said.

She sat very straight, conscious of every vertebra and of her hands, folded, on the other side of the glass. "I want to know why you did it."

"What? Confessed?"

"Whatever you want to tell me."

He couldn't seem to focus on her. He looked massively tired, as if he'd never expected a visitor. "Are you sick, Clayton?"

He kept looking to one side. "They can't kill me," he finally said, so quietly she strained to hear it. "I'll die on them first. So I don't care what happens to me. See, I might as well keep confessing. You want to be my priest, Edith?"

It had been a while since anyone called her by her full name. "I'm sure they'd let you talk to a minister."

"I won't do that. I don't believe in it." He leaned his gaunt cheek on one hand and began to rub his temple slowly with the tips of his fingers. "Did you ever know anybody with AIDS?"

She said "No," and then added, "Not that I knew of."

"Well I've known hundreds of them, seems like. This is not as small a town as you think." He looked almost pleased, saying this. "Yes, I am sick."

She didn't answer, just waited for him to go on.

"I thought with Joe, it would be different. I thought we were safe. But there's no safe sex, really." He looked at her, cockeyed. "You don't want to know this, do you?"

She breathed deeply, but with her eyes she agreed with him.

"Anyway. I knew it must have been me. You may not believe me, Edith, but your husband was faithful. I was his first."

"I believe you."

"And I'd never felt that way about anyone. It scared me. I wanted him to be with me, the time we had left. Only me." He almost smiled, as if it were a big laugh, telling this to his lover's widow. "But Joe wouldn't leave you."

She wished he had, if this was going to happen.

"I don't know if you can understand this, Edith. I've seen men, strong men, turn into weeping babies. It's a terrible disease. You lose everything. My friends had no family; the church wouldn't even bury them. There are protests at their funerals. You lose control of all bodily functions; you go blind."

Edith leaned forward and rested her temples, which were starting to throb, against her fingertips. Clayton kept talking. "I was so mad at Joe for not staying with me. I would have taken care of him if he'd gotten sick, but he refused me. Did you ever love someone so much, and then you couldn't love them anymore, and then it turns on you? Like a drug, it turns from love to hate—"

"No," she said. "That's never happened to me."

"I was so scared," Clayton said, a near-whisper. "So scared he would get sick and die on me. Or on you, and you wouldn't get anything, because the life insurance wouldn't pay. Did you know men turn their insurance into money to pay for their care?

It's a whole industry now. It all gets spent on treatment, which we don't survive anyway."

"I've never heard of that." But of course, she had.

"Anyway, I'm not a monster, Edith. Believe that if you want but I felt for you all, your kids. Especially that Dana. I didn't want you to be left with nothing."

Images of Rwanda again flashed in her mind. "So you went after my husband—"

"I was high. I get high a lot." He shook his head as if these had been the actions of another man.

She just stared at him.

"I always got high when we went out. We all did. Except Joe, he'd never touch stuff."

"And look where that got him."

Clayton pinched at one pitiful bicep with his thumb and forefinger. "It was all over before I knew," he said. "I'm strong. I was strong."

She looked at him and thought, no, you're wrong, Clayton, you're wrong about everything. You're not strong; I'm strong. As she realized this, it, too, was like the first time. She'd put up with Joe for better or worse, way longer than Clayton had. He hadn't the faintest notion of sickness and death because if he did, he'd not have said that other thing he was wrong about. Love turning to hate. She thought, if you once loved someone, you can never really hate him.

"You must hate me now," he said, and it was pathetic the way he said it, this once-strong man turned to a weeping child, the way he'd described others but couldn't see himself. Wrong, wrong about everything. He couldn't die on them; he already had.

"No," she said. "I don't hate you." And she didn't, somehow. She had a far-off memory of first hearing about AIDS, Rock Hudson or something, and wondering if it could be the judgment of God. A very far-off memory now. But how far off was the judgment?

"Did you say you didn't believe in God?" she said.

He snorted. "I don't believe in anything. God is love, shit. God is hate."

"You said you were confessing."

"To you. I need your forgiveness, not some god's."

She could already see him skeletal, like those horrible pictures of people from the Holocaust. She remembered something in a book by Simon Wiesenthal. "I'm not the one who can forgive you," she said.

"Then who is?" He leaned forward on his bony elbows, and looked at her as fiercely as anyone'd ever looked at her in her life. "Who?"

She couldn't look back at him anymore. She rose, feeling pity turn to disgust in her throat. "He's dead. Goodbye, Clayton." And she got out of there as fast as she could, rounded the first corner and vomited into it, her hand ineffectual at her mouth.

Someone stood behind her, handed her a tissue. "Thank you," she said in a choked voice. With what was left of her dignity, she straightened up. "Where's the ladies' room, please?"

"That next door, there," Charlie said.

She couldn't bear to turn around. "Oh, Charlie. I'm so sorry."

"Don't be," he said. "I feel the same way."

She went into the ladies' room, and stayed until she was sure he'd had to get back to work.

The lights over the bathroom mirror were, surprisingly, like those in a theatre dressing room. Edith fixed her makeup, noticed her eyebrows growing astray, debated plucking them, but couldn't find the tweezers in her purse. They must be at home. An old rusty pair, which she'd had at least since the children were little. When they came in from playing in the woods, she'd use the tweezers to pluck any tick she found beginning to make headway in their hair or on their legs. Nobody in her house was going to die of Rocky Mountain spotted fever. She thought of the irony of that. There were so many ways to die.

She'd only ever known one student who died, and he was not her student. The boy had been a kindergartener, her first year of teaching. He'd wanted to visit his sister, a student at the middle school—Edith's school. He had no concept of how far away the other school building was, but in the process of trying to get there he tried to climb over the sewage works that were just an open pit in the back of the elementary school, surrounded by a chain-link fence. Not enough fence. But no lawsuit either. Poor families in 1970 did not sue.

She remembered him, the drowned boy, frozen forever in the yearbook picture—"who attended the kindergarten class." His name escaped her these twenty years later, but not his face. Not his, or Clayton Hornsby's, any more than her own son's.

What happened to these boys? For they were boys. She climbed into the car, her *Newsweek* on the passenger seat where she'd thrown it. Boy warriors hacking each other to death in East Africa, boys drowning, running away, getting high, hammering each other's brains out. She leaned against the steering wheel, wondering how long it would take her to clean up after this bout of tears, because she wanted to go into the Citgo for a Coke.

Chapter 29

She bought a six-pack of Coke to chain-drink. It was a terrible thing to do, still morning, but she had bought a lot of gum too, and intended to chew it. If all her teeth fell out, it wouldn't be sugar's fault.

She had driven Mountain Highway so many times, at least twice every day of her teaching career. The jail was not her usual destination. The road, a little further than she was prepared to go, led to the Cooking Club, and beyond that to the courthouse and wherever else Clayton might end up. That thought made her face hot and she rolled the window all the way down. She set the Coke can against her cheek as she drove, and the condensation mingled with her sweat.

Spring had arrived, was here, and she hadn't welcomed it properly. She wanted to turn the car around, to head out past the jail and the city limits and go back to Unaka Lake, but she hadn't been there but once and wasn't sure she knew the way.

In the driveway she parked and applied the emergency brake,

then wedged bricks under the front tires as she'd done every day for many years. One time one of the kids—she thought it was Dana but it could have been Jeremy—had got bitten by a tick, it had been missed somehow, and Edith in panic and guilt had tweezed it out and it lay there, swollen with blood, looking like a wad of chewed-up gum. She had picked up one of the bricks and smashed the tick in the driveway, over and over again though once would have been enough, and scraped its tick-skin and the black blood of her child across the concrete. She did not remember, now, being surprised at her own violence.

The sun was high, the mist long since burned up. There was clover in the grass and it needed mowing. Edith could smell each blossom, each blade.

She went inside, leaving the screen door open. Dialed the phone while draining the last of her Coke. "Linda, it's Edie."

Out of her other ear, she could hear birds twittering. Linda said, "How are you?"

"Fine." What could she say? "Want to go to the lake?"

There was a silence. Edith pictured Linda plucking at a daisy: I hate her, I hate her not. "Sure. Give me forty-five minutes, okay?"

Half an hour later Edith heard the station wagon pull in. She'd done her eyebrows, though Linda probably couldn't care less. Her scent hung in the air of the bathroom and when she called to Linda to come on in, she was sure Linda noticed it. Edith had dressed down, flannel and jeans, only the smallest black studs in her ears. Of course, her good clothes had already been thrown in the wash. It reminded her of diaper-pail days.

Linda drove with the country station on, not talking. She'd stood in the house, almost at attention, and listened to Edith's description of her shock at the news from Rwanda, how she was going to call Linda but then Charlie called, she couldn't believe it but Clayton..."So guess where I was this morning?" Edith kept talking, no tears. She had to say it, to get out all these words. And she concluded by telling Linda what Clayton had said about hating someone you once loved, and how she told him she wasn't the one who could forgive him.

"No," Linda said, "I don't think you are."

They arrived at the lake, but they weren't the only ones. Three young men were throwing a Frisbee. It was only April but they wore nothing but shorts. Edith could not help but admire their torsos, not yet paying for indulgence in beer, a little pale though. Then she looked over at Linda, and knew that Linda had seen her, seeing them, and a sad smile pulled at the corners of Linda's mouth.

Edith bent to take off her sandals, and walked down to the water. It was cold, but not unbearably so. She nodded in the direction of the young men, who had moved off down the beach. "Think they're gay?"

"I doubt it."

Edith threw a stick in the water. "So what do you think? About, if you loved someone once. I mean, I loved Joe." She spoke fast before Linda could say anything. "I have to talk to someone about this, you're the only one I want to talk to."

Linda slid her sandals off, one foot at a time. "I don't know, Edie. I can see love turning to hate. If you're betrayed enough, if your own family turns on you, your own body."

"If your own neighbors come in the night and attack you."

"Yes." Linda was quiet. "But knowing what Clay did—"

"Clay?"

"—how can I agree with him? But I do."

Edith said, "Then you don't forgive me?"

She was afraid to look at Linda, but forced herself to turn anyway. Linda opened her arms and Edith walked into them. She felt cocooned there, and yet ready to burst into flight.

Back at the brown station wagon, Linda said, "Don't know about you, but I'm hungry." She held up the keys. "Want to drive?"

They had lunch at Edith's house. Only now was she beginning to feel okay about that, about it being her house, and calling it that. It had been her and Joe's house, as distinct from Isabella's; then Jeremy had been born, and Dana, and it became their house. They probably still thought of it as theirs. Well, Dana was graduating from college now. She'd have to start calling before she just dropped in. Edith was startled at this thought, and laughed.

"What's funny?" Linda said, and took a bite of her sandwich.

Edith saw a piece of lettuce on her chin defying gravity, and just laughed harder. Everything was funny...and any minute now she was going to tear up. She could feel it coming. To settle herself, she said, "Is your sandwich all right?"

Linda nodded. "Anything someone else makes is good," she said. "I love pimiento cheese."

Edith had never heard of anyone loving pimiento cheese, but the subject of what was in her refrigerator seemed a safe one.

When they finished, Edith was on her fourth Coke. The caffeine made her bold. "Will you have lunch with me again tomorrow?"

Linda looked at her. "Sure. Where?"

"Burger King?" It was public. Safe.

They made a date for twelve thirty. Spring break was almost over, and Edith wanted to enjoy it. Not that guilt and forgiveness and the Rwanda massacre were enjoyable, but at least it was adult conversation. Next week it was back to eighth graders, and she needed more than Coke to carry her through.

As soon as Linda was out the door Edith called Dana. She intended to leave a message, and this was also new for her, since she hated answering machines and called when she thought Dana or Tomas would be there to answer the phone. But Dana picked up. "Mom, hi," she said. "What's wrong?"

"Nothing." Did something always have to be wrong when she called? "Have you read the news?"

"What news?"

"Rwanda," Edith said, and felt like Uncle Jones, calling to warn her about Kent State.

Dana had heard about Rwanda. She'd even had a real conversation with Tomas about it, their first in months. Tomas said that officer Dana had shouted at could have been a homicidal maniac. Dana said if he was, she wished she could've stopped him.

But to Mom, she just said, "I've been meaning to call you about Florida. I saw Jeremy."

"You did?"

"Yeah. He's doing fine, he wants to see you."

"When?"

"Soon. He's been doing his music, you know; he has a band. They're pretty successful down there."

"Did you hear them play?"

"Some. You should be really proud of him, Mom, he's graduating the same as I am. It's like an apprenticeship."

"What kinds of places does he play at?"

Dana wondered how much her mother could handle. "Oh, you know. Bars."

There was a pause. "He's not on drugs, is he?"

"No, Mom." She rolled her eyes.

"Okay, it's just that I've heard about bars."

Dana took a dig. "What, from the ladies you hang out with?"

"Dana, you have no idea." Mom was shutting the fridge, Dana could hear it. "Guess who I saw?"

"Who?"

"Clayton Hornsby."

Dana fell back on the bed, and with her eyes traced concentric watermarks on the ceiling. "Then you know."

"What do you know, Dana?"

She took a deep breath. "It was Jeremy who found Clayton," she said. "I don't know how long it took. He didn't want to tell you, you know, or blow it. Tracked him down in a gay bar."

"Dana."

"Yeah?"

"Is Jeremy—"

"No, Mom. He's okay. He's not gay, on drugs, nothing."

Sigh. "Thank God."

"What, that he's not gay?"

"Well, makes one of us."

Dana sat up. "What?"

"I need to tell you about Linda," Mom said.

Dana listened, tried to sound surprised. Then Mom asked,

"So how's Tomas?"

"Okay. She's pretty stressed out about going to med school next year."

"Is that hard on you?"

"What? No. I mean, we don't even see each other that much." Dana felt she ought to tell her mother something, so she said, "Actually, I met a guy."

"Oh?" Mom's tone was inscrutable. "Who?"

"Name's Elijah."

"Elijah. Is that a—"

"Yes, he's Jewish, Mom."

"Okay, honey. It's just that, I married a Catholic and—"

"Catholic!" Dana knocked into the rickety table and the phone almost fell off. "I'm not marrying anybody. Besides, I know about Dad."

Mom was silent for a minute. Then she said, "Do you think that's why?"

"Why what?"

"Why I married your father."

"You married him because you loved him," Dana said. "Didn't you?"

"And you kids."

Dana thought of Elijah's pale face and thin lips, of the bronze arms of basketball players. From so little, people started families.

"You did good, Mom," she said.

Next morning the sun broke through, a beam of it across the wall, waking Edith up before the alarm did. Then she remembered she was still on vacation and hadn't set the alarm. Still, it was rare that she woke to the sunrise, that she didn't lie in bed as long as possible, dead to the world, not wanting to move or even open her eyes because it was just another day of school.

She sat up in bed, unsure of how she felt. Men wounded in battle must do this, sit up and ask after their missing limbs, feeling phantom pain. Or women or children, she thought, remembering the horrible articles, the machete scars.

What was she feeling? Pain wasn't the word, it was some other sensation, like the pins and needles when she slept on her arm oddly and now it was letting her know it was there. It was sharp, like her memory. Should she have talked to Dana? Could she blame it on the Coke?

She pulled the robe around her. It was old soft terrycloth, but she felt it prick her skin as if she had a fever. She went straight to the refrigerator. "I'm a Coke addict," she said, and laughed out loud.

She drove to the Burger King. It was right there on that same road that led to the schools, the jail, the lake, and North Carolina if she took it that far. All the way to Charlotte, where you could take a flight to Amsterdam and end up in Arusha. All the cigarettes came from over that way too. Was there anything that didn't remind her of death?

She could hardly sit still in their booth, which was harder than a church pew. "You're wired," Linda said.

"I just figured it out. I'm a Coke addict."

Linda set down the tray of food. "It's Pepsi here," she said. "Though we're Southerners so everything's a Co-Cola. Now, what's going on?"

Edith grabbed a wrapped sandwich and waved her hand. "Let's eat first. I didn't have breakfast."

"You're scaring me."

They ate their burgers, and Edith ate all her french fries and finished Linda's. She went through three packets of ketchup. "Kids at school," she said in a rare pause between bites, "will just throw these on the floor and stamp on them. Oh, that cafeteria. It's like blood, a war zone."

Linda just looked at her.

Edith did not say anything serious until they were out in the parking lot. She squinted in the sun and made no move toward her own car, but escorted Linda to hers. Linda stood with her hand on the station wagon door. "You're not smoking."

"No," Edith said. She'd had enough, but there would be time to tell Linda all that later. "Dana told me Jeremy's doing quite well with his band. He wants to come home and see me."

Linda's eyes were narrow but she might just have been

squinting too. "That's good, that's real good, Edie."

Edith leaned her hand on the hood. "You can meet him."

"What will you tell him?" Linda said. "About me?"

Edith reached out and put her hands on the soft flannel shoulders of Linda's shirt. She leaned in and kissed her on that beautiful mouth, slowly, long enough for all Mountain Highway to see. It was only the parking lot of the Burger King, but it was a start.

Pentecost 1994

At six o'clock on a Monday morning the alarm woke Edith. She had it turned to the public radio station now, jazz or something, not like the annoying beep she'd been waking up to for so many years.

She dressed without company for the first time in three mornings. It was wonderful being alone again, though company was wonderful too.

She and Linda had been to St. Paul's yesterday, where their guests for the service were members of a black Pentecostal congregation. They spoke in tongues, but it was all very quiet and orderly. It had been so long since she'd been to church, longer since she'd felt at home, there or anywhere. They sang very un-Episcopal hymns: "On the day of Pentecost, fire fall on me." Tongues of fire...

Her marriage to Joe had been another language, and she was returning to her mother tongue. Marriage was different, different for everybody and different from what anybody thought. It meant tracing the lines on someone's face and memorizing them. With perfect clarity, the way she recalled that day at the old Comiskey Park, when Larry Doby was at bat. It was the first baseball game Edith had ever been to, and she wore her cap and her glove. Everyone made fun of her for taking her glove, even Uncle Jones. But she was eleven years old and didn't care what any of them thought, not then. Edith—Edie—sat undaunted in the bleachers all that day, and she caught a ball. She caught that ball, by God, and nothing could take that away from her.

About the Author

J. E. Knowles is a native of Upper East Tennessee and a graduate of the University of Chicago. She holds a Diploma in Jewish Studies from Oxford and has published stories, essays and poems in the USA and Canada. *Arusha* is her first novel. Please visit her on the Web at jeknowles.com.